Steps Beyond the Horizon

Lila Ashford

Published by Lila Ashford, 2024.

STEPS BEYOND THE HORIZON

First edition. October 2, 2024.

Copyright © 2024 Lila Ashford.

ISBN: 979-8227693440

Written by Lila Ashford.

Chapter 1: A Wrong Turn

The bustling streets of Maplewood unfold like a vibrant tapestry, woven with the sounds of laughter and the chatter of friendly neighbors. The air is thick with the sweet perfume of blooming magnolias, their pale pink petals dusting the pavement like confetti. As I race past quaint cafés and boutiques, the aroma of freshly brewed coffee mingles with the floral notes, a comforting reminder of home. My heart pounds in time with my hurried footsteps, each beat urging me to reach the dance studio before the first class of the day begins. It's been years since I last performed, but today feels different; a buried passion stirs within me, threatening to break free from its long slumber.

Navigating through traffic is a skill honed by necessity. I dodge a wayward skateboarder, narrowly avoiding a collision with his carefree grin. "Hey! Watch it!" he shouts, but my focus is elsewhere, fixed on the looming brick façade of the studio that now glimmers in the distance like a beacon of hope. I've promised myself that today is the day I reclaim my love for dance, a promise made silently in the depths of my heart, and I refuse to let anything—especially not a skateboarder—stand in my way.

The sun hangs high in the sky, casting warm rays that beckon me to move faster. As I approach the intersection, I catch sight of a 'DANCE STUDIO' sign swinging gently in the breeze, its cheerful letters painted in vibrant hues of orange and teal. With a giddy rush, I step onto the crosswalk, my mind swirling with dreams of pirouettes and grand jetés. But just as I feel a surge of confidence, I realize the light has turned red, forcing me to pause, if only for a moment.

In that fleeting instant, I spot him. He stands against the wall of a nearby building, a tall, rugged figure clad in a worn leather jacket that speaks of countless adventures. His dark curls bounce slightly in the breeze, framing a chiseled jaw that seems to have been carved from stone. And then, there are those eyes—piercing blue, like the deep ocean—drawing me in with a magnetic pull that sends shivers racing down my spine. For a heartbeat, everything around me fades; the bustling sounds of the city are muted, leaving only the soft thrum of my pulse echoing in my ears.

Before I can fully absorb the moment, the light turns green, and I'm swept away in the current of pedestrians. I take one last glance over my shoulder, half-expecting him to be a figment of my imagination, but there he stands, a flicker of amusement dancing in his eyes as they catch mine. Heat rushes to my cheeks, and I feel the weight of his gaze as if it's a tangible force, stirring something deep within me. But time waits for no one, and I push forward, determined to reach the studio.

As I turn down a narrow alley, intending to cut through to the street parallel to the studio, my mind wanders to the daydreams that have plagued me since childhood. Memories of lace-trimmed tutus and scuffed ballet slippers swirl around, each one reminding me of a joy I once cherished. Yet, just as my nostalgia begins to envelop me, I feel the world tilt slightly, as if a hidden hand has nudged me off course. I try to adjust, but it's too late. I crash straight into him.

The impact is startling. I stumble backward, my heart racing as I look up to see that it's the very stranger who had captivated my attention moments before. His expression shifts from surprise to concern as his strong hands reach out instinctively to steady me. I catch a glimpse of his perfectly sculpted features, his rugged charm instantly softened by a playful smirk. "You okay there?" he asks, his voice smooth like honey, wrapping around me like a warm embrace.

Flustered, I take a moment to compose myself, the world around us fading away as I try to find my voice. "Uh, yeah! I mean, I'm fine!" I stammer, my cheeks burning with embarrassment. This isn't how I envisioned my return to the dance world—colliding with a stranger in an alley like some character in a cheesy rom-com.

His laughter is infectious, a deep, rumbling sound that seems to resonate in the very core of me. "Good to know I'm not a total menace," he quips, his eyes sparkling with mischief. There's an easy familiarity in the way he carries himself, as if he's accustomed to being the center of attention without even trying. The banter flows naturally between us, the initial awkwardness melting away as we share a moment that feels both fleeting and monumental.

"You're not a menace, just... unexpected," I reply, a shy smile creeping onto my lips. The alley around us is dimly lit, littered with remnants of the day—old newspapers fluttering like forgotten memories, the distant sound of laughter echoing from the street beyond. Yet, here, in this small pocket of the world, everything seems to pulse with a sense of possibility. Our laughter dances through the air, intertwining with the remnants of my past and the dreams I'm trying to reclaim.

Just as the moment feels poised to deepen, a cacophony of honking horns and shouting voices pulls me back to reality. My heart sinks at the thought of being late. I glance toward the studio, its cheerful façade now seemingly distant and unreachable. "I really should go," I murmur, the weight of my responsibilities pressing down on me.

"Of course," he replies, his tone surprisingly gentle, as if he understands the silent struggle hidden behind my forced smile. "But maybe next time, let's avoid the alley?" There's a teasing glint in his eyes that makes me laugh, a sound that feels foreign yet welcome.

"Deal," I say, a flicker of something unnameable igniting within me.

As I turn to leave, I can't help but steal one last glance at him. He stands there, a solitary figure in the chaotic rhythm of the city, and in that moment, I realize this encounter has already changed something inside me. With a final wave, I step away, my heart racing not just from the rush of the day but from the uncharted territory that lies ahead. The dance studio awaits, but it feels as if I've already begun a dance of my own—one that may lead me to places I've never dared to explore before.

The moment I step into the dance studio, I'm enveloped by the rich, nostalgic scent of polished wood and the faint residue of sweat that hangs in the air like an unspoken promise. Sunlight streams through large windows, casting long shadows across the floor, illuminating the dust motes that twirl lazily in the warmth. The space is alive with echoes of laughter and the rhythmic thud of feet moving in perfect sync. My heart flutters, caught between exhilaration and anxiety as I take in the familiar sight of mirrors lining the walls, reflecting back a younger version of myself—a girl who once believed in the magic of dance.

It's a cozy establishment, newly opened, and the walls are adorned with vibrant artwork depicting dancers in motion, their limbs frozen in beautiful poses that hint at stories untold. I catch a glimpse of a poster announcing the upcoming recital, the title boldly emblazoned in glittering letters. My breath catches at the thought of performing again, a longing igniting deep within me. I take a moment to inhale deeply, letting the atmosphere wrap around me like a warm blanket, and I can't help but smile at the mix of excitement and fear bubbling within.

A chorus of giggles pulls me from my reverie, drawing my attention to a group of young girls in colorful leotards, their hair tightly pulled into buns. They leap and twirl, their laughter ringing out like a symphony, infectious and pure. I can't help but envy their unfiltered joy; they dance with abandon, as if the world around them doesn't exist. In that moment, I remember the intoxicating feeling of freedom that came with every plié and pirouette, the exhilaration that swept through me like a tidal wave each time I stepped onto the stage.

"Hey! You made it!" A voice cuts through my nostalgia, pulling me back to the present. I turn to find Mia, the studio owner, bouncing toward me with the enthusiasm of a child. Her hair, a cascade of fiery curls, catches the light as she approaches, and her smile is wide enough to brighten even the cloudiest day. "I was beginning to think you'd bail on me. I know how tempting it is to stay curled up in bed when it's chilly out."

"Not a chance!" I assure her, my voice infused with the same enthusiasm she exudes. "I've been waiting for this day for so long." The truth is, I have. This studio is a dream come to life, a place where I can finally embrace my love for dance again, and I refuse to let anything hold me back—not even a chance encounter with a charming stranger.

"Great! Let's get started." Mia claps her hands together, her eyes sparkling with excitement. "I've arranged a warm-up class to ease everyone back into it. We have a mix of levels here today, but trust me, you'll fit right in." She gestures toward the other dancers, and I notice a mix of familiar faces—some old friends from my childhood days and others I recognize from the local dance scene.

As we warm up, my body feels both foreign and familiar, muscles awakening as I stretch and bend. Memories flood my mind like an old film reel, the flickering images of past performances—nights spent rehearsing under bright stage lights, the rush of adrenaline before stepping into the spotlight, the bittersweet thrill of applause. The rhythm of the music begins to seep into my bones, and I lose myself in the moment, every worry and hesitation dissolving away.

The class progresses, and I find my rhythm, dancing as if no one is watching. Each movement feels like a brushstroke on a canvas, painting my emotions with every beat. Laughter echoes through the studio, blending with the music as we push ourselves, encouraging each other in a way that feels both competitive and supportive. I feel the walls of doubt that have built up around me begin to crumble, replaced by a renewed sense of purpose.

Mia leads us through a series of combinations, her voice guiding us like a gentle breeze. "Remember to express yourselves! Dance is as much about feeling as it is about technique!" Her words resonate deeply within me, igniting a flicker of courage I thought I'd lost. The idea of fully embracing my passion, of dancing without the weight of expectation, begins to take root.

After the warm-up, we gather in a circle to share our stories. As I listen to others speak about their journeys, I find myself inspired by their resilience. Some have danced their whole lives, while others are returning after years away, just like me. Each narrative is a thread weaving together our collective love for dance, reminding me that I'm not alone in this pursuit. When my turn comes, I take a deep breath, feeling the warmth of camaraderie surrounding me.

"I'm Sarah," I say, the name rolling off my tongue with surprising ease. "I danced for years but stepped away for a while. Life took me in a different direction, but I'm finally back, and it feels like coming home." My voice wavers slightly, but the words feel true, each syllable resonating with the passion buried deep inside.

"Welcome home, Sarah!" Mia exclaims, her enthusiasm infectious. The group erupts in applause, a wave of encouragement washing over me. It's a small gesture, but it solidifies my decision to embrace this moment fully.

After class, as we stretch and cool down, my thoughts drift back to the stranger I collided with earlier. His piercing blue eyes flash in my mind, an unexpected spark in my otherwise predictable day. I wonder if he's nearby, perhaps wandering the streets of Maplewood or nursing a coffee at a local café, unaware of the impact he's had on me. There's a lingering curiosity about him, a sense of unfinished business that tugs at my heartstrings.

As I gather my things and bid farewell to my new friends, the sun begins to dip below the horizon, painting the sky in hues of orange and purple. I step outside, inhaling the cool evening air, the scent of blooming magnolias still lingering. It feels like the perfect ending to a day that has reignited my passion for dance, yet a small part of me yearns for more.

I walk through the streets, my footsteps echoing in the growing quiet. With each step, I feel lighter, as if I'm shedding layers of hesitation and self-doubt. The world around me is alive, the streetlights flickering to life like stars awakening in the twilight. Yet, in the back of my mind, the stranger's blue eyes linger, a vivid reminder that life is full of unexpected twists, and perhaps, just perhaps, it's time to embrace those twists with open arms. The night stretches before me, full of promise, as I wonder what new adventures await in the heart of Maplewood.

The evening air wraps around me like a soft shawl as I stroll through the vibrant streets of Maplewood, each step echoing with newfound confidence. The sun has surrendered to the horizon, leaving behind a canvas splashed with deep indigos and fiery oranges. The sidewalks are alive with laughter and conversation, punctuated by the distant sound of jazz drifting from a nearby bar. I can't help but smile at the familiar sights—the old bookstore with its wooden sign creaking in the gentle breeze, the gelato shop where children's giggles intermingle with the sound of scoops against crisp cones. It feels like a postcard of my childhood, each corner a fragment of a story I thought I'd left behind.

But there's something different tonight, a charge in the air that makes every moment feel ripe with possibility. I find myself wishing to turn down a random street, to explore the nooks and crannies of my hometown that I've overlooked for so long. The studio has breathed new life into me, igniting a desire to reclaim the joy that dance once brought. With each step, the memory of the stranger lingers, the warmth of his laughter still echoing in my mind like a favorite song that refuses to fade away.

Just as I'm about to cross the street to visit my favorite coffee shop, a flicker of movement catches my eye. There he is, the enigmatic stranger, leaning against the brick wall of a small café. He's laughing with a friend, his dark curls tousled, the streetlight illuminating his features like a spotlight on a stage. My heart skips a beat, a rush of exhilaration flooding my senses. The very essence of our earlier encounter fills the air, a playful tension that makes the world around us blur into insignificance.

For a brief moment, we lock eyes, and a thrill runs through me, igniting an unspoken connection that feels almost tangible. My heart races as I consider the possibility of approaching him, of breaking the barrier that fate has constructed between us. But doubt creeps in, whispering caution into my ear. What could I possibly say to him? The last thing I want is to stumble over my words or fumble through some awkward small talk. I think back to the lightness of our earlier exchange and how it ignited something in me that has been dormant for far too long.

Just as I decide to muster my courage, he glances away, his attention returning to his friend. I'm left standing on the sidewalk, a mere spectator to the scene playing out before me, an eager player but not quite ready to step into the spotlight. The moment stretches, taut and electric, and I find myself caught in a delicious indecision. Should I take that leap? The studio's warmth still radiates within me, reminding me that life is too short to let opportunities slip by.

With a deep breath, I take a step toward him, feeling the thrill of anticipation pulsing through my veins. I'm on the cusp of reclaiming not just my passion for dance but a sense of spontaneity that has been buried under layers of routine. My foot lands on the cobblestone, and it feels as if the world slows around me. With each movement, I silently prepare for a conversation that may or may not lead anywhere, but I realize that it's the act of stepping forward that truly matters.

"Hey," I say, my voice steady despite the rapid thump of my heart. His gaze snaps back to mine, surprise lighting up his face before transforming into that charming grin that seemed to draw me in from the moment we collided.

"Hello again," he replies, the easy warmth in his tone making me feel instantly at ease. "I was wondering if I'd see you again after our little mishap."

"I was hoping I wouldn't have to avoid alleys forever," I joke, a playful smile tugging at my lips. "You seem to be the type who can take a wrong turn and still end up in the right place."

He chuckles, the sound rich and inviting, wrapping around me like a familiar melody. "I like that philosophy. Name's Jake, by the way. What's yours?"

"Sarah," I reply, feeling the name roll off my tongue like it's a treasured secret. "I just started at the dance studio downtown."

"Dance? That's awesome! I've always admired dancers," he responds, his eyes lighting up with genuine interest. "So, what brought you back?"

The question hangs in the air between us, inviting me to peel back the layers of my own hesitations. I take a moment, allowing the memories to wash over me—the late nights spent rehearsing, the thrill of performing, the abrupt halt that life threw at me. "I took some time away," I admit. "Life got busy, and I lost touch with what made me happy. But I think I'm ready to find that joy again."

"Finding joy is a worthy pursuit," Jake agrees, leaning slightly closer as if to hear my thoughts more intimately. "It sounds like you've got the right spirit for it."

We chat for what feels like hours, weaving through topics as effortlessly as a dancer glides across the stage. He shares stories of his adventures traveling the country, chasing sunsets and chasing dreams, and I find myself captivated by his passion for life. With every laugh, with every shared story, the initial spark between us grows brighter, illuminating a path that seems to beckon us forward.

As the night deepens, I feel an undeniable connection building, something that feels refreshing and exciting. Yet, part of me remains cautious, wary of the fleeting nature of chance encounters. Still, I can't shake the feeling that this moment might be the beginning of something more—a dance of its own, a rhythm that pulls us closer.

"Would you want to grab coffee sometime? You know, without the risk of colliding in an alley?" Jake suggests, a glint of mischief in his eyes.

"I'd like that," I reply, unable to suppress the smile that blooms across my face. The invitation lingers in the air like the last note of a beautiful song, a promise of more moments like this to come.

As we exchange numbers, my heart swells with the thrill of possibility, and I realize that this chance encounter may just be the spark I needed to reignite the fire within me. The world feels more vibrant, each color more vivid, each sound more harmonious. I leave him standing on that cobblestone street, a sense of hope swirling around me as I walk away, knowing that sometimes, the most beautiful dances begin with a wrong turn.

The city glows softly around me as I make my way home, the anticipation of what lies ahead intertwining with the remnants of my past. The journey to reclaim my love for dance has just begun, but with each step, I feel invigorated, ready to embrace whatever comes next. After all, life is a dance, and I intend to step boldly into the rhythm.

Chapter 2: Rediscovering Old Passions

The studio's doors swing open with a creak, welcoming me into a world where dreams pirouette with reality. The scent of polished wood and faint lavender wafts through the air, mingling with the faintest hint of sweat—a nostalgic reminder of all the hours I spent here, transforming my youthful ambitions into graceful pirouettes. Sunlight spills through the large windows, casting an ethereal glow on the polished wooden floor, illuminating the space like a stage set for a grand performance. Each plank of wood gleams, reflecting the myriad of dreams that have taken flight within these walls. It feels like a sanctuary, a sacred space where stories unfold and the heartbeats synchronize with the pulse of the music.

Lena stands in the center, her vibrant energy radiating as she stretches her limbs with an elegance that seems almost effortless. Her auburn hair, pulled into a messy bun, frames her face, which is illuminated by a smile so genuine it could warm the coldest of hearts. "You're here! I was beginning to think you'd let the world steal you away," she teases, her voice ringing like the chimes of a delicate bell. I can't help but smile back, feeling a flutter of excitement as her infectious enthusiasm washes over me like a soothing balm.

As we settle onto the floor, our bodies stretching and flexing in unison, the old memories flood back like a tide. I can feel the familiar ache in my muscles, a sensation I had long forgotten, yet it feels like an old friend reuniting after years apart. With each stretch, the tension that had woven itself into my body begins to unravel, thread by thread, releasing the knots of anxiety and uncertainty that had settled in my chest since that awkward encounter just moments ago.

"Let's start with the warm-up," Lena suggests, her eyes sparkling with the thrill of the upcoming choreography. The music begins to play, a soft, lilting melody that fills the room, wrapping around me like a warm embrace. The notes dance in the air, inviting me to join them, and I find myself moving instinctively, letting the rhythm guide my body.

As I sway and stretch, I can almost hear the echoes of the past—a cacophony of laughter, the scuffling of shoes against the floor, the whispers of encouragement from my peers. It's as if the walls themselves are alive, breathing in the memories of countless rehearsals, late nights, and dreams that soared high above the clouds. I can almost see the silhouettes of my younger self and my friends, their bodies twisting and turning in perfect synchrony, each one a note in the grand symphony of our shared aspirations.

But amidst the euphoria of the dance, the stranger's image flickers in the corner of my mind, like a half-remembered tune that refuses to fade away. His gaze had been piercing, as if he could see through the layers I had carefully built around my heart. I shake my head, willing myself to focus, to let go of the world beyond these walls. The melody swells, urging me to shed my inhibitions and immerse myself in the artistry of movement.

Lena begins to teach me the choreography, her voice a steady guide as she illustrates each step with grace and precision. I watch her intently, absorbing the fluidity of her movements, my heart racing in time with the music. My body begins to remember the language of dance—the way my feet should land, the tilt of my head, the arch of my back. Each step feels like a conversation, a dialogue between my soul and the universe, rekindling a fire I thought had long been extinguished.

As I lose myself in the choreography, the world outside fades into a distant hum. The mirrors reflect my image, a young woman caught in a moment of sheer bliss, her worries melting away with every spin and leap. There's a buoyancy in my heart, a lightness that comes from reconnecting with something that once defined me. Dance becomes a sanctuary, a place where I can express the unspoken words lodged in my throat, the feelings I often struggle to articulate.

But just as I find my footing, that fleeting memory of the stranger intrudes again, as potent as the scent of the freshly polished floor. I can't quite grasp why he lingers in my thoughts, like a shadow I can't shake. Perhaps it's the intensity of our brief encounter, the way he seemed to peel back the layers of my facade with just a glance. I push it aside, determined to lose myself in the rhythm, to chase the whisper of revival that has begun to pulse through my veins.

With each step, I rediscover a part of myself I thought I had lost to the relentless grind of adulthood. The clinking of jewelry, the soft swish of fabric, the sound of laughter—it all fills the studio, blending into a harmonious backdrop. It's as if the universe conspired to bring me back to this moment, to this space where passion reigns and the mundane is transformed into the extraordinary.

Lena pauses to adjust the playlist, her eyes sparkling with mischief. "Now for the fun part!" she declares, and I can't help but laugh, the sound echoing off the walls, mingling with the music that swells around us. I feel alive, invigorated by the energy swirling within this studio, which feels like a cocoon wrapped in warmth and possibility.

In this sanctuary of movement, I am reminded of who I am, of the dreams that once set my heart alight. The dance is not merely an art form; it is a celebration of life, a reminder that amidst the chaos of the world, there is beauty to be found in the rhythm, in the flow. And as I twirl, surrendering to the music, I know—this is where I belong.

The music swells around me, enveloping the studio like a warm blanket, inviting and familiar. Each note wraps around my body, urging me to surrender to the rhythm. With Lena leading the way, our bodies begin to move in harmony, a tapestry of motion woven together through shared passion. The choreography unfolds like a story, each step revealing a new chapter in this enchanting narrative of rediscovery. I close my eyes for a moment, allowing the melody to wash over me, my feet finding their way instinctively across the polished wood, gliding and dipping as though they had always known this path.

Lena's voice breaks through the haze, guiding me like a lighthouse in the fog. "Remember to breathe! Dance isn't just about the steps; it's about the space you create," she reminds me, her eyes alight with the joy of teaching. I nod, absorbing her words, and take a deep breath, letting the air fill my lungs like an elixir, a reminder that I am here, fully present. As we move, I find my thoughts drifting, leaving behind the shadows of doubt that had clouded my mind for too long. The stranger's piercing gaze slips away, replaced by the comforting familiarity of this space and the exhilaration of dance.

The choreography becomes a playground, each turn and leap transforming my insecurities into an exploration of possibility. I throw my arms wide, reveling in the freedom of movement, feeling like a bird unshackled from its cage. The studio walls seem to hum in encouragement, echoing with the laughter of past students, the whispers of dreams birthed in this very room. I can almost see them, silhouettes darting across the floor, their youthful spirits igniting my own.

As the music shifts, so does my energy. The tempo picks up, and I push myself to keep pace with Lena, whose laughter fills the air like a sweet symphony. "You've got this!" she calls, her voice buoyant. I can feel the warmth of her encouragement wrapping around me like a cozy scarf, and I find myself smiling, heart racing in tandem with the upbeat rhythm. I lose track of time, caught in the ebb and flow of choreography, each move becoming a brushstroke on the canvas of my life.

With every stretch, every spin, I feel the burdens of the outside world beginning to dissolve. The stresses of work, the ghost of that strange encounter, all of it fades into the background, mere whispers against the vibrant pulse of this moment. I am reminded of the countless hours I spent here as a child, practicing for recitals, perfecting every movement, each rehearsal a stepping stone toward a dream I had almost forgotten. The studio transforms into a time machine, taking me back to when my only worry was whether I would land the pirouette or hit the high note in a routine.

But amidst the exhilaration, there's a flicker of uncertainty that refuses to be completely extinguished. The stranger's face flits in and out of my mind like a ghost, an enigmatic presence lurking just beneath the surface of my joy. I had felt a connection, a spark that was both exhilarating and terrifying. The intensity of his gaze had sparked something deep within me, but now, in this vibrant space, I long to push those thoughts aside. I want to embrace the present, to reclaim my passion without the shadows of doubt clouding my heart.

The routine flows effortlessly, and before long, we are drenched in sweat, laughter spilling from our lips like confetti. I can feel my muscles waking up, reminding me of their power and grace, and I relish in this physical awakening. Each leap takes me higher, a release of pent-up energy, and I let the joy of movement pulse through my veins, every heartbeat in sync with the beat of the music.

"Let's add a bit of flair!" Lena exclaims, her eyes sparkling mischievously. She demonstrates a flourish, a dramatic twist of the wrist that adds a new layer of depth to our movements. I watch her, captivated by her enthusiasm, and mimic her gesture, the movement becoming an extension of my own spirit. With every flourish, I can feel the walls of the studio pulse with life, as if they are joining in the celebration of this moment, this rediscovery.

The energy in the room heightens, and as we dance, I find myself breaking through barriers I didn't even know existed. I close my eyes once more, surrendering to the music and letting it lead me. The world fades into a blur, and I feel light, as though I could soar above the ground. I imagine the wind lifting me, the sensation of flying, of being free from the weights that had anchored me for too long. In this moment, I am not defined by my past or by the gaze of that stranger; I am defined by the dance, by the rhythm that pulses within me.

As we finish the routine, breathless and exhilarated, I can't help but burst into laughter. It's a sound that reverberates through the studio, echoing off the walls, a testament to the joy of rediscovery. Lena joins in, her laughter bright and infectious, and we share a moment of pure bliss, two souls connected by the love of dance and the thrill of creativity.

But even as I bask in this warmth, I feel the inkling of a question lingering at the back of my mind. What does it mean to embrace these passions when the outside world seems determined to pull me away? The stranger's presence had brought a spark of curiosity, a challenge to confront the parts of myself I had buried. Would I dare to explore that connection further, to confront the unknown, to see where it might lead me?

For now, though, I push those thoughts aside, focusing instead on the vibrant energy that surrounds me. The studio, with its wooden floors and mirrored walls, has become my sanctuary once more—a sacred space where I can dance my fears away, transforming them into movements that express the joy of being alive. In this moment, the world outside seems far away, and all that exists is the rhythm of my heart, the pulse of the music, and the exhilaration of rediscovering what it means to truly dance.

As the last notes of our routine fade into silence, the studio stands still, a sanctuary cloaked in the soft hum of post-dance euphoria. I take a moment to relish this sensation, breathing in deeply, the air infused with the sweet scent of fresh paint and the lingering aroma of sweat—evidence of our hard work. It feels like a homecoming, and yet, a nagging thought threads its way through my mind, wrapping itself around my heart: how do I carry this newfound passion beyond these walls?

Lena busies herself with adjusting the stereo, and I catch my reflection in the mirror, a mosaic of sweat and smiles. My hair has come loose, tendrils framing my face like a halo, a testament to the joy that has reinvigorated my spirit. But then, as if summoned by my thoughts, the stranger's image flashes before me, his deep-set eyes a puzzle I cannot decipher. He felt like a riddle, enticing and perplexing. What had we shared in that brief encounter? Was it mere coincidence, or was it something more significant, a thread woven into the fabric of my reality?

"Let's take a break," Lena chirps, pulling me from my reverie. She plops down onto the floor, and I follow suit, stretching my legs out in front of me. "Tell me, what's been going on in your life? Besides, you know, avoiding dance classes like the plague?" She nudges me playfully, her eyes sparkling with mischief.

I chuckle, the sound bubbling up like soda fizz. "Life has a funny way of throwing you off balance, doesn't it? I've been... busy." I hesitate, feeling the weight of my words. The truth is, the rhythm of my life had faltered long before I stepped foot in this studio again. Work had consumed me, and my aspirations lay buried beneath a mountain of spreadsheets and deadlines.

"Busy is just code for 'I've forgotten how to live,'" Lena quips, her brow arched knowingly. "You've got to reclaim your time. Dance is not just something you do; it's a part of who you are." Her words hang in the air like a mantra, echoing in the corners of my mind. I can't help but wonder: who was I before I allowed life to sweep me away?

As I sit there, stretching my limbs and basking in the afterglow of dance, I decide that I won't allow myself to be swept away again. I want to uncover those lost fragments of myself, and maybe—just maybe—discover what lies beneath that stranger's enigmatic gaze. With a renewed sense of purpose, I rise to my feet, a smile dancing on my lips. "Okay, I'm ready for more."

Lena beams, a look of triumph on her face, and we dive back into the choreography, my body now fueled by determination and clarity. Each move is a reminder of who I am, a dialogue with my past and a promise to my future. As we flow through the steps, I can feel the boundaries of the studio dissolving, the mirrors becoming portals to a world where my dreams are alive, vibrant, and within reach.

The routine begins to morph into something new—our steps intertwining, a conversation unfolding in motion. Lena encourages improvisation, a spark igniting between us as we layer our movements with personal flair. It becomes less about perfection and more about expression. I allow my body to speak, to sing the words I can't articulate. Each twist and turn feels like peeling back layers of an onion, revealing the raw, unfiltered essence of my soul.

With every leap, I feel lighter, the weight of expectation slipping away. I want to dance for myself, to be unshackled from the roles I've been playing. As we finish the sequence, breathless and laughing, I notice the sunlight beginning to dip lower in the sky, casting a golden hue across the studio. It's a reminder that time moves on, relentless and unyielding, and I want to seize every moment before it slips through my fingers like grains of sand.

As we wrap up the session, Lena gestures toward the window, where the last rays of the day filter through, painting the room in shades of amber. "Let's take it outside," she suggests, her voice brimming with enthusiasm. "Dance isn't confined to four walls; it breathes in the open air, finds new rhythms in the world around us."

I follow her lead, my heart racing with anticipation. We step out onto the small balcony that overlooks a bustling street, the sounds of the city merging with the fading notes of our practice. I can feel the energy buzzing around me—laughter, chatter, the distant hum of traffic—a vibrant soundtrack to our impromptu performance.

"Let go of your inhibitions," Lena encourages, and as if on cue, she begins to move. Her body sways, arms floating gracefully above her head, embodying the very spirit of freedom. I watch, entranced, before joining her, my own body responding to the rhythm of the city. The cool evening breeze wraps around me, a gentle reminder that I am alive, that I am here.

We dance under the sky, the stars beginning to twinkle above like diamonds scattered across a velvet canvas. The world blurs around us as we become lost in the music of our hearts. Laughter bubbles forth, echoing off the walls of the buildings surrounding us. In this moment, I am no longer just a dancer; I am a part of something larger, a melody woven into the fabric of life itself.

As we twirl and leap, I glance up at the stars, their light piercing through the dusk. I am reminded of the vastness of the universe, of the infinite possibilities that await me if I choose to embrace them. The stranger's face flits through my mind again, but this time, instead of uncertainty, I feel a spark of curiosity. What story lies behind those intense eyes? What chapter remains to be written?

"See? This is what it's all about!" Lena calls, her laughter ringing clear like a bell. I can't help but smile, my heart swelling with gratitude for this moment, this rediscovery of passion. The music may have changed, but the dance continues, swirling and spiraling like a ribbon in the wind.

As the final notes of our impromptu performance fade into the night, I find myself standing at the edge of possibility. The studio has become a portal, not just to the past, but to a future shimmering with potential. And in that moment, I vow to embrace the journey ahead, to explore the depths of my desires and confront the stranger who lingers in my thoughts.

With the stars as my witnesses, I will dance my way into the unknown, open to the adventures that await. The rhythm of life is calling, and I am ready to respond, heart wide open, ready to step boldly into the next act of my story.

Chapter 3: A Heartwarming Love Story

The sun dipped low over the Brooklyn skyline, casting a warm golden hue across the cracked pavement of the old dance studio. Inside, the air hummed with energy, alive with the sound of music and laughter. I leaned against the barre, my muscles aching from another long rehearsal, and watched my fellow dancers pirouette through the last movements of a particularly challenging routine. The smell of sweat and chalk mingled, but somehow it felt comforting, a testament to our hard work and shared ambition. Each dancer brought something unique to the floor—Sarah, with her effortless grace and gentle laughter; Malik, who could turn the simplest step into a daring leap; and of course, Lena, who seemed to float rather than walk. Together, we created a tapestry of passion and dreams, vibrant and layered like the graffiti that adorned the building's walls.

Despite the joy that enveloped us, there was a flicker of uncertainty in my heart. The memory of that man from the alley loomed over me, not as a shadow but as an electric spark. His gaze had been magnetic, pulling me in like a tide that refused to recede. Jason. Just the thought of his name sent a thrill coursing through me, as if I could still feel the rough texture of his stubble against my skin, the warmth of his body brushing against mine in that brief moment of chaos. It was ridiculous to dwell on a stranger, but the way he'd looked at me—those eyes, deep and playful—left me feeling both exhilarated and vulnerable.

On that particular afternoon, as the music swelled and the choreography spiraled into its crescendo, I felt his presence before I saw him. It was an undeniable instinct, the kind that makes your heart thud louder than the rhythm of the beat. When I dared to glance up, there he was, leaning casually against the doorframe, arms crossed, a bemused smile playing on his lips. My breath caught, and for a moment, the world around me faded into a blur. Jason had returned, and everything in the room shifted.

"Hey, dancer," he called, his voice smooth and teasing, sending a ripple of warmth down my spine. The other dancers noticed too, their movements pausing mid-step as they turned to gawk at the unexpected interruption. I could feel my cheeks heat as I stumbled through the routine, trying to maintain composure while my mind raced with a mix of embarrassment and excitement.

I returned his smile, a flicker of confidence sparking within me. "What brings you back?" I asked, forcing my voice to be steady, despite the butterflies swirling in my stomach.

"Just checking out the competition," he replied, his eyes glinting with mischief. "You're not half bad, but I'm pretty sure I could give you a run for your money."

His playful banter pulled me in like a magnet, igniting a flicker of challenge in my heart. There was something intoxicating about his confidence, the way he stood there, unabashed and magnetic. I took a moment to appreciate the sharp lines of his jaw, the tousled hair that looked as if it had been sculpted by a gentle breeze, and the warmth that radiated from him, illuminating the dim hallway.

"Care to prove it?" I shot back, feeling a burst of energy surge through me.

His smile widened, revealing a hint of amusement, as if he relished this banter as much as I did. "Maybe one day. But for now, I'd love to see you finish your routine. I'm intrigued."

With renewed determination, I turned my focus back to the practice. The music flowed through me, a current of life and rhythm that pulsed with every beat. I danced as if he weren't there, pouring my heart into every movement, pushing my limits. In that moment, I was not just a dancer; I was a storyteller, each turn and leap conveying the joy, the pain, and the triumph of the journey.

As the final notes faded and I struck my last pose, a wave of applause washed over me, an echo of approval that felt almost surreal. My fellow dancers cheered, but my heart raced for another reason entirely. I turned to find Jason still standing there, his expression a mixture of admiration and intrigue.

"Wow," he said, shaking his head slightly as if trying to comprehend what he'd just witnessed. "You really have something special. I mean, I've seen dancers before, but you... you dance like you're trying to breathe life into the air."

His words wrapped around me, warm and reassuring, and for a moment, I could almost forget the tumult of my past, the insecurities that often clouded my thoughts. Instead, I felt like I was standing on the edge of something beautiful, something vibrant and alive.

"Thanks," I replied, a genuine smile breaking through my earlier nerves. "That means a lot coming from you."

He stepped closer, the distance between us shrinking, the energy palpable. "I'm serious. You're incredible. I can't help but wonder what else you're hiding behind that dance persona of yours."

There was a hint of mischief in his tone, and I felt the flush return to my cheeks. Was he flirting with me? Or was it just the heady mix of adrenaline and admiration? Either way, I was captivated, my heart dancing to a rhythm all its own.

"Perhaps I'll show you," I said, the challenge in my voice mingling with a hint of flirtation.

With that, the world outside the studio faded away, leaving just the two of us, suspended in a moment of possibility. I felt alive, as if this fleeting encounter held the key to something extraordinary, a spark that could ignite a new chapter in my life—one that was filled with passion, dance, and perhaps a little bit of love.

The rhythm of rehearsals became my lifeblood, a pulse that thrummed through my days, infusing each moment with purpose. As weeks slipped by like sand through an hourglass, I found myself entwined in a whirlwind of choreography and camaraderie. Each morning greeted me with the familiar sound of sneakers scuffing against the hardwood floors, the scent of liniment wafting through the air, mingling with the faint echo of old vinyl records spinning in the background. My fellow dancers became my family, their laughter a balm for the insecurities that sometimes threatened to drown me.

We shared stories during breaks, each revelation peeling back layers of who we were beyond the dance. Sarah, with her infectious giggle, revealed that she danced to escape the mundane monotony of her day job in marketing. Malik, always the entertainer, confessed that he dreamed of choreographing for Broadway someday, his ambition burning as brightly as the studio lights. Lena, who seemed to carry a world of grace within her, spoke softly of her mother, a former dancer who had encouraged her to pursue this path, though the weight of expectation sometimes pressed heavily on her shoulders.

Amidst this vibrant tapestry of shared dreams and struggles, Jason lingered in the periphery, a figure I could never quite shake. His playful jibes and keen observations became a welcome distraction from the rigors of practice, and each encounter ignited a spark of curiosity within me. I would catch glimpses of him outside the studio, leaning against lampposts, watching the sunset spill colors over the skyline, a faint smile playing on his lips as if he held secrets I was desperate to uncover.

One rainy afternoon, as the clouds cloaked the city in a gray shroud, I found myself alone in the studio, the only sound the soft patter of raindrops against the windows. My muscles ached, and I was caught between exhaustion and the adrenaline of my morning routine. I decided to practice my solo piece, a lyrical expression of longing and hope, each movement imbued with the weight of my unspoken emotions. The studio was my sanctuary, and as I danced, the world outside faded away, the notes enveloping me like a warm embrace.

Just as I reached the emotional climax of my routine, the door creaked open, interrupting the moment. I turned, breathless and slightly startled, and found Jason standing there, dripping wet and grinning, his hair tousled and eyes sparkling with mischief.

"Nice moves," he called out, stepping into the room like a summer storm that had decided to stick around. "I'd say you've got a little bit of magic in those steps."

I couldn't help but smile, feeling the heat rush to my cheeks. "Thanks, but I'm not sure I'd call it magic. More like a desperate attempt not to trip over my own feet."

"Desperation looks good on you," he replied, his tone teasing yet genuine. He leaned against the wall, watching me with an intensity that made my heart race.

"What are you doing here? Shouldn't you be out there charming the rain?" I gestured to the window, where the droplets danced against the glass like a million tiny ballerinas.

"I came to see if you'd like some company," he said, a playful glint in his eyes. "You know, in case you were planning on wallowing in your own melancholy."

"Wallowing? Please. I'd never be that dramatic," I shot back, though there was a warmth in my chest that told me I didn't mind the intrusion at all.

With a flourish, he grabbed a nearby chair and spun it around to face me, perching himself on it with a casual ease that somehow only added to his charm. "Good. Because I'd hate to ruin my vision of a strong, independent dancer who can't be brought down by a little rain."

As we bantered back and forth, the hours slipped away unnoticed. Jason's humor was infectious, and I found myself opening up to him in ways I hadn't anticipated. We talked about everything—our childhoods, our dreams, even our failures. I discovered that he was a struggling musician, pouring his heart into his lyrics while balancing a day job at a coffee shop, where he sometimes performed open mic nights. There was a sincerity in his voice that made me feel seen, and with each shared laugh, I felt the walls I had carefully constructed around my heart begin to crumble.

"Why dance?" he asked at one point, his tone shifting to something more serious. "What draws you to it?"

I hesitated, the weight of his question pressing down on me. "It's the only time I feel completely alive. When I dance, it's like the world disappears, and all that matters is the music and my body moving to it. It's cathartic."

He nodded, his gaze thoughtful. "That's beautiful. I get that. Music does the same for me."

We fell into a comfortable silence, the only sound the gentle rhythm of the rain outside, a soothing backdrop to our growing connection. I realized how easily he slipped into my life, how the laughter we shared felt like a soft melody that lingered long after the notes had faded.

"I should probably get back to my rehearsals," I said reluctantly, but the thought of leaving this moment with him felt like closing a door I wasn't ready to shut.

"Why don't I join you?" he suggested, his eyes alight with enthusiasm. "I might not be able to dance, but I can cheer you on."

With a playful grin, I replied, "I warn you, my routine might be a little too... expressive for your taste."

"Expressive is exactly what I'm here for," he said, standing up with a flourish. "Lead the way."

As I resumed my practice, I felt him watching intently, his presence a warm ember in the chilly studio. I poured everything into my movements, each leap and twirl infused with the energy of our conversation, the chemistry that seemed to crackle in the air between us. And for the first time in a long while, I felt not just alive but genuinely hopeful.

As I danced, the movements began to intertwine with Jason's presence, creating a rhythm that felt almost like an extension of him—a silent conversation that transcended words. He stood at the edge of the studio, leaning casually against the wall, his arms crossed, an appreciative smile lighting up his face. Each time I glanced his way, I caught a flicker of admiration in his eyes, which fueled my passion. The space transformed around us; the mirrors reflected not just my image but the spark of something new and exhilarating that seemed to swirl in the air.

As the days turned into weeks, Jason became a familiar fixture in my rehearsals. He would drop by at odd hours, often bringing coffee or treats from the café where he worked, turning mundane breaks into joyous interludes filled with laughter and playful banter. The awkwardness that once colored our first encounter dissipated, replaced by a camaraderie that made me feel like I had known him forever. We shared stories of our dreams—his passion for music, my desire to dance my way onto the world stage—and those moments solidified a bond that grew deeper with each interaction.

One evening, after a particularly grueling rehearsal, we found ourselves on the rooftop of the studio, the Manhattan skyline sprawling before us like a shimmering tapestry of dreams. The city pulsed beneath us, a living entity teeming with stories, while the sunset draped everything in hues of orange and violet. Jason leaned against the railing, the wind tousling his hair, and as he began to strum a guitar he'd brought along, the notes floated through the air like whispered secrets.

"Music has a way of making everything feel right, doesn't it?" he said, his fingers dancing over the strings.

I nodded, captivated by the way he poured himself into the melody. "It really does. It's like it understands you when words fail."

He glanced at me, a hint of mischief in his gaze. "Then dance with me."

"Here?" I laughed, the thought of dancing on a rooftop under the open sky feeling wildly exhilarating yet slightly terrifying.

"Why not?" He smiled, the kind of smile that could light up the darkest of days. "Let's make our own stage."

Before I could protest, he set the guitar down and stood, his arms outstretched in an invitation. There was something electrifying about the moment, a thrill that surged through me as I stepped forward. The music began to fill the air around us, and as I twirled, the city became a backdrop to our impromptu performance. I let the music guide me, and every movement felt alive, the rhythm syncing with the pounding of my heart.

He matched my movements, his feet shuffling in time with mine, and for a blissful moment, we were two souls unbound by the constraints of our lives, lost in the joy of pure, unadulterated expression. Laughter bubbled between us as I spun, the cool evening air wrapping around me, invigorating my spirit. It was as if the world had paused to watch our little dance, a celebration of spontaneity and connection, and I felt an overwhelming sense of freedom.

But beneath that exhilaration lingered a fear that loomed large—what would happen when the music stopped? The thought of losing this connection, this electric spark between us, sent a pang through my heart. I took a deep breath, trying to quell the unease that threatened to surface, but Jason's laughter broke through the haze.

"See? You're a natural," he said, panting slightly as we both collapsed against the railing, breaths mingling in the cool air. "We should make this a regular thing. Dancing under the stars, guitar in hand."

"Only if you promise to keep playing," I teased, nudging him lightly with my shoulder.

"Deal," he replied, his expression turning serious for a moment. "But in all honesty, I'm glad I stumbled into that alley. Meeting you feels... unexpected. In a good way."

The sincerity in his voice caught me off guard, and I turned my gaze toward the skyline, my heart fluttering uncomfortably. "It feels that way for me too," I admitted, the words spilling out before I could stop them. "Like you've pulled me into a world I didn't even know I needed."

He was quiet for a moment, and I could feel the weight of his gaze. When I looked back at him, the look in his eyes made my stomach twist in the most exhilarating way.

"Then let's not let this be just a moment," he said softly, his tone earnest. "Let's make it a journey."

The promise hung in the air, and I could almost touch it—the potential for something beautiful, something that could transform my world. As we sat side by side, watching the sun dip below the horizon, I knew deep down that I was ready to embrace whatever this journey might hold.

In the days that followed, we fell into an easy rhythm, our lives intertwining like threads in a tapestry. He would accompany me to rehearsals, and I would cheer him on during his open mic nights at the café. The more I learned about him, the more I admired his passion and dedication. He had a way of bringing light into the darkest corners of my thoughts, gently nudging me to confront my fears about the future.

On a particularly bright Saturday morning, we ventured to the Brooklyn Botanic Garden, the air alive with the scent of blooming flowers. Jason, with his guitar slung casually over his shoulder, strummed tunes that danced with the breezes. I twirled through the flower beds, surrounded by bursts of color, laughter spilling from my lips as petals swirled around us.

"Alright, what's next?" he asked, eyes sparkling with mischief.

"Let's find a secluded spot for a proper jam session," I suggested, my heart racing at the thought of more intimate moments with him.

As we wandered deeper into the garden, we stumbled upon a quiet alcove, the trees arching overhead like a natural cathedral. Jason began to play, and I let myself fall into the music, a whirl of movement and emotion. The world around us faded as I danced freely, completely lost in the rhythm, the melody intertwining with the beating of my heart.

In that moment, I felt invincible—alive and whole, as if every fiber of my being was resonating with joy. When I finally paused, breathless and grinning, I found Jason watching me, his expression a mix of admiration and something deeper.

"Can I be honest?" he said, his voice low and sincere.

"Always."

"I've never met anyone who lights up a room the way you do. You dance like you're unafraid of anything, and it's incredible to see."

I felt a warmth bloom in my chest, a mix of pride and vulnerability. "It's easier to dance like that when I'm with you."

He stepped closer, the distance between us vanishing as he tucked a loose strand of hair behind my ear. The air felt charged, heavy with unspoken words, and for a heartbeat, I thought he might lean in, the world around us blurring into a soft haze.

But then, just as quickly, the moment slipped away, like a dream fading upon waking. "Let's head back," he said, his voice tinged with something I couldn't quite decipher.

As we strolled back through the garden, the day began to cool, the sun casting long shadows as evening approached. I replayed our moments in my mind, a tapestry of laughter and connection, and felt a tug of hope within me. Maybe, just maybe, we were crafting something beautiful together—an unexpected journey that had begun in an alleyway and had spiraled into a vibrant dance of possibilities.

In the weeks that followed, our connection deepened like the roots of a mighty oak, resilient and strong. Every rehearsal felt infused with an extra spark, and each moment spent together blossomed with unspoken promise. There was magic in the air, a tapestry woven from dreams, laughter, and the sweet thrill of the unknown. As I moved through life, surrounded by the vibrant world we were creating, I felt ready to embrace whatever came next. The journey had only just begun, and with Jason by my side, I was eager to see where it would lead.

Chapter 4: Unexpected Collaborations

The sun had dipped below the horizon, casting an amber glow over the rooftop terrace where I found myself perched on the edge of nostalgia. The city skyline sprawled before me, a vibrant tapestry of lights flickering like a thousand fireflies caught in a warm summer's embrace. I had always loved New York in the twilight hours, when the chaos of the day ebbed, and the streets below whispered secrets that danced on the warm breeze. It was a perfect backdrop for the unexpected collaborations that had recently entered my life, and tonight felt particularly electric.

Jason was seated across from me, a picture of charisma wrapped in a fitted denim jacket that accentuated his lean frame. His dark hair fell in soft waves, framing his face, and his piercing green eyes sparkled with the kind of enthusiasm that could ignite the dullest of rooms. He had a way of speaking that made each word feel like a gentle caress, coaxing thoughts and feelings from deep within me. As he shared his vision of an artistic endeavor—a fusion of music and dance that he claimed would be revolutionary—my heart raced. The flickering candles on our table cast shadows that danced as he animatedly spoke, mirroring the whirlwind of emotions swirling inside me.

"I can't just sit back and let someone else take the reins," he said, his voice rich with conviction. "I need someone who can breathe life into my music, someone who understands the language of movement as I do. You have that magic, Emily." His words, though flattering, felt daunting. Did I truly have the magic he sought, or was I merely an echo of who I once was?

The very thought of stepping back into the spotlight after years of quietude was enough to set my nerves alight. Memories of past performances—the bright lights, the roaring applause, the intoxicating adrenaline—flooded my mind, mixing with the fear that had slowly crept in over the years. I had spent so long cultivating a life of comfortable anonymity, a life far removed from the intensity of the stage. But as I sat across from Jason, his presence igniting sparks of inspiration, I couldn't help but wonder if I had the courage to embrace this unexpected opportunity.

"Let's brainstorm together," Jason suggested, leaning closer as if sharing a delightful secret. The air between us buzzed with an unspoken connection that felt both exhilarating and terrifying. "I want to create something that reflects the struggles and joys of the human experience, something raw and real."

His words wove a spell around me, wrapping me in the promise of creativity and passion. There was a magnetism in the way he spoke, his enthusiasm infecting me with a sense of possibility I hadn't felt in years. I could envision it—our ideas intertwining like the intricate choreography of a duet, both of us moving to a rhythm only we could hear.

"Okay," I found myself saying, my voice slightly breathless. "Let's do it." The agreement slipped from my lips like the last ray of sunlight slipping beneath the horizon. The decision felt monumental, a daring leap into the unknown.

The next few days unfolded like a tapestry, each thread woven with laughter and camaraderie as we transformed my modest apartment into a creative sanctuary. We sprawled across the living room floor, the scent of fresh coffee mingling with the sounds of Jason's eclectic playlist that echoed through the air. It was a delightful chaos—papers covered in scribbled ideas, sketches of dance moves, and snippets of lyrics pinned to the walls like vibrant butterflies, fluttering with potential.

With every brainstorming session, I could feel the walls I had built around my heart begin to crumble. Jason's passion was infectious, and I found myself sharing fragments of my past—the elation of performing, the heartache of leaving it all behind. He listened intently, his eyes widening with fascination as I recounted tales of triumphs and failures, the bittersweet dance of life that had led me to this very moment. In return, he shared his own journey—a budding producer navigating the wild, unpredictable world of the music industry, fueled by dreams and aspirations.

As we collaborated, I began to discover the depths of his creativity, a flame that burned brightly beneath his confident facade. He was not just a man with grand ideas; he was a visionary, weaving stories through sound. The more we worked together, the more I realized how aligned our passions were, igniting a fire within me that I had long thought extinguished. It was as if we were two stars colliding, our energies intertwining to create a celestial spectacle of possibility.

The chemistry between us was palpable, sparking moments of levity that often dissolved into fits of laughter. There was a comfortable intimacy in our collaboration, punctuated by playful banter and shared glances that lingered a moment too long. I found myself captivated by his determination and charm, each shared moment drawing me closer to a part of myself I thought I had lost forever.

One evening, as the city buzzed below us, I glanced over at him. Jason was deep in thought, a pen poised in his hand as he scribbled on a notepad, his brow furrowed in concentration. In that moment, something within me shifted. It was the realization that perhaps this wasn't just a collaboration; it was a rediscovery. I was reclaiming my identity, my love for dance, and my passion for creation. I could feel it, a bubbling excitement rising within me, pushing aside the remnants of doubt.

"Let's make this something people will remember," I said, my voice steady as I met his gaze. The conviction behind my words surprised even me. I was ready to dive into this journey, no matter where it led. It was time to embrace the magic of collaboration and creativity, to breathe life into a project that had the potential to become something extraordinary.

As the evening wore on, the city outside became a glittering sea of lights, and I knew, deep down, that this was only the beginning. We were on the cusp of something incredible, a whirlwind adventure waiting to unfold, and for the first time in years, I felt alive.

The days blurred into a delightful symphony of color and sound as Jason and I fell deeper into our collaboration. Each morning, I woke with a newfound energy, the thrill of creating something from the ground up coursing through my veins like a potent elixir. I would sit up in bed, the sunlight spilling through my window, illuminating the chaotic arrangement of notebooks, colored markers, and crumpled sheets of paper that had taken over my living space. My heart fluttered at the thought of what lay ahead, the promise of art waiting just beyond my fingertips.

Jason was an enigmatic whirlwind. He often arrived with a playlist crafted specifically for our sessions, each track designed to evoke the precise mood we needed for our brainstorming. One afternoon, he came in with a song that encapsulated the highs and lows of human experience—a throbbing beat that vibrated through the air and settled into my bones. "Listen to this," he said, his eyes alight with enthusiasm. "Feel how it builds and breaks. There's a story here."

I pressed my headphones to my ears, surrendering to the rhythm. It was a melodic journey, punctuated by soaring crescendos that made my heart race and gentle descents that left me breathless. I could see it—dance interpreting the music's ebb and flow, a choreography that would mirror the struggles and triumphs of life itself. "We could depict the cycle of despair and hope," I murmured, my mind swirling with images of bodies moving in unison, reflecting the intensity of emotions that the music evoked.

"Exactly!" Jason exclaimed, a broad smile breaking across his face. "You understand! I want to capture the essence of human connection through movement. Let's play with the idea of shadows—dancers becoming silhouettes against a backdrop, exploring the light and dark of existence."

As we mapped out our ideas, I realized that I was no longer just a choreographer; I was a storyteller. Each concept unfolded like a petal, revealing layers I had never considered. Jason's passion was contagious, igniting something deep within me that craved expression.

In the evenings, after our sessions, I often found myself lingering in the afterglow of creation, the warmth of our discussions wrapping around me like a cozy blanket. We would share meals at a nearby diner, the kind with checkered tablecloths and neon signs buzzing cheerfully against the darkening sky. We laughed over greasy plates of fries and milkshakes, each sip and bite punctuating our conversation. The diner was a sanctuary where we could let our guards down, tossing around wild ideas while the waitress poured another round of coffee.

One evening, as we shared a plate of fries, I noticed Jason's fingers tapping a rhythmic beat on the table. "You know, I used to play guitar," he said, his voice taking on a nostalgic tone. "In high school, I thought I would be a rock star. I was convinced the world needed my sound."

The hint of vulnerability in his confession surprised me. "What happened?" I asked, intrigued.

"I discovered I was better at crafting sound than making it myself," he replied, a wry smile dancing on his lips. "That realization was a bittersweet moment. But it led me here, to producing, where I can help others find their voice."

There was a beauty in his journey, an acceptance of the winding path that had led him to this moment. I felt an unexpected kinship with him, our shared love for creativity bridging the gap between our vastly different worlds. The more I learned about Jason, the more I felt an affinity growing—a connection that was becoming difficult to ignore.

With each passing day, we fell into a rhythm, our collaboration morphing into something more intimate. Late-night conversations spilled into discussions about our dreams, our fears, and the fragments of our lives we had tucked away, hidden from the world. I shared stories from my childhood, recalling the first time I stepped onto a stage, the thrill of the spotlight igniting a passion that had never dimmed, even as I had retreated into the shadows. He listened, captivated, nodding as I spoke, his gaze intense and unwavering.

"It sounds like dance was always a part of you," he said, his voice softening. "It's beautiful how you've nurtured that passion, even when life pulled you in different directions."

His words wrapped around me like a warm embrace, prompting me to open up further. I confessed my fears—the creeping doubt that I had lost my touch, the uncertainty of whether I could truly step back into the spotlight. "What if I'm not enough?" I admitted, my voice barely above a whisper.

Jason reached across the table, his hand brushing against mine. "You are enough, Emily. Every moment you've spent away from the stage has shaped you into who you are now. You bring depth and understanding to your art. Trust that."

His touch sent a thrill through me, a spark that ignited the air around us. There was something reassuring in his presence, a steadiness that made me believe I could reclaim the parts of myself I had thought lost. We exchanged glances that lingered just a beat too long, an unspoken acknowledgment of the chemistry crackling between us.

As our project progressed, we began to experiment with choreography, spending afternoons in my living room, moving furniture to create a makeshift studio. We flitted from idea to idea, our laughter echoing off the walls as we stumbled through routines that felt just shy of perfect. The music pulsed through the room, filling the space with a vibrant energy that made my heart race.

One evening, I stood in front of the mirror, adjusting the fabric of my favorite leotard—an old relic from my dancing days that still fit surprisingly well. I turned to Jason, who was fiddling with the speaker, his brow furrowed in concentration. "Are you ready for this?" I asked, my voice steady despite the flutter of nerves in my stomach.

He looked up, his green eyes gleaming with excitement. "Ready as I'll ever be."

As the first notes of our chosen song filled the room, I felt an electric current surge through me. I closed my eyes, letting the music wash over me, guiding my body into movement. Every leap, every turn felt like a rebirth, a reclaiming of my identity. Jason watched, his gaze unwavering, as if he were witnessing a phoenix rise from the ashes.

And in that moment, I knew—this collaboration was more than just a project; it was a journey of rediscovery, a path leading back to the very core of who I was. The laughter, the music, the dance—it all wove together, creating a tapestry of emotions that left me breathless, reminding me that sometimes, the most unexpected collaborations lead us exactly where we are meant to be.

Days stretched into vibrant weeks, each one unfurling like the pages of a cherished book, filled with unexpected twists and delightful surprises. Our project began to take shape, blossoming from mere ideas into a living, breathing entity. We spent countless hours immersed in the art of creation, often losing track of time as the sun dipped below the horizon, casting long shadows that danced against the walls of my apartment.

The routine was intoxicating. We would start our afternoons surrounded by a mess of snacks—popcorn, gummy bears, and far too much caffeine. The living room transformed into a bustling creative hub, where every surface overflowed with notebooks brimming with scribbled thoughts and colorful diagrams mapping out choreography. One afternoon, I caught Jason attempting to balance a pencil behind his ear, an exaggerated concentration etched on his face as he scribbled notes about the emotional beats of our upcoming piece. "This is my serious producer look," he declared, causing me to burst into laughter, a sound that echoed through the room, wrapping around us like a warm embrace.

The laughter was a balm, soothing any remnants of my earlier fears. With each passing day, I found myself more immersed in our work, the initial trepidation slowly melting away, replaced by a growing confidence that I could reclaim my place in the world of dance. Each movement we crafted together felt like a conversation—two souls intertwining to express something beyond words, a story woven from the very fabric of our experiences.

One evening, as dusk cloaked the city in shades of lavender and navy, we decided to take our ideas beyond the confines of my living room. The decision came about after a particularly spirited brainstorming session, during which Jason suddenly declared, "We need a real stage. Let's test this out in the park."

Before I knew it, we were off to Central Park, the heart of New York pulsing with life and energy. The vast expanse of green was a welcome contrast to our cluttered indoor sanctuary. We set up near a quiet corner, surrounded by the rustle of leaves and the distant laughter of families enjoying the evening air. The moment felt electric, as if the park itself were holding its breath in anticipation of our performance.

I stood in the open space, a soft breeze tousling my hair, feeling the earth beneath my feet as if it were encouraging me to reconnect with my roots. The world around us faded into a gentle hum as Jason played our chosen song through a portable speaker, the music blending seamlessly with the sounds of the city—laughter, the chirping of crickets, the distant strumming of a guitar.

As I began to move, the choreography we had crafted over the weeks poured from me like a river overflowing its banks. Each step became a declaration, a pulse of life responding to the rhythm of the music. The air was charged with possibility, and as I danced, I felt a familiar warmth radiating from within, the echoes of my past performances urging me on.

Jason watched, his eyes alight with admiration and intensity, as if he were witnessing a magical transformation unfold before him. With every leap and spin, I lost myself in the dance, the music swirling around us like a warm breeze. The city was my audience, the trees my guardians, and for those precious moments, I was utterly free.

When I finished, breathless and exhilarated, the applause came from an unexpected source—an impromptu audience that had gathered, a cluster of onlookers captivated by the unexpected performance. They erupted into applause, their cheers mingling with the evening air, wrapping around me like a cocoon of encouragement. Jason joined in, his clapping thunderous and genuine, his pride palpable.

"You're incredible!" he shouted over the applause, his voice cutting through the clamor. "That was just... wow!"

I couldn't help but beam at his enthusiasm, the adrenaline still coursing through my veins. "I didn't think I could still do that," I admitted, a shy smile creeping across my face.

His expression softened, and for a moment, the world around us faded. "You can do so much more than this, Emily. We're just getting started."

In that moment, I felt the weight of my doubts begin to lift, replaced by a burgeoning belief in myself and the project we were creating. With Jason by my side, I realized I was not merely stepping back into the spotlight; I was reclaiming my narrative, reshaping it into something that reflected who I had become during my time away.

As we made our way back to my apartment, the city alive with lights and sounds, I sensed a shift between us. The chemistry that had simmered beneath the surface during our creative sessions ignited into something more tangible, a warmth that enveloped us. Our shoulders brushed, fingers grazing in a way that sent shivers down my spine.

We returned to our sanctuary, the familiar chaos of notebooks and snacks greeting us like old friends. We settled on the floor, surrounded by the remnants of our creative journey, but this time felt different. The air crackled with an unspoken tension, a realization that our collaboration was evolving into something deeper than just art.

"Emily," Jason began, his voice steady, yet laced with a vulnerability that made my heart race. "I can't ignore it anymore. There's something here, something special between us. I want to explore it."

His words hung in the air, heavy with possibility. I met his gaze, a flurry of emotions crashing within me. The laughter, the creativity, the late-night talks—everything had drawn us together, weaving an intricate tapestry of connection that I had never anticipated.

"I feel it too," I admitted, my voice barely above a whisper, yet resolute. "But... we're in the middle of something big, and I don't want it to get complicated."

Jason nodded, understanding etched on his face. "I get it. But I also believe that what we have could enhance our work. Art is about emotion, right? Maybe we shouldn't shy away from exploring this."

His sincerity was disarming, and as I contemplated his words, I felt the walls I had built around my heart begin to crumble. The potential for something beautiful lay just beyond our fingertips, waiting to be embraced.

"Okay," I said, a sense of courage swelling within me. "Let's see where this goes. Together."

With that, a new chapter unfurled before us, the dance between creativity and connection taking on a life of its own. In the weeks that followed, we dove deeper into our project, our collaboration blossoming into a beautiful blend of artistry and passion. Each movement we choreographed, each note we crafted, was infused with the electric energy that pulsed between us.

The city became our muse, inspiring our work and drawing us closer together. We began to envision performances that transcended the traditional, combining movement with storytelling in a way that would resonate with audiences on a profound level. The lines between our personal and artistic lives blurred, each moment spent together only deepening our bond.

As we prepared for our first public showcase, the anticipation hung in the air like a sweet perfume, rich with possibility. I stood backstage, heart racing, surrounded by the buzz of activity, the warm glow of stage lights illuminating the path ahead.

Jason appeared beside me, his presence grounding and invigorating all at once. "You ready?" he asked, a playful grin tugging at his lips.

I took a deep breath, a smile breaking across my face. "More than ever."

As the curtain rose, the world faded, and we stepped into the spotlight together. The music swelled, and I felt the rhythm pulse through me, guiding my movements as I embraced the stage once more. With every leap and turn, I danced not just for the audience but for us—our shared journey of creativity and connection, a celebration of unexpected collaborations that had brought me back to life.

Chapter 5: Falling Into Step

The diner stood like a beacon of nostalgia on the corner of a sleepy street, its neon sign flickering a gentle invitation to the weary souls passing by. The sun had dipped below the horizon, leaving behind a canvas of deep purples and twinkling stars, each one a tiny reminder of childhood wishes yet to be fulfilled. As I pushed open the door, the tinkling bell announced our arrival, and the warm scent of grilled cheese and sweet cinnamon enveloped us like a welcoming hug.

Inside, the diner was a delightful chaos of mismatched furniture, each piece telling its own story. A faded red vinyl booth nestled against a wall adorned with sepia-toned photographs of the town's history, capturing moments of joy and struggle that resonated with the air of the place. The booths seemed to have personalities; some were plump and inviting, while others leaned slightly, their cushions a tad too worn, echoing whispers of laughter and heartache.

Jason slid into the booth opposite me, a lopsided grin lighting up his face. He was the kind of guy who seemed effortlessly cool, with a tousled mop of dark hair and eyes that sparkled like the soda fountain behind the counter. I felt a flutter in my chest as I watched him shake off the chill of the evening, his casual confidence a balm to my ever-spiraling nerves. It was easy to forget the harshness of the world outside when I was with him, cocooned in this vibrant bubble of fries, milkshakes, and whispered secrets.

As we settled in, the waitress, a petite woman with bright pink hair and a tattoo peeking out from beneath her rolled-up sleeve, ambled over. "What can I get for you two lovebirds?" she teased, her eyes dancing with mischief. My cheeks flamed as Jason chuckled, his laughter like music weaving through the air, pulling me deeper into the moment. "Just two milkshakes and an order of fries, please," he replied, his voice warm and inviting.

"Coming right up!" she chirped before disappearing into the kitchen.

The seconds stretched between us, filled with the hum of conversation and the clatter of plates. I glanced around, absorbing the eclectic charm of the diner—the jukebox in the corner sputtering out classic tunes, a lone patron hunched over a plate of pancakes, and the faint aroma of fresh coffee mingling with the sweetness of desserts.

"So, what's your story?" Jason leaned in, resting his chin on his hands, his gaze intense yet inviting. "How did you end up here, in this quirky little diner on a Thursday night?"

I hesitated, my mind racing through snippets of my life—the pressure of auditions, the fear of failure, the longing for acceptance. But something about the way he looked at me, with genuine curiosity and warmth, made me feel safe. I took a breath, summoning courage from somewhere deep inside. "Well, I guess it all started when I was a kid. I was the one putting on plays in my backyard, forcing my neighbors to watch me reenact scenes from my favorite movies." A smile tugged at the corners of my mouth as I remembered the makeshift stage I had created with old sheets and cardboard boxes.

"Really? A budding actress?" he teased, raising an eyebrow playfully. "I can see it now—the neighborhood's very own Meryl Streep."

I laughed, the sound bubbling up like soda fizz. "Hardly! More like a very enthusiastic wannabe with a flair for the dramatic. I remember the day I decided I wanted to pursue acting seriously. I must have been around fifteen, and I auditioned for this community theater production. I was terrified, but when I stepped on that stage, it was like everything clicked. The lights, the audience, the thrill of becoming someone else for a little while—it felt like home."

Jason nodded, his expression thoughtful. "That's beautiful. It sounds like you've always had a passion for storytelling."

"Yes," I said, my voice softening. "But it's been a struggle, too. Sometimes I feel like I'm chasing a dream that's just out of reach, you know? Like I'm standing on the edge of a cliff, peering into the vast unknown."

He leaned back, considering my words as the waitress returned, balancing two towering milkshakes, their whipped cream crowned with cherries. She set them down with a flourish. "Here you go, lovebirds! Enjoy!"

I couldn't help but laugh again, the warmth of the moment wrapping around us. I took a sip, the cold sweetness tingling against my lips, a delightful contrast to the heat of our conversation. "Thank you!" I called after the waitress as she sauntered away, her pink hair bobbing cheerfully.

"Okay, so what about you?" I asked, eager to turn the spotlight back on him. "What makes Jason tick? What's your story?"

He paused, a flicker of something I couldn't quite place crossing his face. "Well, I grew up in a small town not too far from here, with parents who wanted me to follow a 'safe' career path. They envisioned a future in business or law. But I always felt this pull towards music. I started playing guitar when I was eight, and it became my escape."

As he spoke, I could see the passion igniting his words, illuminating the corners of his mind. "I'd spend hours strumming away in my room, writing songs that nobody would ever hear. It wasn't until high school that I found the courage to perform at open mics. It was terrifying, but exhilarating. I remember one night, I played this song I wrote about a girl who seemed out of reach. And then she walked in."

He paused, a smile dancing on his lips, and I felt my heart quicken, both intrigued and amused. "Did you get her number?" I asked, arching an eyebrow.

"Not exactly," he replied, chuckling softly. "But she inspired me to keep writing, to keep performing. I realized then that music was my way of expressing what words sometimes couldn't convey. It felt like falling into step with a rhythm that was uniquely mine."

In that moment, a spark flickered between us, electric and undeniable. The vulnerability we shared transformed the diner into a sanctuary, a place where dreams collided with reality and laughter filled the gaps of uncertainty. As he reached across the table, his fingers brushed against mine, sending a jolt of warmth surging through me. I couldn't help but smile, a smile that was both nervous and exhilarated, caught in the delightful uncertainty of what lay ahead.

The evening wore on, the diner slowly emptying as the hours slipped into a comfortable routine. The hum of conversations faded, replaced by the soothing croon of a distant jazz tune wafting from the jukebox. It felt as if the universe had conspired to hold us in this moment, allowing the rest of the world to blur into a soft background, while we lingered in the warmth of our shared stories. I watched as Jason leaned back, a thoughtful expression crossing his face, his fingers absently toying with the straw in his milkshake. It was a gesture that struck me as both playful and contemplative, a subtle blend of his laid-back demeanor and the depth that lay beneath.

"Do you ever think about what would happen if we just took a leap?" he mused, breaking the comfortable silence. His eyes sparkled with a mix of mischief and seriousness that made my heart race. "Like, what if we just packed our bags and drove to the coast? No plans, just a couple of friends chasing the sunset?"

The thought hung between us, tantalizing and surreal. I envisioned the open road, the smell of salty air mingling with the sweetness of freedom, each mile a step further away from my insecurities. "That sounds incredible," I said, my voice tinged with longing. "But I'd probably just end up worrying about my job and all the things I should be doing instead."

"Who says we have to worry?" he challenged, a grin spreading across his face, his enthusiasm contagious. "It's just one night. Besides, I think everyone needs a little chaos now and then, don't you?"

He was right. The idea of throwing caution to the wind stirred something deep within me, a yearning for adventure that had been buried beneath layers of practicality. "I could definitely use some chaos," I admitted, my heart fluttering at the thought of breaking free, even if just for a moment.

With our milkshakes nearly finished and the remnants of fries lying neglected on the table, the familiar sensation of vulnerability crept in, mingling with the excitement. I could feel the magnetic pull between us, and every brush of his fingers against mine felt charged with an intensity that made my breath hitch. It was the kind of electricity that ignited a slow burn, teasing the edges of possibility, igniting a flicker of hope that maybe, just maybe, this was something more than friendship.

"What about you?" I asked, diving into the deep end. "What do you want out of all of this? The music, the performances, this crazy dream we're both chasing?"

He leaned forward, his eyes glinting with passion. "I want to feel alive, you know? Music has this way of grounding me, and when I perform, it's like I'm connecting with something bigger than myself. I want to write songs that resonate, that make people feel something real. That's my chaos. What about you? What do you want, really?"

His question lingered, stirring my thoughts like autumn leaves in a brisk wind. I took a moment to reflect, the weight of his gaze urging me to peel back the layers I so often hid behind. "I want to step out of my comfort zone. I want to be brave enough to take risks, to embrace the uncertainty that comes with pursuing something I love," I confessed, my voice barely above a whisper.

A knowing smile crept across his lips, as if he understood the battle I waged within myself. "Then let's do it together. Let's challenge each other to push past the fears that hold us back."

His words resonated like a promise, wrapping around me like a warm blanket on a cold winter night. I felt a surge of courage mingling with my desire for connection, and it was exhilarating. "Okay," I said, my voice steadying. "Let's be brave together."

The air crackled with unspoken understanding, and our hands found each other across the table, fingers intertwining in a quiet affirmation of our shared journey. The warmth radiated from our clasped hands, sending a rush of exhilaration coursing through me, filling the space between us with an intensity that was intoxicating.

Just then, the waitress returned, her bright hair catching the light as she placed the check on our table, shattering our reverie. "You two are too cute," she chimed, winking before bustling off. I blushed, my heart racing at the unexpected interruption.

"Guess we're adorable now," Jason teased, a playful smirk tugging at his lips as he reached for the check.

"Adorable is one way to put it," I shot back, unable to suppress my smile. "Just don't let it get to your head."

"I make no promises," he replied, his laughter ringing out like a melody that echoed against the diner's walls.

After settling the bill, we stood to leave, and as we stepped outside into the cool night air, the world felt different—brighter, more vivid. The stars shone overhead like a sprinkle of diamonds, illuminating the path ahead. I breathed in deeply, the crisp air invigorating my senses, mixing with the lingering sweetness of our milkshakes.

Jason turned to me, his expression serious yet playful. "So, what's the plan? Should we hit the road, or do you think we'll just end up chasing the sunset in our minds?"

I glanced around, feeling a rush of spontaneous energy bubbling within me. "What if we just walked? Let's see where the night takes us. No agenda, no destination—just you, me, and the moon."

His eyes lit up, a spark igniting that mirrored my own. "I love it. Let's wander."

We strolled down the street, the sidewalks beneath our feet alive with the rhythm of our conversation. We shared stories, laughter, and dreams, each word deepening the connection that had woven itself between us like a tapestry of shared experiences. As we walked, I could feel the walls I had built around myself starting to crumble, revealing the vulnerable parts of my heart that I had kept hidden for so long.

Every step felt like a dance, and with each shared glance, I could sense the pull of something extraordinary blossoming between us, weaving itself into the fabric of our lives. The night unfolded like a beautiful dream, each moment more precious than the last, leading us toward a future painted with possibilities.

The night air buzzed with energy as we walked side by side, the world around us bathed in the silver glow of streetlamps. It was as if the stars had descended to join us on our impromptu adventure, twinkling with a conspiratorial glimmer as we meandered through the familiar streets of our small town. The scent of blooming jasmine lingered in the air, wrapping around us like an embrace, intoxicating and sweet, setting a backdrop for our blossoming connection. Each step felt like a leap into the unknown, each glance igniting a spark that kept the fire between us alive.

As we turned a corner, a nearby park came into view, its sprawling expanse illuminated by the soft glow of twinkling fairy lights strung between the trees. The gentle rustle of leaves whispered secrets as we approached, the allure of the park calling to us like a siren song. "Do you want to sit for a while?" I suggested, gesturing toward a weathered wooden bench that beckoned us to take a break from our wandering.

"Absolutely," he replied, his voice smooth like the sweetest melody, resonating with warmth. We settled onto the bench, the wood cool beneath us, and I couldn't help but feel as though we had carved out a small piece of the universe just for ourselves. The sounds of the city faded into a distant hum, replaced by the gentle rustle of the trees and the occasional chirp of a nightbird.

"I love this park," I said, gazing up at the delicate lights. "It feels magical at night, doesn't it?"

Jason nodded, his eyes reflecting the glimmering lights above. "It does. It's one of those places where you can forget the chaos of life, even if just for a moment." He leaned back, stretching his arms behind his head, exuding an effortless confidence that made my heart flutter. "It's like we've stepped into a different world."

In that moment, the weight of unspoken words hung between us, an invisible thread that tethered our hearts together. I turned to him, the questions swirling in my mind, longing to know more about the boy sitting beside me. "What's your favorite thing about performing?" I asked, my curiosity pouring out like an open tap.

He considered my question, his brow furrowing slightly as he thought. "It's the connection," he said finally, his voice taking on a reflective tone. "When I'm on stage, I can feel the audience's energy. It's like this dance, where we're all moving together, sharing something intimate. It's thrilling and terrifying all at once, but when it clicks, it's like nothing else."

His words wrapped around me, resonating deep within my soul. I imagined him under the stage lights, pouring his heart into every note, every lyric. "That sounds incredible. It must feel amazing to share that part of yourself with others," I replied, a hint of envy threading through my words.

"It is, but it's also vulnerable," he admitted, his gaze steady on mine. "There's always a fear of being rejected, of pouring yourself out there and having nobody care. But then again, isn't that the risk of being human? To love, to create, to put yourself out there, even when it terrifies you?"

His insight struck a chord, resonating with the struggles I faced in pursuing my dreams. "I know what you mean," I said, my voice softer. "Sometimes I feel like I'm battling against my own fears, like I'm holding myself back from fully embracing my passion. It's scary to think about failing in front of others."

"Hey," he said gently, turning to face me fully, "what if we flipped that fear on its head? What if instead of fearing failure, we embraced it as part of the journey? Every stumble is just a step closer to finding your rhythm."

His words wrapped around me like a comforting quilt, igniting a flicker of determination within. I nodded, feeling the weight of his encouragement settle on my shoulders, lightening the burden I had carried for too long. "You're right. I want to embrace every moment, even the messy ones."

A playful smile danced on his lips as he leaned closer, his voice dropping to a conspiratorial whisper. "Then let's promise to keep each other accountable. No more holding back, okay? If we fall, we'll pick each other up."

"Deal," I said, grinning as our hands instinctively found each other again, fingers intertwining like the branches of the trees around us. It was a simple gesture, yet it felt monumental, a promise of support and shared dreams.

As the night deepened, we sat in a comfortable silence, letting the magic of the moment wash over us. I watched as the stars shimmered above, the world fading away, leaving just the two of us, lost in our own universe. I realized that this moment, this connection, was becoming a part of me, an integral thread woven into the fabric of my life.

But as the evening wore on, a thought nagged at the back of my mind. I glanced over at Jason, who seemed lost in his thoughts, his expression thoughtful. "What happens when this moment ends?" I asked, my voice barely above a whisper. "What happens when we go back to our normal lives?"

He turned to me, a serious look replacing the lightness in his eyes. "I think it becomes part of who we are. These moments—every laugh, every shared secret—they shape us, even when we go back to reality."

I nodded, feeling a bittersweet ache settle in my chest. I wanted to hold on to this feeling forever, to capture the essence of this night and store it away for the tougher days ahead. "And what if we end up going our separate ways?" I asked, a tremor in my voice.

"Then we promise to make our paths cross again," he replied, his expression unwavering. "Life is too short to let the good stuff slip away."

The sincerity in his words wrapped around me, enveloping me in a sense of hope and possibility. As we sat beneath the blanket of stars, I realized that Jason was no longer just a friend; he was becoming a cornerstone of my journey, someone who dared me to dream bigger and reach higher.

With our hearts entwined in a tapestry of shared dreams, we rose from the bench, ready to step back into the world together. As we walked side by side, the night stretched out before us, full of potential, laughter, and the promise of more adventures yet to come. The path ahead might be uncertain, but together, we were ready to face it head-on, each step falling into perfect rhythm with the other, creating a melody that was uniquely ours.

Chapter 6: A Fractured Past

The sun dipped low over the sprawling plains of Texas, casting a warm, golden hue across the dusty streets of my small town, where the air hummed with the promise of change. I found solace in the simple joys of life, my morning coffee curling steam against the glass of the café where I spent my afternoons. The familiar creak of the wooden door announced my arrival, a sound as comforting as the well-worn leather chair that cradled me, and I nestled deeper into its embrace.

Today, though, the usual buzz of chatter felt different, as if everyone was speaking in a language I no longer understood. I could feel the weight of their eyes lingering on me, assessing my every move. Perhaps it was the shadow of my past that clung to me like a worn-out coat. My thoughts drifted back to those darker days, the kind of memories that whispered doubt into my ear, reminding me of the fragility of trust. Each sip of coffee was bittersweet, the taste mingling with the lingering scent of betrayal that still haunted me.

It wasn't long before Jason strode in, the light shifting around him like an aura, pulling my gaze as if I were magnetized. He had a way of illuminating the dim corners of my world. With his unruly hair and easy smile, he was the kind of man who could turn mundane moments into laughter, but there was something deeper hidden beneath his surface—something that stirred a sense of kinship within me, like two lost souls navigating a world too vast to comprehend alone.

He spotted me immediately, and that warmth spread through the café, brightening the room in a way that felt distinctly unfair. As he approached, my heart fluttered, the remnants of my past clashing with the hopeful present. I smiled, forcing the ghosts of my history back into the shadows, but the weight of my past was a stubborn companion. It loomed over our interactions, casting doubt like a pall over what should have been innocent moments.

"What's on your mind?" he asked, concern etched across his brow as he settled into the chair across from me. His voice, rich and melodic, wrapped around me like a cozy blanket, but it was a blanket riddled with holes, a reminder that I was not entirely safe.

I hesitated, my heart pounding like a drum in my chest. How could I unravel the threads of my history without scaring him away? Memories of betrayal danced behind my eyelids: the sharpness of accusations, the chill of abandonment, the slow erosion of trust until there was nothing left but the barren ground of my heart.

"Just... thinking about the past," I replied, trying to sound casual, though my voice quivered like a reed in the wind. The last thing I wanted was to cast a shadow over our blossoming connection. Yet, there it was—a looming specter that haunted my every thought.

"I get it," Jason said softly, his gaze unwavering. "Sometimes, it feels like the past is a shadow that just won't let go." His eyes reflected a depth of understanding that made my heart ache.

In that moment, I felt a crack form in the fortress I had built around my heart, a fissure wide enough for vulnerability to seep through. "I had a relationship that... well, let's just say it shattered my confidence." The words tumbled out before I could stop them, raw and jagged. "I thought I could trust him, but he betrayed me in a way I didn't see coming. Now, I'm scared to let anyone in, even you."

The air between us crackled with the weight of honesty, the kind of openness that had been absent in my previous life. Jason leaned forward, his elbows resting on the table, the distance between us shrinking. "You're not alone in this. I've been through something similar," he admitted, his voice low and steady, as if we were sharing a secret. "I was in a toxic relationship that twisted my view of love. It took me a long time to feel whole again."

His confession drew me in, a soft tether that pulled us closer together. For the first time, I realized that we were both navigating the jagged edges of our pasts, two broken pieces seeking solace in the shared ache of lost love. My heart ached with empathy, and the shadows that clung to us began to feel less menacing.

"What happened?" I asked, my curiosity overriding my caution. It felt strange to pry into his history, yet it was a relief to share this burden.

He sighed, his eyes darkening momentarily as if the memory had a physical weight. "I was young and naïve, convinced I could fix someone who didn't want to be fixed. The love was intense, but it turned toxic fast. It taught me to keep my guard up, to protect myself at all costs." His gaze met mine, and in that moment, I understood his hesitation.

"It's hard to let someone in when the fear of being hurt again looms large." I couldn't help but feel a surge of gratitude for his openness, as if we were crafting a delicate tapestry of trust between us.

"Exactly," he replied, his smile returning, though it didn't reach his eyes. "But sometimes, you meet someone who makes the risk feel worth it." The implication hung in the air, unspoken yet palpable, igniting a flicker of hope within me.

As we continued to share our stories, the world outside faded away, the café buzzing softly with life around us. For the first time in a long while, the past felt like a distant echo rather than an impending storm. The sunlight streamed through the window, illuminating the spaces between us, and I couldn't help but think that perhaps, just perhaps, we were both on the cusp of something extraordinary—a fragile connection that felt both exhilarating and terrifying. The shadows of our pasts were still there, but they didn't seem so daunting when faced together, side by side.

Evenings in our town had a way of transforming the familiar into the extraordinary. As twilight draped the horizon in shades of lavender and deep orange, I felt an unsettling mix of comfort and anxiety knotting in my stomach. The café was alive with laughter and the aroma of freshly baked pastries, yet my mind drifted to the weighty conversation I had shared with Jason, still resonating like a haunting melody in my ears. We had peeled back the layers of our pasts, exposing the raw wounds beneath, but the fear of opening myself up again gnawed at me. It felt like standing at the edge of a cliff, teetering on the brink of uncertainty.

With every heartbeat, the walls I had so meticulously constructed began to tremble. The specter of betrayal loomed over me, whispering that the past was a persistent ghost, one that had no intention of being exorcised from my life. Jason's kindness only complicated my feelings, each smile from him a reminder of what I could lose if I dared to leap into this new chapter. But as I watched him from across the table, his laughter spilling into the air like bubbles in a glass of champagne, I couldn't help but wonder if it was worth the risk.

The clinking of silverware and the soft murmur of conversations swirled around us, yet I was acutely aware of the world narrowing down to just him and me. His eyes sparkled with an unguarded warmth, as if he were revealing a treasure trove of secrets. But I couldn't shake the feeling that there was more lurking beneath the surface, and each moment spent with him felt like threading through a tapestry of emotions—intricate, beautiful, and fraught with the potential for unraveling.

As the evening wore on, I found myself drawn to the cadence of his voice, the way he spoke about his passions, his dreams shimmering in the light like stars in a midnight sky. "I've always wanted to travel," he mused, his gaze drifting toward the window, where the last rays of sunlight danced upon the pavement. "To see the world and escape the routine. It's like there's a whole universe out there just waiting for someone to discover it."

I couldn't help but smile at his enthusiasm. It was infectious, a reminder that there was life outside the shadows that had cocooned me for far too long. "Where would you go first?" I asked, leaning in, allowing the sparks of conversation to illuminate my doubts.

"Maybe Italy," he replied, his expression transforming as if he were already wandering through the sun-drenched streets of Rome. "The art, the food, the history. It seems like a place where dreams come alive."

"Or where they shatter," I added, a teasing lilt to my voice, but the weight of my words hung in the air between us. He caught my gaze, his brow furrowing slightly, and in that moment, I could see the shadows creeping back into his eyes—the same ones I battled daily.

"Yeah, but isn't that the beauty of it? The possibility of it all?" His voice was steady, yet the tremor beneath it mirrored my own uncertainty. "Sometimes, you have to take a leap, even if you're terrified of the fall."

The truth of his words struck me. How many times had I clung to the edges, afraid to let go, afraid to soar? The fears that had once paralyzed me began to dissolve in the light of his conviction, but it felt like a fragile shift, as though I could fall back into that dark place at any moment.

Jason reached across the table, his hand brushing against mine, sending a ripple of warmth up my arm. "Hey," he said, his eyes softening, "I get it. We've both been hurt, and it's okay to be scared. But maybe it's time we stopped letting the past dictate our future."

A lump formed in my throat as I absorbed his words, the sincerity of his gaze penetrating the barriers I had constructed. "What if I can't?" I whispered, vulnerability cracking my voice like thin glass.

"You can," he assured me, a hint of resolve threading through his tone. "We both can. We just need to take it one step at a time."

It was a simple promise, yet it felt monumental, like we were forging an unbreakable bond with each heartbeat. As he spoke, the world around us faded, the café's chatter becoming a distant hum. All that mattered was this moment, the way his hand lingered on mine, a lifeline in the tumultuous sea of my emotions.

But just as I began to breathe in the possibility of a future untethered from my past, the shadows crept back in, taunting me with memories that refused to let go. The laughter of another time, the promises that had shattered like glass, echoed in the corners of my mind. I pulled my hand away, the sudden loss of warmth igniting a chill.

"I'm sorry," I murmured, unable to meet his gaze. "I don't want to drag you into my mess."

"It's not a mess if you let me in," he replied softly, his words a gentle nudge, urging me to confront the tangled web of emotions that held me captive. "I want to understand. I want to be there for you."

The honesty in his voice broke something within me, a dam that had held back years of hurt and betrayal. Tears threatened to spill, blurring the edges of my reality, but I fought to hold them back. "It's just... I thought I could trust him, but when he left, it felt like the ground vanished beneath my feet. I don't want to feel that way again."

Jason's expression shifted, a mixture of understanding and empathy washing over him. "Trust is hard," he said, his voice soothing. "But not everyone will hurt you. I promise."

In that moment, I glimpsed a glimmer of hope, the threads of possibility weaving into my heart, stitching up the wounds that had long been left exposed. Perhaps Jason was right—perhaps I could learn to trust again. Perhaps this connection, this tentative bond, could be the bridge that led me away from the shadows.

As the evening deepened, I felt a flicker of courage igniting within me, warming the edges of my heart. I didn't know what lay ahead, but for the first time in a long while, I was willing to embrace the uncertainty. With each shared moment, the specters of my past began to fade, leaving behind a fragile but promising dawn that whispered of new beginnings. The café buzzed around us, but the world felt different now—alive with potential and the sweet taste of hope, echoing Jason's words as they settled into the very core of my being.

The moon hung low in the sky, casting a silvery glow over the town, transforming familiar streets into a shimmering path of shadows and light. After that profound evening in the café, I walked home feeling a strange blend of exhilaration and trepidation, as if I were traversing the tightrope of a high-wire act without a safety net. Jason's words echoed in my mind, a soft refrain that whispered the possibility of something new, something hopeful. But as the chill of the night air wrapped around me, the ghosts of my past began to swirl, reminding me that hope was often a double-edged sword.

My feet carried me down the familiar route, past the quaint houses with their porches adorned with rocking chairs and potted ferns. Each step felt heavier, the weight of my history pressing down on me like a suffocating blanket. I paused at a particularly vibrant tree, its leaves a riot of color, and breathed in the crisp air, attempting to steady the tumult within. The warmth of Jason's hand, so recently entwined with mine, felt like a beacon of light piercing the fog of uncertainty, yet I couldn't escape the gnawing fear that surged through me.

What if I couldn't let go of the past? What if I pushed him away before he had a chance to prove himself? The weight of my insecurities was almost tangible, a physical entity I could sense wrapping around my heart.

As I approached my front door, the familiar creak greeted me like an old friend, and I stepped inside, enveloped in the comfort of my cozy home. The smell of lavender from the candle I had lit earlier lingered in the air, mingling with the faintest hint of something sweet from the cookie dough I had forgotten in the fridge. My sanctuary was filled with books, each spine a whisper of untold stories, yet tonight, the tales seemed to blur into one overwhelming narrative of uncertainty.

I sank onto the sofa, the cushions embracing me as I cradled my head in my hands. It was in these moments of quiet that the shadows grew louder, each memory a piercing reminder of how easily trust could shatter. I closed my eyes, willing myself to think of Jason—not as the embodiment of my fears but as the man who had opened up to me with a sincerity that stirred something deep within.

Images of our conversation danced through my mind. His smile, warm and genuine, ignited a flicker of hope amidst the darkness. It was a fragile connection, one that could easily break, but I couldn't help but feel that we were standing on the precipice of something worth exploring. There was magic in the way he spoke, an earnestness that seemed to promise a safe harbor from the storms of our pasts.

The next day dawned bright and clear, a stark contrast to the swirling chaos inside me. I found myself drawn back to the café, the familiarity of it soothing the frayed edges of my nerves. As I settled into my usual spot, the aroma of coffee swirled around me, blending with the tantalizing scent of baked goods. I busied myself with a book, the words blurring together as I anxiously awaited Jason's arrival.

He entered with the same effortless charm that had captivated me from the start, his presence lighting up the room. "Hey there," he greeted, sliding into the seat across from me, a lazy smile spreading across his face. "Hope I'm not interrupting anything too important."

I couldn't help but chuckle, the tension within me beginning to unravel at the sight of him. "Just trying to distract myself," I replied, a teasing glint in my eye. "But you might be more distracting than the book."

"Good to know," he grinned, and I felt a wave of relief wash over me. The previous day's vulnerability hung in the air between us, yet somehow, it felt lighter now, less like a weight and more like a shared secret.

As we talked, laughter flowed easily, weaving through the fabric of our conversation like threads of gold. We shared stories of our childhoods, revealing fragments of ourselves that felt both risky and exhilarating. He spoke of his father's passion for music, how their living room had once been filled with the sounds of guitars and laughter, a stark contrast to the echoing silence that came after his parents' separation. I shared my own tales of family, of a childhood marred by fleeting moments of happiness eclipsed by the weight of disappointment.

But just as the warmth of our connection deepened, I felt the familiar shadows begin to stir once more. As Jason's laughter echoed in my ears, a nagging voice reminded me of the risk I was taking. "What if he leaves too?" I thought, the specter of betrayal creeping back into my mind.

"Are you okay?" Jason's voice broke through my reverie, a hint of concern etched across his brow. "You seem a million miles away."

The urge to retreat into the safety of silence nearly overwhelmed me, but I took a breath, feeling the weight of honesty pressing against my chest. "I'm just... afraid," I confessed, my heart racing as I revealed my vulnerability. "I've been hurt before, and sometimes it feels easier to keep my walls up."

He leaned in, his expression earnest, and the sincerity in his eyes reminded me of why I was drawn to him in the first place. "I get it," he said softly. "But sometimes we have to take the leap, even when we're scared. It's part of being human."

I could see the reflection of my own fears in his gaze, the understanding that came from shared pain. It felt surreal to lay my heart bare before him, yet there was an undeniable strength in that moment—an unspoken promise that we would face our fears together.

As we left the café, the world outside felt different, as if the air had shifted in some profound way. The shadows of the past still lingered, but they no longer felt like chains binding me to old hurts. Instead, they had transformed into stepping stones, guiding me forward into a future ripe with possibility.

The vibrant streets buzzed with life, and the chatter of laughter and joy filled the air. With Jason by my side, I began to sense the potential of what could be—a bond forged not just in shared trauma, but in hope and understanding. I knew the journey ahead would be fraught with challenges, but for the first time, the prospect of love no longer felt like a burden; it felt like an adventure waiting to unfold.

Together, we stepped into the unknown, two souls entwined in a dance of healing and trust. The past might have shaped us, but it no longer defined us. As the sun dipped below the horizon, casting a warm glow across our path, I felt an exhilarating rush of courage rise within me. Perhaps the light we sought was not just in the absence of shadows but in our willingness to confront them, hand in hand, ready to embrace whatever the future might hold.

Chapter 7: Dancing in the Rain

The rhythmic patter of raindrops against the window had become a melody of its own, an intimate serenade that resonated through the empty dance studio. The familiar scent of polished wood mixed with the earthy aroma of wet pavement outside, creating a cocoon of warmth and nostalgia. I could see the soft shadows cast by the overhead lights dancing across the floor, a gentle reminder that even in solitude, the space was alive, ready to cradle the echoes of dreams yet to be realized.

The world outside was drenched in a silvery haze, the sky cloaked in heavy, dark clouds, giving the day a dreamlike quality. It was the kind of afternoon that could easily have felt oppressive, but instead, it infused me with an undeniable sense of possibility. My dance shoes were still laced tight, my body humming from hours of practice, when Jason entered, shaking the droplets from his hair like a playful dog. He flashed that boyish grin, his dark eyes sparkling with mischief, and in that moment, the atmosphere shifted. I could feel a crackling energy in the air, charged and electric, as if the storm outside was merely a backdrop to the tempest brewing between us.

"Hey, you want to take a break?" he asked, his voice light and teasing. There was a challenge in his tone, an unspoken dare that pulled at the corners of my mouth until I was smiling without reservation.

Before I could respond, he stepped closer, his hand brushing mine in a fleeting touch that ignited a flutter in my chest. The studio, usually filled with the soft strains of classical music or the beats of contemporary dance, was now silent except for the rain, as if the universe held its breath in anticipation of what would unfold.

"Let's dance," he suggested, the invitation lingering in the air like the sweet scent of rain-soaked earth. I hesitated for just a moment, my mind racing with the familiar warnings that accompanied any hint of intimacy. But something in the way he looked at me, full of warmth and encouragement, melted those reservations. I nodded, a silent agreement, and before I knew it, he had taken my hand, pulling me into the center of the floor.

We began to sway, our movements unchoreographed yet perfectly in sync, as if our bodies had always known this rhythm. His hands were firm around my waist, guiding me with an effortless grace. I could feel the tension of the day dissipate with every step we took, the outside world dissolving into mere background noise. I let myself forget the mirror, the critical voices in my head that told me I wasn't good enough, and instead focused on the way his laughter mingled with the sound of the rain.

"Isn't it funny?" he said, breaking the silence between us, his breath warm against my ear. "How rain makes everything feel different? Like the world gets a reset button."

I laughed, nodding as I spun away from him, twirling like a leaf caught in the wind. The studio was ours alone, and I felt as if we were the only two people in existence. The music in my head was a symphony crafted by the storm, each note echoing the pounding of the rain, the pulse of my heart. My inhibitions faded into the background, replaced by an overwhelming desire to surrender to the moment.

As I spun back toward him, I caught his gaze, and in that instant, something shifted—an understanding, a connection that transcended words. We were no longer just dance partners; we were explorers of a realm untouched by fear, where vulnerability was not a weakness but a strength. The barriers I had built around my heart were crumbling, piece by piece, like the clouds dispersing above us, revealing glimpses of sunlight that dared to break through.

"Come here," he beckoned, pulling me close again, and I willingly stepped into the warmth of his embrace. It felt like coming home—a safe harbor amid the chaos of my thoughts. The world outside may have been gray, but in that moment, we created our own vibrant universe, a kaleidoscope of colors swirling around us.

Jason's fingers grazed my hair, a tender gesture that sent shivers down my spine. "You know," he murmured, his voice low and soft, "I've always thought that dancing in the rain was a metaphor for embracing life's unpredictability. You just have to let go and trust that you won't drown."

His words resonated deep within me, igniting a flicker of hope I thought had long extinguished. I had spent so much time clinging to the past, to the fear of what could go wrong, that I had forgotten how to dance without hesitation. With him, I felt the urge to break free, to twirl and spin with reckless abandon.

"Then let's embrace it," I replied, my voice barely a whisper as I leaned in closer, our foreheads touching in a moment of shared intimacy. The warmth between us was palpable, charged with unspoken promises and the thrill of something new blossoming in the air.

With a sudden burst of energy, I pulled away and dashed to the window, watching as the rain continued to fall in sheets, drenching the world outside. The droplets raced each other down the glass, their paths unpredictable yet beautiful. "What if we take this outside?" I challenged, glancing over my shoulder at him, my heart pounding in anticipation.

The mischievous grin that spread across Jason's face told me he was all in. In a matter of moments, we were running together, the wooden floors of the studio giving way to the slick pavement outside. We splashed through puddles, laughter erupting from our lips as the rain soaked us to the skin. It was freeing, exhilarating, a rebellion against the mundane. The cold water splattered against my legs, but I felt alive—truly alive—as if every drop washed away the remnants of my fears.

Together, we danced under the stormy sky, each movement igniting a fire within me. I spun and twirled, his laughter echoing around us like the sweetest music. In those fleeting moments, I was no longer a hesitant dancer plagued by insecurities. I was bold, daring, and entirely myself. Jason was my partner in this impromptu performance, our chemistry radiating like sunlight breaking through the clouds.

The rain cascaded around us, turning the world into a blurred palette of color and sound, and I was lost in the magic of it all. It was just him and me, dancing in the rain, the barriers around my heart melting away like ice under the warmth of the sun.

The rain persisted, a relentless rhythm that only deepened the vibrant atmosphere surrounding us. My heart raced in tandem with the cascade of water, our shared laughter cutting through the heavy air, each peal a defiant cry against the monotony of life. It was as if we had stepped into a painting, the colors more vivid, the emotions heightened, every droplet imbued with a sense of purpose. I felt weightless, liberated from the shackles of expectation that often bound me in the dance studio and beyond.

We danced as if no one were watching, though the truth was, it felt like the entire universe was tuned into our little rebellion against the storm. Jason's hand found mine again, and he pulled me closer, our bodies moving with an intimacy that was both exhilarating and terrifying. I could feel the warmth radiating from him, even through the cool rain, an anchor amid the wildness of the moment. The world blurred around us, and I allowed myself to lean into the sensation, trusting him to catch me if I fell.

"You know," he said, breathless as we paused for a moment, our foreheads nearly touching, "there's something magical about being out here, dancing in the rain. It's like we're breaking all the rules." His voice was laced with mischief, but his eyes held a sincerity that pulled me in deeper.

"Like a movie scene?" I teased, my heart fluttering as I searched his gaze. There was something undeniably cinematic about this moment—the dark clouds overhead, the glistening pavement reflecting our joy, the laughter mingling with the soothing sound of the rain. It felt both thrilling and surreal, as if the universe conspired to create this scene just for us.

"Exactly," he replied, his smile wide enough to illuminate the gray afternoon. "Let's make our own story." And with that, he twirled me again, our bodies spinning in harmony as the rain wrapped around us, creating a cocoon of warmth despite the coolness of the air.

In that instant, I understood that life's best moments often emerged from the most unexpected circumstances. As we danced, I found myself lost in a rhythm that went beyond the physical. It was a dance of emotions, each step reflecting a growing connection, a shared experience that seemed to transcend words. The barriers I had built around my heart began to melt like snow under the sun's first light.

We moved together as if we were two halves of a whole, the world outside fading into the background. The rain soaked through my clothes, but I didn't care; I felt alive in a way I hadn't in years. As we spun and twirled, my insecurities and fears were swept away, washed clean by the cleansing rain. The laughter continued to bubble up between us, an infectious energy that made my cheeks ache from smiling.

As the dance evolved, so did our conversation. Each laugh, each playful nudge, revealed something deeper beneath the surface. "So, what's your story?" I asked, curiosity pushing through the carefree banter. "How did you end up here, dancing in the rain like a couple of lunatics?"

He paused, a thoughtful look crossing his face. "Well, I guess I'm just a guy who believes life's too short to take everything seriously.

I used to be pretty rigid, but then something clicked. I realized that spontaneity could lead to the best adventures." His gaze lingered on me, and I felt the warmth spread through my chest. "And who knows? Maybe today is one of those adventures."

"Are you suggesting I'm an adventure?" I laughed, feigning shock. "That's quite the compliment."

Jason chuckled, his eyes sparkling with mischief. "Oh, definitely. You're a storm in the best way possible. Just when I think I've figured you out, you surprise me."

I was taken aback, the weight of his words settling over me like a warm blanket. For so long, I had hidden parts of myself, believing they wouldn't be accepted or understood. But in this moment, under the patter of rain and the weight of his gaze, I felt seen. The realization sent a thrill through me, igniting something deep within.

"Maybe we're both storms," I replied, feeling bold. "Chasing adventure, leaving chaos in our wake."

"Or creating a little magic," he added, his voice softening. "Every storm has its beauty, right?"

He stepped closer, the air thickening between us, and for a fleeting second, the rain became an irrelevant backdrop to the connection unfolding. My breath caught as his fingers brushed against my cheek, a delicate, almost tentative movement. It felt electric, a spark that ignited an uncharted territory in my heart.

The laughter faded as the moment stretched, filled with unspoken possibilities. I could sense the shift, the subtle change in energy, as if we were standing at the edge of something profound. My heart raced, anticipation swirling within me.

But before I could delve deeper into this unexpected intimacy, a rumble of thunder rolled through the air, shattering the moment's delicate tension. We both jumped, laughing nervously as the storm above mirrored the turmoil brewing inside me.

"Maybe we should take this adventure inside," I suggested, my voice slightly breathless. I wasn't ready to let the moment slip away, but I could feel the weight of reality pressing in.

"Yeah, I think the rain might be starting to get a little too aggressive for my taste," Jason joked, his eyes glinting with mischief as he glanced up at the gathering clouds. We turned back towards the studio, the playful energy between us undiminished as we dashed through the rain, our laughter blending with the thunder.

Inside, the world felt transformed. The studio was a sanctuary, a place where the echoes of our laughter and the warmth of our connection could flourish free from the chaos outside. As I shook the water from my hair, I felt a renewed sense of clarity wash over me, as if the storm had purged my doubts and fears.

We were both breathless, the air thick with unspoken words and possibilities. The silence hung heavy, but it was a comfortable quiet, punctuated only by the sound of rain against the windows. I could feel the chemistry crackling between us, thick and tangible, begging to be acknowledged.

Jason took a step closer, a playful grin spreading across his face as he wiped a raindrop from my cheek with his thumb. "You know," he began, his tone shifting from playful to earnest, "today was really special. I didn't expect to find myself here, with you, sharing all of this."

I met his gaze, my heart pounding in my chest. "Neither did I," I admitted, feeling a rush of honesty. It was liberating to express how I felt, to allow myself to be vulnerable in this moment.

He stepped even closer, the distance between us shrinking until I could feel the warmth radiating from him, the electricity palpable. "I think there's something here, between us. Something worth exploring."

With those words, the storm inside me calmed, a sense of peace washing over me. In this warm, inviting space, amidst the soft glow of the studio lights and the lingering scent of rain, I felt as if I had found a kindred spirit, someone who understood the beauty of chaos and the magic of spontaneity.

The possibility of what lay ahead shimmered like the raindrops on the window, beautiful and uncertain. And in that moment, I dared to hope for more.

The warmth of the studio enveloped us, a cocoon woven from shared laughter and the lingering hum of rain outside. My heart thudded in my chest, a drum echoing the thrill of our dance, and as Jason stepped closer, I felt the space between us pulse with a magnetic energy. I had stepped into uncharted territory, and every breath I took tasted of possibility, mingling with the faint scent of rain that clung to my skin.

"I'm glad we escaped the storm," I said, my voice light but edged with a sincerity that made my cheeks flush. "Though I can't say I've ever had a dance partner quite like you before."

His smile widened, revealing a warmth that made the corners of his eyes crinkle. "You're the perfect dance partner, even if you do have a habit of making the rain look like a movie set. I'm just trying to keep up."

Our playful banter felt like an unspoken acknowledgment of the connection we were nurturing, an invisible thread weaving us together amid the chaos of the outside world. I took a moment to observe him—the way his dark hair fell slightly over his forehead, the way his shirt clung to his frame, the hint of a spark in his eye that promised mischief. The air was thick with anticipation, as if the very walls of the studio were holding their breath, waiting for us to take the next step.

Without thinking, I reached out and brushed my fingers against the damp fabric of his shirt, tracing a pattern that seemed to draw us closer. "What if we danced again?" I suggested, my heart racing at the thought of exploring this new intimacy. The idea felt daring, and my pulse quickened at the thought of surrendering to this moment, to this adventure.

"Only if we make it a little more interesting," he replied, his voice low and teasing, a playful glint in his eyes. "How about we incorporate some elements from the choreography we've been working on?"

I raised an eyebrow, intrigued by the idea. "Are you suggesting we improvise a rain dance?"

"Absolutely," he laughed, his enthusiasm infectious. "Let's break all the rules we know. After all, the best dances happen when you throw caution to the wind."

The prospect sent a thrill through me, the idea of combining the technical with the spontaneous—a delicious challenge. I nodded, excitement bubbling within me, and as we stepped back into the center of the studio, I felt a rush of adrenaline mixed with the lingering warmth of our previous dance.

The rain continued to drum against the windows, a steady backdrop to our unfolding adventure. We began to move, our bodies responding to the rhythm of the storm outside. I let my instincts take over, trusting Jason to follow my lead. With every step, every twirl, we infused our movements with the energy of the rain, each gesture echoing the wildness of the elements.

I felt my spirit soar, losing myself in the music of our shared laughter and the echo of our footsteps against the wooden floor. We danced like we were on the edge of something monumental, an exhilarating mix of passion and freedom. The outside world faded completely, the walls of the studio closing in around us, insulating us from the realities that lay beyond.

As the routine evolved, I could feel the shift in the air. Jason's gaze burned into mine, and every glance ignited a fire within me. His movements mirrored my own, our chemistry palpable as we wove between improvisation and the familiarity of our practiced steps. With each pirouette and leap, we pushed boundaries, the spontaneity of our dance matching the unpredictability of the storm outside.

"Okay, now let's take it up a notch," he said, a wicked smile spreading across his face. "How about we do a leap into a spin? It'll be epic."

"Epic sounds good," I grinned, my heart racing as I envisioned the sequence. "But you'll have to catch me."

He stepped closer, his breath warm against my ear as he whispered, "I've got you." That simple promise settled in my chest like a comforting weight, and suddenly, I felt invincible.

We positioned ourselves, and with a shared glance, I took off, my heart pounding in rhythm with the storm. I leapt into the air, the world momentarily falling away as I soared, the adrenaline coursing through my veins. Time slowed, and for a heartbeat, it felt as if I were flying. Then Jason's arms were around me, steady and strong, guiding me safely back to the ground, his laugh mixing with my own as we spun together, the motion dizzying and exhilarating.

"That was incredible!" I exclaimed, breathless as we came to a stop. I couldn't believe how seamlessly we had transitioned from playful to something more profound, the electricity between us crackling with every shared smile and lingering touch.

"Just wait until we get to do that outside," he teased, a glint of mischief returning to his eyes. "I bet we'd create a masterpiece."

"Are you trying to get us struck by lightning?" I shot back, but I couldn't help the laughter that bubbled up inside me. "I think I'd prefer to keep my limbs intact."

He chuckled, a deep, rich sound that sent shivers down my spine. "No promises. But I'd consider it an honor to be your dance partner in the storm. Besides, we're already soaked. What's a little more rain?"

The playful banter and warmth in his gaze gave me the confidence to suggest, "What if we did it? Just a quick spin outside to feel the elements again?"

Jason's grin widened, and without another word, he grabbed my hand, pulling me toward the door. "Let's make a run for it!"

We dashed outside, the rain hitting us anew, a refreshing torrent that soaked us instantly. I reveled in the wildness of the moment, the laughter bubbling from deep within me as we embraced the chaos of the storm. The world outside had transformed—cars glided through rivers of water, the trees swayed like dancers in a grand performance, and the sky overhead crackled with life.

The rain was invigorating, the cold droplets contrasting sharply with the warmth of our bodies as we slipped and twirled around the pavement. The studio's strict lines faded away, replaced by the unrestrained joy of our surroundings. With every splash, every puddle we jumped, we crafted our own little symphony, an unchoreographed dance that felt both rebellious and beautiful.

As we spun under the downpour, I caught sight of Jason's laughter, pure and unfiltered, filling the air around us. It was infectious, drawing me in and igniting a sense of belonging I had been craving for so long. There was no judgment, no walls to break down, just the two of us, soaked and exhilarated, dancing under the vast expanse of a sky that seemed to mirror our freedom.

In that moment, I felt a sense of clarity wash over me. I was no longer just the girl seeking perfection in every step; I was a participant in this chaotic, beautiful dance of life. I was alive, embraced by the rain, and caught in a whirlwind of emotions and laughter that Jason had effortlessly pulled me into.

As we finally slowed, breathless and exhilarated, I turned to him, my heart racing. "This is what it means to truly live, isn't it?"

He nodded, his expression softening as he reached out, brushing a raindrop from my cheek. "Exactly. It's about the moments we create, the spontaneity we embrace. And I have a feeling this is just the beginning."

In the heart of the storm, I realized I had found a partner not just in dance, but in life. The rain might have drenched us, but in its wake, it had washed away my fears, leaving only the vibrant promise of what lay ahead. Together, we stood, soaked to the bone, ready to write our own story, unfiltered and unafraid, dancing under the storm.

Chapter 8: The Unraveling

The sun hung low in the sky, painting the world in golden hues as I navigated the bustling streets of Chicago, the city alive with a palpable energy that thrummed through the air like the heartbeat of a jazz bassline. I could hear the distant sounds of street musicians, their melodies weaving through the labyrinth of skyscrapers, each note a fleeting moment in the city's unending symphony. My heels clicked against the pavement, punctuating my thoughts as I made my way to the café where Jason and I had agreed to meet. The aroma of freshly brewed coffee curled around me, a warm embrace that whispered promises of comfort amid the chaos brewing within.

With each step, the weight of my dual life settled heavily on my shoulders. On one hand, there was the thrill of my blossoming relationship with Jason—his laughter igniting something deep within me, a spark I had long thought extinguished. Yet on the other, there was the haunting shadow of Ava's voice echoing in my mind, tinged with desperation. She had been my anchor in a world that often felt overwhelming, my confidante in the realm of dance and dreams, and now she was drowning in a storm of her own making. As I crossed the street, a vibrant mural caught my eye—a kaleidoscope of colors splashed across a brick wall, depicting a dancer caught in mid-pirouette. It was a beautiful reminder of the artistry that connected us, yet it felt painfully ironic. How could I find my own balance when hers was teetering on the edge?

I slipped into the café, the warmth enveloping me like a soft blanket. The rustic wooden tables were filled with patrons, their laughter and conversations blending into a tapestry of life. But my focus was drawn to Jason, who sat in a corner booth, his dark hair tousled in that effortlessly charming way that always made my heart flutter. His deep-set eyes sparkled with a curiosity that drew me in like a moth to a flame, yet today, they flickered with concern as he caught sight of my approach.

"Hey, you look like you've seen a ghost," he remarked, a teasing lilt in his voice, but I could hear the undercurrent of worry woven into his words. I slid into the booth across from him, the soft leather squeaking under my weight.

"It's just... it's Ava," I confessed, my voice barely above a whisper. The name felt heavy on my tongue, laden with the weight of unspoken fears. "She's really struggling."

Jason leaned in, his expression shifting from playful to serious in an instant. "What's going on? You know you can tell me anything."

The urge to spill everything—to lay bare my heart's confusion—battled with the instinct to protect him from the swirling chaos that threatened to engulf me. "She's in a bad place. She lost her job, and now she's behind on rent. I don't know how to help her without losing myself in it."

His brow furrowed as he processed my words. "Have you talked to her? What does she need?"

The questions bounced around in my mind like pinballs, each one triggering another wave of anxiety. "I've been trying to support her, but she keeps pushing me away. It's like she doesn't want me to see how broken she feels. And then there's us—" I faltered, the tension coiling tightly in my chest. "I want to be here with you, but I can't just abandon her."

Jason's hand reached across the table, his fingers brushing against mine, grounding me in the present moment. "I get it. But you can't pour from an empty cup. You need to take care of yourself too."

His words hung in the air, and I felt the sting of truth in them. How could I juggle both? The late-night calls from Ava, the frantic texts begging for reassurance, all gnawed at my energy like a relentless tide. I loved her, and the thought of her suffering twisted something deep within me. Yet with every ounce of support I extended, I felt the vibrant colors of my budding romance with Jason start to fade.

The café around us felt like it had receded into the background, the laughter and chatter becoming muffled whispers as I wrestled with my thoughts. "I wish I could just fix it," I admitted, frustration creeping into my voice. "But I can't save her from herself."

Jason squeezed my hand, a soft smile breaking through the concern etched across his face. "Sometimes just being there is enough. You don't have to have all the answers."

But as he spoke, a flicker of doubt sparked within me. The late nights spent talking to Ava had drained my spirit, leaving me grappling with my own emotions. How could I offer her a lifeline when I was treading water myself? The realization that I was beginning to lose myself in her chaos felt like a betrayal, both to her and to the love I was beginning to cultivate with Jason.

"Maybe I need to take a step back," I murmured, my heart aching at the thought of creating distance. But the weight of my decision pressed against my chest like a heavy fog.

Jason leaned back, his expression thoughtful. "If you think that's what's best. But don't forget about yourself in the process. You're important too."

As I gazed into his warm eyes, the sincerity radiating from him wrapped around my heart, an anchor amidst the tumult. The world outside continued its rhythmic dance, unaware of the storm brewing within me. And in that moment, I realized that the path forward wouldn't be easy. I would have to confront the fragility of my own emotions, navigating the intricate web of friendship and love, where loyalty and desire intertwined like dancers in a delicate waltz, each step leading me closer to a choice that could unravel everything I held dear.

The next few days passed in a blur, each hour marked by the incessant ping of my phone—a digital reminder of Ava's spiraling crisis that seemed to demand my attention like an unrelenting tide. I found myself in a whirlwind of emotions, caught between the serene comfort of my new romance and the stormy chaos that Ava had invited into my life. I'd wake up in the morning, sunlight streaming through my apartment windows, only to be met by the knot of anxiety tightening in my stomach as I prepared for another day of balancing my heart's desires with the needs of my friend.

Each night, after Jason would drop me off, I'd return to a barrage of messages that felt like tiny daggers, each one digging a little deeper. "Can you talk?" "I really need you." "I'm scared." Those three phrases became my evening soundtrack, underscoring the flickering tension that buzzed in the air like a live wire. I could almost hear Ava's voice trembling on the other end of the line, echoing in my mind long after we hung up. It was in those moments that I wrestled with my emotions, trying to remain the unwavering pillar Ava had always counted on.

One particularly bleak evening, as rain pattered softly against my window, I found myself pacing the living room, feeling like a caged animal. The muted glow of the streetlights outside painted the walls in shades of melancholic yellow. I picked up my phone again, staring at Ava's name on the screen, a bittersweet reminder of the connection we once shared on the dance floor, gliding gracefully in sync with each other. But that harmony felt distant now, replaced by an overwhelming sense of responsibility that threatened to drown me.

When I finally dialed her number, the anticipation twisted my stomach. "Hey, Ava," I greeted softly, hoping to convey some warmth despite the heaviness hanging between us.

"Hey," she replied, her voice fragile, as if each word was laced with the weight of her despair. "I don't know what to do. I feel like I'm losing everything."

"I'm here for you," I reassured her, sinking onto the couch, the cushions enveloping me like a long-lost friend. "Tell me what you need."

"I don't even know," she admitted, a slight hitch in her breath. "I just... I thought I could handle everything. But it's too much."

The air crackled with the tension of unspoken fears, and I could sense her pain radiating through the line, wrapping around me like an icy shroud. I wanted to be the strength she needed, the friend who could offer solutions, but my mind swirled with thoughts of Jason, who was patiently waiting for me to return to our budding romance, our laughter echoing in a world far removed from the turmoil Ava faced.

"I know it feels overwhelming," I said gently, trying to infuse a note of hope into the conversation. "But you're not alone in this. We'll figure it out together."

Yet, even as I spoke, doubt gnawed at my insides. Would I lose myself in her struggle, consumed by her needs until there was nothing left of me to give to Jason? I pictured his warm smile, the way his eyes crinkled when he laughed, and a pang of longing washed over me. But I pushed the thought away, focusing instead on Ava's shaky breaths, as if they were a lifeline pulling me back into the present.

"I just don't want to drag you down," she whispered, and I could hear the weight of her guilt, the desperate wish to shield me from her spiraling reality.

"Please," I urged, my voice firm yet gentle. "You're my best friend. I'd never abandon you when you need me most."

Our conversation continued into the night, the rain tapping against the window as I offered words of encouragement, piecing together a plan to help her navigate through her tumultuous situation. But every time I hung up, I felt a little more frayed, a little more distant from the vibrant connection I shared with Jason. Each night, I would climb into bed, wrestling with the dichotomy of my life, and wonder if I could keep juggling both friendships without losing sight of myself.

Eventually, I could feel the toll it was taking on my spirit. I became a ghost in my own life, moving through days in a fog, my laughter with Jason often tinged with an underlying sorrow that wouldn't fully lift. One evening, as we strolled through Millennium Park, the vibrant greens of the landscape dotted with bursts of colorful flowers, I could see the worry etched across his handsome features.

"Hey, is everything okay?" he asked, his voice low and concerned as we paused by the fountain, water dancing in the fading light.

"Yeah, just... a lot on my mind," I replied, forcing a smile that felt like a mask. I didn't want to burden him with my struggles, didn't want him to see the cracks beginning to form in the foundation of my carefully constructed façade.

But he wasn't fooled. "You know you can talk to me, right?" His gaze was unwavering, searching for the truth hidden behind my bravado.

I hesitated, the urge to unburden myself warring with the desire to protect him from the chaos of my life. "It's just my friend," I finally admitted, the words tumbling out like a confession. "She's going through a really tough time, and I feel like I'm stretched too thin. I want to be there for her, but it's hard."

Jason's expression softened, and he took a step closer, closing the space between us. "You're not a superhero, you know. You don't have to save her alone. It's okay to set boundaries."

His words struck a chord deep within me, resonating with the internal struggle I had been battling. "But what if I let her down?"

"Sometimes letting go is the kindest thing you can do—for both of you." He reached out, brushing a loose strand of hair behind my ear, and the warmth of his touch sent a shiver down my spine, pulling me momentarily away from my spiraling thoughts.

In that moment, the storm within me quieted just a bit, replaced by a flicker of clarity. I realized that I didn't have to carry Ava's burdens alone, nor did I need to sacrifice my happiness to maintain our friendship. I could still be a support without being completely consumed, and perhaps it was time to have a heart-to-heart with Ava about my limits.

As I gazed up at Jason, the realization began to sink in: navigating love and friendship was never going to be easy, but I needed to be honest with myself about what I could offer. The beautiful chaos of life wasn't about perfection; it was about finding balance, a dance in which both partners contributed equally. And maybe, just maybe, with each careful step, I could learn to embrace the beauty in the imperfections.

In the days that followed my conversation with Jason, I resolved to carve out a space where both my friendship with Ava and my budding romance could coexist, albeit uneasily. As I ventured into the intricate dance of managing both worlds, I felt like a performer treading a tightrope high above a tumultuous sea. Each day unfolded with its own unique set of challenges, punctuated by late-night calls that turned into early-morning texts, creating a perpetual cycle of worry and weariness.

The following Friday, under the dusky Chicago skyline, I decided it was time to confront Ava's situation more directly. The air was thick with the promise of summer, the humidity clinging to my skin as I made my way to her apartment—a cozy nook that had always been a haven for both of us, adorned with vibrant tapestries and an eclectic mix of plants that she nurtured like children. But today, as I stood at her door, I felt a knot of anxiety twist in my stomach, the familiar warmth of our friendship now shadowed by the uncertainty of what lay ahead.

I knocked gently, the sound echoing in the quiet hallway, and when she opened the door, the sight of her struck me like a thunderbolt. Ava was a whirlwind of untamed emotions, her hair falling in disarray around her face, eyes darkened by sleepless nights. The stark contrast between her vibrant spirit and her current state was unsettling, and my heart sank at the sight.

"Hey," I said softly, stepping into the dimly lit living room where clutter seemed to reign supreme—empty takeout boxes, crumpled receipts, and clothes strewn about like remnants of a battlefield. It felt like an invasion of her personal chaos, each item a testament to her unraveling.

"Thanks for coming," she mumbled, her voice barely above a whisper as she sank onto the couch, her posture defeated. I joined her, the fabric of the cushion sinking under our combined weight, creating an odd sense of shared burden.

"I'm worried about you," I confessed, feeling the heaviness of my words hang in the air. "You don't have to go through this alone."

Her eyes flickered with emotion, a mixture of gratitude and guilt that tore at my heart. "I know, but I don't want to drag you down with me. You have so much going on—your dance classes, Jason..."

The mention of his name felt like a jarring reminder of the world outside this chaotic bubble we occupied. "Jason understands," I replied firmly. "He wants to help you too. But you have to let us in, Ava. You can't just shut us out."

She sighed, a deep, shuddering breath that seemed to release some of the pent-up tension. "I just feel like I'm failing at everything. I lost my job, my savings are gone, and now I can't even pay rent. I'm so embarrassed."

"Life throws curveballs," I reassured her, trying to keep my voice steady. "But this doesn't define you. You've overcome so much before. Remember our first dance recital? You thought you'd forget the choreography, but you nailed it. This is just another challenge to face."

Ava smiled weakly, the corners of her lips lifting slightly, but the spark in her eyes was still dim. "That was different. This feels... insurmountable."

"Maybe it feels that way because you're trying to climb it alone. Let's make a plan together. We can tackle this one step at a time." I leaned closer, the warmth of her presence reminding me of our countless nights spent dreaming of our futures. "What about looking for a new job? You have so much talent, Ava. We can revamp your résumé and practice some interview skills. And I can help you with your finances. I'm not going anywhere."

The flicker of hope in her eyes ignited a tiny flame in my heart, and for the first time in days, I felt a sense of purpose. We spent hours brainstorming ideas and options, mapping out a plan like choreographers working on a new dance. I felt invigorated, and the weight of my own worries began to lift. In that moment, the bond of friendship felt unbreakable.

As the evening wore on, we indulged in nostalgic stories, laughing until our sides hurt. I could see the stress begin to ebb from Ava's demeanor, her laughter washing over me like a soothing balm. It was a reminder of the light she once carried and the resilience that lay beneath the surface.

But as I returned home that night, the warmth of our connection lingered like a soft glow, the shadows of uncertainty crept back in. Jason was waiting for me, his silhouette framed by the soft light of the lamp in the corner. He looked up as I stepped inside, his face a mixture of concern and relief.

"How did it go?" he asked, the warmth in his voice wrapping around me like a soft blanket.

"It was good," I replied, forcing a smile. "We made a plan. I think she's feeling a bit better."

His expression brightened, but I could still sense the worry lurking beneath the surface. "That's great to hear. But don't forget to take care of yourself too. You're carrying a lot on your shoulders."

I nodded, feeling the heaviness settle back in. "I know, but it's hard to balance everything. I don't want to let her down, but I also don't want to lose what we have."

Jason stepped closer, his gaze unwavering. "You won't lose me. Just remember that you're allowed to have your own life too."

In that moment, the weight of his words settled in. I realized that while I needed to be there for Ava, I also had to honor my connection with Jason. Love was not a zero-sum game; it didn't diminish when shared, but rather multiplied in the light of mutual respect and understanding.

As the weeks rolled by, the routine of managing both friendships became more fluid. I found ways to support Ava while still nurturing my blossoming romance with Jason. Our evenings shifted from quiet reflections to vibrant conversations, filled with laughter and shared dreams. We explored the city together, his enthusiasm infusing new energy into my life.

One night, as we walked along the lakefront, the moon shimmering on the water's surface like a thousand diamonds scattered across a dark velvet blanket, I took a moment to breathe in the beauty around me. "You know," I began, turning to Jason, "I never thought I could find someone who understands the chaos of my life and still wants to be a part of it."

He smiled, his expression softening. "I wouldn't want it any other way. Life is messy, and that's what makes it real."

As we continued our stroll, I felt a renewed sense of hope blooming within me. I realized that love and friendship were not mutually exclusive; they were intertwined, forming a tapestry of connection that could withstand the tests of time.

In the days that followed, as I supported Ava in her job search and celebrated small victories, I learned the importance of balance—not just in my relationships, but in my own heart. Love required vulnerability, patience, and the courage to lean on others while also allowing them to lean on me.

I watched as Ava slowly began to find her footing again, each small triumph igniting a spark of resilience within her. And as I navigated this intricate dance of friendships and love, I understood that both paths were worth walking, hand in hand, each step guided by trust, understanding, and the unwavering belief that together, we could weather any storm.

Chapter 9: A Fork in the Road

The sun hung low in the sky, casting a warm golden hue over the park, where every blade of grass shimmered like a green gemstone in the late afternoon light. I nestled myself onto a bench, the cool wood beneath me offering a grounding contrast to the vibrant chaos of life swirling around. Children's laughter floated through the air like notes from a distant melody, their gleeful shrieks intermingling with the occasional chirp of birds flitting between the blossoming cherry trees. Pink petals danced on the breeze, some landing gently in my lap, a reminder that spring had bloomed into its full, riotous splendor.

As I gazed across the lawn, the colors swirled together, painting a picture of sheer joy. There, a couple strolled hand-in-hand, their fingers intertwined like roots of a long-standing oak tree. Nearby, an older gentleman fed crumbs to a gathering of sparrows, each one flitting in eagerly, their tiny bodies puffing up as they chirped in frantic delight. Yet, amid this tapestry of happiness, my heart felt heavy, burdened by choices that loomed like storm clouds over a bright sky.

Jason's smile haunted me, soft and sincere, with a warmth that enveloped my very soul. His patience was the kind that felt foreign to me—like a soothing balm against the jagged edges of my past. In his presence, I found a sanctuary where I could lay bare my fears and dreams without fear of judgment. I'd always known that friendship was a tender thread, easily frayed, and the thought of weaving it into something deeper with Jason filled me with a mix of exhilaration and dread. The echoes of our laughter replayed in my mind, merging with the unease of my commitment to Sarah.

The sun dipped lower, casting longer shadows across the grass as if trying to illustrate the weight of my indecision. My gaze wandered to the park's winding paths, where a fountain bubbled cheerily, sending sprays of water into the air, glistening like diamonds. Just then, I caught sight of Jason making his way toward me, his silhouette framed by the golden hour glow. The way he carried himself, with a relaxed confidence and a hint of boyish charm, made my heart flutter, yet the thought of my obligations to Sarah pulled at me like a tether I was reluctant to sever.

"Lost in thought?" he asked, his voice a soft rumble that broke through my reverie.

I glanced up at him, caught in the moment as if I were a deer startled by the approach of a hunter. "Just... contemplating the meaning of life," I replied, forcing a smile that felt more like a mask than a reflection of my inner turmoil.

He raised an eyebrow, a playful smirk dancing on his lips. "And what have you concluded? That it's all just a series of bad decisions leading to more bad decisions?"

"Or perhaps it's all just one long series of beautiful moments sprinkled with a few bad decisions," I countered, and for a fleeting second, the weight on my chest lifted, allowing a shared laugh to echo between us.

But as laughter faded into silence, reality loomed larger than life, creeping back in with the urgency of an approaching storm. The easy camaraderie that had always defined our friendship suddenly felt tinged with an unspoken tension. I could sense the change in the air, a shift that signaled an inevitable confrontation of our feelings.

"Hey," he said, leaning against the wooden railing of the bench, his expression serious now, those warm brown eyes locked onto mine. "You've been distant lately. What's going on?"

The honesty in his voice struck me. I opened my mouth to speak, yet the words caught in my throat like thorns in my heart. What was going on? The weight of my secret was suffocating, the guilt of even considering a shift in our dynamic gnawing at me relentlessly. I could feel Sarah's presence like a ghost looming over my shoulder, her smile and laughter intertwining with every thought I tried to voice.

"I don't want to mess things up between us, Jason," I finally admitted, my voice trembling. "You mean a lot to me, and I—"

"And I care about you too," he interjected, his tone firm but gentle, as if he were afraid of breaking something fragile. "But it feels like there's something more here. Something we're both dancing around. Are we really just friends, or is there something deeper?"

My heart raced, a rapid thumping against my ribs as if it were trying to escape. The world around us faded, leaving just the two of us suspended in this moment. Every passing second seemed to echo with the weight of my indecision. His eyes bore into mine, filled with the kind of understanding that made me both comforted and terrified.

"I care about you, Jason. I do," I replied, my voice barely a whisper. "But Sarah is my friend. I can't betray her."

His expression shifted, a flicker of disappointment crossing his features before he masked it with a brave smile. "And I respect that. But you deserve to be happy too. You shouldn't feel guilty about exploring what we could have."

As his words sank in, I felt the pull of conflicting desires tear at my heart. Should I prioritize this spark of something extraordinary blooming between us or the loyalty I felt toward my friend? I was at a crossroads, love and friendship vying for my heart's allegiance, and with every heartbeat, the decision loomed larger.

The laughter and joy that surrounded us faded into a dull hum, replaced by the storm brewing within me, the tension coiling tighter as I grappled with the uncertainty of what lay ahead. It was a decision I could no longer postpone, one that would change everything, and as the sun dipped below the horizon, darkness settled around us, mirroring the weight of the choice that lay before me.

A heavy stillness settled in the air, a hush that felt almost sacred as I wrestled with my thoughts. The vibrant hues of the sunset bled into one another, oranges and purples swirling like an artist's palette left unattended. It was a stunning reminder of the beauty that existed in the world even as my heart grappled with the weight of my choices. I took a deep breath, inhaling the fragrance of blooming magnolias mingling with the crispness of the approaching evening. It was intoxicating, a fragrant elixir that momentarily softened the jagged edges of my uncertainty.

"Can I ask you something?" Jason's voice broke through my spiraling thoughts, grounding me like the firm roots of the oak tree nearby. His gaze was steady, brimming with an intensity that threatened to unravel my defenses. I nodded, though my heart raced with the anticipation of what he might say next.

"Do you ever think about us? Not just as friends, but... more?" His words hung in the air, thick with vulnerability and hope.

I swallowed hard, feeling the weight of his question settle deep in my gut. The way he spoke made it sound so simple, yet the complexities of my emotions twisted around my heart like creeping vines. I studied him, taking in the earnestness etched into his features—the way his brow furrowed ever so slightly, as if he were afraid to hear the answer, or worse, the silence that might follow.

"I do think about it," I confessed, the words escaping before I could call them back. "But it scares me. I've never been good at balancing friendships with... other things."

He leaned closer, his voice dropping to a conspiratorial whisper. "What if you don't have to? What if we could just be? Together?"

His words were like a gentle push against the door of my heart, one I had carefully locked and bolted over the years. The thought of stepping beyond the threshold into something uncharted made my pulse quicken, but the allure of discovery shimmered brightly in the dimming light. The laughter of the children faded into a distant echo, and in that moment, it felt as if we were the only two people in the universe.

"But what about Sarah?" I asked, my voice shaky. The mention of her name brought a fresh wave of guilt, like ice water splashed over my warm resolve. "I can't just disregard her feelings."

"Then don't," Jason replied, his gaze unwavering. "You can still talk to her. You can still figure it out without abandoning one for the other."

His words danced around my mind, igniting a flicker of possibility. What if it didn't have to be an either-or scenario? What if I could honor my feelings for both Jason and Sarah, delicately balancing my heart like a tightrope walker swaying above the crowd? The notion was both exhilarating and terrifying, a dichotomy I struggled to grasp.

"I don't want to hurt her, Jason," I admitted, my voice barely above a whisper. "She's been my rock through so much. I can't just... throw that away."

"I know," he said softly, his expression a mix of understanding and frustration. "But your happiness matters too. You deserve to explore what's in front of you without guilt weighing you down."

The sincerity in his eyes was a balm to my frazzled nerves, and as I took in the beauty of the park, a realization began to blossom within me. I had always been the caretaker of emotions, the one who made sure everyone else felt okay before considering my own heart's desires. But perhaps it was time to carve out a space for myself, to allow the petals of my own needs to unfurl under the sunlight of potential.

The sky deepened into shades of indigo, and the park lights flickered on, casting a soft glow that made everything feel magical, almost surreal. I felt a mixture of hope and fear swirling within me, creating a storm of conflicting emotions. I wanted to reach out, to grasp what Jason was offering, but the thought of Sarah's disappointment loomed large in my mind like a thundercloud ready to unleash its fury.

"Can we take it slow?" I asked, the words tumbling out before I could overthink them. "I need time to figure this out."

"Slow is good," he replied, a smile breaking across his face like the dawn after a long night. "I'll be here, whenever you're ready. Just don't shut me out."

The warmth of his smile ignited a flicker of joy within me, and for the first time in days, I felt a surge of clarity. Maybe taking it slow was the answer—a way to honor both my friendship with Sarah and my burgeoning feelings for Jason without sacrificing either. As I mulled over this newfound resolve, my heart dared to hope.

"Let's enjoy tonight, then," I said, my voice steadier now. "Just the two of us. No expectations."

Jason nodded, and the tension that had gripped us began to melt away. We moved toward the fountain, its rhythmic bubbling providing a soothing soundtrack to our unfolding moment. The water shimmered under the glow of the lights, each droplet catching the light like tiny stars, and I couldn't help but smile at the beauty surrounding us.

As we reached the fountain, I tossed a coin into the water, the small splash reverberating like a wish cast into the universe. Jason watched me with an amused expression, curiosity sparking in his eyes.

"What did you wish for?" he teased, leaning closer, the playful glint in his gaze making my heart flutter.

I grinned, feeling a sense of liberation as I decided to embrace the moment. "If I told you, it wouldn't come true."

"Fair enough," he replied, feigning a dramatic sigh. "But you better make it a good one."

The playful banter felt like a breath of fresh air, washing away the remnants of uncertainty and guilt that had clung to me. For now,

I allowed myself to revel in the joy of his company, to savor the laughter that rang out like music in the air.

We strolled through the park, talking about everything and nothing, our voices mingling with the night sounds of crickets and rustling leaves. I found comfort in the ease of our conversation, the way we fell into a rhythm that felt as natural as breathing. With each step, I felt the burden of my decisions begin to lighten, if only for a moment.

As we wandered past a cluster of food stalls, the enticing aroma of warm pretzels wafted through the air, and Jason's eyes lit up with excitement. "You can't come to the park without having a pretzel," he declared, and I couldn't help but laugh at his enthusiasm.

"Okay, but only if we can share it. I don't want to ruin my dinner," I replied, reveling in the playful banter that had become our trademark.

"Deal," he grinned, his eyes sparkling with mischief as he led the way toward the stand.

In that simple exchange, I felt the walls I had built around my heart begin to crack, allowing the possibility of love to seep in like the soft glow of moonlight. Maybe I was at a crossroads, but with Jason by my side, I felt a glimmer of hope that I could find my way forward. The choices I faced were daunting, but in that moment, surrounded by laughter and the warmth of new beginnings, I realized that perhaps it wasn't about choosing one path over the other; it was about carving out my own road, one filled with compassion, love, and the courage to embrace the unknown.

As we strolled toward the food stall, the enticing scent of soft pretzels mingled with the sweet, sugary aroma of funnel cakes. The vibrant energy of the park enveloped us, with families enjoying picnics and friends basking in the warmth of camaraderie. I could hear laughter and snippets of conversation as we navigated the throng of people, our shoulders brushing occasionally, igniting sparks of electricity that made my heart race.

"Two pretzels, please," Jason called out, flashing a charming smile that had the vendor grinning like he'd just won the lottery. While I leaned against the wooden counter, savoring the momentary stillness, my thoughts danced back to my earlier conversation with Jason—the way he had laid bare his heart, urging me to examine my own. It was a beautiful contradiction: this connection that felt so right, yet was simultaneously cloaked in layers of complication.

With pretzels in hand, we wandered to a nearby bench, one that offered a view of the fountain. The water cascaded down like a glistening veil, illuminated by the soft, ambient lights that dotted the park. As we settled onto the bench, I couldn't help but feel as if I were perched on the edge of something monumental, the night sky stretching out before me like an uncharted territory waiting to be explored.

Jason took a bite of his pretzel, a playful grin stretching across his face. "You have to try this. It's like a warm hug in a bread form."

I laughed, taking a small bite from my own pretzel, the warm dough melting in my mouth, coated in salt. "Okay, I'll admit it's pretty great."

He leaned closer, his shoulder brushing against mine. "See? I knew you'd come around. It's all about the little pleasures in life, you know?"

In that moment, surrounded by laughter, light, and the soft whispers of the evening breeze, I felt a sudden sense of calm. Jason's laughter resonated within me, chasing away the shadows that had lingered. Perhaps this was the clarity I had been searching for—finding joy in the simplest moments while acknowledging the complexity of my feelings.

As we sat there, watching the shimmering water dance in the fountain, the world around us faded into a beautiful blur. I turned my head slightly, catching him glancing at me with an intensity that sent butterflies fluttering in my stomach. "You know," I said, attempting to anchor the moment with a playful edge, "if we keep eating like this, we might need to roll ourselves home."

He chuckled, his laughter rich and warm, and for a brief moment, I allowed myself to imagine what it would be like to lean into this connection fully. I could envision us laughing through evenings spent on park benches, sharing not just pretzels but dreams, fears, and everything in between. But then the image of Sarah flickered across my mind, a gentle reminder of the ties that bound me, the responsibilities I had yet to untangle.

The warmth of the pretzel faded as I grappled with the encroaching thoughts. Jason's voice pulled me back. "What's going on in that pretty head of yours?"

"I just... it's complicated," I replied, running my fingers through my hair, trying to ease the tension creeping back into my shoulders. "I want to enjoy this, but there's so much I need to figure out first."

"Let's take it step by step then," he suggested, his expression softening. "I'm in no rush. I just want to be here, and that includes your confusion."

His words wrapped around me like a warm blanket, comforting yet simultaneously unsettling. What did it mean to be in a space where I was allowed to be confused, where I didn't have to carry the weight of decisions on my shoulders alone? I had built a fortress around my heart, convinced that vulnerability was a luxury I couldn't afford. Yet, here was Jason, dismantling the walls brick by brick with every kind word and gentle smile.

As darkness settled more fully around us, the park transformed into a haven of twinkling lights and whispered promises. Couples strolled by, hand in hand, their silhouettes glowing softly in the ambient light, while the fountain continued its melodic dance, the water sparkling like stars falling into the depths of a cosmic sea.

"Have you ever thought about how we all walk through life carrying our own stories?" Jason mused, pulling me from my reverie. "Each person a chapter in a grand narrative, influencing the others in ways we might not even see."

I contemplated his words, feeling the resonance of truth in them. "I think we all have a responsibility to be mindful of the stories we share. They shape who we become."

"Exactly," he replied, his enthusiasm palpable. "And that's why it's so important to be authentic. It's the only way we can truly connect with others."

His insight made me consider my own story—the tangled threads of friendship and love, loyalty and desire. It was a narrative woven with vibrant threads of joy and darker strands of uncertainty, but it was mine. And maybe it was time I embraced all of it, even the messy parts.

As we continued our conversation, sharing stories about our childhoods, our dreams for the future, and the silly moments that shaped our lives, the weight of my earlier turmoil seemed to lighten. I caught glimpses of his life—the little quirks that made him uniquely Jason, the way his eyes sparkled when he laughed, the passion in his voice when he spoke about his dreams. Each detail drew me closer, building a bridge between the life I had known and the one I was beginning to imagine.

When he spoke about his aspirations, the way he wanted to create art that resonated with people, I felt the kindling of something deeper—a connection that surpassed the boundaries of friendship. It was a spark that ignited a fire within me, a yearning to embrace the possibilities that lay before us.

Yet, even as we shared laughter and dreams, the echo of Sarah's friendship lingered, a quiet reminder of the path I had walked for so long. I realized that navigating these waters wouldn't be simple. There would be heartache, tough conversations, and the inevitable fallout of change, but maybe that was part of life's richness—a tapestry woven from both pain and joy.

As the night deepened, I leaned back on the bench, allowing the cool breeze to wash over me, carrying away the remnants of my confusion. "You know," I said softly, "maybe the best stories are the ones that challenge us, the ones that force us to confront our deepest fears."

Jason turned to me, his expression thoughtful. "Absolutely. It's in those moments of discomfort that we discover who we truly are."

The weight of his words settled within me, illuminating the path forward. I could no longer ignore my feelings or dismiss the budding connection we shared. It was time to embrace the chaos, to accept the intertwining of love and friendship as part of a beautiful, complex journey.

With a newfound determination, I turned to Jason, the vulnerability between us palpable. "I'm ready to explore this," I said, my voice steady. "I don't want to hide anymore."

His smile widened, a mixture of relief and joy lighting up his face. "Good. Because I've been waiting for you to say that."

As we shared another warm pretzel, laughter spilling between us like the soft cascade of water from the fountain, I felt the walls around my heart crumbling. Each moment we shared built upon the last, layering a foundation of trust and understanding.

The park transformed into a sanctuary, a vibrant tapestry of life unfolding around us. I reveled in the warmth of Jason's presence, and as the stars began to twinkle overhead, I realized that sometimes, the most beautiful stories arise not from the clear-cut paths we choose, but from the twists and turns we navigate with those who dare to walk beside us. The journey was just beginning, and as I leaned into the possibilities, I felt a sense of hope ignite within me, illuminating the road ahead.

Chapter 10: The Sound of Silence

The studio felt like a cavern of solitude, an expanse of polished wood and bright lights that once pulsed with the energy of creativity but now stood still, waiting. I took a tentative step forward, the familiar smell of varnish and chalk dust swirling around me, a mixture of past performances and unfulfilled potential. The mirrors lined the walls, reflecting not just my physical form but also the weight of my indecision, each crack in the glass amplifying my internal battle. I had spent countless hours rehearsing here, honing my craft, yet today it felt as if the very air conspired against me, pressing down on my shoulders like a heavy quilt.

As I moved deeper into the studio, my sneakers squeaked against the floor, a sound that felt almost foreign in this silence. I glanced around at the empty spaces where laughter and camaraderie had once thrived. The walls, usually echoing with shouts of encouragement and the shuffling of feet, now absorbed every flicker of doubt I possessed. I longed for the warmth of my friends' voices, the lively banter that had once felt like the heartbeat of this place. Yet, as I stood there, swallowed by my thoughts, I found only echoes of past joys and fears mingling in the air, creating a cacophony of what-ifs.

Then came Lena, a whirlwind of energy and empathy, bursting into my cloud of desolation. She had an uncanny ability to breathe life into the dimmest of moments. The sunlight spilled through the tall windows behind her, casting a halo that framed her dark curls and highlighted the twinkle in her eyes. "You're not alone," she said, her voice a melodic balm that soothed my frayed nerves. It was the kind of statement that grounded me, tethering my spiraling thoughts to the earth.

Lena leaned against the barre, her posture relaxed but her gaze penetrating. "I know what it's like to feel like everything is slipping away," she continued, a hint of vulnerability sneaking into her otherwise vibrant tone. "Remember that time I almost quit? I thought I wasn't cut out for this." Her smile was contagious, even in the midst of my storm. I remembered that moment vividly, her tears glistening like raindrops on her cheeks as she confided her struggles. The way she'd channeled her despair into a performance that left us all breathless was nothing short of magic.

With each word, Lena wove a tapestry of shared experiences and unspoken fears. I could see the struggle mirrored in her eyes, the same uncertainty that now danced in my own. She spoke of nights spent pacing her tiny apartment, rehearsing lines that felt foreign, and of the inevitable breakdown that followed each false start. "But I didn't give up," she insisted, her voice rising with an intensity that ignited the flicker of determination buried deep within me. "I faced it head-on. And so will you."

The flickering light of hope sparked in my chest, growing brighter with each moment. I realized that my fears—those monsters that lurked in the corners of my mind—could be confronted, wrestled with, and ultimately, transformed. "You're right," I replied, feeling the warmth of our shared resolve envelop me like a comforting blanket. "It's time to stop hiding behind my doubts."

With Lena by my side, we moved across the studio, her laughter dissolving the heavy silence that had settled in like a ghost. As I looked into the mirrors again, I saw not just my reflection but the potential to reclaim my confidence. The fear that once paralyzed me began to lose its grip, replaced by a newfound sense of purpose. The sunlight danced along the floor, illuminating the path ahead, guiding me toward the first steps of my journey.

"Let's do something crazy," I said, surprising myself with the boldness of my words. "Let's create a routine that embodies everything we've been through." Lena's eyes sparkled with excitement, her laughter bubbling over like champagne, infectious and effervescent. She agreed without hesitation, already envisioning the choreography that would spring from our hearts and struggles.

We spent hours crafting movements that mirrored the ebb and flow of our emotions. The studio, once a haunting space of silence, now reverberated with the sound of our bodies colliding against the floor, echoing the stories we had to tell. With each turn and leap, we breathed life back into the room, a testament to our resilience and friendship. The mirrors reflected not just our physical forms but the triumph of our spirits as we danced through our fears, transforming them into art.

In the midst of our routine, I caught a glimpse of the vibrant colors surrounding us—the bright blue of the walls, the deep reds of the barre, and the golden beams of sunlight streaming in, illuminating every corner of the studio. Each hue became a brushstroke on the canvas of our journey, a reminder that even in moments of silence and uncertainty, life could burst forth in vivid, breathtaking ways.

As we wrapped up our impromptu session, breathless and exhilarated, I felt a renewed sense of hope blossom within me. The weight of my doubts had been lifted, replaced by the exhilaration of creation and connection. I glanced at Lena, who beamed back at me, her presence a constant reminder that I wasn't alone in this journey.

The studio was no longer just a place of solitude; it had transformed into a sanctuary of possibilities, a space where fear could be confronted, and dreams could be reignited. The echoes of laughter and determination danced around us, wrapping us in their embrace as we prepared to face the challenges ahead, together.

The moment we finished our impromptu routine, the air buzzed with a lively energy that felt foreign yet thrilling. I wiped the sweat from my brow, glancing at the small clock perched on the wall, its hands spinning almost too fast to register. Time had slipped away unnoticed, the worries that had plagued me before now mingling with the exhilaration of movement. The mirror reflected my flushed cheeks, a testament not just to the physical exertion but to a burgeoning sense of clarity. With Lena, each beat of music pulsed through my veins, reminding me that the world was still alive and brimming with possibility.

As we stood in the middle of the studio, I was struck by a wave of inspiration that enveloped me like the softest of embraces. My mind began to race, weaving together threads of ideas and movements, each one more vivid than the last. I could see our routine evolving, blooming into something that captured not only our struggles but also the vibrancy of our friendship. "What if we incorporated elements of our personal journeys?" I suggested, the thought bubbling up with an infectious enthusiasm. "We could tell a story through dance—something raw and real."

Lena's eyes lit up as if I had just revealed a secret treasure map. "Absolutely! We can highlight those moments that made us doubt ourselves, and then show how we rose above them. It's like... a phoenix rising from the ashes, but with jazz hands." She grinned, and I couldn't help but laugh. The imagery was both ridiculous and perfect, encapsulating the essence of what we were trying to achieve.

We spent the next few hours diving into this newfound vision, moving from one corner of the studio to the other, hands outstretched as if inviting the very air to join our dance. I could hear the faint echo of the city outside—horns honking, pedestrians chatting, the distant strum of a street performer's guitar—each sound adding a layer to our creative sanctuary. It felt almost poetic, this juxtaposition of the bustling world beyond the studio's walls and the stillness we were forging within.

In the moments of reflection between our dance sessions, I allowed myself to look deeper into my own experiences. I recalled the times when self-doubt had crept in, those insidious whispers that told me I wasn't good enough, that I didn't belong. Each memory was a sharp reminder of how far I had come and how important it was to acknowledge the struggle. I wanted our performance to resonate with others, to inspire them to face their own fears. It was a revelation wrapped in determination.

As the sun dipped lower in the sky, casting long shadows that stretched like fingers across the studio floor, we decided to take a break. We settled onto the worn-out couch tucked in the corner, a relic from days gone by, its upholstery faded yet somehow comforting. I sank into the cushions, sighing contentedly as the weight of the day's labor began to wash over me. Lena rummaged through her bag, pulling out two water bottles that had somehow been kept cold despite the warmth in the room.

"Here," she said, handing me one. "We've earned this. We've transformed the silence into something spectacular." Her enthusiasm was infectious, and I couldn't help but smile, feeling as though we were on the brink of something monumental.

"Do you remember our first dance class together?" I asked, the memories flooding back as vividly as if they had happened yesterday. "I was so nervous I thought I might throw up right there in the middle of the floor."

Lena chuckled, her laughter echoing against the walls, filling the space with warmth. "You weren't the only one! I thought I'd trip over my own feet and faceplant right into the mirror. But there we were, flailing around like a couple of newborn giraffes. Yet somehow, we made it through."

"That first routine was a disaster," I admitted, recalling our attempts to master the simplest of steps. "But that was the moment I realized how much I loved this. It was messy, but we laughed until we cried. You made me feel like I belonged."

Lena's expression softened, and she reached across the couch, squeezing my hand. "And you've come so far since then. You're not that scared girl anymore. You're fierce, passionate, and ready to take on the world. I see it every time you step into this studio."

Her words washed over me, lifting the veil of uncertainty that had shrouded my spirit. I felt a warmth unfurl in my chest, a blossom of self-acceptance that had been long overdue. "Thank you," I said, my voice catching in my throat. "You don't know how much that means to me."

As we sat in the cozy silence, our shared memories floating around us like confetti, I contemplated how our friendship had become a lifeline. It had been a beacon during my darkest moments, illuminating the path to self-discovery. Each shared laugh and tear had stitched us closer together, creating a tapestry of resilience that I cherished deeply.

The sun had nearly dipped below the horizon, leaving behind a canvas of oranges and purples that painted the windows with a golden hue. I stood and moved toward the mirrors, my reflection shimmering like a work of art, vibrant and alive. "Let's do this," I declared, a newfound resolve sparking within me. "Let's create something that embodies who we are—flaws and all."

Lena rose beside me, her presence a steady anchor as we prepared to dive back into our craft. We stepped away from the couch, our spirits buoyed by the promise of what was to come. With the echoes of our laughter and stories swirling around us, the silence that once felt oppressive transformed into a space brimming with potential. We would not just dance; we would soar. The studio was no longer a hollow shell but a sanctuary of strength, a place where we could carve out our stories and share them with the world.

The music began to play again, and as the notes filled the air, I felt every fear, every ounce of doubt, fall away like autumn leaves surrendering to the wind. Together, we would paint the silence with sound, rhythm, and an unbreakable bond that would resonate long after the last note faded.

As the music swelled, I surrendered to its embrace, the notes weaving through me like threads of silk. Each beat pulsed with life, pulling me into a world where vulnerability transformed into strength. I caught Lena's eye in the mirror, her expression a perfect blend of encouragement and mischief, as if we were conspirators in a delightful escapade rather than two dancers crafting a routine. With a playful smirk, she nodded, and we launched into movement, allowing our bodies to articulate the story we wanted to tell.

The studio transformed with each step we took, the space expanding beyond its physical boundaries. We became two souls intertwined in a narrative, each lift and turn symbolizing the triumphs and trials we faced in our journey. As I spun across the floor, I felt a burst of exhilaration, a freedom that washed over me like a cool breeze on a sweltering day. The world outside faded away, and it was just us—our breaths syncing, our spirits harmonizing in perfect unison.

In one moment, I was a girl grappling with self-doubt; in the next, I was a warrior confronting her fears. With each leap, I soared, imagining the weight of my insecurities being cast off, each movement a rebellion against the silence that had once threatened to consume me. Lena mirrored my energy, her movements bold and fearless, each flick of her wrist a declaration of defiance against the shadows that had lingered too long.

"Let's add that moment when we first realize we can rise above our fears," Lena suggested mid-routine, her breath mingling with the rhythm of our dance. I nodded, a spark of inspiration igniting within me. We shifted the focus of our routine, incorporating elements of playfulness juxtaposed with raw emotion. I envisioned us dancing on the precipice of our struggles, teetering yet resolute, as we spun into a powerful tableau that encapsulated our shared experiences.

As we danced, the studio echoed not only with the sound of our feet but with the essence of our stories—fears faced, battles fought, and dreams chased. The mirrors reflected our raw honesty, exposing the layers of vulnerability that lay beneath our bright exteriors. In that dance, I felt empowered, not just as an individual but as part of something larger—a sisterhood built on trust and resilience.

When the music faded, we collapsed onto the floor, our chests heaving, laughter spilling from our lips like confetti. The adrenaline coursed through me, mingling with the sweat that glistened on my skin, reminding me that I was alive, and fiercely so.

"I think we have something special here," I gasped, wiping the back of my hand across my forehead. The sense of accomplishment surged within me, a reminder of how far I had come since that first hesitant step into this world.

"Let's refine it," Lena replied, her eyes sparkling with mischief. "But first, we need a snack. I'm pretty sure I left half a burrito in my bag."

I couldn't help but laugh, and the sound echoed off the walls like music itself. We trudged over to the corner where our belongings lay scattered, and as Lena rummaged through her bag, I caught a glimpse of the sun dipping below the horizon, painting the windows in hues of pink and gold.

"I can't believe we spent the entire afternoon dancing," I mused, my heart swelling with gratitude. "This place used to feel so intimidating, and now it feels like home."

Lena paused, her hand poised over her half-eaten burrito. "It's because we've filled it with our stories," she replied, her voice thoughtful. "This studio is a reflection of us—messy, beautiful, and ever-evolving. It's a safe space where we can lay our hearts bare, where we can fail and rise again without fear."

With each bite of the burrito, we refueled our bodies and souls, sharing our hopes and fears, dreams and aspirations. We spoke of the upcoming performance, the nervous excitement mingling with the thrill of creation. I felt the familiar knot of anxiety tighten in my stomach, but this time it was accompanied by a sense of purpose. I could visualize our dance—every twist, every turn—and how it would resonate with the audience, a mirror reflecting their struggles and triumphs back at them.

After we finished our makeshift meal, we returned to the floor, the echoes of our earlier laughter still lingering in the air. With renewed energy, we began to hone our routine, the movements flowing seamlessly as if we were carving our narrative into the very air around us. We experimented with dynamics, shifting between moments of tension and release, laughter and heartache, embodying the very essence of life itself.

It was in those hours of creation that I discovered a truth I had long been seeking: vulnerability was not a weakness but a profound strength. Each falter, each moment of hesitation became an opportunity for growth, a testament to our shared resilience. The dance was no longer just a performance; it was an anthem of survival, a celebration of everything we had faced and overcome.

With the final notes of our piece echoing in my ears, I stood in front of the mirror once more, taking in the reflection of the girl who had once been so unsure. I saw her now—not just the hesitant dancer but a fierce warrior ready to step into the light. The shadows that had clung to me began to recede, replaced by a bright halo of determination.

Lena joined me at the mirror, and we exchanged a glance that spoke volumes. In that moment, we were not just friends; we were kindred spirits intertwined by shared dreams and struggles. We had weathered the storms together, and now we stood on the precipice of something incredible—a performance that would not only showcase our artistry but resonate with the hearts of everyone who witnessed it.

As we finalized the details of our choreography, I could already envision the audience sitting in rapt attention, feeling every beat and emotion we poured into our performance. I was no longer just a dancer afraid of the silence; I was a voice, a story waiting to be shared. Together, we would step onto that stage and transform our journey into something beautiful, something that would linger long after the final bow.

In the heart of that vibrant studio, surrounded by the remnants of our laughter and dreams, I felt ready. Ready to embrace the silence, to fill it with sound and spirit, and to dance boldly into the life that awaited me just beyond those mirrored walls.

Chapter 11: Picking Up the Pieces

The air in the small café smelled like freshly brewed coffee and sweet pastries, a perfect concoction that clung to the walls, wrapping us in a comforting embrace. It was the kind of place where laughter floated easily, mingling with the clinking of ceramic mugs and the rhythmic tapping of keyboards. I had always loved this spot, tucked away in the heart of our town, its wooden beams and vintage posters whispering stories of those who'd come before us. Yet, that day, the vibrant energy around me felt muted, dulled by the gravity of my friend's troubles.

Sarah sat across from me, her hands wrapped around a steaming mug that had long lost its warmth. I could see the tremor in her fingers, the way she'd twist the handle of the cup as if it were a lifeline. Her eyes, usually so full of spark, were clouded, distant, as if the weight of the world had settled on her shoulders. The turmoil she faced seemed endless, an unrelenting tide threatening to pull her under. I could feel her fear—a palpable thing, thickening the air between us.

"Just take it one step at a time," I urged gently, keeping my voice steady even as my heart raced. I leaned forward, closing the distance between us. "You don't have to have it all figured out right now."

She nodded, a fragile smile ghosting across her lips, but it didn't reach her eyes. I wished I could lift the burden from her, trade places, if only for a moment. The truth was, I felt anchored to her plight, as if her sadness had become a part of my own skin, and the thought of peeling it away was unbearable. It was a strange kind of intimacy, sharing her struggles while shoving my own concerns into the back of my mind. In those late-night conversations filled with brainstorming and strategizing, I found solace in her company. The chaos of her life created a whirlwind that allowed me to escape my own fears, even if only temporarily.

"Let's focus on what you can do today," I suggested, determined to keep her grounded. "What's the next step?"

Her brow furrowed, and she took a deep breath, the sound like a gentle sigh of defeat. "I need to figure out how to talk to my boss about the promotion. I thought I was ready, but now..." Her voice trailed off, and I could see the self-doubt creeping in like an unwelcome shadow.

"Remember that time you aced that presentation?" I reminded her, leaning back in my chair, trying to rekindle her confidence. "You charmed everyone in that room. You can do this too."

She chuckled softly, a hint of nostalgia lighting her expression. "Yeah, but that was different. This feels so much more important."

"Exactly," I countered, my voice infused with encouragement. "Because it's important, you'll bring your A-game. You always do."

As the hours melted away, we crafted a strategy, each point more intricate than the last, layers of possibility unfolding before us like the petals of a blooming flower. Each success I helped her envision felt like a small victory for both of us, the tension in her shoulders easing with every plan we formulated. Yet, amid our fervent planning, my mind drifted to Jason.

His presence was like a beacon, warm and inviting, but I felt the flicker of guilt snuffing out my enthusiasm. He had reached out several times, checking in with that concerned gaze of his, reminding me of the promise I'd made to explore the connection between us. But how could I do that when Sarah needed me? My commitment to her loomed larger than my budding relationship, an unspoken pact that tethered me to her side.

The sun dipped below the horizon, painting the café in warm hues of orange and pink, casting elongated shadows across our table. "What if I mess up?" Sarah whispered, her voice barely above a breath.

"Then you learn from it and try again," I replied firmly, wanting to anchor her back to reality. "Life isn't a straight line; it's a series of curves and detours. You're not alone in this. I'm right here."

As we packed our things and stepped out into the cool evening air, the world seemed to pulsate with possibility. The streetlights flickered on, illuminating the sidewalk in a soft glow, and I felt a surge of hope wash over me. I wanted to believe in Sarah's potential, to wrap her in confidence as tightly as a comforting quilt, but I couldn't shake the nagging feeling that I was losing something precious in my own life.

Days turned into nights as I continued to help Sarah navigate her challenges. Our evenings were spent buried in strategy sessions, laughter punctuating our conversations like punctuation marks. It was in those moments, sitting on the floor of her living room surrounded by empty coffee cups and crumpled notes, that I felt the chaos of my own life subside. But each smile exchanged felt like a concession in my heart; Jason remained a distant flicker, his warmth beckoning from afar while my attention was locked onto Sarah's needs.

Each time my phone buzzed with his name, my heart would flutter, a small hope igniting, only to be extinguished when I reminded myself of my priorities. I wondered if I was being noble or simply reckless, sacrificing my own budding romance for the sake of someone else. The thought of losing Jason kept me awake at night, a cruel companion in my quest to be the supportive friend Sarah needed.

And yet, in the moments of quiet, when Sarah drifted off to sleep, her worries momentarily silenced, I found myself gazing out her window, lost in the maze of stars twinkling above. I wondered if Jason was looking at the same sky, imagining the same future I had envisioned with him. Would he understand my struggle to balance it all? Would he wait for me to find my way back, to reclaim the pieces of myself that were slowly slipping away? The answer eluded me, tangled in the complexities of love, friendship, and the unyielding pull of responsibility.

The evening air wrapped around me like a familiar embrace as I walked home from Sarah's place, the dim streetlights casting a gentle glow on the sidewalk. Each step felt weighted with the heaviness of unspoken words, emotions coiling tightly in my chest like a spring ready to burst. The chaos of her life had become a comforting noise, drowning out the quieter, more complex concerns of my own heart. Yet with every laughter-filled strategy session, the gaping void left by my unfulfilled connection with Jason seemed to stretch wider.

The clatter of my keys echoed in the silence as I opened my front door, the scent of my candle-lit living room welcoming me home. I paused, taking in the neatness of the space I had crafted, where the chaos of the outside world faded away. My walls were adorned with photographs—snapshots of laughter, places, and people that once filled my life with joy. They were reminders of moments when love was uncomplicated, before it tangled with responsibilities and unspoken commitments.

I sank onto the couch, the cushions embracing me like old friends. A glass of water sat nearby, untouched, as my thoughts churned relentlessly. I flicked on the television, searching for distraction in the glow of moving images, but the words of my favorite show blurred into white noise. Instead, my mind wandered to Jason—his smile, the way his laughter would spark joy in a room, the gentle way he understood the unspoken layers of my heart. He was a puzzle I hadn't yet solved, and every moment spent with Sarah was a moment lost in uncovering those mysteries.

The phone buzzed on the coffee table, jolting me from my reverie. Jason's name flashed across the screen, and my heart danced nervously in my chest. I hesitated, fingers hovering over the screen, caught between the desire to connect and the weight of the obligation I felt towards Sarah.

"Hey, just checking in. How's everything?" His message was straightforward, yet the warmth behind it felt like a hug from a distance.

I contemplated how to respond, wanting to share the good and the challenging. I wanted him to know how much I valued our connection, yet how could I explain the turmoil swirling within me? I settled for a simple reply. "Busy helping a friend. Things are tough, but we're figuring it out."

A few moments passed before his response came. "I'm here if you need to talk. Don't forget to take care of yourself too."

His words were a gentle reminder, a lifeline thrown out into my turbulent waters. But the guilt was a heavier anchor, dragging me deeper into the depths of obligation and friendship. I couldn't help but think how selfish I was being. Here I was, wrapped up in my friend's crisis, while the man who cared for me waited patiently in the wings.

As the days rolled on, I found myself swept deeper into Sarah's world, our late-night sessions becoming a comforting routine. We'd map out her career goals, her dreams interwoven with fears, hopes painted in bright colors amidst the shadows of self-doubt. The more I invested in her journey, the more I recognized the significance of every step she took. It was a reflection of my own struggles, a reminder of the dreams I had stowed away in the back of my mind like forgotten trinkets.

One night, under the soft glow of fairy lights strung above her couch, we broke into laughter, a melody that filled the room with light. "Can you believe I thought that sending a PowerPoint would be enough to impress my boss?" Sarah chuckled, her eyes sparkling with newfound confidence. "It's not like he's going to hand me a promotion just because I can use bullet points!"

"That's the spirit!" I encouraged, clapping my hands in delight. "What you need is a killer pitch—something that'll knock his socks off."

And as we continued to scheme, weaving together her plans like a tapestry, I couldn't help but feel my own dreams stirring, whispering beneath the surface. I wanted to pursue my passion for writing, to explore the stories that bubbled just beneath my skin, waiting to be set free. But with every laugh shared, every doubt quelled, I also felt the gnawing uncertainty that came from neglecting my own aspirations.

That night, as I lay in bed, the stars glimmering outside my window, I reached for my journal. The pages were blank, waiting patiently for the chaos of my thoughts to spill onto them. I wrote about Sarah's triumphs, the way she had begun to reclaim her narrative, each word a testament to her strength. But I also wrote about my own dreams, the flickering embers of stories that demanded to be told. As I penned my feelings, I could almost hear Jason's voice echoing in my mind, urging me to embrace my truth.

"Why are you holding back?" his voice seemed to ask. "You deserve to explore your passions just as much as anyone else."

I closed my journal, feeling lighter. Perhaps it was time to find balance—not just for Sarah, but for myself as well. The thought hung in the air like a tantalizing promise. Could I carve out space for both our journeys?

The next day, as I met Sarah for our usual coffee, the café buzzed with activity. The scent of espresso and warm pastries filled the air, mingling with the laughter of patrons who were blissfully unaware of the internal battles being fought at the tables around them.

"I think I'm ready to talk to my boss," Sarah announced, her voice firm and resolute, the spark of determination igniting within her. "I've got my pitch ready, and I can feel it in my bones."

A smile broke across my face, a surge of pride washing over me. "That's incredible! I knew you could do it."

But as she spoke, my heart tugged at me—a longing for Jason, the gentle reminder of the connection I was neglecting. "You've got this, Sarah," I said, my voice rich with enthusiasm, even as a part of me yearned to reach out to him.

We wrapped up our meeting, her excitement infectious, and as I walked back home, my phone buzzed once more. Jason's message lit up the screen: "Let's grab dinner soon. I miss you."

The warmth of his words enveloped me, and I realized then that perhaps it was time to be brave. It wasn't just about Sarah anymore; it was about finding that delicate dance between support and self-care, about nurturing the parts of myself that had lain dormant for too long.

With newfound determination, I typed back, "How about tomorrow? I'd love to catch up." My heart fluttered as I hit send, a step towards embracing all the parts of my life—friendship, love, and my own aspirations. The world felt a little lighter, the night sky above a canvas of endless possibility.

The next day arrived with a hesitant sun peeking through the curtains, casting gentle rays across my bedroom walls. I could hear the distant hum of the city awakening, its heartbeat resonating through the open window. The aroma of fresh coffee wafted from the café down the street, teasing my senses, and I found myself drawn to the comforting ritual of brewing my own. I moved through the familiar motions, pouring the water, watching the grounds bloom, feeling grounded in the simple act. Yet, beneath that tranquility lay a whirlwind of anticipation, my heart racing at the thought of dinner with Jason.

After a quick shower, I chose an outfit that felt like me—comfortable yet polished. I slipped into my favorite dress, the fabric soft against my skin, and applied a hint of lipstick, enough to draw attention but not distract from the warmth in my eyes. As I stood in front of the mirror, I practiced a smile, hoping to reflect the excitement fluttering in my stomach. Tonight wasn't just about reconnecting with him; it was about reclaiming the pieces of my life that had been overshadowed by Sarah's turmoil.

When I arrived at the restaurant, the ambiance enveloped me in a cozy embrace. Soft jazz floated through the air, and the gentle clink of silverware on plates blended with the low murmur of conversations. The dim lighting cast a golden hue, transforming the space into a haven where laughter and connection thrived. Jason was already there, seated at a small table by the window, his back turned to me as he studied the menu.

As I approached, he turned, and that familiar spark lit his eyes. "Hey, you made it!" he exclaimed, standing up to pull out my chair with effortless grace. I could see the way the light danced in his gaze, and for a moment, everything else faded away.

"I wouldn't miss it for the world," I replied, settling into the chair as the weight of the day slipped from my shoulders. Our conversation flowed easily, laughter bubbling up like champagne as we recounted silly stories from our past. With each shared smile, the chasm that had formed between us during those chaotic days began to close.

"What's been going on with you?" he asked, leaning forward, his expression genuinely curious. "I've missed our talks."

I hesitated, the balance I'd been searching for teetering on the edge of vulnerability. How much could I reveal without overshadowing Sarah's journey? "I've been supporting a friend," I began, gauging his reaction. "She's been going through a rough patch with work, and I've been helping her prepare for a big conversation with her boss."

"That sounds intense," he acknowledged, his brow furrowing slightly in concern. "But it's great that you're there for her. You have a knack for that."

His compliment warmed me, and I felt a flicker of pride. "It has been intense. But honestly, it's a little draining. I think I've been neglecting my own needs," I admitted, allowing the truth to unfurl between us like a delicate flower.

Jason leaned back in his chair, the glint of understanding in his eyes deepening. "It's important to find time for yourself too," he said softly, his tone inviting me to share more. "You can't pour from an empty cup."

The weight of his words lingered, resonating in the corners of my heart. I nodded, contemplating how I had let my own aspirations slip away while focusing on supporting Sarah. "You're right," I murmured, looking down at the table as I traced the rim of my glass with my finger. "I've been so consumed with her struggles that I haven't thought about what I want."

"What do you want?" he asked, his gaze steady, searching.

I could feel the air shift, the question hanging between us like a shimmering thread waiting to be pulled. "I want to write," I confessed, the words tumbling out before I could rein them in. "I've always loved telling stories, but I've pushed it aside. Life just... got in the way."

Jason smiled, a soft light igniting in his eyes. "Then write. No one's stopping you except yourself."

His encouragement wrapped around me, filling the empty spaces that had lingered for far too long. Our meal arrived, the dishes fragrant and beautifully presented, but the real feast lay in our conversation. We dove deep into discussions about dreams and aspirations, each word unraveling the threads of uncertainty that had tangled in my mind.

"So, what's the story that's been itching to get out?" he asked, and I could see the genuine interest etched on his face. I hesitated, caught between the fear of exposure and the exhilaration of sharing.

"It's a romance," I began, a playful smirk tugging at my lips. "One that follows a woman navigating the complexities of love and friendship in a city that never sleeps."

"Ah, a classic," he teased, and I rolled my eyes, laughing. "What's the twist?"

"Well, there's a love triangle," I said, unable to suppress a mischievous grin. "But not in the way you think. It's more about the choices she has to make, the sacrifices she faces for her friendships. It's about finding herself amidst the chaos."

"Sounds like it hits close to home," Jason remarked, his expression turning more serious. "Do you think you'd make those same sacrifices?"

The question hung in the air, a silent challenge that struck a chord within me. I considered it carefully, the enormity of it all washing over me. "I hope not," I replied finally, my voice steady. "I think I'm learning that I don't have to lose myself for others. I can support them without sacrificing my own happiness."

He smiled, a knowing look passing between us that felt almost electric. "That's the first step. Recognizing that you're worthy of your own dreams and desires."

As the evening unfolded, time seemed to lose its grip on us. We spoke of everything—books, music, life goals—our laughter and words weaving a tapestry that felt both familiar and new. I felt my heart lighten, the burden of obligation to Sarah softening as I immersed myself in the connection I had with Jason.

When dessert arrived—an indulgent slice of rich chocolate cake—we both dove in with gleeful abandon, indulging in each bite like children at a candy store. In that moment, the world outside faded away, leaving only the sweet intimacy we were forging.

As we left the restaurant, the cool night air was invigorating, and I could hear the city pulsing around us—cars honking, laughter ringing out from nearby bars, the distant music of street performers echoing in the night.

"Let's walk," Jason suggested, and I nodded, my heart soaring at the thought of lingering a little longer in his company. We strolled down the bustling streets, our conversation flowing effortlessly, the night wrapping around us like a protective cloak.

But as we reached the park, where the trees rustled softly in the gentle breeze, the mood shifted. We paused by a bench, the dim glow of a nearby lamppost illuminating Jason's face. "I've missed this," he said, his voice low and sincere. "Being with you like this."

"Me too," I admitted, my heart swelling. "I didn't realize how much I needed this until now."

He stepped closer, the space between us shrinking. "I want to be part of your journey, all of it. You don't have to feel guilty about balancing your friendships with whatever this is between us."

The sincerity in his voice sent warmth flooding through me, igniting a spark of hope. I could feel the foundation we were building—a space where dreams and connection could coexist without one diminishing the other.

As I looked up at him, the world fell away, and all that remained was the soft glow of his gaze. "I want that too," I whispered, the words emerging like a vow. In that moment, everything clicked into place, a beautiful mosaic of hope and connection that felt both exhilarating and grounding.

The path ahead might still be strewn with challenges, but I finally felt ready to embrace it all. Love, friendship, and the pursuit of dreams could coexist harmoniously if I allowed them to. With Jason by my side, I knew I could navigate the twists and turns of life, no longer fearing the sacrifices that once haunted me. Instead, I could forge a new path, one where I embraced every piece of myself—because I was worthy of every single moment.

Chapter 12: A Dance of Doubt

The rehearsal studio, a cavernous space bathed in the soft glow of flickering fluorescent lights, thrummed with the energy of our collective ambition. Mirrors lined the walls like watchful sentinels, reflecting not just our movements but the flickering embers of our dreams and aspirations. The air was thick with the smell of sweat and determination, a heady mix that lingered long after the music faded. My feet glided across the polished wooden floor, each step echoing with a resonant clarity, yet every beat of my heart seemed discordant with the music that poured from the speakers.

The sound was intoxicating—a pulsing rhythm that called for my body to respond with fluidity and grace. Instead, I found myself trapped in a quagmire of anxiety and doubt. Each pirouette was a battle against the turmoil brewing within me, my thoughts swirling like autumn leaves caught in a whirlwind. I couldn't shake the feeling that my friend's situation was creeping into my bones, a weight that threatened to anchor me to the floor. Her struggles, so palpable and consuming, reached out to me, binding me in invisible threads that choked my passion.

As I stared into the mirror, my reflection morphed into a shadow of who I used to be. The vivacity in my eyes, once bright with dreams of stardom, dimmed into a mere flicker of hope. I tried to focus on the choreography, the intricate steps that had once brought me joy, but every movement felt heavy, every leap a reminder of the emotional turmoil swirling just beneath the surface. Doubt slithered into my mind like a snake coiling around its prey, squeezing tighter with each rehearsal, whispering insidious thoughts that clouded my spirit.

The familiar sounds of our group began to fade into the background as Jason's voice cut through the noise. "What's going on with you today?" His tone was gentle yet probing, a lifeline thrown into the tempest of my thoughts. I could feel the intensity of his gaze, a warm presence that sought to unravel my tangled emotions. Jason had a knack for sensing when something was off, as if he were attuned to the very rhythm of my heart. But today, I was unwilling to share the cacophony of my inner world with him.

"I'm fine," I replied, forcing a smile that felt more like a grimace. I turned away, resuming my place at the barre, willing my body to conform to the movements I once cherished. The music began again, a sweeping melody that should have lifted my spirit. Instead, it felt like a cruel joke, a taunt echoing the stark contrast between the beauty of the dance and the chaos within my soul.

As we moved through the routine, I could feel the tension between Jason and me thickening, an unspoken question lingering in the air. He mirrored my movements with grace, yet his eyes remained fixed on me, searching for an answer that I didn't have. I admired his dedication, the way he poured himself into every step, every beat, as if each dance was a declaration of his passion. It only made my struggle feel more pronounced, like a discordant note in a symphony.

In a moment of frustration, I stumbled, my foot catching awkwardly on the floor. The sudden lapse shattered the delicate illusion I had been trying to maintain. "You're off today," Jason said, concern etched across his features. "Talk to me. What's really going on?"

I bit my lip, the floodgates threatening to burst. My mind raced with memories of my friend, her vulnerability stark against the backdrop of my own self-absorbed chaos. She was grappling with challenges that I couldn't even begin to fathom, and here I was, bemoaning the loss of my rhythm. Was I really going to drag Jason into this mess? The thought felt selfish, yet the weight of my emotions bore down on me like a suffocating fog.

With a deep breath, I finally broke, "It's just... everything. My friend, she's going through a tough time, and I feel like I'm supposed to be there for her, but it's affecting my dancing." The confession spilled out, raw and unrefined, hanging between us like a fragile thread. Jason's expression softened, a mix of empathy and understanding flooding his features.

"You're allowed to feel that," he replied, his voice steady and reassuring. "But you also deserve to dance without that weight dragging you down. It's okay to be vulnerable about it." His words wrapped around me like a comforting embrace, but I could feel the remnants of my hesitation lingering, the fear that I would burden him with my worries.

As the music swelled again, I watched the mirror, my heart torn between the desire to lose myself in the dance and the guilt that had rooted itself deep within. The tempo of the music quickened, and I felt a surge of defiance rising within me. If I couldn't find my way back to joy on this floor, then maybe it was time to share the truth with Jason, to let him in on the chaos that lived beneath my surface.

We resumed the routine, and as I moved, I allowed my heart to guide me. The choreography became less about perfection and more about expression, a cathartic release of the doubts that had plagued me. With each step, I felt the weight of my friend's struggles begin to lighten, if only just a little. In this dance, I sought not just to perform but to connect, to transform the doubt into a dialogue between my body and soul.

As I glanced at Jason, our eyes met, and in that brief moment, I saw the unwavering support shimmering within his gaze. This dance was about more than just choreography; it was about the rhythm of our hearts, the symphony of friendship that flourished even amid chaos. And as we twirled and leapt, I felt a flicker of hope igniting within me, reminding me that even in the darkest moments, there is beauty in vulnerability and strength in shared burdens.

The fluorescent lights above buzzed softly, flickering like the uncertainty that loomed over me. I stood at the edge of the studio, watching my fellow dancers twirl and leap with the kind of abandon I yearned for but couldn't grasp. The hardwood floor, polished to a reflective sheen, captured their movements, framing them in a tableau of grace that felt both enchanting and agonizingly distant. Each flick of a wrist and each pointed toe seemed to mock my inability to simply lose myself in the rhythm.

Jason was at the center of it all, his body a perfect embodiment of the choreography. He spun effortlessly, the music flowing through him like water, while I felt like a stone, stubbornly anchored to the bottom of an emotional well. As I observed him, I caught glimpses of his playful smile, a beacon of light that flickered just beyond my reach. He danced as if nothing existed outside those four walls, yet here I was, shackled by the weight of my friend's struggles.

We were preparing for an upcoming showcase, the anticipation electrifying the air. The audience would be filled with friends, family, and strangers alike, all eagerly awaiting the magic we promised to deliver. But the closer the date loomed, the more paralyzed I felt. The thought of performing under the scrutiny of so many eyes filled me with a dread that coiled around my stomach like a serpent. My feet felt leaden, my heart racing with every beat, and I could only imagine how my friend would react if she knew I was faltering. It felt selfish to even consider my own aspirations when she was drowning in her reality.

The music shifted, a haunting melody that echoed through the studio, and I knew it was time to join in. With each note, I pushed myself forward, seeking to merge with the rhythm. Yet as I moved, I couldn't shake the sense of being an impostor, a dancer masquerading as someone who was once vibrant. I forced a smile, trying to mimic the ease with which Jason glided across the floor, but my movements were stiff and hesitant, as if I were merely a marionette controlled by unseen strings of doubt.

The choreography called for a duet, a dance of intertwined bodies and shared emotions, yet here I was, out of sync with my partner and my own heart. Jason caught my eye, concern etched into his features, and in that fleeting moment, the world around us faded. I could see the questions flickering in his gaze: What was I hiding? Why was I holding back? The connection we shared, once so effortless, now felt strained, each step an echo of my internal conflict.

After another round of practice, we paused for a break, the echoes of the music still reverberating in my ears. As I sat on the cool floor, leaning against the barre, I felt the weight of my thoughts settle heavily on my shoulders. I longed to unburden myself, to share the chaos that swirled in my mind, but I hesitated. Would he think less of me for being so overwhelmed? For feeling torn between my ambitions and my loyalty to a friend in need?

"Hey," Jason's voice sliced through the silence, warm and reassuring. He approached me, his brow furrowed with concern. "You're really not okay, are you?"

His question hung in the air like a challenge. I could feel my heart racing, the familiar urge to deflect rising within me. "I'm just tired," I offered weakly, but even I could hear the hollowness in my own words.

"Tired doesn't make you dance like you're fighting a hurricane," he replied, his voice steady but gentle, as if he were coaxing a wild animal out of its den. "You can talk to me, you know. I'm here."

The sincerity in his voice tugged at something deep within me, a longing for connection, for understanding. But the fear of vulnerability loomed larger than my desire to share. "It's just... there's a lot going on in my life right now," I finally admitted, my voice barely above a whisper. "My friend needs me, and I feel like I'm failing her."

"Hey," he said softly, kneeling beside me so our eyes were level. "You're not failing anyone. You can't pour from an empty cup. You need to take care of yourself first."

His words wrapped around me, a gentle reminder that resonated deeper than I expected. I blinked back tears that threatened to spill, the release of tension so close I could almost taste it. "I just wish I could find a way to balance everything. I want to be there for her, but I don't want to lose my passion for dance. It feels like I'm being pulled in two directions, and I'm terrified of what will happen if I choose one over the other."

Jason's eyes softened, and I could see the gears turning in his mind. "What if you let both parts of you exist at the same time? You can be a good friend and a dancer. It's not one or the other. You can lean on me, and I can help you find that balance. We're a team, remember?"

His words felt like a lifeline tossed into turbulent waters. I nodded, the lump in my throat easing just a fraction. "You're right," I breathed, a sense of clarity washing over me. "I need to find a way to make space for both of these parts of my life."

We sat in silence for a moment, the weight of my fears lifting, if only slightly. The music played softly in the background, a haunting melody that now felt like a promise rather than a burden. In this moment, I realized that sharing my struggles didn't equate to weakness; it was an act of strength, an acknowledgment of the complexities of life that we all navigated in our own ways.

As we resumed practice, the steps felt lighter, the music infused with a newfound vitality. I danced with Jason beside me, his presence a reassuring anchor. The choreography flowed through me, each movement a conversation between our bodies, an exchange of trust and understanding. I felt the doubts begin to recede, allowing the joy of dance to seep back into my veins.

With every twirl and leap, I reminded myself that it was okay to be a little messy, to wade through the uncertainty as long as I didn't have to do it alone. Together, we created a space where our hearts could dance freely, intertwined in a rhythm that was uniquely ours. And for the first time in what felt like forever, I believed that perhaps I could navigate the complexities of friendship and passion, forging a path that honored both.

With the tension from earlier still lingering in the air, our dance took on a new energy, a shared determination that replaced my self-doubt with purpose. Each movement felt more authentic, a beautiful blend of the emotions that swirled between us. Jason and I moved like waves, rising and falling in sync, the music a heartbeat that pulsed through the studio and into my veins. The world outside faded into oblivion, leaving only the two of us and the intricate choreography that became a dialogue between our bodies.

As we leapt and twirled, I couldn't help but steal glances at Jason, whose commitment to the dance inspired me to push through the fog clouding my heart. His unwavering focus ignited a spark within me, awakening the part of my spirit that yearned to dance without reservation. I felt the rush of adrenaline flood my senses, the exhilaration of movement washing over me like a summer rain. The complexities of my friend's situation faded momentarily, and in those moments, I found clarity, a reminder of why I loved to dance in the first place.

But that clarity was like a butterfly, beautiful yet fleeting. As rehearsals continued, I couldn't ignore the quiet dread that sat in the pit of my stomach. With every day that passed, my friend's struggles grew heavier, her calls for support more frequent. I found myself torn between two worlds, each demanding my attention, each pulling me in a different direction. The anxiety that accompanied my passion began to creep back in, lurking at the edges of my consciousness, threatening to unravel the progress I had made.

One afternoon, as we prepared for yet another rehearsal, I noticed Jason's expression shift as he entered the studio. There was a tightness around his mouth, an undercurrent of concern that made me immediately uneasy. "Hey, you good?" he asked, his voice softer than usual.

"Yeah," I replied, but it came out more like a question than a statement. The truth was, I wasn't good, not really. The cracks in my resolve were beginning to show, and I could feel his gaze piercing through the facade I had carefully constructed.

As the music started, I danced with renewed intensity, pouring every ounce of my conflicting emotions into the movements. The choreography called for passion, and I danced as if I were in a tempest, the raw energy spilling over into every turn and leap. But no matter how I tried to lose myself in the rhythm, the anxiety of my friend's situation loomed large, a cloud of uncertainty casting shadows over my every step.

Halfway through our routine, Jason caught my eye again, and this time I couldn't hold back the flood of feelings that bubbled to the surface. I stumbled, losing my footing as the music reached a crescendo. My heart raced, not from the exhilaration of the dance but from the weight of everything I had been bottling up. The moment hung heavy between us, and I knew I had to speak up.

"Jason, I..." My voice cracked, and I took a breath, willing the words to come out. "I'm struggling. With everything. I can't keep pretending that I'm okay."

His face softened, and he stepped closer, the concern in his eyes shifting to understanding. "You don't have to pretend with me. What's going on?"

The dam broke, and suddenly I was pouring out my worries, the fear of losing my passion for dance while supporting my friend. "It's like I'm standing at a crossroads, and I don't know which way to go.

I want to be there for her, but I can't let that overshadow what I love to do."

Jason listened intently, his expression a mix of sympathy and encouragement. "You can find that balance, you know. It doesn't have to be one or the other. Let yourself feel everything, but don't lose sight of who you are."

His words washed over me, a soothing balm for my frayed nerves. I took a moment to collect myself, grounding my thoughts in the familiarity of the dance studio—the scent of polished wood, the coolness of the air, the rhythm pulsing from the speakers.

As I resumed the routine, I realized something profound: my friend's struggles didn't have to define my journey. I could be there for her while still nurturing my own passions. The realization felt liberating, like a weight lifted off my shoulders. I danced with renewed vigor, pouring every ounce of my heart into each movement, and as Jason matched my energy, it felt like we were weaving a tapestry of support, hope, and resilience together.

The days turned into weeks, and the showcase drew nearer. The rehearsal schedule intensified, each session a blend of hard work and creative exploration. The studio became our sanctuary, a place where we could dance away our worries and transform them into art. Each session with Jason sparked a fire within me, reigniting my love for dance. I learned to embrace the fluidity of my emotions, finding strength in vulnerability and comfort in collaboration.

With every leap and every turn, I could feel the bond between us growing stronger, our movements reflecting an understanding that transcended words. In this dance, I found not only a way to express my emotions but also a space where my complexities were welcomed and embraced.

One afternoon, as the sun poured golden light through the studio windows, we paused after a particularly demanding rehearsal. Breathing heavily, I glanced at Jason, his shirt damp with sweat, his hair tousled yet somehow charming. "I feel... lighter," I admitted, a genuine smile breaking across my face.

Jason grinned back, a warm light igniting in his eyes. "That's because you're allowing yourself to be real. And you're an incredible dancer, even when life gets messy."

The sincerity in his voice sent a rush of warmth through me, igniting a spark of joy that I thought I had lost forever. As we began to gather our belongings, a sudden thought struck me. "Thank you for being patient with me," I said, my voice soft but filled with sincerity. "I know I've been all over the place."

"Just doing what friends do," he replied casually, but I could see the flicker of something deeper in his gaze, a hint of vulnerability that mirrored my own. "And besides, this dance is about connection. We're stronger together."

As I left the studio that day, the world felt different. The air was crisp with the promise of autumn, the leaves beginning to shift into vibrant hues of orange and gold. The beauty of the season mirrored my own journey, the emergence of color from a once-muted landscape. I realized that I was beginning to find my rhythm again, not just in dance but in life.

With each passing day, I became more attuned to the balance between supporting my friend and nurturing my passion. I found ways to be there for her, listening and providing comfort, while also carving out time for rehearsals and self-expression. I was learning that it was okay to be multifaceted, to embrace the chaos while still pursuing the things that set my heart on fire.

As the night of the showcase approached, I felt a mixture of excitement and nerves coursing through me. I was ready to step into the spotlight, not just as a dancer but as a friend who had weathered storms and emerged stronger. Jason's unwavering support and understanding fueled my confidence, and I could already picture the performance unfolding—a tapestry of movement and emotion, woven from the complexities of our lives.

When the day finally arrived, the stage felt electric, buzzing with anticipation and the sweet scent of fresh flowers. I took a deep breath, letting the moment wash over me, and stepped into the spotlight with Jason by my side. As the music began, I closed my eyes and let go, surrendering to the rhythm and the connection we had built through our struggles. In that moment, I knew I was exactly where I was meant to be, dancing not just for myself but for the vibrant tapestry of life that intertwined all our stories.

Chapter 13: Breaking the Walls

The sun hung low over the bustling streets of Chicago, casting a golden hue across the city as if the universe had chosen that moment to pause and take a breath. The air was thick with the mingled scents of deep-dish pizza wafting from nearby restaurants and the earthy aroma of fresh rain, a recent gift from a spring storm that had swept through the night before. The towering skyscrapers loomed overhead, their glass facades glimmering in the fading light, a mosaic of reflections that danced against the backdrop of a brilliant cerulean sky. I found myself lost in this urban landscape, my heart pounding to the rhythm of the city as I maneuvered through the crowd, a flurry of bodies caught in their own stories, each one a thread in the vast tapestry of life.

As I stepped into the warm embrace of the dance studio, the familiar smell of polished wood and the faint scent of sweat greeted me like an old friend. The studio was a sanctuary, a space where the outside world faded away, leaving only the echo of my heartbeat and the whisper of dreams hanging in the air. Sunlight poured through the expansive windows, illuminating the polished floor and casting elongated shadows that seemed to stretch and sway with the music already playing softly in the background. The melodies wrapped around me, beckoning me to lose myself in their embrace, to let the notes guide my movements as I slipped off my shoes and surrendered to the pull of the moment.

Jason stood in the corner, a tall figure with tousled hair and an infectious smile that could light up even the grayest of days. He was my partner in dance and in life, a kindred spirit who understood my passion for movement like no one else. His presence was a calming force, a balm to the tumultuous thoughts swirling in my mind. As I approached him, I felt the weight of my worries pressing down, threatening to stifle the joy that dance brought me. I couldn't hide from him; he saw through my carefully constructed facade.

"Hey, you okay?" he asked, his voice a gentle rumble that seemed to resonate within me. There was an urgency in his tone, an unspoken invitation to open up. I hesitated, the familiar tightness in my throat creeping back, but I knew I had to share the storm brewing inside.

With a deep breath, I let the words spill forth, each syllable a release. I spoke of my friend, the struggles that shadowed her every move, the way her laughter felt brittle, like glass ready to shatter. I described the nights spent worrying, the feeling of helplessness that gnawed at me as I watched her fight battles I couldn't see. "It's like I'm drowning in her pain," I admitted, the vulnerability of my confession wrapping around me like a shroud. "I want to help her, but it's suffocating. What if I lose myself in the process?"

Jason's eyes softened, the warmth of his understanding enveloping me like a hug. He listened, nodding slowly as if my words were a delicate dance he was learning to appreciate. "You can love her and still chase your dreams," he said, his voice steady, filled with the conviction I needed to hear. "You don't have to sacrifice yourself. We can find a way to merge both worlds."

His words struck a chord, resonating deep within my heart. In that moment, clarity washed over me like a cleansing tide. I realized that my passion for dance could be a bridge, a way to support my friend while still honoring my own aspirations. As I looked into Jason's eyes, I saw the spark of inspiration flickering there. "What if we used our choreography to tell her story?" I proposed, excitement bubbling up within me. "We could create a piece that captures her journey, the struggles and the triumphs, a celebration of her resilience."

Jason's face lit up, his enthusiasm infectious. "Yes! Dance is a powerful medium; it can heal, inspire, and connect. Let's use our art to shine a light on her experience." The possibilities unfolded before us like the petals of a blooming flower, each idea more vibrant than the last. We began brainstorming, our voices weaving together like threads in a tapestry, the studio alive with our energy.

The music shifted, a haunting melody that seemed to echo the emotions we were trying to convey. I let the notes wash over me, my body responding instinctively, swaying to the rhythm as I envisioned the movements we would create. Jason joined me, his presence grounding yet exhilarating, as we explored the narrative we wanted to express. The choreography took shape, each step a reflection of both my journey and my friend's, our bodies intertwining as we crafted a story that felt raw and authentic.

As we danced, the studio transformed. The mirrors reflected not just our movements but the passion burning within us, a testament to the power of vulnerability and connection. I could see it clearly now: my friend's struggle could be woven into the very fabric of our performance, a reminder that healing often comes from shared experiences, that pain can morph into beauty when given the right outlet. We could raise awareness, inspire others, and perhaps, in doing so, create a lifeline for my friend—a tangible representation of the support that surrounded her.

With each passing moment, I felt the walls that had encased my heart begin to crumble. Jason's laughter filled the studio, a symphony of hope echoing off the walls as we crafted the movements that would bring our vision to life. This was no longer just about dance; it was about community, resilience, and the unbreakable bonds of friendship. As the last notes faded into silence, I knew we had found our purpose, a way to uplift both our spirits and those around us.

The following weeks unfolded like a carefully choreographed performance, each day marked by our growing commitment to intertwine my friend's story with our dance. With every rehearsal, the studio buzzed with a vibrant energy that seemed to pulse through the floorboards. It became a sacred space, infused with laughter and creativity, where the weight of the world felt just a little lighter. The mirrors, once mere reflections of our movements, now held our dreams and aspirations, capturing the essence of what we were trying to convey.

In the beginning, our dance was a chaotic whirlwind of steps, emotions flaring and fading like the flicker of a candle in a breeze. We tossed ideas around like confetti, excited yet uncertain about how to shape the narrative we envisioned. I found myself absorbed in the creative process, my heart racing as I brainstormed movement sequences that would embody my friend's journey. Each morning brought a fresh wave of inspiration, fueled by countless conversations with Jason about the nuances of storytelling through dance. I wanted to capture not just the struggles she faced but also the glimmers of hope that punctuated her story, the moments when she rose above the fray.

As the sun dipped below the horizon, painting the sky in hues of lavender and gold, we often found ourselves lost in the magic of the studio. With the music spilling from the speakers, we'd drift into our own world, bodies flowing seamlessly together, creating a dialogue that transcended words. There was something profoundly intimate about the way we moved, our bodies communicating the pain and joy we both understood too well. Jason would often catch my gaze in the mirror, his eyes reflecting a shared understanding that deepened our connection.

One evening, as we were immersed in our work, the door swung open, and a soft voice broke our concentration. It was Lily, my friend, with a hesitant smile and a spark of curiosity in her eyes. She stepped into the studio, her presence both grounding and invigorating. "What are you two up to?" she asked, her tone light, but I could sense an undercurrent of vulnerability that tugged at my heart.

"Just working on a new piece," I replied, my excitement bubbling over. "We're trying to incorporate your story into our choreography." I watched her expression shift from intrigue to surprise, her brows furrowing in thought. I could see the flicker of uncertainty in her eyes, a reflection of her own struggles. "It's going to be powerful, Lily. We want to celebrate you."

The studio seemed to hold its breath, the silence wrapping around us like a blanket. Jason stepped forward, his enthusiasm spilling over. "We want to capture everything you've been through and how resilient you are. Dance can be a powerful way to heal." His words hung in the air, filled with sincerity.

Lily hesitated, her gaze drifting to the polished floor, as if contemplating her place in this beautiful creation we were crafting. "I don't know if my story is worth telling," she finally murmured, her voice barely above a whisper. A pang of heartbreak struck me; how could she not see the strength in her journey?

"It's worth telling," I said firmly, stepping closer to her. "You've faced so much, and we want to share that strength with others. Your struggles resonate more than you realize." A flicker of hope sparked in her eyes, and in that moment, I knew we were embarking on something transformative.

Slowly, we invited her into our creative process, sharing the movements we had developed. I felt a rush of joy as we began to incorporate her into the choreography, allowing her to express her emotions through movement. As she joined us, the dance took on a new life, the steps blossoming into a vivid tapestry of experiences. We laughed, stumbled, and cried together, the boundaries of our friendship dissolving in the face of our shared vulnerability.

Lily's laughter echoed in the studio as she attempted to mimic one of Jason's exaggerated movements, her confidence growing with each passing moment. She began to understand that her story was not just hers alone; it was interwoven with ours, a collective narrative of resilience and hope. The choreography morphed from a mere performance into a living, breathing expression of everything we were grappling with—an honest portrayal of pain, healing, and the power of friendship.

As the weeks progressed, I felt a palpable shift within myself. The weight of my own worries began to lift, replaced by a sense of purpose. I realized that supporting my friend didn't mean sacrificing my dreams; rather, it infused my passion with new life. The dance became a conduit for healing, not only for Lily but for me as well. With each rehearsal, we shed layers of doubt, embracing the beauty of our shared struggles.

We danced through the night, the lights dimmed low, leaving only the glow of the city outside filtering through the studio windows. The melodies morphed into anthems of our lives, echoing the rhythm of our hearts as we surrendered to the music. Every leap, every twirl, became an act of liberation—a defiance against the fears that threatened to hold us captive. Jason's presence beside me felt like a lifeline, anchoring me in the tumult of emotion swirling around us.

In those moments, I could see it clearly—the magic of connection that blossomed between us. The dance wasn't just about executing steps perfectly; it was about sharing our souls, our struggles, and our victories with the world. We were not just telling a story; we were inviting others to witness the beauty of vulnerability, the strength found in unity.

With Lily immersed in our choreography, her laughter weaving through the dance, we became a force to be reckoned with. The walls that once felt so daunting began to crumble, revealing a path forward illuminated by the light of our shared journey. We were building something extraordinary, not just for ourselves but for everyone who had ever felt the weight of the world pressing down upon them. As the final notes of our song echoed in the studio, I understood that our dance was a celebration—a tribute to resilience, friendship, and the healing power of love.

The days slipped away like sand through my fingers, each one more vibrant than the last as we honed our choreography. The studio transformed into a sanctuary, a place where creativity thrived and our spirits danced in unison. The once-clear glass mirrors, which had merely reflected our movements, now became a portal through which we shared our souls. Each rehearsal was an act of discovery, peeling back layers of fear and doubt while revealing a raw beauty that had long been obscured by the everyday chaos of life.

One evening, we gathered for an extended rehearsal, the sun casting long shadows across the floor as it dipped behind the city skyline. The atmosphere was electric, charged with an unspoken anticipation as we prepared to incorporate more of Lily's story into our movements. Jason's infectious enthusiasm set the tone, his eyes sparkling with excitement as he described the rhythm we could harness to capture the essence of her struggles.

"Let's use the music as a canvas," he suggested, his voice a melody itself. "Each note can represent a part of her journey—the highs and the lows, the moments when she felt lost and those when she found her strength." I nodded, the concept igniting a fire within me, pushing me to visualize the dance as a living, breathing expression of what we had all experienced.

Lily stood to the side, her gaze flitting between us, a mixture of awe and apprehension painted across her features. I could see her mind racing, grappling with the weight of our intentions. I stepped toward her, my voice a gentle whisper, "You're a part of this. We want you to feel free to express yourself, to let your emotions guide the dance."

As the music swelled, we began to move, the sounds enveloping us like a warm embrace. I watched as Lily stepped forward, hesitantly at first, then with more confidence as the rhythm swept her up. Her movements were tentative, like a fragile bird testing its wings for the first time. We mirrored her, creating a safe space that urged her to soar. I could see her expression shift, the tension in her shoulders easing as she immersed herself in the moment.

The dance became a tapestry of emotions, a rich blend of joy and sorrow, hope and despair. Each step we took was an exploration, an unveiling of the struggles that had once felt insurmountable. We wove Lily's story into our choreography, letting her pain transform into something beautiful—a narrative of resilience that resonated deeply within us all. I was moved by how, with every leap and turn, she was reclaiming her narrative, taking ownership of her struggles, and allowing them to shape her into someone stronger.

Hours melted away as we rehearsed, our laughter ringing through the studio, mingling with the music, a symphony of shared experiences. I lost myself in the dance, the movements flowing effortlessly, my heart swelling with pride as I witnessed Lily's transformation. She became more than just a friend; she was a warrior, and the studio was our battlefield where we fought together against the demons that threatened to consume us.

The choreography blossomed into a full-fledged performance, and with every practice, we began to solidify our vision. Our initial sketches of movements evolved into powerful sequences that told a story worth telling. I imagined the audience, transfixed, drawn into the web of emotions we had spun. Each performance would be a celebration not only of Lily's journey but also of the bonds we had forged—an ode to the power of love and friendship.

As we approached the date of our first showcase, excitement coursed through me like wildfire. The studio buzzed with preparations, the air thick with anticipation. Jason and I spent hours discussing costumes and lighting, envisioning how to create an immersive experience for our audience. I wanted them to feel the weight of our story, to breathe alongside us as we navigated the highs and lows. We decided on flowing fabrics that mirrored the ebb and flow of emotions—light and airy for the moments of hope, darker hues for the depths of despair.

On the night of the performance, the studio transformed into a haven of creativity, the walls draped with sheer fabrics that fluttered like spirits caught in the breeze. The air was electric, a palpable energy tinged with nervousness and exhilaration. Friends and family filled the seats, their faces alight with anticipation. I could see Lily in the corner, her eyes wide, a mixture of fear and excitement swirling within them.

As the lights dimmed, I felt a rush of adrenaline. We took our places, the music swelling around us, and with a shared glance, we began. Each movement was a conversation, a dialogue between our bodies and the story we were telling. I poured my heart into every step, urging Lily to do the same, to let go of her inhibitions and embrace the beauty of vulnerability.

The audience was captivated, their breaths hitching at moments of intense emotion, their eyes wide with wonder. I could feel the energy shift as the choreography unfolded, the movement weaving through the air like an unbreakable thread. With each leap, we shared the burdens we had carried, the tears we had shed, and the laughter that had pulled us through. The dance became a visceral experience, transcending the physical to tap into the emotional realm, and I could feel our story resonating with each viewer, pulling at their heartstrings.

As we reached the crescendo, I caught Jason's eye, and in that moment, I knew we had succeeded. Together, we had crafted something profound, a celebration of resilience, a testament to the strength found in friendship. We finished the performance with our hearts racing, breathless and alive, the audience erupting into applause that echoed through the studio like a warm embrace.

Lily stood at the edge of the stage, tears glistening in her eyes, a radiant smile breaking across her face. In that moment, I realized we had done more than share our story; we had illuminated a path of healing, both for ourselves and for everyone who had ever felt lost in the shadows. The weight of the world had shifted, and I felt lighter, unburdened by the fears that had once threatened to engulf me.

As the night wore on, surrounded by the warmth of friends and the glow of shared triumph, I understood that we had not just performed a dance; we had woven our souls into a masterpiece of healing and hope. Together, we had broken down the walls that had confined us, emerging stronger, more connected, and ready to face whatever challenges lay ahead. This was only the beginning, a new chapter in our lives where love and friendship would forever be the guiding lights.

Chapter 14: The Stage is Set

The sound of the music reverberates through the studio, wrapping around us like a warm embrace. It fills the air, cascading off the walls adorned with mirrors reflecting our every movement. I inhale deeply, letting the sweet notes wash over me as I close my eyes, surrendering to the rhythm. It's a familiar sensation, a tingling anticipation that dances beneath my skin. This space, infused with the memories of countless rehearsals, feels like a home where creativity flourishes and friendships blossom.

Laughter bubbles up, a melody unto itself, as Sarah attempts yet again to master the choreography. Her frustration, a tempestuous spark, is quickly quelled by Jason's easy charm. He twirls around her, a playful grin illuminating his face, his movements effortless, like he's gliding across an invisible floor. "You've got this!" he encourages, his voice smooth like the bassline that thrums through our feet. It's impossible not to smile at their banter, a delightful dance of teasing and encouragement that encapsulates the spirit of our little troupe.

As the music swells, my body instinctively finds its place in the choreography, and I'm swept away by the beauty of the moment. Each leap, each turn, becomes a brushstroke in a painting of our shared journey. I feel the heat of the studio envelop me, a comforting cocoon where I can shed the weight of the outside world. Outside, the sun casts its golden hue over the bustling streets of Chicago, a stark contrast to our little universe. Inside, we are cocooned in a vibrant tapestry of dreams and aspirations, the air thick with the scent of sweat and determination.

With every rehearsal, the choreography evolves, our movements intertwining like the roots of a mighty oak, strong and resilient. Sarah's laughter rings out, a joyous chime that lifts my spirits. She is the heart of our ensemble, her infectious enthusiasm breathing life into the room. Each stumble she encounters is met with a chorus of support, a testament to the bonds we've forged. I marvel at how our vulnerabilities have become our strengths, stitching us together in a tapestry rich with color and texture.

Then there's Jason, a constant source of grounding energy. His presence has a way of calming the storm within me. I glance at him, and our eyes meet, a shared understanding passing between us, unspoken yet profoundly felt. There's a light in his gaze that ignites something deep within my chest, something that whispers of possibility and uncharted territories. Each time we dance, I feel the connection between us deepen, a tether woven from shared laughter and unguarded moments. It's as if we're speaking a language only we understand, our bodies telling stories that words could never capture.

In our shared space, I can't help but reflect on the journey that brought us here. Memories of long nights filled with uncertainty and moments of doubt swirl in my mind. Yet, as I stand in the studio, surrounded by my friends, I know we've crafted something beautiful from those fragments of struggle. This performance isn't just a tribute to Sarah; it's a celebration of our resilience, a testament to the love that flourishes in the face of adversity.

As rehearsals progress, we begin to weave Sarah's story into our performance. The narrative takes shape, a tapestry rich with emotions and experiences, each movement echoing the highs and lows of her journey. I watch as she pours her heart into every step, her passion illuminating the stage like a beacon. It's not just a dance; it's a narrative of survival, a tribute to the strength found in vulnerability. The studio, once merely a space for practice, transforms into a sacred ground where stories unfold and dreams take flight.

Our routines become rituals, the music serving as a heartbeat that synchronizes our movements. We lean into each other, drawing strength from our shared experiences. With each rehearsal, I find myself not just dancing but embracing a part of Sarah's spirit, allowing her journey to become entwined with mine. I can feel the weight of her struggles in my own bones, each leap a reminder that we carry our pasts with us, yet they do not define us.

As the final rehearsal approaches, a palpable energy fills the studio. Excitement mingles with nerves, a potent cocktail that heightens every sensation. I can almost taste the anticipation in the air, a sweet tang that ignites my senses. The mirrors reflect a kaleidoscope of emotions—excitement, trepidation, love—each expression telling its own story. Jason catches my eye again, his smile reassuring, and I'm reminded that we're in this together.

The day of the performance dawns bright and clear, the sun spilling gold across the cityscape like a painter setting to work on a canvas. I can feel the energy crackling beneath my skin as I lace up my shoes, a ritual that grounds me in the moment. This isn't just a performance; it's the culmination of our shared journey, a celebration of everything we've become. As I step into the studio, the familiar scent of sweat and wood fills my lungs, invigorating my spirit.

With every heartbeat, I am reminded of the love that has brought us here—the laughter, the tears, the countless hours spent refining our craft. This performance is our love letter to resilience, a testament to the unyielding bonds of friendship. I take a deep breath, ready to step onto the stage where our stories will intertwine, where our struggles will transform into art. In this moment, I know we are not just performers; we are creators, weaving a tapestry of hope and love that will resonate far beyond the confines of this studio.

With the curtains drawn and the studio transformed into a realm of possibilities, the air thickens with the heady scent of ambition and freshly polished wood. The overhead lights cast a golden hue across the floor, illuminating the dust motes that dance like fireflies in the twilight. Each step I take echoes the heartbeat of the space, a rhythmic pulse that resonates with the energy we've poured into our art. As we gather in a circle, a familiar excitement mingles with nervous anticipation, the laughter and chatter melding into a harmonious symphony.

Sarah sits cross-legged in the center, her vibrant spirit radiating warmth like a sunbeam breaking through a cloudy sky. I watch her as she speaks, her hands animatedly painting pictures in the air, guiding us through her narrative. There's a raw honesty in her voice that pulls at my heartstrings, a gentle reminder of the trials she has faced and the courage it took to rise from them. It's as if she is inviting us into her world, sharing her vulnerabilities like precious treasures. The air grows thick with emotions, each story thread weaving seamlessly into the fabric of our performance.

"Let's make this real," she says, her eyes sparkling with determination. "I want everyone to feel what I felt." Her words strike a chord within me, igniting a fire that propels me forward. In that moment, I realize that our dance isn't merely a series of movements; it's a conduit for her journey, a chance to breathe life into her experiences and transform pain into beauty. We lean in closer, and I can feel the warmth of her spirit enveloping us, wrapping us in a shared resolve to honor her story.

As we begin to practice again, I notice Jason moving alongside me, his presence a grounding force amid the whirlwind of emotions. Our movements synchronize, a silent conversation unfolding as we navigate the choreography. His laughter dances through the air, a light-hearted melody that makes my heart flutter. Each time our bodies connect, whether in a gentle embrace or a dynamic lift, I feel a surge of energy coursing between us, electric and palpable. It's as if we're creating a tapestry of unspoken words, our dance a bridge between souls that transcends the ordinary.

We dive deeper into the choreography, allowing our bodies to embody the pain and joy woven through Sarah's story. Every leap is a leap of faith, every turn a chance to reclaim lost pieces of ourselves.

The studio transforms into a realm of transformation, where we shed our fears and insecurities like old skin, revealing the vibrant, raw essence beneath. I catch glimpses of Sarah's strength mirrored in my own reflection, a potent reminder that we are all capable of rising from our struggles, one step at a time.

The days slip by like grains of sand through my fingers, each rehearsal drawing us closer together, tightening the bonds of friendship and creativity. We push each other to new heights, our movements becoming more than mere choreography—they morph into an expression of our collective spirit. I relish these moments of vulnerability, the beauty of sharing our scars, both visible and hidden. Together, we create a safe haven, a sanctuary where we can explore the depths of our emotions and emerge stronger.

As we refine our piece, the narrative begins to take shape, a vivid tapestry that encapsulates the essence of struggle and triumph. The music swells, each note resonating with the weight of our experiences. The once-ordinary studio now brims with the energy of our dreams, the floor transformed into a stage where our stories will unfold. I glance at Jason, and the warmth in his gaze ignites something deep within me. There's a connection that goes beyond the dance, a shared understanding that speaks to the depths of our souls.

In the quiet moments between rehearsals, I find solace in our conversations. We often steal away to a cozy café nearby, nestled in the heart of the city, where the aroma of fresh coffee mingles with the laughter of patrons. The barista, a lively woman with a passion for latte art, creates intricate designs atop our drinks, adding a touch of whimsy to our afternoons. We sip slowly, savoring the bittersweet flavors while sharing our dreams, fears, and the little moments that make life exquisite.

One afternoon, as the sun casts a golden glow through the window, I watch Jason as he talks about his own journey—his aspirations, his fears, and the delicate balance he seeks between art and reality. There's a vulnerability in his words that captivates me, a genuine desire to connect beyond the surface. I realize that our friendship is evolving into something profound, a bond steeped in authenticity and shared experience.

"What if we wrote our own story?" I propose, my voice barely above a whisper. "What if we wove our dreams into the performance, creating something entirely new?" The idea hangs in the air, shimmering like the afternoon light. His eyes widen, a spark igniting in their depths, and I know he feels it too—the electric potential of our creative spirits intertwining, ready to burst forth into a vibrant tapestry of art.

From that moment on, we embark on a journey of co-creation, crafting a narrative that is as much ours as it is Sarah's. We brainstorm late into the night, our minds alight with ideas as we laugh and scribble notes, our excitement contagious. Each stroke of our pens, each sketch of a movement, becomes a brush with possibility, a chance to breathe life into our dreams.

The studio morphs once again, becoming a playground for our imagination. We dive headfirst into the creative process, our bodies moving in sync, reflecting the newfound energy between us. With each rehearsal, we explore new layers of expression, allowing our vulnerabilities to spill forth onto the stage. The choreography evolves, a living entity that pulses with the heartbeat of our shared stories.

As we prepare for the upcoming performance, I can't shake the feeling that we are on the brink of something monumental. The culmination of our efforts feels like a symphony, a harmonious blend of struggle, resilience, and the unyielding bonds of friendship. I steal a glance at Jason, our eyes locking in a moment of understanding. We are crafting something far greater than ourselves, a legacy woven into the very fabric of the dance. In this sanctuary of creativity, I know we are forging a connection that will resonate long after the music fades, a testament to the power of art and the strength of the human spirit.

With each rehearsal, the music seeps deeper into our bones, becoming a familiar rhythm that syncs with our very heartbeats. The studio transforms into a stage not just for performance but for exploration, a canvas where we paint our emotions with every movement. Our costumes, once mere fabric draped over chairs, now hang like vibrant ghosts waiting to be summoned. Each color whispers a part of Sarah's story, echoing her journey through pain and joy. The fabric catches the light, shimmering with the promise of what's to come, a tangible reminder of the beauty we are striving to create together.

In the moments between sets, laughter erupts like fireworks, brightening the air and infusing it with life. Jason's humor, quick and clever, never fails to elicit giggles from Sarah and me. He has an uncanny ability to ease the tension that sometimes clings to us like mist, transforming our nerves into a shared camaraderie that feels almost sacred. One afternoon, while we're sprawled on the floor, panting and slightly out of breath, he launches into an impromptu rendition of a popular song, substituting the lyrics with whimsical commentary about our dance moves. It's ridiculous and perfect, and we find ourselves doubled over with laughter, the kind that makes your stomach ache and your cheeks burn.

As we move into the final weeks of rehearsal, the pressure mounts, but so does the exhilaration. We gather more frequently, often spilling into the dimly lit corners of our favorite café, where the barista knows our orders by heart. The rich aroma of freshly brewed coffee and the sugary scent of pastries swirl around us, fueling our late-night brainstorming sessions. I often find myself gazing out the window, watching the bustling city life unfold beyond the glass, a world alive with stories, just like our own. Each face passing by carries its own narrative, a reminder that our performance is just one of many tales waiting to be told.

One evening, as the sun sets and bathes the café in hues of orange and pink, we dive deeper into the heart of our narrative. "What if we incorporated elements of our own stories?" I suggest, feeling a surge of excitement. "Let's let the audience feel the connections we've built." Jason nods enthusiastically, his eyes alight with possibility. We begin weaving fragments of our lives into the choreography, allowing our personal struggles and triumphs to find expression in the dance. Sarah's eyes shine with determination as she shares her struggles, her voice steady despite the weight of her words. We listen intently, captivated by the raw honesty that flows between us.

Incorporating our stories feels liberating, a release of the burdens we've carried. As we develop the choreography, I realize that each step, each leap, becomes an embodiment of our collective spirit. It's not merely about movement; it's about sharing the essence of who we are and what we've overcome. The studio pulses with energy, each practice session feeling more like a celebration than a rehearsal. With every ounce of vulnerability we lay bare, I feel the choreography morph into something transcendent, an outpouring of our souls manifesting in the form of art.

The day of the performance arrives, shimmering with anticipation and the electric buzz of creativity. The city outside is a riot of color, the streets alive with the sounds of laughter and chatter. I pull on my costume, the fabric hugging me like a second skin, a reminder that I am part of something larger than myself. As I look in the mirror, I see not just my reflection but the culmination of our collective journey, every struggle and triumph etched into my features.

When we arrive at the venue, the atmosphere crackles with excitement. The stage, adorned with twinkling lights, beckons like a siren calling us home. I can feel the thrum of the audience's energy, an invisible current connecting us all in that moment. The lights dim, and my heart races, a wild creature trapped within my chest. With a quick glance at Sarah and Jason, I draw strength from their presence, knowing that we're not alone on this journey.

As the music begins to play, the world fades away, and we step onto the stage, the spotlight warming my skin. The audience blurs into a sea of faces, their anticipation palpable, and I allow the music to envelop me, guiding my movements. With each step, I channel Sarah's resilience, her laughter, and her tears, pouring our shared stories into the choreography. I feel the weight of every struggle, every moment of doubt, transforming into a powerful force that propels me forward.

Jason's presence beside me is electric, our movements fluid and instinctual as we weave through the narrative we've crafted together. The dance feels like a dialogue, a conversation of souls communicating in a language beyond words. As we twirl and leap, I can sense the audience leaning in, captivated by the story unfolding before them. There's a unity in our performance, a bond forged from shared experiences, and I can feel the energy radiating from the stage, connecting us all.

As the music swells, I lose myself in the rhythm, letting go of any fear or hesitation. In that moment, I am not just performing; I am living and breathing the essence of our journey. The movement becomes a catharsis, a release of everything I've ever held back. With every spin, every leap, I embrace the joy and pain, allowing them to coalesce into something beautiful.

The performance reaches its climax, and I can see Sarah's face, a mixture of pride and joy lighting her features. I know that this is not just our story; it is hers, an homage to her strength and resilience. As the final notes linger in the air, the applause erupts like thunder, enveloping us in warmth and acceptance. We bow together, hearts swelling with gratitude, knowing that we have shared a piece of ourselves with the world.

Backstage, the air buzzes with the afterglow of our performance. Laughter and chatter fill the space, a chorus of voices celebrating our collective achievement. Jason pulls me into a tight embrace, and in that moment, I feel an overwhelming sense of connection. This journey has woven us into a tapestry richer than I could have ever imagined.

In the weeks that follow, we reflect on the performance, the connections we forged, and the stories we shared. Our friendship deepens, grounded in the understanding that we are all a tapestry of our experiences, resilient and beautiful in our imperfections. And as we continue to dance through life, I know that this chapter will forever be etched in my heart, a reminder of the magic that happens when creativity and love intertwine, creating a masterpiece that transcends the stage.

Chapter 15: Twists and Turns

The sun hung low in the sky, casting a golden hue over the small town of Ashwood, where I had built my life in a quaint little studio on the edge of Main Street. My days revolved around the hum of the café next door, the scent of roasted coffee beans wafting through my window and mingling with the tang of fresh paint and wood shavings from my latest projects. It was the kind of place where laughter echoed down the cobblestone streets, where the friendly waves from neighbors felt like a warm embrace, and where dreams felt tangible—like the vibrant canvases I splashed color onto every day.

But that familiar comfort began to fray as a dark cloud loomed over my closest friend, Emily. We had weathered storms together—failed relationships, job losses, and the ever-present struggle of chasing our creative aspirations—but this felt different. The news she had received just hours earlier crackled like static in the air. It was a grim reminder of how fragile life could be, how a single moment could shatter the delicate glass of happiness we had so painstakingly crafted.

As I stood in my studio, brushes still dripping with paint and canvases waiting to be born into something beautiful, the silence felt deafening. Emily's usual bright smile had dimmed to a shadow of its former self, her vibrant spirit fading like the pastel hues of dawn giving way to a stormy afternoon. I could see her retreating into herself, pulling away like a flower wilting in the sun. The warmth I'd always associated with her began to feel like a distant memory, and the weight of her despair pressed down on me, igniting a fierce determination to help her rise again. I could do this. I had to.

The next few days morphed into a blur of muted colors and heavy-hearted conversations, the café bustling with life just outside my door while Emily sat across from me, a hollow shell of the person

I adored. I reached out, grasping for the right words, but they eluded me like smoke slipping through my fingers. Each attempt felt like throwing a lifeline into a churning sea only for it to be swallowed by the waves.

"Just let me help you," I pleaded one afternoon, my voice breaking the suffocating silence. "I'll be here, every step of the way."

But Emily's eyes, once sparkling with mischief and light, held a depth of sorrow I struggled to penetrate. "I don't want to drag you down, Clara. You have so much to look forward to," she whispered, her voice barely more than a fragile breath.

As much as I wanted to fight her on it, I understood. There was an unspoken bond between us, a mutual recognition that our dreams were intertwined. Yet, in this moment, I felt an overwhelming responsibility to pull her from the brink of despair. This wasn't just about her anymore; it was about the shared history of laughter and tears that had built the foundation of our friendship. I would not abandon her now.

The tension began to seep into my relationship with Jason as well. At first, it felt innocent—a slight distance here, a lingering glance at Emily when I should have been focused on him. But soon, it bubbled over into something more tangible, something I couldn't ignore. I could see it in Jason's eyes, the flickering flame of frustration turning into an all-consuming fire.

"Clara, I need you to be present," he snapped one evening, the words cutting through the warm glow of our shared space. The studio, usually a sanctuary filled with creativity and joy, felt charged with an electricity I hadn't anticipated. "I feel like I'm competing with her sorrow."

The weight of his accusation struck me, and I could feel my chest tightening as I struggled to formulate a response. I had always admired Jason's straightforwardness, his ability to voice his feelings so clearly, but right now, all I could feel was an overwhelming surge of guilt and anger. "It's not a competition! She's my best friend! She needs me," I fired back, my voice echoing off the studio walls.

His jaw clenched, the air thickening with every word unspoken. "And what about us, Clara? I thought we were building something together."

The accusation hung in the air, heavy and unyielding. I wanted to tell him that I was just trying to be the friend Emily needed, but my loyalty felt like a double-edged sword, cutting into the burgeoning love I felt for Jason. The room pulsed with unspoken words, and I could see the lines of frustration etched across his face, mirroring the confusion swirling in my heart.

"I can't just walk away from her," I said, the tremor in my voice betraying the strength I was trying to project. "You don't understand what she's going through."

"Maybe I don't," he replied, frustration spilling over into an edge of desperation. "But I can't stand here and watch you disappear into someone else's grief."

It was a raw moment, a confrontation that stripped away the layers of our relationship and laid bare the fears and insecurities we both clung to. I could feel the heat of my own emotions rising, swirling into a tempest of anger and love, despair and hope. But there we stood, two people caught in the middle of a storm neither of us had anticipated, both fighting to find a way forward without losing what we held dear.

In that charged silence, I realized the truth: loyalty and love could coexist, but only if I was willing to embrace the chaos that came with them. I took a step closer to him, grounding myself in his presence. "I'm here, Jason. I just need you to understand that this is hard for me too."

And as the sunlight filtered through the studio window, illuminating the dust motes dancing in the air, I felt a flicker of hope amid the tension. Maybe there was a way to bridge the gap between love and friendship, to weather the storm together. But first, I had to help Emily find her way back to the light, even if it meant navigating the complexities of my heart in the process.

The days unfolded like a tattered book, each chapter filled with the turmoil of emotion, the pages worn from the weight of unspoken words and unrelenting worries. Emily's despair seemed to seep into the very fabric of my studio, dulling the once vibrant colors that adorned my walls. I could no longer drown myself in brushstrokes, each stroke now feeling hollow, as if the canvas itself recoiled from the heaviness in the air. My fingers longed to create, yet every idea slipped through my grasp like the sand that filled the hourglass of time, leaving me with nothing but the shadows of what used to be.

Outside, the town pulsed with its usual rhythms—children laughing as they chased one another down the street, the tantalizing aroma of baked goods wafting from the bakery down the road, the sounds of life continuing unabated. But within my four walls, it felt as if a storm raged. I had watched Emily slip deeper into a cavern of solitude, her laughter a mere echo of the joyful symphony it once was. The vibrant discussions about our dreams, plans, and art had dwindled to strained silences, punctuated only by the occasional sigh that escaped her lips like the air deflating from a balloon.

One evening, as the sun dipped below the horizon, spilling its fiery orange across the sky, I made my way to her favorite spot in the park, a secluded bench that overlooked the river. The water shimmered in the fading light, reflecting the last vestiges of day like a mirror to her soul. I found her there, staring blankly at the water, as if seeking answers in the currents that flowed endlessly. The sight of her like this tightened something deep within me, a visceral reminder of the bond we shared and how far it had slipped into the abyss.

"Hey," I whispered, careful to keep my voice light, even as my heart felt like it was lodged in my throat. I sat beside her, the bench creaking softly under our combined weight. "How about we take a walk? The sunset is beautiful tonight."

Emily turned her gaze slowly toward me, her eyes shimmering with unshed tears that glistened like the fading sun. "I don't know, Clara. I'm not sure I can just pretend everything is okay."

I reached for her hand, intertwining my fingers with hers, a gesture of solidarity that seemed so simple yet carried the weight of my commitment to her. "You don't have to pretend. I'm here for the hard stuff too. Just let me in."

With a shuddering breath, she nodded and pushed herself up from the bench, her shoulders slightly less hunched than before. As we walked side by side, the warmth of the summer breeze whispered through the trees, carrying with it the scent of blooming jasmine that wrapped around us like a comforting embrace. We strolled along the riverbank, our footsteps in sync, creating a rhythm that echoed the pulse of our friendship.

"Do you remember the summer we spent painting those massive murals in the old library?" I asked, trying to spark a flicker of that old Emily. "We thought we were the next great artists. I still can't believe how wild we were, thinking we could change the world one stroke at a time."

A ghost of a smile danced on her lips, and I felt a glimmer of hope. "Yeah, I remember. We were a mess—paint everywhere and no idea what we were doing. But it felt good, you know? It felt like we were making a difference."

"That's because we were," I affirmed, my heart swelling with determination. "You still are. Just because you're facing something tough doesn't mean you're not strong, Em. You've always been my anchor."

She paused, her gaze drifting back to the river. "But what if I can't find my way back? What if I'm too far gone?"

The vulnerability in her voice tugged at me, and I could see how deeply she battled her own demons. "Then I'll be your compass," I vowed, the words flowing from my heart. "You don't have to do this alone. We'll navigate this storm together."

As I spoke, I felt the familiar warmth of determination settling in my chest. I had to believe that together we could find the light again, that we could reclaim the vibrant colors that had faded from her spirit. We stood in silence for a moment, the river's gentle murmurs surrounding us, until Emily finally broke the quiet with a hesitant, "Okay. I'll try."

Her words felt like a lifeline, a tiny flicker in the vast darkness that had enveloped her. We continued our walk, side by side, each step grounding us in the moment and reminding us of the strength of our bond. Yet, even as we began to reconnect, I felt the tension between Jason and me still brewing beneath the surface, a storm waiting to break.

That evening, I returned to the studio, a glimmer of hope igniting within me. I poured my energy into a new canvas, the brush gliding across the surface with a renewed sense of purpose. I splashed colors—bright yellows, bold blues, and fiery reds—each stroke a celebration of Emily's resilience and the promise of better days to come. Yet, in the back of my mind, I could still feel the unacknowledged rift with Jason looming over me like a thundercloud.

A few days later, Jason found me amidst the chaos of my creativity, paint splattered across my apron and hair, a testament to the frenzy of emotions I was navigating. He leaned against the doorframe, arms crossed, his expression unreadable. I could sense the tension in the air even before he spoke.

"Clara, can we talk?" His voice held an edge, a seriousness that made my stomach twist.

"Of course," I replied, setting my brush down and wiping my hands on a rag, the paint smearing like the uncertainty swirling between us.

He stepped inside, the warmth of his presence filling the room. "I've been thinking a lot about everything," he started, running a hand through his hair, the gesture a familiar sign of his frustration. "I don't want to feel like I'm competing for your attention, but I also don't want to feel like an afterthought."

I swallowed hard, the weight of his words crashing over me like waves against the shore. "I never wanted you to feel that way. I've just been trying to be there for Emily," I said, my voice soft yet firm. "She's going through something really tough."

"I get that, but I need you too," he replied, his tone shifting from frustration to vulnerability. "I want to support you in helping her, but I also need you to support us. Can we find a balance?"

His plea echoed in my heart, a resonance of the love I felt for him battling against my commitment to Emily. I took a step closer, feeling the charged air between us. "I want that too, Jason. I really do."

The tension hung like a thread, thin yet unbreakable, and I could see the hope flickering in his eyes. "Then let's figure it out together. I don't want to be the one you turn to only when things are easy. I want to be there for the messy parts too."

With that simple admission, the storm that had been brewing between us began to settle. We had reached an understanding, a shared commitment to weather the complexities of our lives, both for each other and for Emily. And in that moment, surrounded by paint and canvases, I felt the first hints of clarity amidst the chaos, a reminder that love and friendship could coexist in this intricate dance we were navigating.

The resolve between Jason and me blossomed in the aftermath of our confrontation, yet the world around us remained ensnared in the lingering tension. Each day brought new challenges, as Emily began to cautiously wade back into the waters of her life. Her laughter, once so full-bodied and contagious, returned in soft, tentative bursts, like the shy sun breaking through a cloudy sky. I was determined to hold onto that hope, to encourage her as she started to reclaim the pieces of herself that had scattered like autumn leaves in a brisk wind.

Still, my focus on Emily weighed heavily on my relationship with Jason. I could feel his eyes on me, an unspoken question lingering in the air, waiting for the right moment to surface. It wasn't that I didn't want him there; rather, it was as if the universe conspired to keep us on separate paths, even as they wove closer together. Each evening, we'd slip into a routine of shared dinners, laughter, and the subtle exchange of glances that spoke of unacknowledged affection. Yet there were moments when the laughter would falter, when I could sense Jason's frustration lurking just beneath the surface, ready to bubble over.

One brisk evening, we decided to venture into the heart of Ashwood for a local art show—a yearly tradition that gathered the community together to celebrate creativity and expression. The atmosphere buzzed with excitement, a cacophony of voices blending with the clinking of glasses and the rustling of paintbrushes being showcased. Stalls overflowed with vibrant artwork, each piece telling a unique story, much like the myriad of emotions swirling within me.

As we wandered through the gallery, I found myself caught up in the vibrant displays, the colors calling to me, igniting my passion. My fingers itched to create, to let the hues swirl together in an explosion of expression. I glanced back at Jason, who stood a few paces behind, his brow furrowed as he scanned the crowd, searching for something—or someone—that I couldn't quite grasp.

I stepped closer to a stunning abstract piece, its chaotic strokes and vivid colors capturing my imagination. "Look at this one," I exclaimed, hoping to draw Jason into my enthusiasm. "It's like the artist poured their entire soul onto the canvas."

He nodded absently, his gaze still drifting over the attendees, and my heart sank. The gap between us felt palpable, an invisible barrier that kept us tethered yet distant. In that moment, I realized how my efforts to help Emily had inadvertently created a rift, one I desperately wanted to mend.

"Jason," I said, my voice barely rising above the din of the crowd. "Are you okay?"

He finally turned his attention toward me, a flicker of surprise crossing his face. "Yeah, I'm fine. Just... thinking."

"About what?" I pressed, my curiosity piqued.

"Just everything," he replied, his tone casual yet edged with something deeper. "It's good to see you helping Emily, but I miss you, you know? The us that we used to be before all this."

His honesty tugged at my heartstrings, and I could feel a pang of guilt settling in my chest. I stepped closer, leaning in so I could whisper without drawing attention. "I'm trying to be there for her. I promise, I want to find a balance. I need you to be patient with me."

He searched my eyes, the intensity of his gaze sending a warm shiver through me. "I want to support you. I really do, but I need to know you're still here, with me."

I nodded, feeling a rush of affection surge within me. "I'm here. I'm always here. Let's find a way to make this work."

As the evening wore on, I allowed myself to be swept up in the vibrant atmosphere, relishing the laughter and the shared stories of fellow artists. My worries began to melt away, and for a fleeting moment, the tumult within me quieted. I found myself lost in conversation with other creatives, their enthusiasm infectious, their stories weaving a tapestry of shared struggles and triumphs.

Yet, amidst the joy, I couldn't shake the feeling of Jason's eyes on me, a constant reminder of the tension simmering beneath the surface. I glanced back at him, noting the way his smile didn't quite reach his eyes. It dawned on me that he, too, was fighting his own battle, trying to navigate his place in my world that had recently been rocked by change.

Suddenly, a commotion broke out near the back of the gallery. A crowd gathered around a small stage where a local band was about to play, the energy electric and inviting. Without thinking, I reached for Jason's hand, intertwining our fingers as we maneuvered through the throng. The warmth of his grip sent a flutter through me, a reminder of the connection we shared, even amidst the chaos.

The band began to play, their music filling the space with a joyous melody that stirred something deep within me. As I swayed to the rhythm, I felt the weight of my worries begin to dissipate, replaced by a sense of freedom and exhilaration. I turned to Jason, pulling him into the dance, and for a moment, the world around us faded, leaving just the two of us in a bubble of shared laughter and music.

As the night wore on, the atmosphere thickened with excitement and camaraderie. My heart swelled with hope, the realization that I could be there for Emily while also nurturing my relationship with Jason. It was possible to weave the threads of both their lives into a tapestry that reflected my love and commitment to each. I was learning to balance the delicate act of supporting my friend without losing myself—or the connection that had begun to blossom between Jason and me.

But just as the evening reached its zenith, the unexpected twist I had feared finally materialized. I received a message from Emily, her words terse yet heavy with emotion. "Can we talk? I need you."

A rush of apprehension flooded my veins, the night's joy fading momentarily. I felt Jason's presence beside me, the warmth of his body contrasting sharply with the chill that settled over me. He could sense my change in demeanor, his gaze steady as he studied my face.

"Is everything okay?" he asked, concern etching deeper lines into his forehead.

"I don't know," I replied, a tremor in my voice. "I need to go."

Before he could respond, I squeezed his hand gently, letting the connection linger for just a moment longer. "I'll be back. I promise."

With that, I hurried through the crowd, my heart racing, anxiety spiraling in my chest. I fought to push back the dread that threatened to consume me, clinging instead to the hope that I could help Emily rise once more, as I had vowed to do.

The cool night air embraced me as I stepped outside, the stars twinkling like distant promises overhead. I hurried to my car, the engine purring to life as I raced to meet my friend. The road ahead was uncertain, but I felt a renewed determination coursing through my veins. I would navigate this twist in our lives, intertwining our fates while learning to embrace the chaos that came with love and friendship.

And as I drove into the night, I realized that sometimes, the most beautiful masterpieces are born from the messiest of moments, and perhaps we could paint our own masterpiece, filled with vibrant colors of resilience, hope, and unwavering love.

Chapter 16: An Unexpected Performance

The stage is set, and I can feel the anticipation crackling in the air like static before a summer storm. The vibrant hues of crimson and gold dance across the velvet curtains, catching the light like fireflies caught in a jar, illuminating the faces of friends and family who fill the seats before me. It's as if each individual has become a part of this collective heartbeat, their breaths suspended in time, waiting for our performance to breathe life into the room.

The scent of freshly polished wood mingles with the faint perfume of hairspray and excitement, wrapping around me like an embrace. I take a moment to glance over my shoulder at Jason, his presence beside me both grounding and exhilarating. He's wearing that familiar cocky grin, the one that makes my heart race even as it fills me with an urge to shove him playfully. In the chaos of our recent argument, I had almost forgotten this—how effortlessly our chemistry ignites, illuminating the shadows of our discord. Our eyes lock, and in that fleeting exchange, a silent apology hangs between us, ready to be articulated through movement rather than words.

As the lights dim further, plunging us into a world punctuated only by the warm glow of the stage lights, a wave of calm washes over me. I inhale deeply, filling my lungs with the hope that our choreography could transcend our past misunderstandings. We've spent countless hours rehearsing, each repetition layered with nuances and textures we've crafted through both laughter and frustration. Now, all that remains is to let it flow.

With the first notes of the music unfurling like a blossoming flower, we step forward together, our feet gliding over the polished floor as if it were a river of silk. Each movement unfolds with a purpose, an unspoken story that spills from my heart into the air, drawing the audience into our world. The rhythm of the music pulses through me, a lifeline binding my thoughts and emotions into the choreography. It's a dance of opposites—joy intertwined with sorrow, hope mingling with despair.

We leap and spin, our bodies weaving an intricate tapestry of connection and disconnection. I can feel the audience leaning in, captivated by our performance, their expressions reflecting the ebb and flow of our emotions. I catch glimpses of familiar faces—my mother, her eyes glistening with pride; my best friend, clutching a bouquet of wildflowers, a silent promise of support; and even the distant figure of my former dance teacher, who always believed in my potential. Each encouraging gaze fuels my energy, wrapping around me like a warm blanket, reminding me of why I love this art form—the ability to convey a world of feelings without uttering a single word.

As the music swells, I lose myself in the rhythm, allowing the choreography to carry me. Jason mirrors my every move, his body responding to the slightest shift in my weight, and for a moment, it feels as if we're one entity, a fusion of light and shadow. The air is thick with the electricity of our unspoken connection, and I can sense the story we're telling—the story of love, loss, and the audacity of hope. With each twirl and dip, I release my frustrations, the weight of our argument dissipating like mist under the morning sun.

The audience is rapt, their applause like thunder rolling across the mountains, echoing the beats of my heart. In this sacred space, I shed my doubts, allowing myself to be vulnerable, to share a piece of my soul through every expression and gesture. I can feel the warmth of the spotlight on my skin, the gentle breeze of movement lifting my hair, carrying with it the energy of the room. The performance becomes a dialogue—a conversation where words are unnecessary, where every pirouette speaks volumes.

As we reach the climax of the piece, our movements become more frenetic, a beautiful chaos of limbs and emotions. I glance at Jason, and in that moment, he catches my eye with an intensity that makes my heart skip. His smile is a beacon, guiding me through the tumult of feelings. Together, we throw ourselves into the final sequences, our bodies rising and falling, an ocean of movement. I can feel my breath quickening, my body aching from the exertion, but it's a sweet pain—a reminder of what it means to be alive, to feel every inch of my existence.

With the final note ringing out, we collapse onto the stage, breathless and exhilarated. The applause erupts, enveloping us like a tidal wave of warmth, and in that moment, I understand the true magic of performance. It's not merely about the steps or the technique; it's about the connection forged between us and the audience, the way we've shared a glimpse of our hearts in those fleeting moments. The rapture of their cheers fills the hollow spaces where doubt once lingered, washing away the remnants of our argument and replacing them with something far more profound.

As the lights dim and the curtain falls, I can still hear the echoes of their applause resonating within me, a powerful affirmation of what we've accomplished together. The performance wasn't just an expression of our artistry; it was a healing balm, an unexpected reminder that love, even when tangled in conflict, has the power to transcend and transform.

The applause lingers in the air, wrapping around me like a comforting shawl, its warmth slowly settling into the pit of my stomach. As I catch my breath, a mixture of exhilaration and vulnerability surges through me. Jason, still grinning like a Cheshire cat, leans in, and for a fleeting second, our shoulders touch—a simple gesture that ignites a spark. It's a reminder that even amidst the chaos, we're still tethered to one another, our fates intertwined by the strings of this performance and the shared history that brought us here.

Backstage, the energy shifts. The euphoria of the stage transforms into the clammy tension of reality. The hum of chatter reverberates through the dimly lit corridor, mixing with the sound of my heart still racing from the adrenaline. Friends and family, their faces glowing with pride, flit about, and I can hear snippets of praise—words like "breathtaking" and "captivating" weave through the air like delicate threads. I want to bask in the glow of their admiration, yet a shadow of doubt hovers just at the edges of my mind. What if this was merely a momentary spark, a fleeting glimpse of something that might never return?

In the midst of my internal tug-of-war, I hear the unmistakable sound of laughter—Jason's, mingling with a few others as they congregate in a corner. Curiosity piqued, I move toward the sound, my heart fluttering with uncertainty. I catch sight of him animatedly reenacting a particularly ridiculous moment from our rehearsals, his exaggerated expressions drawing chuckles from the small gathering. It's a sight I can't help but admire, the way he pulls people in, making them feel at ease with the mere cadence of his voice and the warmth of his smile. But beneath that charm, I sense the weight of our earlier conflict still lingering in the air.

"Come on, you have to see this!" he calls out to me, his eyes glinting with mischief. He steps aside, revealing a makeshift circle that has formed around him. "I was just telling them about the time you almost tripped on stage when we were rehearsing that one sequence!"

My cheeks flush with embarrassment, but laughter bubbles up inside me, spilling forth before I can contain it. That moment, that clumsy slip where I stumbled but somehow transformed it into an exaggerated pirouette, has become part of our shared folklore. I can't help but join in the camaraderie, reliving the moment through our laughter, letting the joy wash over me like a refreshing wave on a hot summer day.

As the laughter dies down, I catch his eye, and in that instant, I know we're both trying to bridge the gap that our argument carved between us. With unspoken words, we reaffirm our connection, reminding ourselves of the foundation built not just on the stage but in the countless hours of practice, shared dreams, and occasional disagreements that make us more than mere dance partners. I'm acutely aware of the delicate dance we're now performing, both in our personal lives and in this whirlwind of emotions.

The atmosphere shifts once more as people begin to filter out, their smiles lingering as they collect coats and purses, their excitement spilling over into animated conversations about what they've just witnessed. I lean against the wall, letting the warmth of the night wrap around me, allowing the cacophony to fade into a gentle murmur as I reflect on the evening. The tension that had gripped me before our performance is replaced by a sense of belonging, a feeling that perhaps we've all shared in something greater than ourselves.

Suddenly, a voice breaks through my reverie. "Hey, you two! We're heading out for ice cream. You in?" It's Lucy, my best friend, her blonde curls bouncing as she approaches, her eyes sparkling with mischief. Behind her, a small group nods eagerly, their enthusiasm palpable.

The thought of ice cream after such an emotional whirlwind seems both surreal and perfect. I glance at Jason, his expression a blend of surprise and delight. "Count me in!" he exclaims, an infectious grin spreading across his face. The warmth that had sparked between us earlier reignites, and I can't help but smile back, my heart feeling lighter.

As we step outside into the cool night air, the world feels transformed. The stars are scattered across the sky like shards of broken glass, glinting down at us with an invitation to revel in our youth. The chatter of my friends creates a soundtrack that makes the night feel alive, each laugh a note in our shared symphony. We walk to the nearby ice cream parlor, the promise of sweet indulgence adding a bounce to our steps.

The parlor is a tiny, charming establishment, its bright neon sign flickering like a heartbeat against the twilight. Inside, the scent of waffle cones and sugary delights mingles with the laughter of patrons, creating an atmosphere that feels like a warm hug. I scan the colorful menu, contemplating the endless possibilities, from classic vanilla to adventurous flavors like lavender honey and midnight fudge. The choices swirl in my mind, mirroring the whirlwind of emotions I've navigated through tonight.

"Okay, everyone, I'm going to go bold and get the salted caramel brownie!" Lucy declares, practically bouncing on her toes, her enthusiasm infectious. The others follow suit, each selecting their flavor with gleeful abandon, while I'm left trying to sift through my options, the pressure mounting. What would be the perfect flavor to encapsulate this evening?

Eventually, I settle on a rich chocolate mint—comforting yet vibrant, much like the evening itself. When it's finally my turn to order, the server flashes a bright smile, and I feel a surge of warmth as she hands me my cone, a delightful swirl of mint chocolate goodness perched on a perfectly crispy cone.

As I step back into the bustling night, the first taste is a rush of coolness that dances on my tongue, an explosion of flavor that seems to echo the vibrancy of the evening. I turn to find Jason already indulging in his scoop of strawberry cheesecake, his eyes widening in exaggerated delight as he moans dramatically, drawing laughter from our friends.

"Isn't this just the best way to celebrate?" I ask, taking in the glow of his smile against the backdrop of the night, the casual comfort of our friends surrounding us. He meets my gaze, and in that moment, something unspoken passes between us—a mutual understanding that we've emerged from the storm of our earlier argument, more resilient, more connected than before.

The night unfolds in a haze of laughter and indulgence, the trivialities of the day dissolving as we share stories and jokes, creating memories that will linger long after the ice cream has melted. Beneath the stars, surrounded by friends, I realize that tonight isn't just a celebration of our performance; it's a testament to the resilience of relationships, to the unexpected moments that carve out a space for healing and connection amidst the chaos of life.

As the night wears on, the remnants of our performance continue to linger in the air, vibrant and alive. The laughter and chatter of my friends provide a comforting backdrop, a sweet symphony that drowns out any lingering doubt about my earlier worries. The ice cream parlor buzzes with energy, a quaint little establishment adorned with vintage posters of ice cream advertisements from decades past, each one telling its own story. The walls, painted in cheerful pastels, invite laughter and joy, wrapping us in a cocoon of nostalgia.

Jason is animated, his expressions morphing from exaggerated glee to mock horror as he recounts an incident from last summer when we both found ourselves tangled in a series of misadventures during a group road trip. The way he describes my infamous attempt to navigate while we blasted music from the 80s makes me laugh until tears prick at the corners of my eyes. His storytelling captivates not only me but our entire group, drawing us all closer, weaving a tapestry of memories that bind us together.

As the evening light softens and deepens into twilight, we spill out onto the streets, our laughter echoing against the brick façades of the old buildings that line the avenue. The city feels alive, a symphony of distant car horns and murmured conversations, the hum of life pulsating around us. The stars twinkle above like scattered diamonds, and I can't help but reflect on how something so simple as a performance can ignite this powerful connection among us, reminding me that we are never truly alone in our struggles.

"Let's head to the park," Jason suggests, a glimmer of excitement in his eyes. The park is only a few blocks away, a sprawling oasis in the heart of the city, where the sounds of laughter and music can blend with the rustling leaves and chirping crickets. The group agrees, and with each step, I feel an invisible thread weaving through us, binding our spirits together.

As we arrive, the park unfolds like a secret garden, illuminated by scattered lanterns that flicker like fireflies in the cool night breeze. The laughter of children playing in the distance mingles with the gentle rustle of leaves overhead, creating an atmosphere that feels almost magical. We find a patch of grass and spread out, the earth cool beneath us, providing a comfortable anchor in this urban escape.

Settling into a circle, we dig into the remnants of our ice cream, exchanging half-melted cones and flavors, our laughter mingling with the night air. The chatter flows easily, stories tumble over one another, each anecdote brightening the night with warmth. It's in moments like these, wrapped in the glow of friendship, that I feel an undeniable truth rising within me: we're all fighting our own battles, yet we stand together, a collective army against the weight of the world.

In the midst of our camaraderie, I notice Jason watching me with an intensity that pulls me from the lively banter. He leans closer, his voice low and sincere, "You were incredible tonight. You really poured your heart into it." The sincerity in his gaze catches me off guard, and my heart beats faster as I consider the deeper implications of his words. His admiration feels like a soft breeze, cooling the lingering heat of the performance that still burns in my chest.

"Thanks," I reply, trying to match his sincerity but feeling a flurry of nerves dance in my stomach. "It was cathartic, you know? Like I could finally breathe again." My words tumble out, vulnerable but laced with an understanding that this is a shared experience, an echo of our earlier struggles.

"I get it," he says, nodding, a shadow of understanding passing between us. "It's like we were able to create something beautiful from all the chaos." There's a softness in his voice that resonates, and for a moment, the noise of the park fades into the background, leaving just the two of us in this shared bubble of reflection.

Suddenly, a small child runs past us, laughter ringing out like a bell, pulling me back into the moment. The innocence of their joy reminds me of why I love dance and performance—how it has the power to capture the ephemeral beauty of life and transform it into something tangible, something that can connect us all. The thrill of the stage is intoxicating, yes, but the afterglow of that connection is where the real magic lies.

As the night deepens, the stars begin to twinkle more brightly, as if winking down at us. The group falls into a comfortable rhythm, teasing and joking, but I can't shake the warmth of the moment shared with Jason. I catch him watching me again, his expression a mix of admiration and something deeper, something unspoken.

Lucy interrupts my thoughts, her voice playful and teasing. "Alright, everyone! Who's up for a game of truth or dare?" The suggestion is met with a chorus of agreement, the competitive spark igniting a fresh wave of excitement. The circle shifts, and suddenly, the atmosphere is charged with anticipation, the earlier reflections of vulnerability blending seamlessly with youthful exuberance.

We begin with a few truths, each revelation pulling us closer, unraveling layers of our personalities that had remained hidden. The stories reveal little quirks and shared secrets, moments that solidify our bonds even further. But when it's Jason's turn, he smirks, the glint in his eye promising mischief. "I dare you to perform your best dance move right here, right now!"

Laughter erupts around the circle, and I can feel my cheeks flush, a mix of excitement and embarrassment blooming within me. Yet, there's something liberating about the challenge, and I glance at Jason, the dare sparking a playful challenge between us.

With a deep breath, I stand, the world around me fading as I allow the music that resides in my heart to guide me. I feel the rhythm pulsing beneath my skin, a beat that echoes the laughter and chatter of my friends. With each movement, I channel the energy of the performance we shared earlier, letting it flow freely through me. I spin, leap, and glide, my body becoming an extension of the joy surrounding me.

The laughter becomes an applause, and as I finish, breathless and elated, I see the delight in their eyes. But it's Jason's expression that draws me in—the way he watches me, the admiration evident in every detail of his gaze. In that moment, I realize this night is more than just a celebration of our performance; it's a testament to the connections we've forged, the love that swells between us, and the unexpected ways we can find ourselves renewed through art and friendship.

As I sink back onto the grass, laughter bubbling up uncontrollably, I feel an overwhelming sense of gratitude wash over me. This vibrant, chaotic night has stitched together the frayed edges of my heart, reminding me that even amidst turmoil, there's always a chance for healing, laughter, and connection. And perhaps, just perhaps, it's those very moments that create the most beautiful performances of all.

Chapter 17: The Aftermath

The night air crackled with a mixture of excitement and uncertainty as we stepped off the stage, the last echoes of applause fading into the velvety darkness that enveloped the city. The bright lights of the theater still flickered in my mind, dancing alongside the confetti that swirled through the audience, shimmering like a cascade of dreams. Each sparkly flake that fell seemed to whisper sweet nothings about triumph, yet my heart felt heavy, a lead weight tethered to the ground. Despite the electric thrill of our performance, a chill of reality settled over me like a fog, shrouding the glow of success.

Jason's exuberance, however, lit up the gloom around us. He spun, arms outstretched, basking in the afterglow, and for a moment, I envied his ability to simply revel in the moment. He called out to the others, laughter spilling from his lips like a bubbling brook, and I watched him, caught in a poignant paradox. He was a spark in the darkness, yet my heart ached with the knowledge that somewhere out there, in the shadows of my mind, my friend lay vulnerable and alone.

"I can't believe we did it!" Jason beamed, his voice booming through the narrow hallway of the theater, filled with echoes of past performances and memories long forgotten. "Tonight was magic!" He wrapped an arm around my shoulders, pulling me into the warmth of his side, but the comfort was fleeting, dissipating like steam from a morning coffee, leaving a bitter taste in its wake.

I nodded, forcing a smile to dance upon my lips, but inside, my heart thudded with unease. It felt as if I were standing at the edge of a precipice, peering into a dark abyss. "Yeah, it was great," I replied, but my voice felt thin, almost translucent, and Jason's bright gaze quickly detected the hollowness behind my words.

"Hey," he said softly, drawing me to a secluded corner of the backstage area, a world cloaked in shadows, save for the golden glow of the stage lights seeping through the curtains. "What's really going on? You're not yourself." His concern pierced through the veil of my bravado, forcing me to confront the worry I had been shoving deep down, like a secret too painful to surface.

I sighed, the sound escaping my lips like a deflated balloon, and stared at the ground as if it held the answers I sought. "It's just... I'm worried about Sarah. She was so excited for tonight, and now..." My voice trailed off, choked by the weight of my fears. "I don't know how she's going to cope with everything." The words hung in the air, palpable and heavy, reminding me of the fragility of happiness in the face of adversity.

Jason's expression shifted, the lightheartedness in his eyes dimming as he absorbed my confession. "You know she's strong, right? She's gotten through so much already." He reached out, brushing a lock of hair behind my ear, the gentle gesture sending a cascade of warmth down my spine. Yet, that warmth couldn't chase away the cold tendrils of worry coiling around my heart.

"I know," I replied, my voice barely above a whisper. "But I can't shake this feeling. It's like I'm watching her struggle from a distance, and I'm helpless to do anything." Tears threatened to spill, and I blinked rapidly, willing them to retreat. I hated feeling vulnerable, especially in front of him, yet something about this moment felt unguarded and raw, a fragile connection growing stronger in the face of uncertainty.

Jason stepped closer, closing the gap between us, and in that instant, the world around us faded into the background, leaving just the two of us in our fragile cocoon of unspoken words and unresolved feelings. "You're not helpless," he said, his voice steady and unwavering. "You're her friend. Just being there for her means more than you realize." His eyes bore into mine, earnest and fierce, and I felt a flicker of hope ignite within me, a small flame against the encroaching darkness.

But the weight of unspoken feelings lingered in the air, wrapping around us like an embrace, and for a fleeting moment, I allowed myself to lean into him, to feel the warmth of his presence enveloping me. We shared a tentative embrace, the world outside forgotten, the harshness of reality softened by the moment of intimacy. I could smell the faint trace of his cologne mingled with the scent of fresh paint and wood from the set, a comforting reminder of the space where dreams were born.

"I don't want to lose her," I admitted, my voice muffled against his shoulder. It felt like a confession, a release of all the bottled-up fears that had been simmering beneath the surface. "She's been there for me through everything. I just... I don't want her to feel alone." The honesty spilled from my lips, leaving me feeling vulnerable yet oddly liberated.

He pulled back slightly, our faces inches apart, the connection palpable and electric. "You won't lose her," he reassured me, his gaze steady. "And you're not alone in this. We'll figure it out together." The promise hung in the air, tangible and comforting, and in that moment, I realized just how much I had come to rely on him, how his presence had anchored me through the storms of life.

Yet, even as the warmth of his words wrapped around me like a soft blanket, the lingering shadow of worry loomed, a reminder that our battle was far from over. In the vibrant world around us, colored by the bright lights and laughter, the uncertainty of the future loomed large, reminding me that even amidst joy, sorrow often wove itself into the fabric of life.

The atmosphere in the theater was still thick with remnants of laughter and lingering applause, but I felt more like a ghost haunting the vibrant hallways than a participant in the celebration. The stage lights flickered off, leaving behind an eerie glow that seemed to pulse in time with my anxious heart. Jason's words, though meant to comfort, floated around me like confetti caught in the wind—beautiful but ultimately insubstantial. I watched as he rejoined our friends, their joyous laughter ringing like chimes in the crisp night air, but I couldn't shake the shadows looming over my heart.

As I stepped outside, the cool night air wrapped around me like a comforting shawl, the bustling streets of Chicago alive with energy. The city thrummed with life—the scent of deep-dish pizza wafted from nearby pizzerias, mingling with the sweet aroma of roasted chestnuts from vendors. Cars whizzed by, their headlights casting brief glimmers on the pavement, creating a mosaic of lights that felt like a metaphor for the evening: bright, beautiful, and ultimately fleeting. Yet, the charm of the city only served to amplify the emptiness gnawing at my core.

I leaned against the brick façade of the theater, trying to inhale the evening's ambiance, but all I could taste was anxiety. The chatter of my friends blurred into an indistinguishable hum, their joy a stark contrast to my inner turmoil. The laughter and camaraderie felt like a vivid painting, vibrant yet disconnected from the monochrome of my thoughts. Each laugh seemed to pierce through my worry, yet I couldn't bring myself to join them, trapped in a maelstrom of what-ifs and should-haves.

And then I spotted her, Sarah, drifting toward us like a wayward star. Her smile, usually bright enough to illuminate the darkest corners of my heart, faltered as her eyes met mine. It was a fleeting moment, but I felt the weight of her sadness pierce through the haze of celebration, heavy and tangible. In that instant, the world around me faded into silence, the laughter becoming a distant echo. The pulse of life thrummed like a heartbeat, quickening as I pushed off the wall and moved toward her.

"Hey," I said softly, my voice barely above a whisper. The warmth of the crowd felt a universe away as I reached her. "You made it."

"Yeah, just couldn't miss it, could I?" she replied, but the attempt at levity felt thin, stretching precariously over the abyss of her pain. Her usual spark was dulled, shadowed by something deeper, something I couldn't quite grasp.

I searched her eyes, hoping to find a glimmer of the strength that had always been her hallmark, but instead, I saw a storm brewing. "Are you okay?" I asked, feeling the words tumble out as if they were too heavy to be kept inside. The vulnerability in her expression made my heart ache.

She shrugged, a gesture that felt like a weighty dismissal, yet I could see the truth clinging to her like a second skin. "Just tired, I guess. The whole thing was a lot." Her words felt like a flimsy shield against the truths that lay just beneath the surface. I wanted to reach out, to wrap my arms around her and shield her from whatever storm was brewing, but I felt paralyzed, unsure of how to break through the barriers she had put up.

As we stood there, the night continued to unfurl around us—cars blared their horns, couples strolled hand in hand, and street musicians played soulful melodies. The world moved forward, blissfully unaware of the turbulence swirling in our small corner. I longed to draw her into the warmth of friendship, to remind her that she wasn't alone, yet my own insecurities clashed with the urge to be strong for her.

"Wanna get out of here? Just for a bit?" I suggested, my voice tentative yet filled with determination. I wanted to break the fragile cocoon we found ourselves in, to pull her away from the laughter that felt so alien to her at that moment. There was a coffee shop just a few blocks down that stayed open late, its inviting glow beckoning like a lighthouse in a storm. I remembered countless nights spent there, sharing secrets over steaming mugs, the aroma of coffee mingling with dreams and whispered fears.

She hesitated, her gaze drifting back to where Jason and the others were mingling. A flicker of longing crossed her face, a desire to belong even in her turmoil. "I don't want to ruin your night," she murmured, her voice almost lost in the cacophony around us.

"You won't," I replied, my heart racing with a mix of desperation and hope. "We'll make it our night. Just you and me. No expectations." I offered her a smile, one that I hoped could bridge the distance between us. The warmth of our friendship had been forged through laughter and tears, and I yearned to revive that connection, to remind her of the bond we shared.

After a moment that felt like an eternity, she nodded, albeit reluctantly. "Okay. Just for a little while." Relief flooded through me, a buoy in the turbulent sea of emotions swirling within her.

As we walked, the city buzzed around us, a living organism, each pulse of life reverberating through the streets. We meandered past brightly lit storefronts, their window displays showcasing the latest fashions and trinkets, vibrant colors that clashed with the monochrome of our thoughts. The sound of clinking glasses and laughter spilled out from nearby restaurants, a reminder of the life we had momentarily set aside.

I led us to the coffee shop, its familiar warmth enveloping us as we stepped inside. The barista greeted us with a friendly smile, the smell of freshly brewed coffee wrapping around us like a favorite blanket. We settled into a small booth in the corner, the world outside falling away as the comforting hum of conversation surrounded us. I ordered two steaming mugs of hot chocolate, hoping that sweetness would bring a flicker of warmth to Sarah's heart.

As the rich, velvety drink slid across the table, I watched her take a tentative sip, the steam curling around her face like a soft embrace. For a moment, the tension in her shoulders eased, and I felt a spark of hope. "You used to love this," I reminded her, my heart aching to see even a hint of her old self. "We spent hours here, solving the world's problems over hot chocolate and pastries."

She chuckled softly, the sound like music to my ears, though it lacked the vibrant energy that had once defined her laughter. "Yeah, and look at us now—more problems than we could ever hope to solve." Her gaze drifted to the window, where the city shimmered in its night attire, a stark contrast to the chaos swirling in her mind.

"Sometimes, it feels like the problems just keep piling up," I said, my voice gentle. "But that doesn't mean we have to face them alone." The words hung in the air, resonating between us, and I watched as she wrestled with her thoughts, the conflict evident in her eyes.

The warmth of the chocolate enveloped us, a sweet cocoon in which we could share our truths without the fear of judgment. The world outside faded, leaving just the two of us, bound by friendship and the shared understanding that life often didn't go according to plan. I reached across the table, my hand brushing against hers, a simple touch but charged with the promise of support and understanding.

"Let's talk about it," I urged, my heart pounding with the hope that this could be a turning point for her. I wanted to peel back the layers of worry that surrounded her, to show her that vulnerability was not a weakness but a strength we could share. "Whatever it is, I'm here. I want to help."

In that moment, I could see the walls she had built around herself beginning to crack, the flickering flame of hope igniting in her eyes. I held my breath, waiting for her to take the leap, to trust me with the weight she carried. It felt like a delicate dance, teetering on the precipice of connection, and I yearned for her to step forward, to embrace the solace of our friendship.

The warmth of the coffee shop enveloped us, a sanctuary from the frigid night air outside, yet the cozy ambiance felt like a thin veil over the turmoil brewing beneath the surface. I watched as Sarah traced her finger along the rim of her mug, her gaze flitting from the rich brown liquid to the window where the bustling street stretched out, teeming with life. In the dim light, her features seemed softer, the harsh lines of worry and stress momentarily blurred by the warmth of the hot chocolate. There was a moment when the silence hung thick between us, charged with unspoken fears and lingering hope, a delicate thread connecting our hearts in this fleeting bubble of camaraderie.

"What's really going on with you?" I finally asked, my voice a soft intrusion in the enveloping quiet. I leaned in closer, searching her eyes for the answers that lay just beneath the surface. The city outside pulsated with life, but inside, I wanted to create a different kind of vibrancy—a tapestry of shared experiences and vulnerabilities.

She exhaled slowly, a breath laden with the weight of her burdens. "It's just... everything feels so overwhelming," she admitted, her voice barely above a whisper. "I thought this was going to be a fresh start, but instead, it feels like I'm drowning in expectations and worries." The honesty in her tone cut through the air like a knife, raw and powerful.

I nodded, empathy flooding through me as I reached across the table, my fingers brushing against hers again. "You don't have to do it alone. We've faced tough times before, remember? You're stronger than you think." The reassurance felt like an anchor, grounding us both in the reality that despite the chaos swirling around her, she had a solid foundation in our friendship.

Her lips twitched at the corners, a flicker of a smile trying to break through. "I remember those late nights filled with endless possibilities and dreams," she said, a wistful glint in her eye. "But now... now it's like I'm stuck in a loop, and I can't seem to find a way out." The vulnerability in her voice was palpable, and I felt a pang of sadness for her, knowing how easily dreams could become entangled in the web of reality.

The barista approached, interrupting our moment, and I seized the chance to refill our mugs, hoping the warmth of the cocoa might thaw the chill settling in her heart. The rich, velvety drink seemed to bring a sense of comfort, and as I stirred the foam, I couldn't help but feel a surge of determination. "We can find that way out together," I said, my heart racing with the conviction of my words. "We'll navigate this maze side by side, and I'll be your compass."

Her eyes widened slightly, the flicker of hope reigniting within them. "You really mean that?" she asked, her voice trembling with uncertainty. I nodded, feeling the weight of my promise hanging in the air. "Absolutely. I'll always be here for you, no matter how tangled the path gets."

As she took another sip, the steam curled around her face, creating an ephemeral halo that momentarily masked her worries. "I guess I just thought once I left that part of my life behind, I could start fresh," she said, her voice gaining strength. "But I didn't realize the past doesn't just vanish. It leaves marks, like a fingerprint on my heart." The metaphor resonated with me, a reminder of how our experiences shape us, for better or worse, like shadows that cling to our souls.

"Those marks can be beautiful, you know," I said, my tone playful, hoping to lighten the mood. "They tell our stories, each line a testament to our resilience." I smiled, and she couldn't help but return the gesture, the warmth of our friendship bridging the chasm of her worries.

"Maybe you're right," she mused, a thoughtful glimmer in her eyes. "Maybe they're not scars but badges of honor." The shift in her perspective was like watching a sunrise, the colors of her spirit warming the corners of my heart.

We settled into a comfortable rhythm, exchanging stories about the past that we had once shared—laughing about inside jokes, reminiscing about our wild ambitions, and dreaming aloud about the futures we yearned to create. It was cathartic, a balm for the wounds we had both endured, and I felt the space between us fill with unspoken understanding.

Just then, the coffee shop door swung open, letting in a gust of chilly wind that carried the sound of distant music. I glanced outside and spotted a group of street performers, their instruments creating a lively melody that danced through the air like the flutter of butterflies. It was contagious, and I felt my spirit lift, the infectious energy compelling me to share that moment with Sarah.

"Let's go," I said impulsively, my heart racing with excitement. "Let's join them!" I slid out of the booth, pulling her along with me. She hesitated, glancing back at the warmth of the coffee shop, but I saw the spark of spontaneity igniting within her.

As we stepped outside, the cool air hit us like a refreshing wave, invigorating and alive. The street performers were a colorful mosaic of talent—musicians strumming guitars, a dancer twirling with reckless abandon, and a juggler who tossed flaming batons high into the air. The vibrant energy of the crowd surged around us, pulling us in, and for the first time that night, I saw Sarah's eyes widen with genuine excitement.

"Come on!" I called, tugging her forward as we danced to the rhythm, the worries of the world melting away with every beat. We moved together, laughter spilling from our lips, our friendship a beautiful tapestry woven with resilience and joy. The music swirled around us, wrapping us in its embrace, and for that moment, it felt like we were invincible, as if nothing could touch us.

As we twirled and spun, I caught glimpses of our past selves in the way we moved—carefree and vibrant, unburdened by the weight of adulthood. With each laugh, I felt the chains of worry loosening their grip on Sarah's heart, the colors of her spirit shining brighter in the dim light of the street. She radiated a joy that had been missing, and I couldn't help but feel my own spirit lift alongside hers.

Eventually, we settled on the sidewalk, panting and exhilarated, the remnants of the performance swirling around us like confetti in the air. Sarah leaned back against the cool brick wall, her chest rising and falling as she caught her breath, a wide grin plastered across her face. "That was amazing!" she exclaimed, her eyes sparkling with newfound vitality.

"I knew you had it in you!" I replied, my heart swelling with pride for her. "You just needed a little push."

"Maybe I needed more than a push," she said, her tone mischievous. "Maybe I needed you to drag me into the wild." Her laughter rang like music in my ears, and I couldn't help but join in, the sound echoing off the walls and dancing into the night.

As the festivities continued around us, a sense of camaraderie blossomed between us, a reminder of the bond that had weathered the storms of life. The shadows that had once loomed over our hearts began to fade, replaced by the warmth of shared experiences and laughter. In that moment, I realized how resilient we were—two friends navigating the intricate dance of life, hand in hand, determined to embrace whatever challenges lay ahead.

With the music still thrumming through our veins, we turned to face the world anew, our hearts intertwined in a symphony of hope and strength, ready to conquer the next chapter together. The future stretched before us, bright and uncharted, but for the first time in a long while, I felt ready to embrace it with open arms, our laughter trailing behind like a comet's tail, lighting up the path ahead.

Chapter 18: A Fork in the Heart

The park unfolds before me, a canvas splashed with the vibrant colors of autumn. Leaves, in hues of gold and crimson, flutter to the ground like confetti celebrating a secret festival. The crisp air is tinged with the earthy scent of damp soil, mixed with the sweetness of the remaining blooms. I take a deep breath, the chill biting at my cheeks, awakening a sense of clarity as I remember that dance—the spontaneous, unfiltered joy of splashing through puddles with Jason, laughter spilling from our lips as if the world had conspired to give us that moment, to hold it aloft like a trophy. Those memories are both a comfort and a weight, tugging at the edges of my heart as I navigate this labyrinth of emotions.

My heart feels like a compass spinning wildly, unsure of which direction to take now that my friend has pulled away. Each step through the park is heavy, laden with the realization that sometimes, even the closest bonds can fray. I glance over to the swing set where we used to push each other, our feet brushing the clouds as we laughed in reckless abandon. The chains creak softly, a melancholic reminder of what once was, a gentle echo of our joy now turned hollow.

As I walk further down the winding path, I catch sight of a couple on a bench, sharing whispers that flutter into the air like tiny butterflies. Their eyes dance with affection, and for a moment, I'm envious of their effortless connection. The juxtaposition of their love against my solitude feels stark; it's like watching a film reel of happiness while I stand behind the screen, separated by a layer of glass that refuses to shatter. I force my gaze away, unwilling to let the warmth of their intimacy seep into my already wounded heart.

I find solace beneath a large oak tree, its branches sprawling out like welcoming arms. The rough bark feels grounding beneath my fingers, a testament to resilience. I sink onto the damp grass, the coolness seeping through my jeans, and close my eyes, letting the sounds of the park envelop me. Children's laughter rings out like chimes, punctuating the air with innocence. Nearby, a dog barks, its joyful yips mingling with the soft rustle of leaves. Each sound is a reminder of life continuing in all its chaotic beauty, while I sit here, feeling like an intruder in my own existence.

And then there's the silence, the kind that amplifies the echo of my thoughts. I can't help but replay the conversation with my friend over and over again, each word resonating painfully within me. "I can't keep dragging you into my mess," she had said, her voice trembling with vulnerability. I had wanted to argue, to push against her wall of pride, but instead, I felt the weight of her truth. There's a distinct cruelty in love sometimes, where the greatest act of care is to step back, to give someone the space they believe they need, even when it tears you apart.

The memory of Jason flickers in my mind, the way he smiled, the warmth of his presence a gentle reminder of safety. He had always been the light in my darkness, illuminating the corners of my insecurities with his laughter and charm. I remember the way his eyes crinkled when he laughed, like he was in on a secret that the rest of the world had yet to discover. In the midst of this emotional turmoil, I realize how deeply I've fallen for him. My heart beats with a rhythm that feels both exhilarating and terrifying, a silent acknowledgment of feelings I've tried to suppress in the name of practicality.

A gentle breeze kisses my skin, coaxing me to open my eyes. I glance up, spotting the clouds shifting lazily across the sky. They morph into shapes that remind me of all the moments Jason and I shared—the way we'd lie on the grass, searching for constellations that didn't exist, lost in the magic of each other's company. My heart clenches at the thought of him, the way his presence felt like home, the way his laughter was a balm for my wounds.

In the midst of my reverie, I spot a flash of color out of the corner of my eye. A little girl, no more than six, is racing toward the swing set, her pigtails bobbing with each determined stride. Her bright red coat stands out against the muted backdrop of the park, and there's something about her unfiltered joy that pulls me from my thoughts. She clambers onto the swing, her laughter ringing out like a bell as she flies through the air, arms outstretched as if she could reach the sky. I can't help but smile at her unadulterated delight, a stark contrast to the weight that presses down on my chest.

In that moment, something shifts within me. Perhaps love is not just about holding on or letting go. Maybe it's about embracing the messiness of life—the way it intertwines with joy and sorrow, the way it compels us to grow and change. I've loved fiercely, and I've lost even more profoundly, but there's still beauty in the chaos, a vibrant thread of resilience that runs through every experience.

I rise from the ground, the coolness of the grass still clinging to my legs, and begin to walk again. Each step feels lighter, a deliberate choice to embrace the uncertainty of what lies ahead. The park, once a backdrop for my memories, transforms into a landscape of possibilities. The laughter of the little girl echoes in my ears, a reminder that life continues to unfold, that even in moments of solitude, there's a heartbeat, a rhythm that pulses with hope. I don't know what tomorrow will bring, but I'm ready to face it—ready to weave my story into the tapestry of this vibrant world, one step at a time.

I stroll past the café with its quaint outdoor seating, the scent of fresh coffee mingling with the faint aroma of pastries wafting through the air. The chatter of patrons fills the atmosphere with a lighthearted buzz, but I resist the temptation to pause. Instead, I continue my trek through the park, my sneakers crunching over fallen leaves, their crispness echoing my own fragile state. I notice a painter at work beneath the nearby willow, each stroke of his brush capturing the golden light filtering through the branches. He seems lost in his craft, the world around him fading into a blur of color and sound, and for a moment, I envy his singular focus. It's a stark contrast to the chaos swirling within me, a reminder that art can offer solace when life feels overwhelming.

As I pass by the pond, I catch sight of ducks gliding effortlessly across the surface, leaving ripples in their wake. Their quacks punctuate the air, a playful banter that draws a smile from me despite my heavy heart. I sit on a nearby bench, watching them paddle about with such unburdened joy. How simple their lives must be, driven by instinct rather than the complexities of human emotions. I lean back, letting the cool breeze tease my hair, as I ponder the choices that have led me here, in this moment, wrestling with the ghosts of my heart.

I pull out my phone, the screen illuminating my face like a beacon in the dusk, and scroll through the photos I've taken over the past few months. Each image tells a story, fragments of laughter and joy intertwined with flashes of heartbreak. There's a picture of Jason, hair tousled and grin wide, a snapshot of carefree bliss captured during one of our spontaneous adventures. I can almost hear the echo of his laughter in my mind, a sound that has become a symphony in my memories. A pang of longing twists in my chest as I linger on that photo, wishing I could freeze time and stay lost in that fleeting moment forever.

But life is relentless in its forward march, and I am reminded of the conversations I had with my friend just days ago—her fears, her hesitations, and the vulnerability she wore like a second skin. She had always been the stronger one, the rock amid the storm, and now, seeing her retreat into herself felt like losing a part of me. I glance up, the sky turning a dusky purple, and I can't help but wonder if her heart, too, is struggling beneath the weight of unshared burdens.

Determined to embrace the evening, I rise from the bench, leaving behind the fleeting comfort of nostalgia. I navigate the winding paths of the park, allowing the cadence of my footsteps to guide my thoughts. The golden glow of lampposts begins to flicker to life, casting soft halos around the trees, and I relish the enchanting atmosphere, each step illuminating a new possibility.

The playground nearby is alive with children, their laughter bouncing off the metal jungle gym, echoing like bells in the night. I find myself drawn to their innocence, their ability to lose themselves in the simplest of joys. A group of kids plays tag, their shrieks of delight ringing through the air, while a couple of parents hover nearby, sharing amused glances as they sip their coffee. One father tosses his son into the air, catching him mid-laugh, a picture of pure, unfiltered love. My heart aches with the weight of that affection, a bittersweet reminder of what it feels like to be fully known and cherished.

I can't help but think of Jason again. Would he be here, his eyes bright with mirth, reveling in the carefree joy of a child? Would he join in the laughter, or perhaps lean back against the fence, watching with that quiet intensity that made my heart flutter? The memory of his touch lingers on my skin like an indelible mark, each brush of his fingers a spark that ignites the warmth of my affection.

As I continue to wander, I find myself at a small gazebo nestled among flowering shrubs, the air thick with the heady scent of jasmine. It feels like a secret haven, a place where the world fades away, and I can lose myself in thought. I step inside, the wooden floor creaking beneath me, and allow myself a moment to breathe, to let the weight of my emotions spill out into the twilight.

I lean against the railing, staring out into the gathering darkness, where shadows dance between the trees. My thoughts drift to my friend and the painful decision she's made to distance herself. I wish she could see the strength in vulnerability, the power of sharing one's burdens with those who care. But perhaps this is part of her journey, a path she must tread alone for now. The acceptance feels like a bittersweet pill to swallow, but I know love sometimes requires us to let go, even when our hearts protest.

Suddenly, a rustle catches my attention. I turn to see a young couple entering the gazebo, hand in hand, their shared smiles bright enough to light the night. They giggle softly as they lean into one another, their presence an intoxicating mix of tenderness and joy. I step back to allow them their moment, the warmth of their connection igniting a flicker of hope within me. Their love feels alive and tangible, a reminder that despite the heartache, beauty continues to exist in the world.

I slip away from the gazebo, retracing my steps through the park. The laughter of the children has dimmed, and the air has turned cooler, but my heart feels a little lighter. As I pass the café again, I hear the soft notes of a guitar drifting through the open window, serenading the evening with a familiar melody. Without thinking, I step inside, drawn by the music, the warmth of the space wrapping around me like a comforting embrace.

The small café is a world of its own, filled with mismatched furniture and art adorning the walls—a collage of creativity that feels inviting. I take a seat at the bar, the surface warm beneath my hands, and allow myself to be swept away in the atmosphere. The barista, a young woman with bright blue hair, greets me with a warm smile, her energy contagious. I order a hot chocolate, craving its sweetness to soothe my heart, and as I wait, I listen to the gentle strumming of the guitar, feeling the notes resonate deep within me.

I glance around, observing the patrons lost in their conversations, their eyes sparkling with connection. In this cozy haven, the world feels right, even as my heart wrestles with its own dissonance. And for a moment, I allow myself to dream of a future filled with laughter, love, and the courage to embrace every twist and turn that life has to offer.

The café wraps around me like a well-worn blanket, each corner radiating a familiar warmth. I settle into my seat, my fingers wrapping around the delicate porcelain mug as I await the hot chocolate that promises to soothe my frayed nerves. The melody from the guitar weaves through the air, a tapestry of notes that seems to echo the confusion and hope churning inside me. I let my gaze wander, catching snippets of laughter and soft conversations around me. An elderly couple, their hands intertwined like roots of a well-established tree, exchange knowing smiles, while a group of friends animatedly discuss weekend plans, their excitement palpable.

As I sip my drink, the rich chocolate floods my senses, a sweet reprieve from the turmoil I've been navigating. It's a momentary balm, but it's fleeting, just like the carefree days I shared with Jason. Each sip draws me deeper into contemplation, and my mind drifts to the paths we take in life—the choices that define us, sometimes even the ones that feel like they lead to dead ends. I imagine Jason's face lighting up with laughter, his easygoing nature drawing everyone in like a moth to a flame. I miss that. I miss him.

The barista approaches, her vibrant blue hair a burst of color that momentarily distracts me from my thoughts. "How's the hot chocolate?" she asks, a friendly spark in her eyes. I nod enthusiastically, feeling the warmth spread through me. "It's like a hug in a cup," I reply, my voice lighter than I expected. She grins, the kind of grin that suggests she knows the weight of the world but chooses to carry it with a sense of humor.

"Glad to hear it! You know, we have a secret recipe for the whipped cream if you want to try it next time." Her casual offer feels like an invitation to return, and I find myself smiling back at her. There's something about this small exchange, the connection of shared moments, that comforts me amid my swirling emotions.

Outside, the sun dips lower on the horizon, casting a golden hue across the park that filters through the café windows, illuminating the wood grain of the tables and creating a dreamy glow. I glance back at the couple from earlier, now leaning in closer, their whispers quiet but their intentions clear. There's something beautifully intoxicating about witnessing the early stages of love, that giddy excitement of possibility tinged with the sweetness of hope.

And yet, the memory of my friend lingers like an unwelcome shadow. I can't shake the feeling of helplessness that came with her decision to push me away. The thought of her facing her struggles alone tugs at my heart, a persistent ache that refuses to be silenced. I wonder how many moments like these we allow to slip away, how many connections we sacrifice for the sake of pride. Wouldn't it be easier if we could just lean on one another, to share the burdens and let the weight distribute itself among those who care?

I finish my hot chocolate, the last sip bittersweet, and set the cup down, resolving to make a change. I rise from my seat, glancing around the café one last time before stepping back into the cool evening air. The park greets me with the vibrant sounds of nature settling into the dusk, the chirping of crickets serenading the fading light. As I walk, the uncertainty clinging to my heart begins to dissolve into determination. I don't want to be the person who stands by while someone I care about struggles alone.

I head toward the swings, their chains creaking gently in the wind, echoing the rhythm of my racing thoughts. There's a child still swinging, pumping her legs with all the might her small frame can muster. The sheer joy radiating from her makes me smile, a reminder of the innocence I sometimes forget exists beneath layers of adult complexities. I watch her, enchanted by her unfiltered delight, and I realize that maybe this is what I need to embody—pure, unabashed joy.

The night settles in as I begin to wander the park, determined to find my friend. Each step is guided by the memory of her laughter, a melody that is both haunting and beautiful. I think back to all the times we shared, our spontaneous adventures and deep conversations that ran late into the night. Those memories ignite a fire within me, fueling my resolve to reach out to her again.

With renewed purpose, I reach for my phone and send her a simple message: "I miss you. Let's talk." I hit send, the weight of my vulnerability settling comfortably on my shoulders. This is love in its truest form—the willingness to expose my heart despite the fear of rejection. The seconds tick by, each one heavier than the last, but I refuse to let uncertainty drag me down.

Suddenly, my phone vibrates with a response, and I pause mid-step. "I'm sorry for shutting you out. Can we meet?" A wave of relief washes over me, intertwining with the remnants of anxiety.

I quickly type back, suggesting a nearby café that has become our favorite spot. It's a place steeped in shared memories, where the walls hold the echoes of our laughter and the aroma of coffee mingles with the warmth of friendship.

As I make my way toward it, I allow the beauty of the night to envelop me. The moon hangs high in the sky, a glowing orb that casts a silvery light over the park. I smile at the thought of rekindling our connection, of peeling back the layers of hurt and misunderstanding. I remind myself that love is messy, that it often requires us to step into the fray, to be vulnerable even when we feel like we're losing ground.

When I finally reach the café, the sight of my friend waiting at a table by the window tugs at my heart. She looks up as I approach, her expression a mixture of apprehension and hope. I take a seat across from her, the familiar warmth of our friendship filling the space between us.

"Hey," I say softly, the tension between us palpable yet slowly beginning to dissipate. She smiles faintly, a flicker of the light I've missed in her eyes.

"Hey," she replies, her voice trembling slightly.

As we settle into a comfortable silence, the world outside becomes a blur, and I know, in this moment, we're both ready to face the mess together, weaving our stories back into a tapestry of laughter and shared strength. And as we begin to talk, I realize that even in the shadows, love finds a way to shine, illuminating the path ahead, guiding us home.

Chapter 19: Whispers of Hope

The café buzzes with life, a vibrant tapestry of chatter, clinking cups, and the low hum of a guitar strumming softly in the corner. The sun filters through the large windows, casting a warm golden glow over the rustic wooden tables and the mismatched chairs that have seen better days. Each piece of furniture seems to carry a story, just as I carry mine, full of longing and hesitance. The air is heavy with the rich aroma of coffee—bold, earthy, with a hint of sweetness from freshly baked pastries that beckon me like an old friend. This was our place, where laughter once spilled like the sugar from the small ceramic bowls on the tables, and where secrets were exchanged like tender glances.

Sitting at our usual spot, I fidget with the frayed edge of the napkin, my heart a drum echoing in my chest. I watch as he walks through the door, a tall silhouette against the bright sunlight, his hair tousled, and a smile that could still ignite my heart. Jason always had that effect on me, as if he held a spark capable of lighting up the dimmest of corners in my life. Today, however, there's an air of uncertainty around him, a veil of quiet reflection that hangs like fog. He approaches, his eyes searching mine, a mixture of hope and guardedness swirling within those depths.

"Hey," he says, his voice low, warm like the coffee we used to share. He slides into the seat across from me, and in that moment, the distance between us feels insurmountable yet tangible.

"Hey," I reply, my throat tight as if the very word could shatter the delicate silence. We sit there, two souls tethered by the past, both hesitant to breach the surface. I take a deep breath, inhaling the heady scent of roasted beans and the familiar warmth of his presence, and begin to unravel the thread of my thoughts.

"I'm sorry," I say, my voice barely above a whisper. "I didn't mean to pull away. It just felt like everything was spinning out of control, and I didn't know how to hold on."

He nods, his gaze steady, a mix of understanding and sadness reflected in his eyes. "I felt it too," he admits, his hands clasping the coffee cup as if it could anchor him. "When you stepped back, I thought maybe I should too. But that didn't make it easier."

As we exchange these confessions, the café around us fades into a blur. The sound of laughter from a group at the next table feels distant, the clatter of dishes dissolves into the background. We're in our own world, suspended in time, where the only thing that matters is the honest connection we've fought to regain.

"I've missed this," he continues, his fingers tracing the rim of his cup absentmindedly. "Us. It's like I've been walking around in a fog, trying to find my way back to something familiar. I thought I'd forgotten how to feel."

The words strike a chord deep within me, resonating with my own feelings of displacement. It's the vulnerability we often hide behind, the shared loneliness that binds us together. In this moment, the cracks in our hearts seem to align, like puzzle pieces finally finding their place.

"I felt lost too," I confess, my heart swelling with a mix of hope and fear. "I didn't realize how much I relied on our moments together until they were gone. It's like...everything else faded, and I was left in the dark."

He reaches across the table, his hand brushing against mine, sending a jolt of warmth through me. It's a simple gesture, yet it carries a weight of promise, a reminder that we're not just talking about the past—we're building a bridge to the future.

Our conversation flows easily now, words cascading like the gentle stream in the park where we used to walk. We share our dreams, weaving tales of where we hope to go, what we aspire to become, and the fears that hold us captive. He speaks of wanting to travel, to explore the world beyond our small town, while I admit my yearning to write, to craft stories that would resonate with others like his words resonate with me.

The sun dips lower in the sky, casting long shadows across the café as the evening begins to envelop us in its embrace. The barista brings us fresh cups, and we clink them together lightly, a toast to our renewed connection. "To new beginnings," Jason says, his smile brightening the dimming light, and I can't help but mirror his enthusiasm.

As we leave the café, the cool evening air wraps around us, refreshing yet familiar, filled with the scent of autumn leaves and the distant echo of laughter from passing pedestrians. I look up at the sky, where the first stars are beginning to twinkle, and I can't shake the feeling that something significant is unfolding.

He takes my hand, our fingers intertwining, and for the first time in what feels like ages, I breathe deeply, feeling a weight lift. With every step we take, the whispers of hope fill the spaces between us, weaving an invisible thread that binds our hearts together anew. The challenges we face still loom ahead, but together, they seem more surmountable. As if love, in its purest form, could conquer any obstacle life throws our way.

In that moment, beneath the fading light of the day and the burgeoning glow of the stars, I realize that this is what it means to truly connect—to share fears, dreams, and a sense of purpose that transcends time. And as we walk toward the uncertain horizon, I can't help but feel a flicker of excitement for what lies ahead, ready to embrace whatever comes next.

The city streets are painted in hues of twilight, where shadows stretch and dance with the fading light. As we stroll down the familiar path, Jason and I find ourselves enveloped in a cozy bubble of warmth, each step releasing the last remnants of doubt I had clutched so tightly. The lingering scent of coffee still clings to us, mingling with the cool evening breeze that brushes against our cheeks, reminding me of the comfort we've both craved.

He leads the way, his fingers interlaced with mine, as if he's afraid to let go, and I share that sentiment. The rhythm of our footsteps echoes against the pavement, a soft, rhythmic heartbeat that grounds us in this moment of rekindled connection. Streetlamps flicker to life, casting a soft glow that illuminates the path ahead, revealing the scattered autumn leaves swirling like confetti around our feet, celebrating our reunion.

"Do you remember that Halloween when we dressed up as superheroes?" he asks suddenly, a twinkle lighting up his eyes. I can almost see the kid in him, the boy who made me laugh so easily and unforgettably. The memory springs to life, vivid and joyous, and I can't help but laugh.

"How could I forget? You insisted on being the 'ultimate' hero, wearing that ridiculous cape while I was just trying to be Wonder Woman," I tease, nudging him playfully with my shoulder. He chuckles, the sound warm and rich, wrapping around me like a favorite blanket.

"Hey, it was a great cape! I thought it gave me superpowers," he defends, mock indignation on his face, and I can't help but roll my eyes, laughing at the sheer innocence of that moment. We had spent that night racing through the neighborhood, filled with candy and laughter, the world feeling limitless.

Those innocent times weave through my mind, an intricate tapestry of youthful joy and whimsical aspirations. I wonder how we had allowed the weight of adulthood to smother the vibrant colors of our past. It's in this shared laughter, though, that I begin to understand the power of revisiting those memories—the way they can act as stepping stones toward healing.

As we wander toward the park, I catch glimpses of children playing, their shrieks of laughter piercing through the evening air. A game of tag unfolds under the watchful eyes of parents, each child darting about with carefree abandon, the essence of freedom palpable. I yearn for that simplicity, that unfiltered joy, and for a moment, I imagine running beside them, the weight of the world lifted from my shoulders.

"Shall we?" Jason asks, his eyes gleaming with mischief, and before I can protest, he's pulling me toward the grassy expanse, the scent of damp earth and grass welcoming us. We join in the playful chaos, darting between the swaying bodies, and I can feel the adrenaline coursing through my veins, igniting a long-dormant spark of excitement.

For a fleeting moment, I forget everything—the anxiety, the insecurities that had plagued me during our time apart. Instead, I revel in the joy of the present, of reconnecting with a piece of myself that had been tucked away. Jason's laughter is infectious, and it spills over into me, igniting a warmth that wraps around my heart. We dart through the throng of children, dodging and weaving like two playful shadows, giggling as we tumble to the grass, breathless and alive.

Once we settle, lying side by side, the stars begin to emerge, dots of light painting the canvas of the night sky. I tilt my head back, the expanse feeling infinite above us, and the calmness envelops me like a gentle wave. "You know," I say, turning to Jason, "sometimes I think about how far we've come, and how easy it was to lose sight of what mattered."

He nods, his gaze drifting toward the heavens. "It's like we got caught up in the rush of everything—work, responsibilities. It can be suffocating." There's a solemnity in his tone, a reflection of the burdens we both carry, and I can feel the gravity of his words.

"I guess I was afraid," I admit, the truth spilling from my lips like a hidden treasure. "Afraid that if I opened up, I'd get lost in the chaos again." The vulnerability hangs in the air between us, heavy yet freeing, and I can sense him processing my admission, weighing it with his own fears.

"Me too," he finally says, the sincerity in his voice pulling at my heartstrings. "But sitting here, it feels like we're finding our way back—like there's a light guiding us home."

And just like that, the whisper of hope becomes louder, reverberating through the quiet night. It's in these shared truths, this delicate honesty, that I realize how much we've both grown, how our struggles have shaped us into the individuals we are today.

The park around us seems to fade, the world narrowing down to just the two of us, nestled in our cocoon of understanding. The laughter of the children becomes a distant echo, the stars above our witness as we traverse the uncharted territory of our hearts.

"I'm glad you reached out," Jason says, his voice low and sincere, the shadows of doubt that had lingered dissipating like mist in the morning sun. "I was terrified of losing you completely, of letting this slip away."

I squeeze his hand, the warmth igniting a flicker of resolve within me. "We can't let that happen again. I want to be in this, whatever 'this' is, together."

And in that moment, the path ahead opens up, vast and inviting, with the promise of adventure and laughter woven into its fabric. No longer do I feel the weight of uncertainty dragging me down. Instead, there's a lightness, a buoyancy that propels us forward.

The night continues to unfold, and as we share stories, dreams, and fears, I can't help but wonder what else lies ahead in this new chapter. The whispers of hope dance in the air around us, and I am reminded that love, despite its challenges, can create a world filled with endless possibilities.

The evening deepens, and the city transforms as if under a spell. The streetlights glow with a gentle luminescence, illuminating the path as Jason and I stroll side by side, our hands still entwined. With each step, I feel the warmth radiating between us, a silent affirmation that we are no longer drifting apart but finding our way back to each other. The sounds of the city fade, and the world shrinks to just us—two hearts navigating the complexities of love, loss, and everything in between.

As we walk, I can't help but notice how the city takes on a more intimate character at night. The hustle and bustle of the day melts away, revealing a softer side—one that cradles the laughter of couples strolling along the sidewalks and the hushed conversations spilling out from nearby restaurants. Each corner we turn feels like a doorway to another shared memory, each flickering light a reminder of the moments that have shaped our relationship.

"Remember that time we got caught in the rain?" I ask, a smile creeping onto my lips as I recall the spontaneous adventure that turned a mundane day into something magical. The memory is vivid, as if it happened only yesterday.

Jason chuckles, his laughter rich and infectious. "How could I forget? We were drenched, running for cover under that awning while trying to protect our coffee!" His eyes sparkle with mirth, the shared memory radiating warmth that banishes any lingering chill in the air.

"We ended up laughing so hard that I almost forgot how cold I was," I reply, shaking my head at the absurdity of our youth. "We were so wrapped up in each other that the world faded away."

"Exactly," he says, nodding in agreement, "that's what I've missed the most—how everything else just disappeared when we were together."

With that simple statement, something inside me shifts. It's as if the weight of the past—of misunderstandings and the silence that had crept between us—begins to lift. In its place, a sense of clarity emerges, a realization that we are not only reconnecting with our past selves but also crafting a new narrative together.

We find ourselves wandering toward the riverfront, the gentle lapping of water against the shore mirroring the rhythm of our hearts. The moon hangs low in the sky, casting a silvery glow over the rippling surface, and for a moment, I'm lost in the beauty of it all. It feels like a scene from a movie, the kind that makes your heart swell with hope, yet here we are, living it.

"Let's sit for a while," Jason suggests, gesturing toward a bench that overlooks the water. I nod, grateful for the chance to pause and take in the moment. As we settle, the cool metal beneath us contrasts with the warmth of our joined hands, and I feel a surge of contentment wash over me.

The city glimmers around us—reflections of lights dancing on the water, a symphony of soft sounds that create a soothing backdrop. I take a deep breath, letting the serenity of the evening envelop me. "This feels like a dream," I whisper, almost afraid to break the spell.

"It really does," he agrees, his gaze fixed on the water, lost in thought. After a moment, he turns to me, a more serious expression settling on his features. "I want you to know that I've been working on myself while we were apart. I've realized how important it is to communicate, to really talk about what we feel, rather than letting it fester."

His honesty resonates deeply within me, a chord struck in the symphony of my heart. "I've been doing the same," I reply, my voice steady. "It's hard to put yourself out there, to be vulnerable. But I see now that without that openness, we can't grow."

Jason nods, the moonlight casting shadows across his face, highlighting the sincerity in his eyes. "I want us to be better—together. No more running away. I want to build something real, something that lasts."

The sincerity of his words washes over me, filling the gaps that doubt had created. "I want that too," I admit, my heart racing with the promise of new beginnings.

We sit in comfortable silence for a moment, allowing the weight of our words to settle between us, before he continues, "Let's make a pact. No matter what life throws at us, we promise to face it together. We can't let fear dictate our choices anymore."

I smile at his earnestness, feeling the truth in his proposition resonate with my own desires. "Agreed," I say, squeezing his hand tighter. "Let's promise to always communicate, to be honest about our fears and our dreams. I don't want to lose you again."

He leans closer, his voice a whisper as if sharing a secret with the universe. "No matter what happens, I'm here. You're my person, and I won't let go."

In that moment, the air crackles with a newfound energy, a promise that wraps around us like a delicate thread, binding us closer together. The uncertainties that lay ahead seem a little less daunting, the shadows of the past fading as we step into the light of possibility.

As the night wears on, we share stories, hopes, and even a few fears that still linger like stubborn ghosts. The conversation flows effortlessly, punctuated by laughter and the occasional soft sigh as we uncover pieces of ourselves that had been hidden. It's a slow unveiling, like peeling back the layers of an onion, each revelation bringing us closer, each word echoing with the intimacy of shared experiences.

The stars twinkle above, and I lean back against the bench, feeling lighter than I have in ages. It's as if the universe is conspired to remind us of the beauty of second chances and the magic of love that can heal even the deepest wounds. I catch Jason's eye, and in that moment, I see a future woven with threads of hope and dreams—a future that feels both exciting and attainable.

The moon hangs high, a silent guardian of our revelations, and as I sit beside Jason, I realize that this is what it means to truly connect—to embrace the complexities of love and to let the whispers of hope guide us forward. The night stretches out before us, brimming with possibilities, and I know, without a doubt, that together, we can navigate whatever challenges life may present.

In this moment, enveloped by the night, I feel as if I've finally found my way home—not just to Jason, but to myself. As we sit side by side, our dreams and fears entwined, I can't help but smile at the future waiting just beyond the horizon. Whatever awaits us, I'm ready to face it, hand in hand with the person I've always been meant to share this journey with.

Chapter 20: The Calm Before the Storm

The sun dipped below the horizon, casting a warm, golden hue over the expansive Los Angeles skyline, a shimmering patchwork of glass and steel that held the dreams of countless souls. As the shadows lengthened, I sat cross-legged on the worn wooden floor of our studio, surrounded by a vibrant array of canvases, brushes, and half-finished sculptures that bore witness to our collective passion. The scent of turpentine mingled with the faint aroma of coffee, creating an intoxicating blend that fueled our creativity. My heart thrummed in rhythm with the bustling city outside, each beat resonating with the frenetic energy that pulsed through the streets below.

Jason stood a few feet away, his gaze fixed on a particularly vivid painting splashed with hues of cerulean and burnt sienna. It was a representation of chaos, swirling shapes and lines that seemed to cry out for attention. Yet, as I watched him, I could see the tension lurking in the corners of his mouth and the tightness in his shoulders. His hands, so skilled and confident, trembled slightly as he adjusted the easel. I reached for my own canvas, trying to channel the unease that mirrored his. With each stroke, I sought to capture the bittersweet sensation of fleeting moments, the beauty intertwined with the anxiety that clung to us like a heavy fog.

Despite the uncertainty swirling around us, our rehearsals were becoming a ritual, a cathartic escape that allowed us to weave our lives together through art. We had decided to collaborate on a showcase, a project that promised to elevate our work and open doors to new talent, new opportunities. The anticipation was palpable, yet the weight of my friend's struggles hung like a dark cloud over our creativity. Lucy had been battling her demons, and I found myself constantly torn between supporting her and pushing forward with my own aspirations. It felt as if we were all teetering on the edge of something momentous, and I could sense the storm brewing just beyond the horizon.

The studio came alive with the sounds of laughter and the rustle of paintbrushes as fellow artists trickled in, each one bringing a unique spark to the atmosphere. I loved this space, our sanctuary, where we could shed our masks and share our rawest selves with one another. Yet, the laughter felt distant as I caught Jason's eye, and we exchanged a knowing glance that spoke volumes. There was an unspoken understanding between us, a bond forged through our shared vulnerabilities and the unsteady ground we navigated. He moved closer, the scent of paint and sandalwood enveloping him as he whispered, "What if we take a break? Get some fresh air?"

Grateful for the distraction, I nodded, my heart racing at the thought of stepping outside the comforting chaos of our sanctuary. We strolled hand in hand down the bustling streets of downtown, the air thick with the sounds of city life—honking horns, snippets of conversations, and the distant strumming of a street musician's guitar. The vibrant murals that adorned the walls seemed to echo the unfiltered essence of our surroundings, each stroke of paint telling a story of resilience and hope. As we walked, I let the energy of the city wash over me, infusing me with a sense of purpose.

We settled on a bench nestled in a small park, the faint sounds of laughter from children playing nearby adding a touch of innocence to the urban landscape. The park was a hidden gem, a slice of tranquility amid the chaos, where the laughter of friends mingled with the rustling leaves overhead. I leaned back, feeling the sun's gentle warmth on my skin, and exhaled slowly, as if releasing the tension that had been coiling tightly in my chest.

"Do you ever think about how far we've come?" Jason mused, his voice a soft murmur as he studied the clouds drifting lazily across the sky. "From those late-night sessions in the apartment to this—our own studio, a showcase to look forward to." His eyes sparkled with a mix of nostalgia and hope, and I felt my heart swell with affection for him. He had become my anchor in the storm, the steady presence that kept me grounded when everything around us felt precarious.

"Absolutely," I replied, my voice barely above a whisper as I tucked a loose strand of hair behind my ear. "But sometimes I wonder if we're just on borrowed time. Like, what if it all falls apart?" The words spilled out before I could stop them, the vulnerability slipping through the cracks of my carefully constructed façade. Jason turned to me, his expression softening, the flicker of doubt I had seen earlier momentarily replaced by something resolute.

"Then we build it back up," he said, his tone unwavering. "That's the beauty of art, of life. It's all about creating something new, no matter how many times we stumble." His confidence enveloped me like a warm blanket, and I felt my fears begin to dissipate, if only slightly. The storm may have been looming, but perhaps there was solace in knowing we had each other to navigate through it.

As the sun dipped lower, painting the sky in hues of orange and pink, I felt a renewed sense of determination. We were artists, after all, resilient in our pursuit of beauty amid chaos. Whatever challenges lay ahead, we would face them together, ready to embrace the calm before the storm.

The days melted into one another, the sweet cadence of routine gently lulling me into a false sense of security. Mornings were greeted with the rich aroma of freshly brewed coffee, the clinking of paintbrushes against glass palettes punctuating the quiet solitude of the studio. We painted, sculpted, and molded our ideas into tangible forms, each stroke an intimate dance between intention and emotion. I often lost myself in the rhythm of creation, relishing the way the colors seemed to sing on the canvas. Yet, beneath this vibrant surface, the undercurrents of my concerns stirred like an impending storm, unsettling the calm.

Jason had a way of coaxing beauty from chaos, and I cherished our collaborative moments. His laughter reverberated through the studio like a familiar song, grounding me when self-doubt crept in like an uninvited guest. Still, there were instances—glimmers in the twilight of our interactions—when I sensed a fissure in his confidence. The way he bit his lip while contemplating a piece or the brief moments of silence that stretched just a little too long felt like harbingers of something unwelcome. I had to wonder if my anxieties were clouding my perception or if he was, too, feeling the weight of unspoken fears.

One particularly sultry afternoon, we decided to take a break from the studio, drawn by the allure of the nearby Venice Beach. The sun hung high, casting a golden sheen on the lively boardwalk, where artists and street performers showcased their talents. The salty breeze intertwined with the tantalizing aroma of kettle corn, wafting through the air like a siren's call. It was a place where creativity thrived, where people came to lose themselves in the beauty of spontaneity. We strolled along the sandy path, our fingers intertwined, as waves crashed rhythmically against the shore, a steady heartbeat in the midst of our chaotic lives.

We found a patch of sand near the water's edge, the grains warm beneath us as we settled down to absorb the atmosphere. The beach was a vibrant tapestry of life; children squealed with delight, chasing the surf as it ebbed and flowed, while couples strolled hand in hand, their laughter mingling with the cries of seagulls overhead. In that moment, I felt a sense of belonging, a kinship with the world around me. I turned to Jason, his sun-kissed skin glistening with beads of seawater, and felt a rush of affection that warmed me from the inside out.

"Do you remember our first trip to the beach?" I asked, laughing as I nudged him playfully with my shoulder. "We thought we were artists, but we just ended up covered in sand and ice cream."

He chuckled, the sound a low rumble that sent a thrill through me. "I think I still have a picture of you with chocolate all over your face. A masterpiece in its own right." His teasing smile was infectious, and I felt a rush of warmth, a flicker of the joy we had shared back then. It was comforting, a gentle reminder of the simplicity we often overlooked in the hustle of our artistic pursuits.

As the sun began its descent, painting the sky with streaks of lavender and fiery orange, I caught sight of a busker nearby, strumming a guitar with a soulful intensity. The music floated through the air, wrapping around us like a soft embrace. I closed my eyes, letting the melody wash over me, every note resonating with the bittersweet longing I had been feeling. The world around me faded, and for a moment, it felt like the music held the answers to all my questions.

Jason leaned closer, his voice barely above a whisper. "Let's create something inspired by this moment," he said, his eyes glinting with excitement. "The colors, the sounds, everything. We can capture this feeling."

A thrill raced through me at the thought of blending our experiences into our art, creating a piece that would transcend the ordinary and reflect our shared journey. I nodded eagerly, already envisioning how we could weave together the essence of the beach with our own stories. "What if we incorporate elements of our lives—the colors we see, the sounds that linger?"

He grinned, his enthusiasm contagious. "Yes! We can use layers to represent the complexity of our emotions. The storm brewing beneath the surface could be a central theme, perhaps with brighter colors swirling above to signify hope."

As the final rays of sunlight dipped below the horizon, we began to sketch our ideas in the sand, our fingers dancing together in the grains. It felt like we were weaving our dreams into the fabric of the earth itself, capturing the fleeting moments that made life so vibrantly chaotic. With each mark, I felt a renewed sense of purpose, as if the universe was aligning, urging us to embrace the tempest that lay ahead.

The sun had vanished, leaving a canvas of stars twinkling above us, illuminating the beach in a soft glow. We sat in silence, the rhythmic sound of waves crashing against the shore melding with the gentle strumming of the busker's guitar. It was an exquisite moment suspended in time, a brief respite from the challenges looming just beyond the horizon.

But as I glanced at Jason, a shadow flickered across his face, momentarily overshadowing the joy that had filled the space between us. His brow furrowed slightly, as if grappling with thoughts that clashed with our beautiful surroundings. "I just... I want this to be perfect," he murmured, almost to himself, the vulnerability in his voice sending a pang through my heart.

"Perfection isn't the goal, Jason," I reassured him, reaching for his hand. "It's about authenticity, about being true to ourselves and our journey. That's what connects us to our art—and each other."

He looked at me, the doubt in his eyes momentarily eclipsed by a flicker of understanding. In that instant, the world fell away, leaving just the two of us, vulnerable yet connected, riding the waves of our uncharted emotions. The beach, once a chaotic blur of sounds and colors, transformed into a sanctuary where we could be raw, unfiltered, and honest.

The music continued to drift through the air, the night alive with possibilities. And as we gazed out at the vast, endless ocean, a quiet determination settled within me. We would navigate whatever storm awaited us, together, bound by our art and an unwavering belief in the beauty of the journey ahead.

The beach had left an indelible mark on our hearts, a lingering echo of laughter and shared dreams that danced on the edges of my consciousness. As the evening wore on, we returned to the studio, the air heavy with unspoken words and creative fervor. The darkness outside clung to the windows like an unwelcome specter, but inside, we were wrapped in a cocoon of our own making. The dim light of the studio illuminated the canvases that had become extensions of ourselves, each one a testament to our struggles, hopes, and triumphs. I set to work immediately, feeling the remnants of the beach still swirling around us, guiding my brush with an urgency I hadn't felt in weeks.

The rhythm of our brushes against the canvases became a dialogue, a way of communicating the thoughts we often left unsaid. Jason's energy pulsed through the room as he immersed himself in his work, the vibrant colors exploding from his palette as he captured the essence of the evening we had just shared. I marveled at his talent, the way he breathed life into every stroke, transforming emotions into visual symphonies. And yet, a nagging sensation clung to the edges of my thoughts—a reminder that while we were enveloped in our creativity, the world outside was shifting beneath us.

Late into the night, I glanced at Jason, who was lost in his own artistic reverie, the intensity of his focus drawing me in. The shadows played tricks on his features, illuminating his cheekbones and casting a gentle light over the soft waves of his hair. My heart fluttered with a mixture of admiration and concern. This was the man who had captured my heart and who now stood at the precipice of something monumental, his potential unfolding before us like a flower daring to bloom amidst the chaos.

"Jason," I said softly, breaking the silence that had settled over us like a blanket. He paused, paintbrush hovering over the canvas, and turned his attention toward me, his expression a blend of curiosity and warmth. "How are you feeling about everything? The showcase, the work... us?"

He sighed, a sound that felt heavy with unexpressed thoughts. "I don't know. Some days, I feel like we're on the brink of something incredible, and other days, it feels like a house of cards waiting to collapse." His honesty struck me, resonating with the very essence of my own doubts.

"Yeah, I get that," I replied, my voice barely above a whisper. "But isn't that what makes it all worth it? The risk? The unpredictability? It's like standing at the edge of a cliff, right before you leap into the unknown."

A flicker of understanding ignited in his eyes, and for a moment, we shared a silence filled with possibilities. I couldn't help but admire how his mind worked, how he articulated the complexities of our shared journey. The weight of our ambitions rested heavily on our shoulders, but in this small studio, we had created our own universe—one filled with color, passion, and vulnerability.

As the clock ticked into the early hours of the morning, we lost ourselves in our art, the tension from earlier melting away with each brushstroke. The world beyond our walls faded into obscurity, leaving only the raw essence of our creativity. With each stroke, I began to weave our fears into the fabric of my painting, layers of color and emotion reflecting the storm brewing just beneath the surface.

Yet, as dawn approached, a knock on the studio door jolted us from our reverie. The sound was sharp, jarring against the gentle hum of our artistic flow. I exchanged a glance with Jason, a mix of apprehension and curiosity shadowing our expressions. He hesitated, then moved to open the door, revealing Lucy, her figure illuminated by the soft glow of morning light.

Her expression was a tapestry of emotions—concern, hope, and an underlying sense of urgency that made my heart race. "Hey, can I come in?" she asked, her voice barely breaking the silence.

"Of course," I said, stepping aside to let her in, my heart sinking slightly as I noticed the worry etched on her face. This was the moment I had been dreading, the one where everything we had built together teetered on the brink of uncertainty.

"I didn't mean to intrude," she said, glancing at the scattered canvases that littered the floor. "But I felt like I needed to talk to you both. I've been struggling, and it's getting harder to keep pretending everything's okay."

The vulnerability in her voice wrapped around us like a cocoon, binding our three souls together in that moment. I stepped forward, instinctively reaching for her hand, squeezing it gently as I met her gaze. "You're not alone, Lucy. We're here for you, no matter what."

Jason nodded, his expression softening as he stepped closer. "We're all in this together. Whatever you need to share, we're ready to listen."

Lucy exhaled shakily, her shoulders slumping as if the weight of the world had pressed down on her. "I don't want to bring you both down, but I feel like I'm losing myself. The pressure to succeed, to keep up with everything—it's suffocating. And it's hard to watch you both thrive while I feel like I'm sinking."

Tears glistened in her eyes, and my heart ached for her. She had always been the strong one, the anchor in our group, and seeing her so vulnerable stirred a fierce protective instinct within me. "You've always been our rock, Lucy," I said softly. "But even rocks can erode over time. It's okay to feel this way. It doesn't make you any less of an artist or a friend."

Jason added, "We'll figure this out together. Maybe we can help each other. The showcase is coming up, and we can incorporate your ideas into our pieces. You have so much to offer, Lucy, and we need your voice in this."

Lucy looked up at us, uncertainty mingling with hope in her expression. "You really think so? I feel like I've lost my way."

I stepped forward, wrapping my arms around her, pulling her into a comforting embrace. "We'll help you find it again. Your perspective is invaluable, and we won't let you go through this alone."

As we held each other, the weight of the moment settled upon us like a warm blanket. It was a quiet reminder that storms would come, but together we could weather any tempest.

With the sun rising outside, the light flooded the studio, illuminating the colors we had been so passionately creating. I felt a shift within me, a spark igniting hope as we prepared to face the challenges ahead. This was just the beginning of our journey, a chance to reclaim our paths while supporting one another through the darkness. The world outside was vast and uncertain, but within these walls, we had each other—our sanctuary amidst the chaos. And as we began to craft a new vision, blending our art, struggles, and aspirations, I knew we were forging something extraordinary, a testament to the power of friendship and creativity.

Chapter 21: Unexpected Revelations

The sun dipped below the horizon, spilling golden hues across the sprawling expanse of the American Midwest. Dust motes danced in the last rays of light, caught in the air like tiny fireflies amidst the fading warmth. The studio, nestled on a quiet street of clapboard houses adorned with swinging porch swings and vibrant flower boxes, buzzed with anticipation. My heart thudded in syncopated rhythm with the pulsing bass filtering through the floorboards. It was a cozy yet charged atmosphere, one where dreams took flight amid the scent of sweat and ambition.

As I adjusted the fabric of my rehearsal skirt, the soft, worn material brushing against my legs like a gentle reminder of countless hours spent in this space, I could almost hear the echoes of past performances swirling around me. Each corner of the studio held a memory—an ensemble of laughter, tears, and unyielding determination. Lena, with her fiery spirit and captivating stories, had become my confidante, weaving tales of dancers who had faced trials akin to mine. Her voice, rich and textured like a tapestry, transported me to a world where pain transformed into beauty.

"Do you know about Mabel?" she had asked me one afternoon, her emerald eyes sparkling with mischief. "She was a powerhouse in the 80s, faced injuries that would have broken lesser dancers. But instead of giving up, she turned her pain into a masterpiece." I leaned in closer, captivated. "She danced her story, every movement laced with raw emotion. It was like she was painting with her body."

Those words resonated, wrapping around my heart like a comforting embrace. Suddenly, my struggles didn't feel insurmountable; they felt like an integral part of my artistic journey. I was not just a dancer; I was a storyteller, and my choreography could convey the depths of my experiences. The revelation ignited a spark within me. What if my own journey could inspire others? The thought pulsed through my veins like adrenaline, invigorating and terrifying in equal measure.

That evening, as twilight blanketed the studio, I found myself alone, the gentle hum of the overhead lights a soft companion in my solitude. I stood at the center of the wooden floor, the polished surface reflecting the fading light like a mirror to my soul. Closing my eyes, I let the music wash over me, its rhythm echoing the beating of my heart. The melodies intertwined with my memories, each note a thread in the fabric of my existence, pulling me deeper into my own narrative.

I began to move, my body following the guidance of the music, every step a deliberate act of creation. My memories surged to the surface—moments of triumph and despair, the laughter of friends, the sting of rejection. The choreography flowed from me like a river, carving its path through the landscape of my spirit. I became both the dancer and the dance, each movement a brushstroke on the canvas of my life. I felt the warmth of the studio embrace me, the walls pulsating with the energy of my artistry.

The door creaked open, a familiar figure entering the space, casting a long shadow across the floor. Jason stood there, his presence both grounding and exhilarating. He had a way of watching that felt like he was peeling back the layers of my soul, uncovering the rawness I often kept hidden. As I continued to move, I caught his gaze, the intensity of his admiration igniting a fire within me. I poured every ounce of emotion into my performance, feeling the boundaries between us blur as our artistic spirits intertwined. His appreciation was like a lifeline, connecting me to the deeper essence of what I was creating.

"Keep going," he urged softly, his voice a whisper amidst the rhythm. "You're telling a story that needs to be heard." His encouragement wrapped around me, giving me the confidence to delve further into my vulnerability. The dance evolved, morphing from a mere expression of my struggles into a profound exploration of resilience and hope. I could feel the room around me fade away, the world outside the studio disappearing as I embraced this journey of self-discovery.

With each movement, I could see fragments of my life crystallize into clarity. The pain I had endured, the moments I felt invisible, and the triumphs that punctuated my journey—all of it intertwined seamlessly into a narrative I could finally own. I was no longer just a dancer; I was the embodiment of a tale that needed to be shared, a voice echoing through the silence that often cloaked the struggles of so many others.

As I reached the climax of the choreography, a surge of emotion coursed through me, the kind that demands to be shared. I opened my eyes and found Jason standing at the edge of the room, his expression a mix of awe and understanding. In that moment, I realized that my story was not just mine to tell; it belonged to anyone who had ever felt marginalized or lost. Through the artistry of dance, I could carve a space for those voices to resonate.

When the final note faded into silence, I stood breathless, my body humming with the remnants of my performance. Jason stepped forward, his smile wide and infectious, a beacon of support in the dim light of the studio. "That was incredible," he said, his voice thick with emotion. "You've taken something deeply personal and turned it into something powerful. You're going to inspire so many."

His words hung in the air, a promise of what lay ahead. For the first time in a long while, I felt a flicker of hope ignite within me—a quiet assurance that the journey ahead would be marked not just by my struggles but by the strength I would harness to illuminate the path for others.

The following days unfurled like the pages of a well-worn book, each one revealing a new layer of excitement and uncertainty. The countdown to the showcase hung in the air, palpable and heavy, a ticking clock that thrummed with the heartbeat of our anticipation. With each sunrise, I felt the urge to practice pulse through my veins, the choreography transforming from a collection of movements into a lifeline that connected my soul to the stage. The studio became my sanctuary, a place where the echoes of laughter and sweat mingled with the fragrance of polished wood and the lingering scent of chalk from the floor.

Lena's stories replayed in my mind like a film reel, each dancer's struggle serving as a testament to resilience. I found myself captivated not just by their triumphs but by the ways they navigated their darkest moments. Mabel's tenacity ignited a fire within me that refused to dim. As I choreographed, I became a curator of my own narrative, blending sorrow and strength into each movement, transforming the agony of doubt into a breathtaking declaration of hope. The dance became a ritual, a sacred practice through which I unearthed the scars I had carefully tucked away.

One afternoon, after a particularly grueling rehearsal, I flopped onto the worn couch in the corner of the studio, the fabric cool against my overheated skin. Jason settled beside me, a playful grin lighting up his face. He always had this magnetic energy, a spark that made the room feel alive. "You know, you really should consider a career in writing," he teased, nudging me with his elbow. "Those choreographic musings of yours are practically poetry."

I chuckled, brushing my damp hair out of my eyes. "If I did, I'd probably pen a novel about all the ways I trip over my own feet." The truth was, writing had always been a private indulgence, a secret I kept hidden behind layers of self-doubt. But as Jason laughed, a warm sound that wrapped around me like a familiar blanket, I felt a flicker of possibility. Maybe there was a way to bridge my love for dance with the written word, to capture the stories that moved through my body in a form that others could hold in their hands.

Our conversations flowed effortlessly, like the intricate patterns of a well-executed pirouette, each word spinning gracefully into the next. I shared my dreams of choreography infused with narrative, how the emotions of my past could shape a performance that resonated with others. Jason listened intently, his eyes shining with understanding. "You're not just a dancer; you're a storyteller," he said, his voice steady and sincere. "Your experiences give your movements depth. That's what makes your art so compelling."

His faith in me was like a warm tide, washing over my insecurities and washing them away, leaving behind a sense of clarity. I found myself longing for more moments like this, for conversations that sparked creativity and ignited inspiration. Perhaps I wasn't meant to fit into any preconceived mold; perhaps my path was one of weaving together various threads of artistry.

As we sat in the fading light, the sun painting the studio in hues of amber and rose, I felt a surge of gratitude. Jason had a way of illuminating the world around me, revealing the beauty in the mundane. He spoke of the struggles he faced in his own artistic endeavors—how rejection was as much a part of the creative process as inspiration. Each story he shared resonated, echoing my own fears and aspirations, reinforcing the notion that we were kindred spirits navigating our artistic journeys together.

The next day, with the showcase drawing ever nearer, I decided to take a leap. I began incorporating small elements of spoken word into my choreography, weaving together snippets of my own reflections and experiences. Each rehearsal became an exploration, an opportunity to fuse the lyrical with the physical. The studio transformed into my canvas, and I danced with abandon, expressing the complexities of my emotions through every flourish of my limbs. The movement flowed through me like a river, carving pathways in the landscape of my soul.

As I practiced, I could feel the rhythm of my heart aligning with the pulse of the music. Each step became a declaration, each leap an act of defiance against the fears that had once held me captive. I envisioned the audience, their faces illuminated in the soft glow of the stage lights, waiting to be swept away by the story I was about to tell. My narrative was evolving, moving beyond mere performance into something profound—an invitation to share in my journey.

With each passing day, my confidence blossomed like the wildflowers that peppered the fields outside the studio. I reveled in the act of creation, in the way my body moved with newfound freedom. I was no longer just a dancer, confined to the constraints of technique; I was an artist, daring to bleed my truth into the fabric of my art. The intimacy of movement combined with the weight of my words was intoxicating, and I couldn't help but wonder what the audience would feel when they witnessed my evolution on stage.

The rehearsal before the showcase arrived, and as I stood before the mirror, I caught a glimpse of the dancer I had become. The reflection looking back at me was no longer shadowed by doubt; it was vibrant and full of life, ready to take flight. My heart raced with anticipation, each thump echoing the rhythm of my resolve. I closed my eyes, letting the music envelop me, each note a call to embrace the power of my voice—both spoken and unspoken.

When I opened my eyes, Jason stood at the edge of the studio, his expression a blend of admiration and encouragement. As I began to move, I poured everything into the choreography, each motion infused with the energy of my journey. I was no longer just performing; I was living my story, and with each step, I felt the audience already reaching out, eager to grasp the essence of what I had to offer.

The day of the showcase arrived cloaked in an electric atmosphere, the air thick with anticipation that hung like the hum of a low note from a well-tuned piano. The sun emerged lazily from behind a curtain of clouds, casting a warm glow that ignited the vibrant colors of the city. The streets outside the studio thrummed with energy, voices rising and falling like the undulating waves of a symphony. I could feel that energy wrapping around me, urging me forward, pulling me into the heartbeat of the moment.

Dressing for the performance became a ritual, a sacred act of preparation that transformed the ordinary into the extraordinary. I stood in front of the mirror, the fabric of my costume shimmering under the studio lights. Each bead glinted like the stars I had always dreamt of reaching, a constellation of aspirations sewn into the very seams of the outfit. As I adorned myself, I became acutely aware of the significance behind every choice: the way the skirt flowed around my legs, the way the colors echoed the emotions I intended to convey. I was no longer just preparing for a performance; I was preparing to share a part of my soul.

As I applied my makeup with a steady hand, I lost myself in the reflection, searching for the dancer who had once felt uncertain, unsure if she belonged on this stage. But now, there was a fire ignited deep within, illuminating every facet of who I had become. My eyes sparkled with determination, mirroring the vibrant energy of the city outside. I could almost hear the distant sounds of the audience gathering, their chatter a warm breeze that rustled through the curtains, teasing the fabric of my resolve.

The backstage area buzzed with fellow dancers, each one a vibrant thread in the tapestry of our collective endeavor. Laughter mixed with nervous whispers, the air thick with shared dreams and unspoken fears. I found Lena in the corner, her eyes bright and reassuring. "Remember, you're not just telling your story; you're inviting them into your world," she said, her words settling over me like a soothing balm. I nodded, her unwavering support fortifying my spirit. The warmth of camaraderie filled the space, reminding me that we were all in this together.

When it was finally my turn, the moment felt surreal. As I stepped onto the stage, the spotlight enveloped me in a cocoon of brilliance. The audience, a sea of faces blurring together in a mosaic of anticipation, fell silent, the tension palpable. I could feel my heart racing in my chest, the echo of its beat thrumming through my body. Each breath I took became a whispered promise, a commitment to lay my truth bare before them.

As the music swelled, I closed my eyes for a fleeting moment, allowing the melody to wash over me, its familiar embrace igniting the embers of my spirit. The opening notes resonated like a call to arms, urging me to unleash the narrative I had woven through countless rehearsals. I began to move, each step a conversation with the audience, each turn an exploration of the emotions that had guided my journey.

My body became a vessel, flowing seamlessly through the choreography, an extension of my heart and mind. I poured everything into that dance, every ounce of joy, heartache, and determination merging into a performance that felt like a living testament to my growth. I envisioned Mabel, Lena, and every dancer who had come before me, their spirits guiding me as I embraced the power of storytelling through movement.

As I twirled, the fabric of my skirt billowed around me, creating a visual metaphor for the turbulence of my experiences. Each leap was a triumph, each landing a moment of resilience, and the transitions became a graceful dance between the shadows of doubt and the light of possibility. The audience was with me, their breaths synchronized with my movements, their energy a tangible force propelling me forward.

When I reached the climax of my performance, words spilled from my lips, unplanned yet urgent, pouring out in a raw, poetic expression of my truth. "We are the stories we tell, woven from our pain, our dreams, our very essence." The words hung in the air, heavy with meaning, binding me to the audience in an unspoken connection that transcended the boundaries of stage and seat.

As the final notes faded, I stood in silence, the weight of the moment hanging around me like an echo. The applause that erupted felt like a warm wave crashing over me, enveloping me in affirmation and acceptance. I blinked back tears, overwhelmed by the beauty of vulnerability and the power of sharing one's truth. Each clap was a reminder that I was not alone; my journey had resonated, weaving itself into the hearts of those who had come to witness it.

When I finally stepped off the stage, the adrenaline coursing through my veins, Jason was waiting for me, his eyes glistening with pride. "That was incredible," he said, pulling me into a fierce embrace. I could feel the warmth radiating from him, a comforting presence that grounded me in the aftermath of such an emotional whirlwind. "You were amazing out there. You turned your pain into art, and you made it shine."

In that moment, surrounded by the echoes of applause and the lingering notes of my performance, I felt a profound sense of fulfillment. I had shared not just a dance but a piece of myself. The vulnerability I had embraced transformed into strength, a testament to the resilience of the human spirit.

The night carried on, laughter and celebration blending into the fabric of the evening. We gathered with our fellow dancers, the room abuzz with stories and shared experiences. I felt a sense of belonging that had eluded me for so long, a community bound by our shared struggles and triumphs. We were artists, storytellers, each with our unique narrative woven into the greater tapestry of this world.

As the night drew to a close, I stepped outside, the crisp night air wrapping around me like a reassuring hug. The stars twinkled above, a reminder of the infinite possibilities that lay ahead. I took a deep breath, the weight of the evening settling comfortably on my shoulders. I was ready to embrace the journey that awaited, armed with the knowledge that my story was powerful, worthy, and capable of inspiring others. In that moment, I felt the promise of the future bloom within me—a vibrant seed of hope, ready to take root and flourish.

Chapter 22: Crossroads of Trust

The neon lights flickered above me as I stepped onto the bustling streets of New Orleans, the air thick with the sweet scent of magnolias and the salty tang of the nearby Mississippi River. It was one of those evenings where the vibrant chaos of the city pulsed through every cobblestone, every crevice of the lively French Quarter. I could hear the distant notes of jazz swirling through the humid air, wrapping around me like a lover's embrace, beckoning me to forget my troubles, to lose myself in the rhythm of a place that thrived on stories. But tonight, the melodies felt discordant against the frantic beat of my heart.

The call had come just hours ago, a jagged whisper through the phone that shattered my world like a dropped glass ornament. Lucy was in trouble. I could hardly breathe as I raced through the crowded streets, weaving between tourists with their eager laughter and locals whose laughter was tempered by the weight of survival. Each step was a prayer, a desperate plea to the universe that she would still be okay when I arrived. I had always thought of New Orleans as my sanctuary, a haven where my dreams could blossom amidst the vibrant chaos, but now it felt like a maze, each turn leading me further away from the sanctuary of my dreams and deeper into a place of shadows.

As I approached her apartment, I could see the flickering light through the window, a beacon of hope that was gradually dimming. It was a modest building, the paint peeling like the skin of a sunburnt tourist, with wrought iron balconies draped in climbing ivy. I had spent many evenings here, sharing laughter and dreams over cups of chicory coffee and half-eaten beignets, the sound of Lucy's laughter lighting up even the darkest corners of my heart. But tonight, as I climbed the stairs, each creak of the wood beneath my feet felt like a drumbeat of dread.

The door swung open, revealing Lucy, her eyes wild and red-rimmed, as though she had been crying for hours, or maybe days. My heart plummeted at the sight of her disheveled hair, clinging to her forehead like the tendrils of despair that wrapped around her. I wanted to gather her in my arms and erase all the hurt that had etched itself on her delicate features, but the moment was electric, fraught with unspoken accusations and buried feelings.

"Where have you been?" Her voice cracked, each syllable laced with betrayal. "I thought you were my friend, but you've been too busy chasing your dreams to notice that I'm drowning."

The sting of her words pierced through me, sharper than any knife. I opened my mouth to defend myself, to explain how my upcoming showcase had seemed like a once-in-a-lifetime opportunity, but the words crumbled in my throat. Instead, I stepped inside, the air heavy with tension and the lingering scent of burnt coffee. The flickering light cast shadows on the walls, elongating her silhouette as she stood there, arms crossed defiantly, the very picture of hurt and anger.

"I'm here now," I finally managed, my voice softer than I intended. "I'm here for you."

But it wasn't enough. Not for her. Not for me. The silence that followed felt suffocating, wrapping around us like the humid air outside, thick and cloying. I took a step forward, my heart racing as I tried to bridge the chasm that had formed between us. "Please, just tell me what happened. I want to help."

Her expression softened momentarily, the hardness in her eyes giving way to a flicker of vulnerability. "It's too late for help. You wouldn't understand. You've been living your dream while I've been stuck here, trying to keep my head above water."

Each word fell like a stone between us, weighing heavily on my chest. The showcase loomed in my mind, a reminder of my aspirations, but I couldn't shake the guilt clawing at me. I had fought so hard for my place in this world, but at what cost? The dreams I had nurtured now felt tainted, twisted by the reality of my friend's suffering.

Lucy's hands trembled as she clutched a worn-out photo of us from last summer, smiling beneath the dappled shade of a magnolia tree, the sunlight illuminating our carefree spirits. "This is who we used to be," she murmured, her voice barely a whisper, filled with a deep sorrow that echoed through the space between us. "Now, I don't even know who I am anymore."

The vulnerability in her words pierced through the fog of my confusion. In that moment, I understood: her struggles were not just her own; they had become entwined with my ambitions, binding us in a tapestry of dreams and disappointments. I wanted to reach out, to tell her that it was okay to feel lost, that I too had felt the sharp sting of ambition turning against me, yet here I was, frozen, unsure of how to mend what felt irrevocably broken.

"Lucy," I finally said, my voice steadying with resolve. "You're not alone in this. I promise I won't abandon you again. We can figure this out together."

As the words spilled from my lips, I could see the walls around her heart begin to crack, the anger ebbing slightly as she searched my eyes for sincerity. We were at a crossroads, caught in a moment that felt both fragile and monumental, teetering on the edge of trust and betrayal. Would she believe me? Would she allow me back into her world, the world I had momentarily stepped away from in pursuit of my dreams?

The room felt smaller, the walls closing in as we stood there, two souls grappling with the weight of their choices, and I couldn't help but wonder if we could rebuild what had been lost, or if we were fated to remain just shadows of our former selves, forever haunted by the echoes of our decisions.

I stood in the dim light of Lucy's apartment, the air thick with unspoken words and lingering resentment. The photo she clutched slipped from her fingers and fluttered to the floor like a leaf in the wind, a poignant reminder of happier times. I bent to pick it up, the glossy surface reflecting a version of ourselves that felt like a lifetime ago. The laughter captured in that snapshot felt like a distant echo, fading against the backdrop of our current reality.

"Why did you have to go after your dreams?" Lucy's voice trembled, and I could see her clenching her fists, the tension coiling like a spring ready to snap. "It feels like you left me behind. What was so important that you couldn't be here for me?"

Her words stung, each syllable reverberating in my chest, making it hard to breathe. I wanted to tell her that pursuing my dreams had never been about abandoning her, but the truth was murky, a tangled mess of ambition and fear. I had painted a picture of success, of vibrant showcases and accolades, but beneath it all lay the haunting knowledge that I had turned my back when she needed me most.

"I never meant to leave you behind," I whispered, the sincerity of my voice surprising even me. "I thought I could balance everything, but I see now how naive that was. You're my best friend. I should have been here."

The flickering light above us cast a surreal glow, illuminating the tears that glistened in her eyes. I felt a deep-seated urge to bridge the distance between us, to reach out and reassure her that I was still the same person, but I was met with the realization that trust, once fractured, didn't mend easily.

She turned away, her back to me, and I could feel the weight of her despair hanging heavy in the air. "It's not just about you, you know. It's about everything that's been happening. I didn't want to pull you into this mess, but now..." Her voice trailed off, a fragile whisper tinged with frustration.

The city outside continued its rhythmic pulse, the sounds of laughter and music bleeding through the walls, mocking our moment of turmoil. I longed to step outside, to lose myself in the festivities, to forget the storm brewing within our fragile bond. Yet, here I was, rooted in place, the very foundation of our friendship at risk.

"What can I do to help?" I asked, my voice low and earnest. "I'm here for you, Lucy. Let me in. Let's figure this out together."

She turned slowly, her expression softening, and for a brief moment, I saw the glimmer of the girl I had grown up with, the one whose laughter had always been the soundtrack to my life. "I just feel like everything is spiraling out of control. I thought I could handle things on my own, but I'm drowning. I made choices that have consequences, and I don't know how to fix them."

Her confession hung between us like a fragile web, delicate yet strong, and I felt a flicker of hope. Perhaps this was the moment we could start to rebuild, to untangle the mess we had found ourselves in. "Talk to me," I urged, desperate to show her that vulnerability wasn't a weakness but a bridge to understanding.

Taking a deep breath, she sank onto the worn couch, the fabric threadbare and faded, echoing the weariness etched on her face. "I got involved with people I shouldn't have. They made promises—promises I thought would lead to something good. But now, I'm not sure who I can trust, and I can't even recognize myself anymore."

As she spoke, the weight of her choices unfurled like the petals of a wilting flower, each layer revealing the depth of her struggle. The streets of New Orleans felt distant, the colors muted in the face of her pain. My heart ached for her, the helplessness gnawing at my insides.

"Tell me who they are," I urged gently, the urgency rising in my voice. "We can go to the police, or I can help you get away from them. You don't have to face this alone."

She shook her head, her dark hair falling in disheveled waves around her face. "It's not that simple. They're not just strangers; they're people I thought were friends. I was trying to be part of something bigger, to feel alive again after everything that happened last year."

The shadows of the past crept into the room, filling the spaces between us. I knew of the dark time she had endured, the losses that had weighed her down, the grief that had threatened to consume her. "Lucy," I said softly, "you don't have to prove anything to anyone. You are enough, just as you are. We can find another way."

Her eyes met mine, and I could see the flicker of hope battling against despair. "It's hard to remember that sometimes," she admitted, the tremor in her voice betraying her struggle. "Everything just feels so overwhelming."

I moved closer, sitting beside her on the couch, feeling the warmth radiating from her presence. "I'm here. Let's take it one step at a time. Start with what happened—everything you can remember."

The seconds stretched into minutes as she began to speak, her words spilling forth in a torrent, painting a vivid picture of the choices that had led her into the shadows. I listened, every word pulling me deeper into her world, the colors shifting from vibrant hues to shades of gray. Each revelation felt like a piece of a puzzle, a glimpse into the turmoil she had faced alone.

With every sentence, I felt the barrier between us begin to crack, the isolation giving way to a fragile connection built on shared struggles and unguarded truths. The air around us shifted, a soft warmth settling like a blanket, offering solace amidst the storm.

As she recounted her story, I reached out, taking her hand in mine, a simple gesture filled with promise and understanding. We were two souls navigating a labyrinth of confusion, but together, perhaps we could find a way through the darkness, step by hesitant step. The road ahead was uncertain, but at that moment, I knew we were no longer alone.

As Lucy poured her heart out, the atmosphere in the small apartment shifted, a potent blend of desperation and resilience filling the air. Her words painted a chilling picture, each sentence dropping like a stone in a still pond, sending ripples through the very fabric of our friendship. I had known her as a whirlwind of laughter and unyielding optimism, the girl who could turn any mundane afternoon into an adventure. But now, the light in her eyes flickered like the dying flame of a candle, barely holding on against the overwhelming darkness.

"I got involved with a crowd that seemed exciting, like a way to escape the dull ache of reality," she continued, her voice trembling as she recalled the details. "They were charismatic, always throwing parties in swanky places, their lives glittering like the baubles hanging from the Christmas tree. At first, it was thrilling. I thought I had finally found a place where I belonged."

I could almost see the allure she described, the glitzy parties filled with laughter and clinking glasses, a vibrant tapestry woven from threads of reckless abandon and fleeting joy. But beneath the surface, I sensed the undercurrents of danger, a swirling vortex threatening to pull her under. "And then?" I prompted gently, squeezing her hand for encouragement, urging her to keep going.

"Then I started noticing things," she said, her brow furrowing in concentration as if forcing herself to sift through the fog of memory. "People disappearing from the scene, whispers in the shadows. At first, I thought it was just the kind of drama that comes with that lifestyle. But when I saw someone I trusted get hurt—really hurt—I knew I had to get out."

The weight of her confession settled heavily on my chest. Each revelation chipped away at the foundation of that sparkling facade she had been living behind. I felt a surge of protective instinct coursing through me, the same fierce loyalty that had always bound us together. "Did you tell anyone? The police?"

She shook her head vehemently, her dark hair swaying like a pendulum. "I couldn't. I thought I could handle it alone. I didn't want to drag you into my mess, especially with your showcase coming up. I kept thinking, if I just play it cool, it will all blow over. But it didn't."

The vibrant sounds of New Orleans outside faded into a background hum, a mere backdrop to the storm swirling within our small sanctuary. "Lucy, you shouldn't have had to carry this alone," I said, my voice thick with emotion. "I wish you had reached out sooner. You don't have to fight this battle by yourself anymore."

Her gaze softened, and I could see the walls she had built around her heart begin to crack, the hope that had been buried under layers of guilt and shame starting to peek through. "What do I do now?" she whispered, her voice barely audible over the distant laughter and music filtering through the window.

I took a deep breath, feeling a sense of clarity emerge from the chaos. "We need to go to the police. You need to tell them everything. We can find a safe way to get you away from these people." I paused, weighing my next words carefully. "But first, we should figure out who we can trust. There might still be people within that circle who genuinely care for you. If you can identify them, we can devise a plan."

Lucy's eyes glimmered with the slightest hint of hope. "What if they retaliate? What if they come after me?"

A shiver ran down my spine at the thought, but I forced a reassuring smile. "We'll cross that bridge when we come to it. For now, let's focus on taking back your life. You deserve to feel safe, to reclaim that spark that makes you, well, you."

A soft nod from her sent a rush of warmth through me. It felt like stepping onto solid ground after being tossed in a tempest. As we began brainstorming a plan, I could feel the weight of the world lifting ever so slightly, the air between us charged with renewed determination.

The vibrant chaos of the city beyond our walls became our soundtrack, a reminder of the life we wanted to return to. The aroma of gumbo wafted through the streets, mingling with the laughter and the clinking of glasses, whispering promises of joy and connection. It was easy to forget, in those moments, that darkness lingered just outside our reach.

With newfound resolve, we began mapping out our steps, piecing together a strategy that felt both exhilarating and terrifying. We outlined trusted friends, potential allies who could help us navigate this storm, names scribbled hastily on the back of an old envelope that had once contained a takeout order. Each name felt like a lifeline, a tether to the vibrant life we both craved.

As the night wore on, we transformed the apartment into a war room, the flickering light from the lamp illuminating our determined faces. I shared stories from my life, reminding Lucy of her strength, of the fire that had once ignited her spirit. Each laugh we shared slowly rekindled the warmth that had been extinguished, weaving us back together with threads of friendship and shared purpose.

But just as the darkness began to lift, a sharp knock at the door sent a jolt of fear racing through me. The sound echoed ominously in the stillness, a stark reminder of the dangers lurking just beyond our fragile bubble of safety. Lucy froze, her expression a mixture of dread and uncertainty.

"Who could that be?" she breathed, her voice barely above a whisper.

I stood, instinctively moving closer to her, a silent vow to protect her echoing in my heart. "Let me check," I replied, my heart pounding as I approached the door, every instinct on high alert.

As I peered through the peephole, my pulse quickened. A familiar face stared back at me—Jared, the charming, reckless friend we had both known in our youthful escapades, a glimmer of trouble wrapped in a smile. Panic surged within me, memories of our past flooding back, the wild nights filled with laughter and an intoxicating sense of freedom. But there was something in his gaze that set my nerves on edge.

"What do we do?" Lucy whispered urgently, her hand grasping mine tightly.

"Stay behind me," I instructed, my voice steady despite the chaos swirling in my mind. With a deep breath, I opened the door, stepping into the unknown, ready to confront whatever awaited us on the other side.

"Hey! Long time no see!" Jared greeted with his signature grin, the kind that had always made my heart flutter and my instincts scream. But as I looked deeper into his eyes, the glint of mischief seemed to mask something darker, something potentially dangerous.

"Jared," I said, forcing a smile, my heart racing. "What are you doing here?"

He leaned casually against the doorframe, his demeanor deceptively relaxed. "Just thought I'd check in on you two. Heard some whispers around town. Figured you could use a friend."

His words dripped with false sincerity, and I could feel Lucy tensing behind me. This was the moment we had feared, a crossroad where trust hung precariously in the balance. Would this be a path to safety, or would it lead us deeper into the shadows?

The vibrant chaos of New Orleans continued to pulse outside, the laughter and music a distant reminder of life beyond our struggle. In that moment, we stood at the edge of uncertainty, ready to face whatever lay ahead together.

Chapter 23: Chasing Shadows

The streets of Maplewood, once brimming with the vivid hues of autumn leaves, now felt like a faded canvas, washed out by the weight of my thoughts. The golden light of the late afternoon sun spilled lazily over the cobblestones, casting long shadows that mirrored the turmoil within me. Each step I took echoed the lingering tension of my earlier confrontation with Lily, my friend who had become more of a sister than a mere companion. The conversation haunted me, its words replaying in my mind like a broken record.

Jason, ever the gentle soul, had tried to soothe my frayed nerves with his comforting presence. His kind eyes and soothing voice could turn even the most distressing moments into gentle reminders of hope, but right then, they did little to quell the storm inside. I felt like I was adrift on a choppy sea, and no anchor could keep me from drifting further into despair. My feet moved instinctively, guided by the rhythm of my restless thoughts, as I found myself in front of an old theater. Its once-vibrant marquee, now a flickering shadow of its former glory, beckoned me inside with a mix of nostalgia and curiosity.

Pushing through the heavy wooden doors, I was enveloped by the musky scent of aged wood and dust. The dim light struggled against the gloom, casting ghostly shapes across the faded velvet seats that had borne witness to countless performances. I ran my fingers along the railing of the grand staircase, tracing the intricate carvings that had dulled with time, each groove a testament to the stories that had unfolded on this very stage. The silence was palpable, but it was a comforting kind of silence, the kind that holds the weight of dreams long forgotten.

As I stepped onto the stage, the worn floorboards creaked beneath my weight, a reminder of the vibrant life that had once flourished here. I could almost hear the laughter, the applause that had filled this space, and I found myself longing to step back into a time when dreams seemed limitless. The faded red curtains hung like a heavy shroud, whispering secrets of passion and ambition, daring me to confront the shadows that loomed over my heart.

In that moment, something shifted within me. I thought about Lily and the rift that had formed between us, a chasm of misunderstandings and unspoken truths. We had once been inseparable, our laughter echoing through the halls of our shared memories, but now it felt like we were two ships passing in the night, lost to our own fears. I knew I had to bridge that gap, to confront my own insecurities that had driven a wedge between us.

I closed my eyes and let the memories wash over me. The vibrant colors of our friendship, the late-night conversations filled with dreams, and the way we had supported each other through thick and thin—they flickered like the fading lights of the marquee outside. With each breath, I inhaled the scent of hope mixed with regret, a bittersweet concoction that tasted like the remnants of childhood innocence. It was time to reclaim my narrative, to rewrite the story that had veered off course.

As I opened my eyes, the stage before me transformed. I imagined it bathed in bright lights, filled with an audience hanging on every word, every movement. I envisioned myself stepping into the spotlight, fearlessly owning my truth, my flaws, and my vulnerabilities. The ghosts of past performances whispered encouragement, their echoes urging me to take that leap, to stand tall and face the world unapologetically.

But first, I had to confront the person who had become my greatest challenge: myself. The insecurities that had plagued me were the very shadows I had to chase away. I thought about the moments of doubt that had seeped into my soul—the times I had doubted my worth, questioned my dreams, and allowed fear to dictate my choices. I had let the opinions of others cloud my vision, blurring the path that once felt so clear. It was time to break free from those chains, to shed the weight of guilt that clung to me like a second skin.

With a newfound resolve, I stepped closer to the edge of the stage, feeling the cool wood beneath my bare feet. The silence enveloped me, and I breathed in deeply, allowing the stillness to settle around me like a comforting blanket. I envisioned myself as the lead in a grand production, my heart racing with anticipation. I was no longer merely an observer; I was the protagonist of my own story, the one who could rewrite the script.

In this sacred space, I imagined the words I needed to say to Lily, the apology I longed to give, and the bridge I wanted to rebuild. I would not shy away from the truth, nor would I hide from the confrontation that lay ahead. Instead, I would embrace it, knowing that vulnerability was not a weakness but a strength—a power that could transform relationships and heal old wounds.

As I lingered on the stage, a sense of clarity washed over me, illuminating the path forward. The theater, with its faded grandeur and whispered secrets, became my sanctuary—a place where I could reclaim my narrative, confront my fears, and chase away the shadows that had threatened to consume me. In the dim light of that once-grand stage, I discovered the spark that had been buried beneath layers of doubt and regret. I felt like an artist reclaiming her canvas, ready to paint a vibrant future filled with color and possibility.

With that realization, I stepped back, allowing the stage to absorb my fears, my insecurities. The theater had witnessed countless stories of love, loss, and redemption, and now it would bear witness to my own transformation. I felt the warmth of hope blooming within me, and as I left the stage, I knew it was time to step back into the world, ready to face whatever awaited me—starting with a heartfelt conversation with Lily.

As I stepped out of the theater, the late afternoon sun blazed down on Maplewood, igniting the golden hues of the trees lining the streets. The contrast was stark; outside, the world pulsed with energy while I felt like an intruder in my own skin, tethered by the weight of unspoken apologies and fears. Each step away from the theater felt like shedding a layer, revealing a rawness that left me vulnerable to the myriad of emotions swirling within.

My feet led me to Willow Park, a serene sanctuary that had always been a refuge for me. The park was alive with families enjoying picnics, laughter mingling with the gentle rustling of leaves overhead. Children raced around, their squeals of joy echoing in the air, while couples shared quiet conversations on benches, hands intertwined. I couldn't help but envy their ease, their ability to be present in the moment, unaware of the shadows that danced just beyond their laughter.

I settled onto a weathered bench, its wood warm from the sun, and inhaled deeply, allowing the crisp, autumnal air to fill my lungs. It smelled of earth and the fading sweetness of summer, a scent that always carried with it a hint of nostalgia. I closed my eyes and let the sounds of the park wash over me—laughter, the soft rustle of leaves, and the distant sound of a guitar strumming a familiar tune. In this moment of stillness, I tried to gather my thoughts, to unravel the tangled ball of guilt and regret that had taken root in my chest.

Lily's face flickered in my mind, her bright smile and the way her laughter lit up a room. I could still feel the sting of our argument, the words that had flared up between us like sparks from a fire. How had we allowed our friendship to slip through our fingers, like grains of sand? The thought of losing her made my stomach churn. It wasn't just a friendship; it felt like losing a part of myself.

A gentle breeze stirred the leaves above, carrying the laughter of children and the sweet notes of the guitar player nearby. I opened my eyes, drawn to the sight of a girl, no older than seven, spinning in circles on the grass, her dress flaring out around her like a colorful flower in bloom. She stumbled, giggled, and fell into the soft grass, her laughter pealing like a bell, pure and unfiltered. It struck me then how freely she embraced joy and how easily she could shake off the little setbacks that would leave me reeling. I longed to reclaim that innocence, that buoyancy of spirit that felt so elusive.

It was in that moment of watching her that I realized I had a choice. I could allow this moment of confrontation with Lily to consume me, or I could transform it into an opportunity for growth, a chance to deepen our connection rather than fracture it. With renewed determination, I pulled out my phone and stared at the screen, my heart racing as I thought about reaching out. The idea of sending a message felt daunting, but perhaps it was the very thing I needed to do.

After a few moments of deliberation, I opened a blank message and started typing, my fingers dancing nervously over the screen. "Hey, can we talk? I've been doing some thinking." The words seemed so small, yet they held the weight of my uncertainty and desire for reconciliation. My thumb hovered over the send button, a hesitation creeping in. What if she didn't want to talk? What if she felt the same weight of our argument, the tension of unresolved feelings? But then I remembered the girl spinning in the grass, the way she had fallen but gotten right back up, unafraid.

With a deep breath, I pressed send and watched as the message disappeared into the digital ether, carrying with it my hopes and fears. The relief that washed over me was both exhilarating and terrifying, like standing at the edge of a cliff, ready to leap into the unknown. The park around me continued to bustle, oblivious to my moment of reckoning. I leaned back against the bench, closing my eyes once more, allowing myself to be carried away by the sounds of life surrounding me.

Time slipped by like a whispered secret, and when I finally opened my eyes again, the sun had dipped lower in the sky, casting an amber glow that wrapped the park in a warm embrace. I felt a gentle vibration in my pocket, the familiar sound of a notification pulling me back to reality. My heart raced as I pulled out my phone, anticipation knotting in my stomach. It was a reply from Lily.

"Sure, I'd like that. When?"

The simplicity of her words brought a rush of relief, but it was laced with an undercurrent of anxiety. I wanted to choose the right moment, the right place—somewhere that felt safe for both of us. Willow Park had always been a sanctuary for me, but perhaps it needed to be more than just a backdrop for our conversation. I typed back quickly, my mind racing. "How about tomorrow? We can meet at The Brew House?"

The Brew House was our go-to spot, a cozy little café with mismatched furniture and the enticing aroma of freshly brewed coffee mingling with the sweet scent of pastries. It was a place filled with laughter and warmth, where we had shared countless cups of coffee and late-night talks about our dreams and fears.

"Sounds perfect. See you at noon?" she replied, and with that, the shadows began to lift.

I felt lighter, as if a weight had been unburdened from my shoulders. Tomorrow would be our chance to heal, to peel back the layers of misunderstanding and frustration, and to rekindle the connection that meant so much to both of us.

With a smile, I stood up, feeling the warmth of the sun on my face, a reassuring embrace from the universe. The park, alive with energy and laughter, felt different now—less like a sanctuary for my fears and more like a celebration of possibility. As I began to walk home, the shadows of doubt faded behind me, replaced by a growing sense of hope. I could see a glimmer of light breaking through the clouds of uncertainty, and for the first time in days, I felt ready to step into it, ready to face whatever came next.

The morning light filtered through my window like a timid guest, coaxing me from the depths of restless sleep. I awoke with a flutter of anxiety in my stomach, the events of the day ahead swirling in my mind like leaves caught in a gust of wind. Today was the day I would meet Lily at The Brew House, our favorite café, a place where the aroma of coffee danced in the air like a familiar melody. It was more than just a café; it was a patchwork of memories stitched together with laughter, secrets, and the bittersweet flavor of friendship.

As I slipped into my favorite oversized sweater—a cozy, knit embrace that felt like a hug from an old friend—I ran through the possible scenarios in my mind. What if she was still upset? What if we stumbled over our words, struggling to navigate the rough terrain of hurt feelings and misunderstandings? But deep down, a quiet confidence began to unfurl. This was our chance to rediscover the bond we had nearly lost, to unearth the pieces of our friendship buried beneath layers of tension.

The crisp air outside was a refreshing reminder of fall's approach, and the streets of Maplewood buzzed with life. I strolled past storefronts adorned with colorful displays, the windows decorated with pumpkins and autumn leaves. The laughter of children echoed from a nearby park, their joy infectious and brightening the gray edges of my nerves. With each step toward The Brew House, I felt the weight of the past few days begin to lighten, replaced by the hopeful flutter of anticipation.

Upon entering the café, I was greeted by the familiar cacophony of chatter and the rich scent of roasted coffee beans. The eclectic mix of mismatched furniture, with its cozy nooks and worn-out couches, embraced me like an old blanket. I spotted Lily seated at our usual table, a steaming mug cradled in her hands. She looked up, her eyes meeting mine, and for a fleeting moment, everything fell away—the tension, the hurt, the misunderstandings. In that instant, it was just us, and the warmth of nostalgia wrapped around me.

"Hey," I said, my voice barely above a whisper as I approached the table.

"Hey," she replied, her tone softer than I had expected. There was a hint of a smile on her lips, but her eyes reflected a storm of emotions. I slid into the chair across from her, the distance between us still heavy, but I felt the first cracks in the wall that had separated us.

"I'm glad you came," she said, her gaze drifting to the window, watching as leaves danced their way to the ground.

"I almost didn't," I admitted, my heart racing. "I've been thinking about everything we said. I didn't mean for things to spiral out of control."

Lily nodded, her fingers nervously tracing the rim of her mug. "Me too. I guess I just felt... I don't know, abandoned? Like you were moving on without me."

Her words pierced through the air, raw and honest. The vulnerability in her voice cut deeper than I had anticipated. "I would never abandon you, Lily. You're my best friend. I was just so caught up in my own head that I forgot to look around and see how you were feeling."

For a moment, silence enveloped us, heavy with unspoken truths. I watched her as she looked down at her coffee, her thoughts drifting like the autumn leaves outside. She took a deep breath, her shoulders relaxing slightly. "I guess I was feeling lost too. It's hard to find our way sometimes, especially when everything around us is changing."

The truth in her words resonated within me. Change was inevitable, but the way we navigated it could either forge deeper connections or create rifts that threatened to tear us apart. I reached across the table, my hand brushing against hers, a tentative gesture of reconciliation. "Can we start over? I want to hear how you've been. I want us to be okay again."

Her eyes flickered with surprise at the contact, and I could see the tension in her shoulders begin to dissipate. Slowly, she nodded, her smile returning, and the warmth that filled the space between us began to thaw the chill that had settled in my heart. "Yeah, I'd like that."

As we spoke, the conversation flowed more easily, weaving through our fears, hopes, and the challenges that lay ahead. We laughed at shared memories, the absurdities of our teenage years, and the inevitable awkwardness that comes with growing up. It felt like a balm, healing the wounds that had festered between us.

In the midst of our chatter, I caught sight of the barista, a young woman with vibrant purple hair and a contagious smile, who had been eavesdropping on our conversation. "You two sound like you're having a breakthrough," she chimed in, her eyes sparkling with genuine joy. "If you need any help keeping the good vibes going, I recommend the cinnamon bun latte. It's basically happiness in a cup."

We exchanged a laugh, and I felt a spark of warmth surge within me. The simple connection with the barista, the way she recognized the shift in our energy, reminded me of the small joys that could often slip through the cracks of life's chaos.

As we continued to talk, I noticed how the morning light began to change, casting a golden glow across the café. The atmosphere felt charged with possibilities, and I sensed that we were on the verge of something beautiful—a renewal of our friendship, a redefinition of what it meant to be there for one another.

Eventually, the conversation turned to our dreams, the aspirations we had tucked away amid the struggles of the past few months. "I've been thinking about pursuing that design course," Lily confessed, her eyes lighting up at the thought. "It's something I've always wanted to do, but I let fear hold me back."

"That sounds amazing! You should definitely go for it," I encouraged, my heart swelling with pride for her. "You have a talent for it. I've always admired how you see the world in color."

"And you, my friend, have a gift for storytelling," she countered playfully. "You've always had a way with words, capturing life in a way that makes it feel vibrant."

Her compliment warmed me, igniting a flicker of inspiration that had been dormant. "Maybe we should find a way to collaborate," I suggested, my imagination racing. "You could design covers for my stories, and I could weave narratives that reflect your artistic vision."

"Now that sounds like a project worth pursuing!" she exclaimed, her excitement palpable. "We could make something truly unique together."

As we discussed our ideas, the café around us faded into a backdrop, our laughter and chatter creating a world of our own. It felt as though we were reclaiming lost time, stitching together the fabric of our friendship with every word.

The world outside was busy with the hum of life, but inside, we found our own rhythm—a harmonious blend of dreams, vulnerability, and the promise of what lay ahead. I realized then that our friendship, like the leaves falling from the trees, had gone through its own seasons of change. But just as the trees would bloom again in spring, so too could we.

As the sun began to dip lower in the sky, casting a warm glow through the café windows, I knew this moment marked a new chapter in our story. We were ready to chase away the shadows, to embrace the complexities of life together, and to redefine what it meant to be friends. It felt like the beginning of a beautiful journey—one where we would support one another, face the challenges head-on, and create a masterpiece out of the chaos that life had thrown our way.

With a heart full of hope and laughter dancing between us, I knew we would navigate this unpredictable world together, hand in hand, ready to embrace whatever came next.

Chapter 24: Rebuilding Bridges

The park was alive with the vibrant colors of late afternoon, the sun draping a warm, golden hue over the sprawling lawns and crooked paths. The air, thick with the mingled scents of freshly cut grass and blooming honeysuckle, seemed to hold its breath in anticipation of our meeting. I had chosen this place for a reason, a sanctuary where laughter once floated freely like the autumn leaves that now danced around me. Today, however, the laughter felt suspended, replaced by an unspoken weight pressing heavily on my chest.

As I approached the weathered wooden bench, I caught sight of Sarah, her familiar figure nestled among the shadows cast by a towering oak. The sunlight played upon her hair, illuminating the strands like threads of gold against a canvas of deep green. But despite the beauty surrounding us, her expression told a different story—her eyes reflected a tempest of emotions swirling just beneath the surface. I could sense the remnants of our friendship floating like fragile paper boats on an unforgiving river, caught in the turbulent currents of our unspoken grievances.

Taking a deep breath, I let the sounds of chirping birds and rustling leaves envelop me, grounding my resolve as I stepped closer. "Hey," I managed, my voice quaking slightly. "Thanks for coming."

"Of course," she replied, her tone flat, the weight of our history hanging between us like a thick fog. "I wouldn't have missed it."

The silence stretched uncomfortably, wrapping around us as I settled onto the bench, the wood cool against the warmth of my palm. I fiddled with the frayed edges of my sweater, a nervous habit I hadn't been able to shake. The familiar warmth of her presence was still there, but it felt distant, like a fading photograph where the colors had begun to bleed into one another.

"I wanted to talk about everything," I said, my heart racing as I searched for the right words. "I know I haven't been around. Life got... busy."

"Busy," she echoed, her eyebrows raised skeptically. "That's one way to put it."

I flinched at the bite in her tone, a reminder of the hurt I had caused. "I'm sorry. I really am. I didn't mean to make you feel like you didn't matter. You do matter, Sarah. You always have."

As the weight of my words hung in the air, I watched her expression shift, the edges of her frustration softening just a little. Her eyes shimmered with unshed tears, reflecting a mixture of relief and lingering pain. "It's just been hard, you know?" she confessed, her voice wavering. "I felt abandoned. Like I was stuck in quicksand while you were off chasing dreams."

I felt the sting of her words cut deep, each one resonating with an undeniable truth. "I didn't mean to leave you behind. I got caught up in my own chaos and lost sight of what really mattered—us." The admission hung between us, heavy and raw.

Her gaze dropped to her hands, fingers twisting together as if searching for comfort in their embrace. "I guess I just... I didn't know how to reach out. I thought you were too busy for me."

"No one is too busy for a friend who needs them," I countered gently, a spark of determination igniting within me. "You're worth the time, Sarah. You always have been."

A small smile flickered across her face, tentative yet hopeful, as if the sun had peeked through the clouds just for us. "You remember the summer we spent at the lake?" she asked, a hint of nostalgia creeping into her voice. "We used to stay up late, talking about everything and nothing at all, wrapped in our dreams."

I nodded, warmth flooding my chest as memories flooded back. The sun-soaked afternoons spent splashing in the water, the way laughter would bubble up uncontrollably, echoing across the still surface. "Those were the best days. We were invincible."

"Yeah," she replied, a wistful sigh escaping her lips. "I miss that. I miss us."

The confession hung in the air, weaving an invisible thread connecting our hearts once more. "Then let's fix this," I proposed, my voice filled with a newfound resolve. "Let's rebuild what we've lost. I promise I won't disappear again."

Her eyes glistened with unshed tears, the vulnerability in her gaze striking a chord within me. "I want that too," she whispered, her voice thick with emotion. "But it's going to take time."

"I'm ready," I assured her, squeezing her hand gently, feeling the warmth of our shared memories flow between us. "Let's start fresh. I want to hear everything—the struggles, the victories, all of it. I want to be there for you like you've been there for me."

The vulnerability of the moment enveloped us, the noise of the park fading into a gentle hum as we shared our stories, each revelation drawing us closer together. I learned of her late-night struggles and the weight of expectations pressing down on her shoulders like an anchor. In turn, I opened up about my own battles—fears, insecurities, the relentless pursuit of success that often came at the expense of my most cherished relationships.

Laughter spilled from our lips, mingling with tears as we recounted silly moments, weaving them into a tapestry of resilience and friendship. In this sacred space, beneath the canopy of the oak, we began to stitch the fabric of our friendship back together, thread by thread, moment by moment.

In that beautiful, messy conversation, I realized that while life might steer us along divergent paths, it didn't have to sever the bonds we had built. Rebuilding bridges was hard work, but we were willing to put in the effort. As the sun dipped lower in the sky, casting a warm glow around us, I knew this was just the beginning of something beautiful.

The sun dipped lower on the horizon, casting long shadows that danced around us as we shared our stories, each word weaving a fragile thread back into the fabric of our friendship. With every laugh, I felt the walls I had built around my heart slowly crumble, exposing the vulnerabilities I had kept hidden beneath layers of self-doubt. In Sarah's laughter, there was a release, an acknowledgment that perhaps I wasn't the only one feeling adrift in a sea of uncertainty.

As twilight approached, the park transformed into a canvas of deep purples and warm oranges, the colors bleeding together like the emotions swirling inside us. The air turned crisp, a gentle reminder that change was inevitable, but so was the possibility of rebirth. I found myself wanting to hold on to this moment, to trap it like a butterfly under glass. I could see the light flickering in Sarah's eyes again, and I felt a spark igniting within me—a renewed commitment to cherish the bonds that tether us to one another.

"I've been working on a project," I confessed, my voice a mix of excitement and nervousness. "It's about friendship—how it evolves, how it can fray and yet still be beautiful. I want to incorporate our stories, our struggles, everything."

Her brow furrowed slightly, a hint of skepticism dancing in her eyes. "How would you even do that?"

"I want to create something tangible," I explained, leaning closer, the ideas pouring forth like an overflowing fountain. "A series of paintings or maybe even a mixed-media installation. I want it to resonate, to show the rawness of friendship—the way it can be both fragile and fierce."

She was silent for a moment, the cogs in her mind visibly turning. "That sounds amazing," she finally said, her voice barely above a whisper. "But will you really capture all of it? The heartbreak and the healing?"

"Every bit of it," I promised. "I want to honor our experiences, even the messy parts. I think that's where the real beauty lies."

As I spoke, her smile widened, a spark of inspiration igniting within her. "You always had a way of finding the good in everything. It's one of the things I admire about you."

The warmth of her compliment enveloped me, and I couldn't help but feel a swell of pride, a desire to be that person for her as well. "We can do this together," I suggested, the idea blooming like a wildflower in the cracks of concrete. "You could share your side of things too—what you've been through. I know it hasn't been easy."

She hesitated, chewing her lip as if weighing the gravity of my suggestion. "I'm not sure I'm ready to share all of that. What if it's too painful?"

"Pain is part of the process," I reassured her, my voice steady. "And who knows? It might help others feel less alone. Sometimes putting our struggles into words gives them less power over us."

The park was gradually emptying, the sounds of laughter and conversation fading into the distance, leaving behind an almost serene silence. The breeze picked up, rustling the leaves overhead, as if the world itself was encouraging us to take this leap. I caught a glimpse of her hesitation turning into contemplation, a flicker of understanding illuminating her features.

"What if we start small?" she proposed, her voice gaining strength. "I could write down some thoughts, just for me. You could illustrate it. Then we can see where it goes."

I grinned, the excitement bubbling up like a fizzy drink ready to spill over. "That sounds perfect! We can create a whole narrative, visualizing our journey through art. It'll be a living testament to our resilience."

As we talked, the atmosphere shifted; the air was filled with possibilities, each word carrying the weight of hope and renewal. I could see the tentative lines of our past weaving into the bright threads of our present, and it filled me with an energy I hadn't felt in what seemed like forever. In the sanctuary of the park, we began to sketch the outlines of our new path, carving out a shared space in a world that often felt chaotic and unforgiving.

Our laughter rang through the twilight, cutting through the shadows like a beacon of light. We spoke of memories, of the moments that had built us—her quiet determination as she tackled each obstacle and my restless creativity, always yearning to express the inexpressible. Each memory unearthed another layer, revealing the depth of our connection and the beauty in our imperfections.

As darkness draped its cloak around us, the first stars blinked into existence, scattered like promises across the sky. I leaned back against the bench, taking in the sight of my friend, illuminated by the soft glow of the streetlamps. There was a peace settling within me, a sense of certainty that the road ahead, though uncertain, was ours to travel together.

"I can't believe we let things get so out of hand," Sarah murmured, her voice thoughtful. "How did we let that happen?"

I shrugged, trying to shake off the weight of regret. "Life gets busy, you know? We forget to check in, to remind ourselves that we're not alone in this."

"And maybe we think we have to do it all by ourselves," she added, her gaze steady. "But we don't. We never did."

The revelation hung in the air, grounding us in a reality we had both overlooked for too long. In the dim light, I reached out, taking her hand in mine, our fingers intertwining like the branches of the trees above us. The warmth of her grip was a silent promise that we wouldn't let distance creep between us again.

With our hearts laid bare, we began to envision the future. The laughter and tears we had shared were mere threads in a much larger tapestry—one that we were both ready to weave anew. There was magic in the air, a tangible sense of possibility that wrapped around us like a soft embrace, urging us to step forward, to reclaim the friendship that had always been worth fighting for.

The night deepened around us, a rich tapestry of indigo and black, dotted with the shimmering gems of stars. Their twinkling seemed to pulse with the rhythm of our laughter and the warmth of our renewed connection. I could hardly believe how swiftly our conversation had transformed from tentative apologies to the giddy excitement of artistic collaboration. The world around us was alive, the distant sounds of city life echoing softly, a backdrop to our intimate moment.

We sat for a while in companionable silence, the darkness wrapping around us like a well-worn blanket. I relished the tranquility, my heart finally unburdened from the weight of uncertainty. The park, once a site of tension, had morphed into our sanctuary, where we could share our hopes without judgment, where our stories could intertwine and flourish.

"You know," Sarah mused, breaking the silence, "I've always admired how you see the world. It's like you paint it with a brush of optimism."

I chuckled softly, brushing a loose strand of hair behind my ear. "It's a facade, mostly. I just try to find beauty where I can, especially in the chaos."

"Isn't that what art is all about?" she replied, her enthusiasm shining like the moon emerging from behind a cloud. "Taking the chaos and turning it into something meaningful?"

Her words sparked a flame within me, igniting a vision of the project we could create together. "Exactly! I can picture it now—a blend of your written reflections and my artwork. We could create a gallery that showcases not just the beauty of our friendship but the messiness of life itself."

The prospect of it was thrilling. My mind raced with ideas, colors, and textures, the canvas of our creation expanding with each moment. "Imagine a piece that represents your struggles, something raw and visceral, while mine reflects the light we find in each other," I continued, my voice bubbling with excitement. "We could even invite others to contribute their stories—expand it beyond us. It could become a community project."

The spark of inspiration in Sarah's eyes grew brighter, illuminating her face with renewed energy. "I love that! A collaborative effort where everyone's voice matters. It could be so powerful."

As we brainstormed, the stars above bore witness to our budding plans. Each idea flowed seamlessly, building upon the last like an intricate dance. We spoke of creating installations that would invite viewers to engage, to connect with their own emotions and experiences. Maybe even a soundscape to accompany the visuals—recordings of laughter, whispers, and tears, all blending together to create an atmosphere that felt alive.

Time slipped away unnoticed, the cool night air sending gentle shivers through us, urging us to turn our dreams into action. "Let's meet regularly to flesh this out," I suggested, my heart pounding at the thought of pouring our hearts into this venture. "We can sketch out our ideas, write together, and start gathering stories from friends and family."

"Agreed," Sarah replied, her face alight with determination. "This is exactly what I need right now—to dive into something meaningful. It feels like the perfect antidote to everything I've been feeling."

In that moment, I saw a glimpse of the old Sarah I had missed—the one who thrived in creativity and connection, unafraid to explore the depths of her emotions. It filled me with hope, the realization that our friendship could become a conduit for healing, not just for us, but for anyone willing to join our journey.

As the moon rose higher in the sky, casting a silvery glow across the park, we made plans, our voices weaving through the crisp night air like threads of a tapestry. The world felt charged with possibility, each passing moment a reminder that life was meant to be shared, that connection was the antidote to loneliness.

"Okay, I need to ask," Sarah said suddenly, a playful glint in her eye. "What's your ultimate goal with this project? Is it just about friendship, or is there something deeper?"

I paused, the question settling in my mind like the first frost of winter. "Honestly? I want to explore the complexities of relationships—the joy, the heartache, the healing. Life isn't just about the happy moments; it's about the full spectrum of experiences. If I can capture that and help others feel seen in their struggles, then I'll consider it a success."

A thoughtful silence enveloped us, and I could see her processing my words. "That makes sense. I've been feeling so much lately, and I want to channel that into something constructive. I think this project could be that outlet."

"Exactly!" I exclaimed, feeling a surge of excitement. "We can make something that resonates with everyone, something that sparks conversations."

As we continued to brainstorm, the conversation shifted from the serious to the whimsical. We began to craft narratives around each piece we envisioned, creating characters that embodied our struggles and triumphs. Laughter bubbled up as we exchanged ridiculous ideas, imagining an installation dedicated to the art of failing spectacularly, complete with oversized props and interactive elements that invited viewers to share their own flops.

"I can see it now," I laughed, "a giant inflatable failure where people can bounce around and learn that it's okay to mess up."

"That's brilliant!" Sarah responded, her laughter infectious. "We should definitely have a 'fail wall' where people can leave sticky notes with their biggest flops. I mean, who wouldn't want to celebrate their failures?"

The more we laughed, the more I realized how healing this was for both of us. We were not just reclaiming our friendship; we were building something extraordinary—a project that would be a living testament to resilience, creativity, and the undeniable bond we shared.

As the first hints of dawn began to break over the horizon, painting the sky in soft pastels, we reluctantly acknowledged the time. "We should probably head out before they lock the park," I said, glancing around at the deserted paths.

"Yeah," Sarah agreed, her voice tinged with reluctance. "But I feel like we just scratched the surface of what we can create together."

"Absolutely. This is just the beginning," I promised, my heart swelling with hope. "Let's meet again tomorrow? I want to dive deeper into our ideas."

"I wouldn't miss it for the world," she said, her smile bright against the dimming light.

As we walked toward the park exit, the chill of the night air began to retreat with the promise of a new day. The path ahead felt brighter than ever, a ribbon of possibility unfurling before us. I looked over at Sarah, her presence beside me a comforting reminder that I was no longer alone in my journey. Together, we would transform our challenges into art, forging a connection that would only grow stronger in the light of our shared dreams.

Chapter 25: A Dancer's Heart

The studio door swings open with a creak that echoes in the silence, and I step into a world alive with the scent of polished wood and echoes of laughter from years past. Sunlight pours through the large, dusty windows, casting playful shadows across the floor, where scuff marks tell stories of countless rehearsals and dreams realized. Here, the air is thick with possibility, a canvas waiting for my brush strokes. My heartbeat quickens as I see Jason at the far end, his silhouette framed by the soft golden light, a beacon drawing me in.

Today feels different, as if the universe conspired to align our paths perfectly. Jason's body moves fluidly, every muscle honed and precise, like a finely tuned instrument. I can't help but admire the way he dances, his movements filled with an innate grace that makes even the simplest gestures seem profound. He glances up, and our eyes lock. The tension in that moment hangs like a delicate thread, stretched taut between us. His gaze carries a warmth that envelops me, igniting something deep within—a spark I can no longer ignore.

"Ready to get back to it?" he asks, his voice smooth, infused with a playful edge. The way he grins, that crooked smile that feels like a secret shared just between us, sends a shiver of anticipation through my limbs.

I nod, taking a deep breath, grounding myself in the moment. Each step I take toward him feels like a leap of faith, my body almost humming with excitement. I feel liberated, unshackled from the weight of my insecurities. The world outside the studio fades into a distant memory, and all that exists is the connection we share, pulsing with an unspoken understanding.

As we begin, I can feel the energy shift in the room. The music swells, its notes wrapping around us like a warm embrace, and I lose myself in the rhythm. Each beat resonates in my chest, igniting my limbs with life. We weave through the choreography we've spent countless hours perfecting, our bodies moving in perfect sync, like two halves of a whole. The narrative unfolds seamlessly, a tale of passion and struggle told through the elegance of dance.

With each pirouette, I feel the world slip away, leaving behind only the sheer joy of movement. Jason matches my energy, his presence anchoring me as we explore the choreography, pushing the boundaries of our styles. We glide, spin, and leap, our bodies responding instinctively to the music that seems to flow through our very veins. There's a beautiful intimacy in our dance; every brush of our hands ignites a fire, every shared breath draws us closer.

I've always believed that dance has a language of its own, one that transcends words and expresses what we often cannot say aloud. In this moment, as we entwine ourselves in each other's rhythm, it feels as though we are confessing our dreams, fears, and desires with every movement. The music swells, enveloping us in its embrace, and I can almost hear our hearts beat in unison.

A sudden turn brings us face to face, inches apart, our breaths mingling in the space between. The chemistry between us crackles, electric and intoxicating. My pulse races, and I see the flicker of something deeper in Jason's eyes—a reflection of my own longing, a shared secret that dances just beneath the surface. I want to reach out, to close that distance and see if the spark ignites into a flame, but uncertainty tugs at me, weaving doubt into the fabric of our connection.

"Let's take it from the top," he says, his voice steady, breaking the moment but leaving a trail of tension in its wake. I nod, willing my heart to settle as we fall back into the dance. The music swells again, and I immerse myself, pouring everything I have into our performance, channeling my emotions through each movement.

As the routine unfolds, I begin to lose myself in the narrative we're creating. We tell a story of resilience, of overcoming obstacles and finding beauty in the chaos. With each leap, I feel the weight of my fears lifting, replaced by a burgeoning sense of hope. Dancing with Jason, I feel seen, truly seen, in a way I never imagined possible.

He reaches for me, his hand warm against mine, guiding me into a spin that sends a rush of exhilaration through my body. The world outside ceases to exist as I embrace the moment, feeling light and weightless. In the depths of my heart, I realize that this isn't just about dance; it's about finding solace in the connection we're forging, a tether in the midst of life's uncertainties.

The song crescendos, each note swelling like my heart, pounding in rhythm with the movement of our bodies. I sense the shift, the undeniable bond growing between us. We share knowing glances, unspoken words that linger in the air like delicate threads connecting us, weaving a tapestry rich with emotion. The moment stretches, suspended in time, and I am caught between wanting to cling to it and fearing what it could mean.

With one final spin, I find myself back in his arms, breathless and alive. The intensity of our gaze holds promises, uncharted territory filled with unspoken possibilities. I can't help but smile, the warmth of his presence igniting a flame of hope that flickers brightly within me. This isn't merely a dance; it's a glimpse into something profound and beautiful, an invitation to explore the depths of our connection beyond the confines of the studio.

As the final notes linger in the air, I can feel the reality of our situation pressing down like a weight on my chest. What comes next? The unknowing terrifies me, yet there's an undeniable thrill in the uncertainty, a call to embrace whatever it is that lies ahead. For now, though, I allow myself to be fully present in this moment, dancing not just with my body but with my heart wide open, ready to receive whatever magic may come our way.

The final notes of our routine fade, leaving the studio wrapped in a hushed stillness, the air thick with the remnants of our shared energy. I stand there, breathless, my heart thrumming like a live wire. Jason's presence lingers close, warm and inviting, as if he could absorb my racing pulse simply by being near. I wonder if he feels it too—the connection that's grown between us, swelling with each beat of the music and every shared glance.

"Let's take a break," he suggests, a hint of a smile playing at the corners of his lips, as if he knows the effect he has on me. I nod, but my mind races, thoughts spiraling as I turn away to catch my breath. I'm surprised by the mixture of exhilaration and anxiety swirling inside me. Dance has always been my escape, a language I spoke fluently, yet here I am, standing at the precipice of something far more complicated.

I walk to the mirrored wall, the reflections of our movements still dancing in my mind, but the glass also reflects the flutter of uncertainty in my stomach. What if this chemistry is just an illusion, a fleeting spark meant to fizzle out once the music stops? What if stepping beyond the confines of our friendship would ruin everything we've built? The thoughts nag at me, unrelenting, as I watch Jason stretch, muscles rippling beneath his skin, a captivating sight that pulls me back into the present.

I turn away, determined to shake off the spiraling doubts, and instead focus on the rhythmic thud of my heartbeat, steadying myself. A moment of silence passes between us, charged with unspoken words, and I take a deep breath, inhaling the familiar scent of the studio—the faint tang of sweat mingling with the comforting scent of polished wood.

"You know, I think we really captured something today," Jason says, breaking the silence, his voice warm and rich, drawing me back into our shared space. I glance over, meeting his gaze, and there's a flicker of pride in his expression that makes my heart swell.

"Yeah, it felt good," I reply, trying to keep my tone casual, but I can hear the breathlessness in my voice. "Like we're finally finding our rhythm."

His eyes brighten, and he steps closer, the space between us shrinking until the warmth of his body radiates against mine. "I knew you had it in you," he says, sincerity lacing his words. "You're a natural." There's a softness to his tone that makes me feel seen, valued, and I can't help but blush under his praise.

"I appreciate that," I murmur, surprised by the weight of his compliment. "But it's really a team effort."

Jason shakes his head, his dark hair falling into his eyes in a way that's both charming and infuriatingly distracting. "No. This is all you. I just... I get to ride along on your talent."

We share a moment of laughter, the tension easing slightly, and I feel lighter, buoyed by his easy camaraderie. Still, beneath the surface of our banter, I sense an undercurrent, a tension that lingers, waiting for the right moment to break through.

He gestures toward the corner of the studio where our bags are tossed haphazardly, and I follow his gaze. "Want to grab some water? I could use a break before we dive back in."

I nod, my throat suddenly dry, and we walk together, our footsteps echoing softly on the wooden floor. The studio is adorned with posters of famous dancers, their graceful forms frozen in time, but it's hard to focus on anything other than the heat radiating from Jason beside me. As we reach our bags, I rummage for my water bottle, my fingers brushing against the cool plastic, grounding me as I try to shake off the whirlwind of emotions spiraling through me.

"Do you ever think about what's next?" he asks casually, taking a sip from his own bottle, eyes flicking to the floor, as if contemplating the weight of his question.

I pause, feeling the gravity of the moment settle around us like a heavy blanket. "What do you mean?" I ask, trying to sound nonchalant, but my heart races as I brace myself for what he might say.

"Like, after the performance. What happens when the lights go down and the audience leaves?" He looks at me, the intensity of his gaze sending a thrill through my chest. "I mean, what do you want to do? What's your dream?"

The question hangs in the air, and for a moment, I'm caught off guard. My dreams have always been about dance—each pirouette, each leap, a step toward a shimmering future—but I've never truly voiced them out loud. There's a freedom in sharing my aspirations, a weight that lifts as I consider the possibilities.

"I want to perform, of course," I begin, my voice gaining strength. "But I also want to teach. I want to help others find their voice through dance, to experience that same liberation I feel when I'm on stage."

His expression shifts, admiration flickering in his eyes. "You'd be a great teacher," he says earnestly, and I can feel the warmth of his words wrap around me like a cozy blanket. "You have a gift for it."

"Thanks," I reply, a shy smile tugging at my lips. "What about you? What's next for you after this?"

He leans against the wall, a thoughtful look crossing his face. "I've been thinking about trying out for a company. Maybe take my dancing more seriously. I've always wanted to do something big, something that makes an impact."

A flutter of excitement dances in my stomach. "You'd be incredible in a company. You have the talent for it."

Jason chuckles, but there's an edge of seriousness to his tone. "It's a big leap, though. A lot of competition. What if I don't make it?"

I step closer, a sudden surge of conviction swelling within me. "You will," I say firmly, the words spilling out before I can second-guess myself. "You've put in the work. You have the passion, and that counts for so much. Don't doubt yourself."

His gaze meets mine, and for a heartbeat, the world around us fades. There's an honesty in his eyes that makes my heart race, a depth that reaches beyond the surface, hinting at dreams and fears alike. The moment stretches, heavy with possibilities and uncharted territories, and I can feel the warmth of connection wrap around us once more.

"Thanks, I needed that," he says softly, and the sincerity in his voice sends a rush of warmth through me.

Just then, the studio door swings open, breaking our reverie. A wave of chatter floods in, and the moment dissipates like smoke in the wind, leaving me with the lingering taste of what might have been. I watch as our fellow dancers begin to fill the room, their laughter and energy a stark contrast to the intimate cocoon we had created.

But as the music starts again, a sense of purpose fills me anew. The studio, with all its memories and aspirations, stands as a testament to the journeys we've taken and the ones yet to come. With Jason by my side, I know that whatever challenges lie ahead, I am ready to embrace them, ready to dance through life with an open heart.

The chatter of fellow dancers fills the studio, blending with the rhythm of the music as we prepare to dive back into our routine. I can feel the vibrant energy of the room wrap around me like a well-loved blanket, a sense of belonging that's as comforting as it is invigorating. The studio has always felt like my sanctuary, each corner steeped in memories of laughter, sweat, and unyielding determination. Today, however, it feels different, infused with the unspoken tension between Jason and me—a current that hums beneath the surface, urging me to explore it further.

We gather in a circle to discuss our upcoming performance, our voices overlapping like the melodies we strive to master. I listen, nodding and chiming in, but my mind wanders back to the moment we shared. I can't shake the feeling that something has shifted, that our connection has deepened in a way that defies logic. I catch Jason's eye across the room, and my breath catches in my throat. There's an understanding there, an acknowledgment of the feelings simmering just beneath our friendly banter.

As rehearsal progresses, we move through the choreography with an intensity that feels electric, each movement sharper and more deliberate than before. I'm hyper-aware of his every gesture, the way his muscles ripple as he executes a turn, how his brow furrows in concentration. My own body responds instinctively, mirroring his energy as we navigate the complexities of our routine.

"Let's try it with more emotion," our choreographer instructs, his voice cutting through the air like a knife. "Imagine you're telling a story. What do you feel? Let that guide you."

The words resonate deep within me. Dance has always been about expression, about laying bare my soul through movement, but today I feel an urgency, a desire to pour every ounce of my being into our performance. I glance at Jason, and he meets my gaze, the intensity of his eyes igniting a spark of inspiration.

As the music swells again, I let my heart lead. I feel each note reverberate through my body, a visceral connection that spills into every twirl and leap. Jason matches my energy, our movements entwined as we dance not just as partners but as two halves of a single entity. We share glances filled with unspoken words, fleeting touches that send shivers racing down my spine. With every dip and spin, I feel our connection grow, blooming like wildflowers breaking through the cracks of concrete.

But just as I allow myself to get lost in the moment, doubt creeps in. What if this connection, this chemistry, is a mere figment of my imagination? The thought unsettles me, and I find myself hesitating, my movements faltering for a split second. Jason notices immediately, his eyes narrowing with concern, and it makes my heart race in a way that both thrills and terrifies me.

"Hey," he says softly, his voice slicing through the haze of uncertainty. "You're doing great. Just focus on the dance, and let everything else fade away."

His words are like a lifeline, pulling me back to the present. I nod, taking a deep breath, willing myself to banish the lingering insecurities. I push through, pouring everything I have into the dance, surrendering to the rhythm, the emotion, the beauty of it all.

As we finish the routine, the room erupts into applause, and I can feel the adrenaline surging through my veins, a cocktail of joy and exhaustion. I search for Jason's gaze, and when our eyes meet, there's a spark—a shared understanding that transcends the applause around us. He grins, that charming smile lighting up his face, and I can't help but smile back.

"See? You nailed it," he says, his breath warm against my cheek.

"Thanks to you," I reply, the words slipping out before I can temper my enthusiasm. "You always bring out the best in me."

The moment lingers, charged with possibilities, and I wonder if he can feel the same electric current that seems to crackle between us. But before I can delve deeper into the moment, the rehearsal is interrupted by the arrival of our dance coach, her presence commanding attention with an effortless grace.

"Alright, everyone," she calls, her tone authoritative yet encouraging. "Great work today! Let's take a quick break, and then we'll run through the routine one more time before we wrap up."

As the group disperses, I slip away to the side, trying to collect my thoughts. The echoes of our dance reverberate in my mind, leaving me breathless and exhilarated. I lean against the wall, closing my eyes for a moment, allowing the sounds of the studio to wash over me.

Jason approaches, his expression softening as he leans against the wall beside me. "You okay?" he asks, genuine concern etched in his features.

"I am," I assure him, opening my eyes to meet his gaze. "Just... processing, I guess. Today felt different."

"It did," he agrees, a hint of a smile on his lips. "In a good way, right?"

I nod, feeling my cheeks flush at the thought of what might be brewing beneath the surface of our friendship. "Definitely in a good way."

There's a moment of silence as we stand side by side, the air thick with unspoken words. I can feel the tension building again, a palpable force drawing us closer.

"Listen," he says, breaking the spell, "I know we've talked about our dreams, but I want you to know that I believe in you—like, really believe in you. You're going to shine in this performance."

His words ignite something deep within me, a fire of determination mixed with hope. "And you," I say, my voice steadier now, "you're going to blow everyone away. I can see you on that stage, a spotlight shining just for you."

He chuckles, the sound rich and warm. "Now you're just making me blush."

We share a laugh, and in that moment, I realize how effortless this connection is, how easily we slip into comfortable banter. But as the laughter fades, I feel the weight of our words hanging in the air, filling the space with something deeper, something we're both afraid to name.

"Do you think we'll get a chance to perform together again after this?" I ask, trying to keep my tone light, but my heart races at the thought.

"Absolutely," Jason replies, a glimmer of mischief in his eyes. "This is just the beginning. We're a team now, right? Plus, I have a feeling we'll find ways to collaborate in the future."

The prospect fills me with hope, and I can't help but smile. "I'd like that."

Just then, the rehearsal call echoes through the studio, and we both straighten, the moment dissipating like mist. As we return to the center of the room, I can't shake the feeling that this is a turning point, a threshold we're standing on, waiting to step into something new.

As the music starts again, I allow myself to get lost in the moment, knowing that whatever comes next, I am ready. Ready to embrace the dance, the connection, and whatever magic lies ahead. Each note reverberates through me, resonating with the promise of tomorrow, and I know I want to dive headfirst into this beautiful, chaotic journey—whatever it may hold. The studio becomes a canvas once more, and I'm determined to paint it with the colors of my dreams, side by side with Jason, as we explore the uncharted territory of our hearts.

Chapter 26: Moments of Clarity

The night is thick with anticipation, an electric current running through the air, palpable enough to ignite the senses. The studio hums with an undercurrent of chatter, laughter spilling from the audience like the sweet notes of a well-played piano. Each face that fills the seats holds its own story, woven into the fabric of this moment, this shared experience, as they come together under the glowing chandeliers that shimmer like stars suspended in the ceiling of our dreams.

I stand backstage, the cool concrete floor beneath my feet grounding me amidst the whirlwind of excitement. The walls pulse with the sounds of distant music, notes dancing through the air, teasing the edges of my consciousness. Each beat thuds against my chest, echoing the rhythm of my heart, a metronome counting down to the crescendo of our performance. The smell of freshly polished wood mingles with the faint, intoxicating aroma of anticipation—an olfactory reminder that I am standing on the threshold of something profound.

Jason stands beside me, his presence a steady anchor in the ocean of noise. His hands find mine, warm and reassuring, drawing me closer as if sharing an unspoken pact. His gaze, sharp and unwavering, searches mine, grounding me in the moment. There's a vulnerability in his eyes, a shared recognition that tonight is not merely a showcase of our talents; it's a celebration of everything that has brought us here—the late-night rehearsals, the moments of doubt, the joy of discovery, and the gentle nudges from one another when we felt too weak to take another step.

As the lights dim, a hush falls over the crowd, transforming the atmosphere into something almost sacred. My breath quickens, but in that breath, I feel the weight of our journey crystallize into clarity. This stage isn't just a platform; it's a canvas upon which we will paint the intricate patterns of our stories. Every stumble we've endured, every triumph we've celebrated, has culminated in this moment. And as I glance at the faces of those who have come to support us—friends who've laughed with us, family who've cried with us, and mentors who've guided us—the realization settles in my bones. This isn't just my story; it's ours.

The curtain rises slowly, revealing the wooden stage bathed in a warm glow, the soft luminescence creating an ethereal backdrop that beckons us forward. As we step into the light, I feel the rush of adrenaline flooding my veins, each heartbeat synchronized with the pulsating energy radiating from the audience. It's as if we've been transformed, every ounce of doubt melting away, leaving only the purity of purpose behind.

The first notes of music spill into the air, a gentle swell that carries us away, each sound wrapping around us like an embrace. I can see the faces before me, a sea of anticipation and encouragement, and I realize I am not alone. We are a collective, woven together by shared aspirations and dreams, each note a thread binding us in a tapestry of expression. As Jason and I begin to move, every gesture becomes a dialogue, a conversation that transcends words. The choreography flows through us, our bodies speaking a language honed through countless hours of practice and passion.

With each step, the weight of our struggles slips away, replaced by the buoyancy of joy that comes from simply being alive in this moment. The rhythm pulses beneath our feet, an invisible current lifting us higher, guiding us through the story we've crafted together. I feel my spirit soar as I lose myself in the dance, each movement an extension of my heart, a testament to everything I have fought for.

The audience watches with rapt attention, their eyes glistening with shared emotion. I can feel their energy, a tangible wave that washes over me, bolstering my courage. As Jason twirls me into a spin, the world blurs, and I am enveloped in a cocoon of light and sound, a whirlwind of expression that feels both exhilarating and terrifying. In those moments of dizzying freedom, I understand what it means to be truly alive—to embrace vulnerability, to dance with abandon, and to let the music flow through me.

The performance builds to its climax, a fever pitch of emotion and energy that seems to resonate deep within the hearts of everyone present. I see my mother in the front row, her eyes shimmering with pride, her smile a beacon guiding me through the whirlwind of adrenaline. The memory of her gentle encouragement echoes in my mind, reminding me of all the times she believed in me when I struggled to believe in myself. It's a thread that connects us, an unbreakable bond that transcends the stage.

As we approach the final moments of our performance, I feel Jason's hand tighten around mine, a silent acknowledgment that we are not just two individuals performing; we are partners in this journey. With one last leap, we land together, the world around us falling silent as the final note hangs in the air like a lingering promise. In that stillness, the reality of what we've created washes over me, a wave of satisfaction mingling with relief.

The applause erupts like a storm, a torrent of sound that washes over us, lifting us to our feet. It's a wild, thunderous celebration of our shared journey, a tribute to every moment we've poured into this performance. The lights sparkle around us, illuminating the joy etched on our faces as we take our bows, hearts pounding with exhilaration. In that sea of sound and light, I understand: this is not just an end but a new beginning, a fresh chapter in a story that continues to unfold.

As the applause begins to wane, I catch my breath, the heat of the spotlight still radiating off my skin like the last glow of sunset clinging to the horizon. With every bow, I feel the weight of countless expectations lift, transforming into an intoxicating cocktail of relief and triumph. The world around me blurs into a gentle haze, and for a moment, I'm suspended in time, surrounded by the warmth of appreciation and the soft hum of post-performance chatter. It's a cocoon of belonging, the kind that wraps around your heart and makes you forget about the worries of the outside world.

The audience begins to disperse, but their energy lingers like the final strains of music hanging in the air, a gentle reminder of our shared experience. I glance over at Jason, who is still beaming, his smile so infectious it could light up even the dimmest of corners. We exchange a knowing look, one that speaks volumes without the need for words. In that moment, I feel a deep connection not only to him but to everyone in the room, each person carrying a piece of our journey with them as they depart.

"Let's find your family," Jason suggests, pulling me toward the backstage area where friends and loved ones await. I nod, my heart racing in the aftermath of the performance. The rush of adrenaline begins to ebb, replaced by an overwhelming gratitude for the people who have supported me throughout this journey. As we weave through the throng of well-wishers, laughter and chatter swirl around us, a vivid tapestry of emotion, each thread representing a connection made, a moment shared.

The backstage area is a kaleidoscope of activity, with dancers adjusting their costumes, hair stylists cleaning up brushes and products scattered across tables, and stagehands rushing around, packing away props and equipment as if they were preparing for battle. The air is thick with the scent of sweat and perfume, mingling in a chaotic symphony of human experience. It's both exhilarating and chaotic, and in the midst of it all, I spot my mother, her eyes sparkling with pride, a lighthouse cutting through the fog of excitement.

"Mom!" I call out, my voice breaking slightly as I rush toward her. She envelops me in a warm embrace, her familiar scent—coconut and vanilla—filling my senses. It's a comfort that melts away the lingering adrenaline, grounding me once more in the reality of my accomplishments.

"You were amazing!" she exclaims, her voice trembling with emotion. "I can't believe how far you've come!"

I smile, overwhelmed by her enthusiasm, feeling as though the universe had aligned perfectly for this moment. "I couldn't have done it without you," I say, pulling back to look into her eyes. The admiration reflected in her gaze speaks of late-night talks and shared dreams, of sacrifices made and lessons learned. She's the one who helped me navigate the choppy waters of self-doubt, the one who taught me to dance through the storms.

"Let's get a picture," she says, and before I can respond, she whips out her phone, pulling me close again. Jason slides in beside us, a good-natured grin plastered on his face as my mother captures the moment, her fingers dancing over the screen. The click of the shutter is like the snap of a memory being forged, one I will treasure forever.

As we pose, my heart swells with a sense of belonging, of having finally carved out a place for myself in the vast tapestry of life. Just then, a group of fellow dancers rushes over, their faces flushed with excitement and camaraderie. They wrap us in their jubilant energy, sharing compliments and anecdotes about our shared journey. Laughter bubbles up as they recount our most ridiculous rehearsal moments—like the time I tripped over my own feet and landed in a heap, a spectacle that would have made a perfect blooper reel.

"Do you remember that?" I laugh, shaking my head at the memory. "I thought I was going to die of embarrassment!"

"But you got right back up," Jason interjects, nudging me playfully. "That's what makes you a true performer."

As the conversation flows, I bask in the warmth of friendship and shared dreams. We've forged bonds through countless hours of practice, each dancer a thread in this vibrant tapestry. I realize, with a swell of pride, that we are not just performers; we are a family, bound by passion and perseverance.

As the evening unfolds, I take a moment to step outside, needing a breath of fresh air after the sensory overload of the night. The city is alive with energy, the streets pulsating with life, bathed in the soft glow of streetlights. I lean against a lamppost, closing my eyes and letting the cool breeze brush against my skin, grounding me in this newfound reality. The distant sounds of laughter and music blend with the faint hum of traffic, a comforting reminder that life continues beyond the stage.

Just then, I hear footsteps approaching, and I open my eyes to see Jason stepping outside, his face alight with the same exuberance that filled the studio. He leans against the lamppost beside me, a comfortable silence enveloping us, the chaos of the showcase fading into the background.

"I can't believe we did it," he says, breaking the silence. There's a sparkle in his eye, a reflection of the joy we've shared. "It felt like magic up there."

I nod, feeling a warmth spread through me, a shared sense of accomplishment that lingers in the air between us. "It really did. I think this is just the beginning for us." My voice is steady, confidence surging through me like the wind rustling the leaves overhead.

As the world around us continues to pulse with life, I realize that the journey ahead is filled with endless possibilities. Each breath I take is infused with hope, a promise of what's to come, and as Jason stands beside me, I can't help but feel that whatever challenges lie ahead, I am ready to face them. Together.

The night air wraps around us, cool and invigorating, as Jason and I linger beneath the lamppost, the soft glow casting a warm halo over our faces. It's a sharp contrast to the intensity of the studio, a moment of stillness where the cacophony of our triumph fades into the background, leaving space for contemplation. As laughter echoes from within, a soft symphony of joy, I can't shake the feeling that this evening is merely a precursor to something far grander.

"Have you thought about what's next?" Jason asks, his tone light yet probing, the hint of a challenge in his words. "I mean, after this?"

I tilt my head back, gazing at the stars sprinkled across the indigo sky, their twinkling reminders of dreams yet to be realized. "Honestly? I've been so focused on this showcase that I haven't really planned beyond tonight." My voice is laced with a hint of uncertainty, a whisper of vulnerability that lingers in the air between us.

Jason shifts closer, his shoulder brushing against mine. "What if we could take this—everything we've worked for—and turn it into something more?" His words hang in the air, thick with possibility, like the unspoken thoughts that flutter in the corners of my mind.

"What do you mean?" I ask, intrigued but cautious, my heart racing at the thought of stretching my ambitions beyond the confines of the stage.

"What if we created our own show? Something that tells our stories, showcases our growth, and brings in the people we've met along the way?" His enthusiasm is contagious, sparking a flicker of excitement within me.

The idea dances in my mind, tantalizing and terrifying all at once. I envision a vibrant performance, alive with movement and emotion, weaving together the experiences and dreams of all the dancers I've come to know. "You mean like a community showcase?" I ask, testing the waters.

"Exactly! A platform for emerging talent, a celebration of the journey we've all taken. It could be so powerful, bringing people together."

I can see the fire in his eyes, his passion igniting my own dormant aspirations. "We could incorporate storytelling elements, share our struggles, our breakthroughs," I muse, the vision growing clearer. The idea begins to take shape, blossoming like the flowers in the park we often danced in during our rehearsals, each petal a piece of our collective narrative.

"Let's do it," I say, the words spilling out before I can rein them in. A thrill courses through me, igniting a spark that had long lain dormant. "Let's make it happen."

With newfound determination, we step back into the studio, the warm lights beckoning us like old friends. The energy within has shifted, a vibrant undercurrent that hums with possibility. Friends and fellow dancers continue to mingle, their voices a tapestry of stories interwoven with laughter and joy. I spot some of my classmates gathered in a corner, animatedly discussing their performances, and I can't help but feel a surge of pride for what we've accomplished together.

"Hey! Can we have your attention for a second?" I call out, raising my voice just enough to catch their interest. The chatter begins to die down, and a few heads turn in our direction.

Jason steps forward, a confident smile spreading across his face. "We're thinking of starting something new—something that can showcase not just our talents but also the incredible journey we've all been on."

The room buzzes with curiosity, and I feel a rush of adrenaline as I continue, "We want to create a community showcase, where we can tell our stories through dance, invite others to share their journeys, and really connect with one another."

The responses are immediate—eyes widen, smiles break across faces, and the buzz of excitement grows.

"I love it!" someone shouts from the back, and another dancer, Emma, chimes in, "We should have it at that outdoor amphitheater! It's perfect for summer evenings."

Ideas begin to swirl like the leaves caught in a playful breeze, each suggestion more vibrant than the last. We bounce concepts off each other, our laughter mingling with the thrill of shared dreams. I feel a sense of belonging deeper than I've ever known, a tapestry of hopes woven together as we move forward, driven by passion and the thrill of creation.

As the night unfolds, the showcase evolves from a mere idea into a tangible vision, a shared commitment that binds us all. The energy in the room swells, wrapping us in a collective embrace that promises to carry us forward, and I feel a sense of liberation in our shared purpose.

"Let's plan a meeting," Jason suggests, his excitement infectious. "We can brainstorm, bring in everyone's ideas, and make this a reality."

I can hardly contain my enthusiasm. "Absolutely! I can take care of the flyers and get the word out. We'll make sure everyone knows they're welcome to join us."

In that moment, as we stand in the middle of the studio, surrounded by the warmth of friendship and the vibrant pulse of creativity, I know we are on the brink of something extraordinary. This is no longer just about individual talent; it's about building a community, a platform where dreams can flourish.

As the last of the audience trickles out, their laughter echoing down the hallway, I take a moment to absorb the magic of it all. The studio, once just a space for rehearsals, now feels like a sanctuary of possibility. I can almost see the invisible threads weaving between us all, connecting our dreams, our struggles, and our stories into a beautiful tapestry of shared experience.

Jason nudges me playfully, pulling me from my reverie. "Ready to celebrate?"

I grin, the excitement bubbling up inside me like champagne ready to spill over. "Absolutely. Let's do it!"

As we step into the cool night, the stars above seem to twinkle in agreement, as if the universe itself is cheering us on. The world is wide open, a canvas waiting for us to paint our dreams across it, and with Jason by my side and my friends supporting us, I know this is just the beginning of an extraordinary journey. Together, we will dance into the future, each step echoing with the promise of what lies ahead.

Chapter 27: The Power of Performance

The stage glowed with a soft, warm light, casting shadows that danced like phantoms across the worn wooden floor. I stood backstage, heart racing, my breath coming in shallow bursts as the faint thrum of music seeped through the heavy curtains. It was the kind of night that promised magic, where every fiber of my being tingled with anticipation. The scent of fresh paint from the backdrop mingled with the lingering aroma of popcorn from the lobby, creating a heady mix that somehow felt like home.

I glanced at my reflection in the cracked mirror. My hair was pinned in a messy bun, wisps escaping to frame my face, and my cheeks glowed with the nervous energy that electrified the air. I smoothed down my costume—a simple, flowing dress in deep cerulean that whispered of the ocean. The fabric shimmered under the stage lights, catching the glint of my spirit as I prepared to pour everything into this performance. It wasn't just a routine; it was a testament to the struggles my friend Claire faced, a vivid embodiment of her battles, her resilience.

As we waited for the cue, I caught sight of Claire in the wings. She was wrapped in her own bubble of calm, her gaze fixed on the stage as if she were peeling back the layers of her own reality, ready to step into something greater. Her eyes sparkled with a mixture of fear and fierce determination, and I couldn't help but feel a swell of pride for her. We had been through so much together—years of laughter, tears, and the kind of late-night talks that stretch into the early hours of dawn, each word a brick in the foundation of our friendship.

The announcer's voice crackled through the speakers, reverberating like the pulse of the city beyond the theater's walls. "Ladies and gentlemen, welcome to the Annual Spring Gala of the Lincoln Center for the Performing Arts!" My pulse quickened, a drumbeat echoing in my ears as the spotlight illuminated the stage, a beacon of opportunity. It was time.

With a deep breath, we stepped into the light. The audience's energy surged forward, wrapping around us like a warm embrace. I could see faces—some familiar, others strangers, all eager to witness the tale we were about to weave. The music swelled, a rich tapestry of strings and piano that cradled us in its embrace, guiding our every movement.

Our choreography unfolded like a story, each step a word, each turn a sentence that led to a crescendo of emotions. I felt the weight of my body as I leaped across the stage, the ground pushing back against my feet, urging me to soar higher. The fabric of my dress fluttered around me, echoing the crashing waves that had inspired this dance. I pictured Claire's journey—the storms she had weathered, the calm she had fought to maintain. Every pirouette whispered her name, every gesture spoke of her courage.

The audience was captivated, their collective breath held in anticipation. I could see a mother clutching her daughter's hand, a couple nestled together in the front row, their eyes reflecting the journey we took them on. In that moment, we were all connected—strangers united by the raw power of performance. I felt Claire's spirit merge with mine, her heart beating alongside my own as we danced for her, for us, for everyone who had ever fought to rise above their circumstances.

As the tempo shifted, our movements became more frantic, more urgent. The music roared, a wild storm that matched the tumultuous emotions coursing through me. I could almost hear Claire's voice in my mind, reminding me of the times we had spent on the sidelines, whispering secrets and dreams while the world rushed by. She had always been the dreamer, while I was the doer, and now, we were both immersed in this moment of creation, both willing our dreams into existence.

The climax approached, a moment suspended in time as we reached the pinnacle of our performance. My heart swelled with an overwhelming sense of triumph and vulnerability, and for a heartbeat, I felt as if I were flying. The world melted away, leaving only the rhythm of our bodies moving as one, a language spoken without words, an expression of everything that had led us here.

And then, as the final notes rang out, a hush fell over the theater. We froze in place, every muscle tense, every breath suspended as we held the last pose—a tableau of resilience and hope. The silence stretched, and for a fleeting moment, I feared we had lost them. But then, like the breaking of dawn, a thunderous applause erupted, filling the space with sound and warmth.

A wave of exhilaration washed over me, a flood of relief mingling with disbelief. We did it. The curtain fell slowly, a curtain of dreams woven from sweat and sacrifice, and in that moment, I felt something deep within me shift. We had created a connection that transcended words, a bond forged through art and authenticity.

As the applause cascaded around us, I caught a glimpse of Claire's face, radiant with joy, her eyes shimmering like the stars we had often gazed at together on those late-night rooftop escapades. We had turned her struggle into a narrative that sang, that danced, and it felt as if we had shared a part of ourselves with every soul in that audience. It was a gift that kept giving, a reminder that even in the darkest of times, there existed a flicker of light, a spark of resilience that could ignite the flame of hope.

The applause roared like a distant storm, echoing through the dim corridors as I stepped off the stage, still riding the high of the performance. My heart raced, a vibrant pulse that matched the rhythm of the music that still hummed in my ears. The world outside the theater seemed to shimmer with possibility, the kind of electric energy that vibrated in the air after a shared moment of magic. I glanced back at Claire, who stood enveloped in a flurry of congratulatory hugs and whispered praises. Her face glowed, illuminated by the stage lights that had just moments ago cast her in a heroic glow.

As I made my way through the throng of excited dancers and supportive friends, I couldn't shake the feeling of being in a bubble—caught between the exuberance of our shared success and the looming reality that awaited us outside those theater doors. The walls of the Lincoln Center seemed to pulse with the echoes of our performance, a sanctuary that sheltered our dreams for just a little while longer. Each step I took felt weighted, the reverberations of our dance still pulsing in my veins.

Once in the green room, I let out a breath I didn't realize I was holding. The walls were adorned with photographs of past performances—dancers frozen in time, capturing the essence of moments that had taken place long before we were ever a part of this space. I traced my fingers along the framed images, imagining the laughter and heartache behind each one. The art of performance felt like a conversation across time, where every dancer added their verse to a collective narrative of passion and pain.

Claire ambled over, her cheeks flushed with a mixture of exhaustion and exhilaration. "Did you see their faces?" she gushed, her voice a buoyant melody that lifted my spirits even higher. "They were with us, every step of the way!"

"Absolutely," I replied, smiling at her infectious enthusiasm. "You were amazing out there. I don't think I've ever seen you dance like that."

She beamed, the kind of brightness that chased away any lingering shadows of doubt. Her transformation from a timid girl who once feared the spotlight to a radiant performer was nothing short of miraculous. I felt a swell of pride; we had done this together. It was more than a performance—it was a chapter of our lives written in motion, a testament to resilience that echoed far beyond the stage.

As we sat on a faded couch, our bodies still humming from the adrenaline, I could hear the chatter of the after-party filtering through the walls. Laughter floated in the air, mingling with the clinking of glasses and the gentle strumming of a guitar somewhere in the background. It was a celebration not just for our performance but for every late-night rehearsal and early morning stretching session. The triumph was bittersweet; the knowledge that tomorrow would bring a return to the mundane loomed over me like a cloud waiting to burst.

"Do you ever wonder what it would be like to dance in a big production?" Claire mused, her eyes sparkling with the promise of a dream yet to be realized. "To perform for an audience in Paris or New York?"

"Every day," I admitted, feeling a warmth spread through my chest at the thought. "But I also love these small moments—the intimacy of sharing our story in a space like this. It feels personal, you know?"

"True," she conceded, but her gaze drifted toward the door as if it might open to reveal a world of possibilities just waiting for us. "But think of the stories we could tell in a bigger venue. The impact we could have!"

The thought sent a thrill through me, but also a pang of anxiety. "What if we don't fit in that world?"

Claire leaned closer, her sincerity wrapping around me like a cozy blanket. "But we will! We just have to believe it, step by step. Like we did tonight."

I could see the determination in her eyes, a reflection of my own hopes and fears. In that moment, the boundaries of our ambitions began to blur, and a shared vision started to crystallize in the air between us. Perhaps the future was more than just a distant dream. Perhaps it was a tangible path we could carve together.

As the night wore on, we joined the throng of dancers who had gathered in the lobby, where laughter and joy bounced off the walls. A makeshift celebration had begun, with snacks and drinks sprawled across the tables. Familiar faces mingled with newcomers, and I felt the warmth of community wrap around me, a safety net forged from shared passions and unyielding support.

I spotted Ryan, our choreographer, who was laughing heartily with a group of dancers. He had a way of bringing out the best in us, challenging us to push our limits while creating a space where we could express ourselves freely. I made my way over to him, my heart still racing from the performance.

"Ryan!" I called, weaving through the crowd. "We did it! Thank you for believing in us!"

He turned, his face lighting up at the sight of me. "You were both phenomenal! I've never seen that kind of energy radiate from the stage before. You two have something special."

A flush of pride bloomed in my chest as we shared a quick embrace. "It felt incredible! We really connected with the audience."

"Keep that fire alive," he encouraged, clapping my shoulder. "You're destined for great things. Just remember, the stage isn't the limit; it's just the beginning."

His words resonated deep within me, filling the empty spaces where doubt lingered. I looked around at the jubilant faces, each person a thread in the vibrant tapestry of our dance community, and suddenly, the future didn't seem so daunting. It was an open door, waiting for us to step through and seize whatever awaited on the other side.

In the midst of the laughter and the celebration, I felt a sense of belonging, a whisper that told me we were not alone in this pursuit. Together, we were creating something more profound than dance; we were weaving a narrative that intertwined our lives and dreams, one step at a time.

The energy of the after-party enveloped me like a warm blanket, every laugh and cheer resonating in my bones. As I leaned against the refreshment table, I took a moment to absorb the scene—the buzzing laughter, the clinking glasses, and the undeniable joy that hung in the air. The smell of rich chocolate from the mini pastries mingled with the sharp tang of fizzy drinks, creating a sensory overload that felt like a celebration not just of our performance but of life itself.

"Hey, do you want to take a group picture?" A voice sliced through my reverie, pulling me back to the moment. It was Mia, a fellow dancer with an effervescent personality and an unyielding smile. Her camera was poised, ready to capture the joy of the night. I nodded enthusiastically, catching Claire's eye and motioning her over.

As we gathered, a mix of familiar faces and newfound friends encircled us, each one reflecting a unique journey that had brought them to this moment. The camera clicked, and laughter erupted, weaving a tapestry of memories that would linger long after the night ended. I felt the warmth of camaraderie surge through me as we posed and joked, the bond forged through sweat and effort strengthened by shared success.

Once the picture-taking frenzy calmed, Claire sidled up to me, her expression contemplative as she surveyed the bustling room. "What's next for us?" she mused, her voice a gentle whisper amidst the vibrant chaos. "This can't be it."

The question settled in my mind like a pebble dropped into still water, ripples of possibility spreading outward. I had long fantasized about what lay beyond this intimate world of community and support. "We could try to audition for that summer festival," I suggested, feeling a rush of excitement at the thought. "They're looking for fresh talent."

Her eyes lit up with a fiery intensity. "Yes! And what if we even start our own workshop? Teach what we've learned and inspire others to find their voice through dance?"

The idea resonated with me. Our struggles, our victories—these were not just our stories; they could become the foundation for others who needed that same spark. I envisioned a studio filled with eager faces, bodies moving in rhythm, creating their own narratives.

As we chatted about our dreams, the atmosphere shifted. The sounds of laughter and music faded, replaced by the whispers of our ambitions. We were no longer just two friends celebrating a performance; we were dreamers on the precipice of something greater, crafting a vision that was as tangible as the air around us.

Hours slipped by, marked by the ebb and flow of laughter and heartfelt conversations. I found myself floating from one group to another, absorbing snippets of life, listening to stories that resonated with my own. Each dancer carried a piece of their journey within them—some had faced adversity, others had chased dreams that felt just out of reach. In that space, vulnerability blossomed into strength, and I realized we were not just performers; we were storytellers, each movement a chapter in an ever-evolving narrative.

As the night deepened, I noticed a group huddled together in a corner, their faces animated with discussion. Drawn by curiosity, I edged closer, overhearing snippets about an upcoming competition. The words "New York" and "stage" floated around like confetti, igniting a spark of excitement in my chest. A competition meant exposure, potential, and a chance to showcase our story on a larger scale.

Claire caught my gaze, her expression mirroring my own enthusiasm. "What do you think?" she asked, her voice barely above a whisper. "Should we dive in?"

With the energy of the night swirling around us, it felt like a perfect moment to leap into the unknown. "Let's do it!" I replied, the decision forming a tangible bond between us, a shared commitment to embrace the challenge.

We spent the remainder of the evening discussing strategies and brainstorming ideas for our submission piece. The chatter of our fellow dancers became a backdrop to our planning, their excitement blending seamlessly with our own. The more we talked, the more the possibilities unfurled before us—a sprawling canvas waiting for the brushstrokes of our creativity.

The night wore on, but the thrill of our conversation kept us energized. As I glanced around the room, I saw that we were not alone in our ambitions. The passion among us was palpable; each dancer was searching for their next breakthrough, their next moment to shine. We were all artists, each sculpting our lives through the language of movement, our aspirations converging in a shared dance of determination.

Finally, as the festivities began to wind down, I stepped outside for a breath of fresh air. The cool night air kissed my skin, invigorating me and drawing the vibrant energy from the celebration into a quieter space of reflection. The stars sparkled overhead, twinkling like diamonds scattered across velvet. I closed my eyes, feeling the cool breeze tousle my hair as I soaked in the serenity of the moment.

Claire joined me, her presence a comforting anchor. "Tonight felt like a turning point, didn't it?" she mused, her voice soft yet confident. "We've opened a door, and I don't think we can close it now."

"No," I agreed, a smile tugging at my lips. "It's wide open, and it's exhilarating."

We stood together in companionable silence, two dreamers at the edge of a precipice, the unknown stretching before us like a vast ocean. The sound of laughter and music faded into the background, replaced by the rhythm of our shared heartbeat, a reminder that whatever lay ahead, we would navigate it together.

As we returned inside, the lights flickered, casting a warm glow on the faces of our friends. Their laughter wrapped around us like a cocoon, and I felt an overwhelming sense of gratitude. This was my world—one filled with passion, creativity, and relentless determination. I knew we were on the cusp of something remarkable, and for the first time in a long while, the future didn't seem frightening; it felt like an exhilarating adventure waiting to unfold, step by step.

With a renewed sense of purpose, I locked eyes with Claire, and we both smiled, knowing that our journey was just beginning. We were not just dancers; we were architects of our own destinies, ready to pen our next chapter on whatever stage awaited us.

Chapter 28: After the Spotlight

The warmth of the stage lights lingers on my skin, a faint reminder of the adrenaline rush that surged through me just moments before. The applause, a distant echo now, leaves a bittersweet taste on my tongue, mingling with the tang of sweat and the fragrance of freshly polished wood from the stage beneath my feet. Backstage, shadows loom, shifting in the dim light, casting long silhouettes that dance with the fading echoes of our performance. I take a deep breath, the air thick with the scent of makeup and the metallic tinge of the stage's rigging.

Jason stands beside me, his eyes glinting with the exhilaration of our shared triumph. We embrace tightly, the warmth of his body grounding me amidst the whirlwind of emotions swirling within. He smells of cedarwood and a hint of something citrusy, a lingering reminder of the soap we both used before the show. In his presence, I find solace. The weight of our journey—the endless rehearsals, the late-night talks, the moments of doubt—feels tangible, wrapping around us like a well-worn blanket.

As we pull apart, a sliver of uncertainty creeps in, cold and unwelcome. I catch sight of the critics filtering through the heavy backstage curtain, their expressions as sharp as the ink they wield. A knot forms in my stomach, tightening with each step they take, the clicking of their pens echoing in my mind like the ticking of a clock counting down the seconds until judgment. They swarm like locusts, hungry for anything they can dissect, their notebooks ready to capture every flaw, every misstep, as they advance on our oasis of victory.

Some critics offer praise, their faces animated as they recount the highlights of our performance. I soak in their words, allowing myself to float momentarily in the comfort of their approval. But then I hear it—a whisper that cuts through the applause, as sharp as a glass shard against my skin. "Did you see her absence during the rehearsal period? Can she truly embody the character if she didn't put in the time?" The words linger in the air, heavy with accusation, tainting the jubilance of the moment.

I try to shake it off, to brush aside the doubts creeping in like unwelcome weeds, but they latch onto me with an insidious grip. I'm aware of my shortcomings, the moments when I faltered. This time of reflection isn't a place of repose; it's a battleground where self-doubt wrestles with the spirit of triumph. I can feel the applause that had once enveloped me fading into a ghostly echo, replaced by the harsh scrutiny of those who wield the power to shape perceptions with their words.

As I move deeper into the chaos of backstage, I'm drawn to a makeshift mirror that stands tall against the wall. I approach it, a moth to the flame, seeking to reclaim the spark that feels dimmed. My reflection greets me, and I take a moment to absorb the sight. My hair, a cascade of curls, is slightly disheveled, framing my face in wild tendrils that echo my turbulent emotions. The makeup, intended to enhance the character I portrayed, now feels like a mask, an armor that both protects and suffocates. My eyes, usually bright with ambition, now glisten with uncertainty, as if they too are searching for a way to express the tumult within.

The world outside the mirror pulses with life, the chatter of the cast and crew mingling with the critiques. My heart thuds in rhythm with the noise, each beat a reminder of my desire to belong, to be recognized not just for this performance but for the relentless effort behind it. I've poured my soul into this role, into every word spoken and every emotion evoked. Yet, standing here, I feel as if I'm on the precipice, teetering between success and the fear of being cast aside.

"Hey," Jason's voice breaks through my reverie, pulling me back from the depths of self-reflection. He steps closer, his brow furrowed with concern. "You okay?"

I manage a smile, albeit shaky, as I respond, "Just taking it all in. It's a lot, you know?" The honesty in my tone surprises me, a crack in the facade I've built around my vulnerability.

He nods, understanding flickering in his eyes. "You were brilliant tonight. Don't let anyone make you doubt that. We did this together." His hand finds mine, squeezing it reassuringly, igniting a spark of warmth that momentarily wards off the chill of doubt.

In that moment, I realize that the path to acceptance—both from others and within myself—will not be without its hurdles. The critics may question my commitment, but they cannot touch the passion that has burned in my heart since I first stepped onto a stage. I glance back at the mirror, taking a deep breath as I commit to stepping away from the lingering shadows of self-doubt.

Jason's presence steadies me, a beacon amidst the chaos. Together, we navigate through the whirlwind, side by side, not as mere performers but as comrades in this vibrant world of art and expression. The backstage energy hums with anticipation, the palpable excitement of what's next. There's a thrill in the air, a whisper of possibility, urging me to push past the noise and step into my own narrative.

With each step we take back into the fray, the fears that had threatened to consume me begin to dissolve, replaced by the recognition that every artist faces judgment. I remind myself that I am more than the whispers of critics; I am the stories I tell and the heart I pour into my craft. And perhaps, just perhaps, that is enough.

The buzzing energy backstage is a delicate fabric woven from anticipation and anxiety, thickening the air around us. The backdrop, a faded canvas adorned with the remnants of past productions, stands like an ancient sentinel, bearing witness to countless dreams birthed and broken. I take a moment to absorb it all—the murmurs of fellow cast members mingling with the sharp clicking of cameras, the sporadic laughter punctuating the tension as everyone floats between celebration and critique.

As the evening unfolds, my mind dances between fleeting memories of joyous moments and the gnawing doubt that seems to find its way into every crevice of my thoughts. The mingling aromas of fresh paint and unwashed costumes create a familiar yet disorienting scent, a reminder of both my triumphs and the sacrifices that have shadowed my journey. I spot a group of actors huddled together, their faces animated with excitement, recounting their favorite parts of the performance, and a pang of longing hits me. I wish I could join them, revel in their joy, but the weight of the critics' words clings to me like an unwanted cloak.

"Let's go grab a drink," Jason suggests, nudging me gently. His voice cuts through the haze, laced with an infectious optimism that I both admire and envy. I nod, appreciating his unwavering support, and we weave our way through the labyrinth of backstage, our path illuminated by the warm glow of flickering lights.

The bar is a small haven amid the chaos, nestled in a corner of the studio, where the chatter blends with the clinking of glasses. The ambiance shifts, and I feel a hint of normalcy wash over me as we take our seats, the plush leather stools a welcome respite. The bartender, a woman with wild curls and a welcoming smile, raises an eyebrow at us as she pours two generous glasses of red wine.

"To us," Jason says, lifting his glass high, his eyes shining with sincerity. I can't help but mirror his gesture, our glasses clinking together, a celebratory sound that momentarily drowns out the cacophony of voices around us. The first sip of wine warms me, its velvety texture wrapping around my tongue like a comforting embrace.

"I mean it, you were incredible out there," he continues, leaning in closer, his voice dropping to a conspiratorial whisper. "You need to believe that. Those critics don't know the half of it." I can see the genuine passion behind his words, and for a moment, the storm inside me subsides.

But then the doubts creep back in. "But what if they're right?" I reply, my voice barely above a whisper. "What if I've been coasting on borrowed talent? They say I didn't deserve to be up there, that my absence during rehearsals was a sign I didn't care." The confession spills out before I can catch it, a torrent of insecurities that I've tried so hard to contain.

Jason's expression shifts, his brow furrowing as he processes my words. "You're being too hard on yourself. It's easy for people to forget the sacrifices we make when they only see the final performance. You've poured your heart into this, and that's what matters." His words resonate within me, a gentle reminder that art is a reflection of one's spirit, not merely a checklist of rehearsals and appearances.

"Maybe," I murmur, taking another sip of my wine, feeling the rich flavor linger, if only to distract myself from the swirling thoughts. The clamor of the bar surrounds us, filled with the laughter and camaraderie of fellow performers, and I can't help but wish for a slice of their carefree joy.

Jason continues to share stories, anecdotes from our time rehearsing, weaving a tapestry of memories that spark joy in my heart. I lean back in my seat, allowing the warmth of his presence to envelop me. I watch as his gestures grow animated, his hands dancing through the air as he recounts a particularly funny moment when our stage manager nearly lost her mind over a forgotten prop. The laughter spills from my lips, a much-needed release, and I find myself enveloped in the comfort of his company.

As the night wears on, the atmosphere becomes a swirl of laughter and excitement, the shadows of doubt retreating further into the corners of my mind. I catch glimpses of familiar faces—other cast members letting loose, the strains of a soulful ballad playing softly in the background, coaxing them onto the makeshift dance floor. The bar transforms into a hub of celebration, the air thick with the aroma of sweet cocktails and fried finger foods, a delightful mix that sings of indulgence.

"Let's join them," I suggest, surprising even myself with the spontaneity of my words. The idea of dancing, of surrendering to the music and letting go of the burdens that weigh me down, feels exhilarating. Jason's eyes widen with delight, and he doesn't hesitate to stand, pulling me up with him.

The music swells, wrapping around us like a warm embrace, and I find myself moving to the rhythm, the laughter of my peers igniting a fire within me. The dance floor, lit with colorful lights that cast a warm glow on the faces around us, feels alive, pulsating with the energy of creativity and camaraderie. Each step I take loosens the knots of tension, each sway of my body shedding the layers of self-doubt that have clung to me like an unwelcome guest.

As I spin around, I catch sight of Jason, his smile infectious as he dances with unrestrained joy. The laughter and cheers from our friends mingle with the music, a symphony of acceptance that washes over me. In that moment, I realize that the critics' words hold no power over me; they are but whispers against the chorus of laughter and love that surrounds us.

I lose myself in the music, in the movement, and the joy of simply being present. The worries that had plagued me fade into the background, replaced by the connection I feel with my fellow performers. Together, we celebrate our achievements and embrace our imperfections, reveling in the glorious chaos that is art.

With each beat of the song, I let go of the fears that had threatened to consume me, finding solace in the rhythm of my heart and the camaraderie that weaves through our lives. I choose to embrace this moment, knowing that the journey ahead may still be fraught with challenges, but tonight, I am simply a part of something beautiful.

The rhythm of the music thrums through my veins, and I lose myself in the joyous abandon that envelops the room. Laughter spills freely, each note a reminder that we are a collective of dreamers, artists crafting our narratives with every step we take on this makeshift dance floor. Faces swirl around me, each one illuminated in bursts of color from the flickering lights, their expressions a mix of euphoria and camaraderie that pierces through the lingering doubts in my mind.

As I twirl under the shimmering lights, I catch a glimpse of Jason, who is fully immersed in the moment, his laughter spilling over like a glass filled to the brim. His joy is infectious, and it draws me closer, reminding me that this—this shared experience—is why I fell in love with the stage in the first place. I pull him into a twirl, and we spin together, our bodies moving in sync as if we were dancing to an unspoken melody, one that celebrates our journey through the highs and lows of this artistic life.

With each passing moment, I feel the weight of criticism lift, replaced by the buoyancy of connection. The voices of the critics become mere whispers, overshadowed by the vibrancy of my peers, who dance and celebrate not just our achievements but the very essence of who we are. We are artists, flawed yet passionate, dedicated to the craft that binds us together like threads in a rich tapestry.

Between the swirls of color and sound, I find myself gravitating toward a small group gathered near the bar. Their laughter is bright and effervescent, a contrast to the heaviness I had carried earlier. I approach, drawn in by the magnetic energy they exude. As I step closer, the light catches the sparkle in a woman's eyes, her laughter a clear chime that cuts through the crowd. She introduces herself as Lily, a dancer with a talent for making even the most mundane moments feel extraordinary.

"Are you coming to the afterparty at Mason's?" she asks, her voice filled with enthusiasm. "It's going to be epic! Just wait until you see the space—it's this amazing rooftop with the skyline as our backdrop. You can't miss it!"

Mason's rooftop? I've heard whispers of the place, a hidden gem where the city unfolds beneath you like a breathtaking canvas, the lights twinkling like stars in the sky. The allure of it wraps around me, enticing me to leave behind the remnants of doubt that had plagued my earlier hours.

"Count me in!" I reply, the exhilaration bubbling up within me as I consider the prospect of celebrating not just our hard work but the very essence of artistry itself. Jason nudges my side, his grin wide, and I can see the excitement reflected in his eyes.

As the party begins to wind down, we gather our things and make our way outside. The cool night air greets us, refreshing and crisp, a welcome change from the warmth of the studio. The city unfolds before us, the sounds of the streets mingling with the chatter of our group, each voice a note in this symphony of urban life. We navigate through the alleys, the cobblestones beneath our feet echoing the rhythm of our hearts, pounding with anticipation as we approach Mason's rooftop.

Once we arrive, the sight is even more breathtaking than I had imagined. The rooftop is adorned with twinkling fairy lights, creating a magical ambiance that transforms the urban landscape into something out of a dream. The skyline stretches before us, an intricate mosaic of shimmering glass and steel, rising majestically against the night sky. I inhale deeply, filling my lungs with the scent of adventure mixed with the faint aroma of street food wafting from nearby vendors.

Lily leads us to a cozy nook draped in string lights, where the laughter of fellow artists fills the air, blending seamlessly with the distant sound of music that dances through the night. I take a moment to absorb the scene, my heart swelling with gratitude for this vibrant community that celebrates creativity in all its forms.

The night flows effortlessly, filled with conversations that flit from the profound to the absurd, laughter punctuating the air like fireworks. I find myself seated next to Jason, our shoulders brushing against each other, creating a warmth that feels both comforting and exhilarating. As we share stories and toast to our triumphs, I can feel the camaraderie enveloping me like a warm embrace.

Amid the revelry, I catch sight of the city skyline, a reminder of how far we've come. Each shimmering light tells a story—a dream realized, a battle fought. In this moment, I'm reminded of the resilience that courses through each of us. We are artists, woven together by our struggles and our victories, sharing the weight of our aspirations.

Later, as the stars twinkle above us and the laughter begins to fade into the distance, I find a moment of stillness. Standing at the edge of the rooftop, I gaze out at the sprawling city, feeling an inexplicable connection to its heart. The gentle breeze brushes against my skin, and I let it wash over me, cleansing me of the doubts that had once consumed me.

In that quiet moment, I reflect on the journey that has brought me here—the late nights filled with rehearsals, the moments of vulnerability on stage, and the friendships that have blossomed along the way. Each experience has shaped me, molded me into the artist I am today. The critics' words no longer have the power to diminish my spirit; instead, they become a part of my narrative, a testament to my growth.

As I turn back to the gathering, I see the faces of my fellow artists illuminated by laughter, their joy infectious. I feel a sense of belonging that ignites a fire within me, a reminder that we are all in this together, each of us striving to tell our stories, to make our mark on the world.

I rejoin the group, laughter spilling forth like music, and I realize that I am ready to embrace whatever comes next. The spotlight may shift, the critics may judge, but I am anchored in the love of my craft and the support of those around me. Tonight, I choose to celebrate not just the art but the community it fosters, the beauty of connection that transcends doubt.

In this moment, I am more than a performer; I am a storyteller, a dreamer, and I am home.

Chapter 29: The Heart's Compass

The sun dipped low, its golden rays spilling across the porch like melted butter, warming the weathered wood beneath me. I leaned back in my chair, feeling the gentle sway of the swing beside me, an old relic that creaked with the weight of memories. My eyes scanned the horizon, where the sky turned to a watercolor masterpiece, each brushstroke a reminder that life was in constant motion, forever shifting like the clouds above. As the world transformed from day to night, I felt a stirring deep within me, an echo of the vibrant rhythms that had once dominated my life.

It had been days since the showcase, the adrenaline rush still coursing through my veins. Jason, ever the optimist, insisted that I had something special, a spark that could light up any stage. He had watched me dance with a fervor that made my heart race, his admiration palpable, yet I couldn't shake the uncertainty that clung to me like a shadow. My dreams had once flickered with brilliance, but now they felt muted, as if shrouded in fog.

I closed my eyes and let the sounds of the evening envelop me: the distant laughter of children playing in the streets, the soft rustle of leaves swaying in the warm breeze, and the faint hum of cicadas serenading the twilight. It was a symphony of life, a reminder that I was part of something greater than myself. Each note resonated within me, awakening a yearning to create, to express, to find my place within this sprawling, chaotic world. Yet, I found myself at a crossroads, hesitating at the precipice of what could be.

In the stillness of that moment, I thought of my friends, the ones who danced through life beside me, their laughter a balm for my restless soul. We had shared countless hours in the dimly lit studio, the mirrors reflecting not just our bodies but our dreams and fears. Each pirouette, each leap, was a testament to our shared passion, but it was more than that; it was a tapestry woven with threads of friendship and support. I remembered the countless late nights spent rehearsing, our sweat mingling on the floor, our voices echoing as we challenged each other to push beyond our limits. It was in those moments that I felt truly alive, but now that vibrancy seemed distant.

A flicker of determination ignited within me, illuminating the path I had been afraid to tread. Why should I choose between my love for dance and the bonds I cherished? They were intertwined, part of the same beautiful fabric of my life. Dance was not merely a pursuit; it was a way of connecting, of giving back, of sharing the joy that had been gifted to me. I could embrace both my passion and my commitment to my friends, intertwining them in a way that felt authentic and fulfilling.

The sun finally sank beneath the horizon, leaving behind a canvas of indigo and silver, the stars twinkling like diamonds scattered across velvet. I stood up, brushing off the remnants of indecision that clung to me, a tangible representation of the weight I had carried for too long. With each step away from the porch, I felt lighter, as if I were shedding the layers of doubt that had held me captive. I was ready to take a leap, not just of faith, but of purpose.

My heart raced as I envisioned a journey that would blend my passion for dance with a desire to help others. I could teach, inspire, and share the joy that movement had brought into my life. The idea took shape in my mind like a dance itself—fluid, dynamic, and filled with possibility. I imagined a community workshop, where I could guide others to find their rhythm, to discover the beauty of expressing themselves through movement. The thought electrified me, sending ripples of excitement through my veins.

The next morning, I found myself at the local community center, the scent of freshly painted walls mingling with the warmth of sunlight streaming through large windows. The space was bright and inviting, a blank canvas waiting for the strokes of creativity to be applied. As I stepped inside, my heart raced with anticipation. This was the beginning of something new, something that felt like home. I could almost hear the whispers of my friends encouraging me, their laughter echoing in my ears, urging me to take the plunge.

With each passing day, the vision grew clearer. I reached out to local schools, inviting students to join my workshops, to explore the joy of dance without the pressure of competition. I poured my heart into the curriculum, blending various styles to create a tapestry of movement that celebrated individuality. We would explore not just technique, but the stories each dancer carried within them. I wanted to create a space where everyone could feel seen and heard, where their unique voices could shine through the rhythm of their bodies.

As the weeks unfolded, I found myself surrounded by eager faces, each one reflecting a spark of curiosity and excitement. I felt alive as I led them through warm-ups and improvisation, their laughter ringing like music in the air. Each step we took together was a reminder that dance was not just about perfection; it was about connection. The room filled with energy, a vibrant pulse that echoed the heartbeat of our shared experience.

And in that whirlwind of movement and laughter, I discovered something profound. The more I taught, the more I learned about myself. I was not just a dancer; I was a guide, a mentor, and a friend. I watched as the students blossomed, their confidence growing with each class. It was a mirror reflecting back the joy that had once ignited my own passion for dance. I felt their triumphs as if they were my own, and in that, I found a new purpose.

The journey had only just begun, and as the seasons shifted, so did my understanding of what it meant to truly dance. It was not confined to a stage or a spotlight; it was a way of life, a celebration of the moments we shared, the stories we told, and the connections we forged. And as the moon rose high, casting its silvery glow upon the world, I realized I had found my heart's compass, guiding me toward a future that was both exhilarating and beautifully unpredictable.

The weeks slipped by like grains of sand through an hourglass, each one bringing fresh energy to the community center. The spacious studio transformed into a sanctuary, its wooden floors gleaming under the bright lights, a perfect stage for dreams to unfurl. The laughter of children echoed off the walls, creating a backdrop to the choreography of our lives. I found myself in this vibrant mix, a conductor orchestrating movements that painted joy across every eager face.

It was a crisp Friday afternoon when I introduced a new concept to my students—storytelling through dance. The idea had simmered in my mind like a well-seasoned broth, rich with flavor and promise. I wanted to show them that every leap and spin could narrate a tale, transforming emotions into movement. The excitement in the room was palpable as I explained the plan, and I watched as eyes widened with the thrill of possibility.

"Imagine you're characters in a story," I said, my voice brimming with enthusiasm. "You can be anything—heroes, villains, dreamers. Every step you take is part of your narrative." I demonstrated a sequence, my body flowing like water, tracing arcs in the air that mirrored the ebb and flow of emotions. They followed suit, their young bodies mirroring my movements with tentative grace. The studio filled with an electric energy, a beautiful cacophony of creativity and collaboration.

As the days rolled into weeks, our classes evolved into a tapestry of expression and connection. I encouraged the students to share their stories, to draw inspiration from their own lives. One afternoon, a shy girl named Mia stepped forward, her hands trembling slightly. With a gentle nod from me, she began to dance, her movements delicate yet fierce, like a flower unfurling in a storm. She portrayed a journey through loneliness, each step resonating with a weight that was almost palpable. The room fell silent, absorbed in her tale. By the time she finished, tears glistened in my eyes, and a round of applause erupted, filling the space with warmth and appreciation.

It became a ritual to create a new narrative each week, exploring themes of friendship, loss, resilience, and love. The kids poured their hearts into their performances, their laughter mingling with heartfelt expressions. Dance was no longer just an art form; it was a vessel for connection, a way to explore the depths of human experience. I found my heart swelling with pride as I watched them evolve—not just as dancers, but as storytellers, brave enough to share their truths.

Yet, beneath the surface of this joy, a familiar tension gnawed at me. My dreams of becoming a professional dancer had not dimmed; they lurked in the corners of my mind, whispering sweet nothings that echoed my earlier ambitions. It was a delicate balancing act, and I often found myself standing on a tightrope, caught between my aspirations and my newfound purpose. Each time I laced up my shoes, the ache in my heart reminded me of the stages I had longed to conquer, the applause I had yearned to hear.

One evening, after class, Jason stopped by, his face bright with enthusiasm. "You have to see this!" he exclaimed, pulling out his phone to show me a video of an upcoming dance competition. The screen lit up with flashes of color, dancers swirling across the stage, each move sharper and more expressive than the last. My breath caught in my throat as I watched, the familiar pang of longing surfacing within me. "You should enter, you know. You're amazing, and this could be your moment!"

His words wrapped around me like a warm blanket, igniting a flicker of hope. But the weight of my responsibility at the community center pressed down on me like an anchor. I had become a mentor, a guide, and the thought of stepping away felt like abandoning my students at the precipice of their own journeys.

Jason noticed my hesitation, his brow furrowing in concern. "What's holding you back? You can't ignore your own dreams. You have to chase them."

"I know, but..." My voice faltered as I searched for the right words. "These kids need me. They're finding their voices through dance, and I can't just leave them."

He leaned against the doorframe, his expression softening. "You can do both, you know. You can dance and teach. Your passion doesn't have to be an either-or situation."

Those words echoed in my mind long after he left, resonating with the truth I had begun to embrace. I could weave my dreams into the fabric of my current reality, letting them coexist harmoniously. Perhaps the dance competition was not a departure from my commitment but rather an extension of it—a chance to inspire my students by demonstrating the very spirit of pursuit I hoped to instill in them.

The next day, I found myself in the studio, the air thick with anticipation as I shared my decision with the students. "I'm entering a dance competition," I announced, my heart racing. "And I want each of you to join me in this journey." The room erupted in cheers, their enthusiasm spilling over like a joyful fountain, and in that moment, I felt a renewed sense of purpose.

In the weeks leading up to the competition, the atmosphere shifted. We became a team, united by a common goal. Together, we worked tirelessly, blending their narratives into a cohesive performance that told a collective story. As I taught them the choreography, I could feel my own excitement building, a phoenix rising from the ashes of my self-doubt.

The energy in the studio crackled with potential as we rehearsed late into the evenings, the sounds of our laughter mingling with the music. I saw the joy reflected in their faces, the confidence blossoming with each movement. As I watched them, I couldn't help but marvel at the transformation that had occurred not just within them, but within myself as well. I was no longer standing on a precipice; I was dancing on solid ground, embracing the vibrant chaos of my life with open arms.

The night of the competition arrived, and the air was thick with excitement, charged with the kind of energy that made your skin tingle. Dressed in shimmering costumes that caught the light like stars, we stood backstage, the sound of our heartbeats mingling with the rhythmic thrum of the crowd. I looked around at my students, their eyes bright with anticipation, and in that moment, I knew that this was not just about me; it was about us, a testament to the power of dreams, friendship, and the indomitable spirit of dance.

The stage shimmered under the warm glow of the lights, each beam illuminating the faces of my students, their expressions a mixture of excitement and nervousness. The hum of the audience seeped through the curtains, a living entity that thrummed with anticipation. I stood backstage, feeling the coolness of the walls pressing against my back, and glanced at the intricate costumes we had chosen together. Each fabric, each sequin, told a story—a collective narrative woven through laughter, sweat, and countless hours of rehearsal. This was it, our moment to shine, a testament to every late night and early morning we had poured into this journey.

As the first act concluded, the applause rolled over us like a wave, filling the air with a palpable energy. I could see my students peeking through the curtains, their eyes wide, their hearts pounding with the thrill of the unknown. The performance space pulsed with life, a canvas where stories were painted with movement, where silence transformed into a symphony of sound. This was more than a competition; it was a celebration of everything we had created together.

When our turn came, the stage manager signaled, and my heart soared, urging me forward. As we stepped into the light, the world faded away, leaving only the music and the rhythm that flowed through us like a current. I led them onto the stage, feeling their energy harmonize with mine, a dance of souls intertwined in a moment of pure magic. The audience faded, and all that remained was the movement—the glides, the leaps, and the swirling grace that transcended the mundane.

The choreography we had crafted came to life, a narrative unfolding with every step. We danced through the highs and lows of life, embodying joy, sorrow, and resilience. I watched as Mia, the shy girl who had initially hesitated to share her story, radiated confidence, her movements fierce and unrestrained. Each dancer transformed into a storyteller, their expressions conveying a thousand emotions in the span of a few beats. Laughter erupted as we pirouetted through moments of playfulness, and the audience joined in the joy, their claps punctuating the air like fireworks.

As we reached the finale, the crescendo of our performance echoed around us, and I felt the energy of my students surge, a powerful force igniting our movements. In that moment, I understood that this was what I had been seeking all along—the intertwining of passion and purpose. I was not just leading them; we were part of something greater, a collective heartbeat that resonated in perfect harmony.

When the final pose hit, we held it for what felt like an eternity, a tableau of dreams and determination. The applause crashed over us like a tidal wave, pulling us back to reality. I could hardly breathe as the audience erupted into cheers, the sound enveloping us like a warm embrace. We had done it; we had transformed our fears into triumph, our stories into dance.

Backstage, the thrill of adrenaline coursed through me as my students jumped and squealed, their joy spilling out like confetti. I pulled them in for a group hug, feeling the warmth of their bodies pressed against me, a tapestry of support and friendship woven together in that moment. "You were all incredible!" I exclaimed, my voice brimming with pride. Their faces glowed, their smiles bright against the backdrop of the stage lights, and I felt an overwhelming rush of gratitude wash over me.

As we waited for the judges to announce the results, I couldn't help but reflect on the journey we had taken together. This wasn't merely about winning trophies or accolades; it was about discovering who we were and what we could achieve as a team. In our shared experience, we had built something beautiful—an unbreakable bond forged through sweat, laughter, and the courage to share our stories.

Finally, the moment arrived, and the air crackled with tension as the announcer took the stage. "And the award for Best Performance goes to...!" My heart raced, each beat echoing the hopes of the students beside me. The name of our group filled the room, and a collective cheer erupted, drowning out the rest of the world. I felt my breath catch in my throat as I realized we had not only performed; we had won.

The trophy gleamed under the stage lights, a symbol of our hard work and resilience. As I held it aloft, my students crowded around me, their laughter mingling with the applause, a jubilant symphony celebrating our victory. It was a moment suspended in time, a snapshot of pure joy that would forever be etched in our memories. We were not just dancers; we were dreamers, and we had turned our aspirations into reality.

As the excitement gradually settled, we gathered our belongings, chatting animatedly about our next steps. The studio had become our second home, a place where dreams were nurtured, and I felt a sense of responsibility to ensure it continued to thrive. I shared my ideas for future workshops and performance opportunities, eager to keep the momentum going.

Mia approached me, her eyes shining with newfound confidence. "Can we do another performance like this?" she asked, her voice brimming with eagerness. "I want to keep dancing and telling stories!" Her enthusiasm ignited a spark in the others, and soon they were clamoring for more—more classes, more performances, more chances to explore the art of storytelling through movement.

In that moment, I felt a surge of purpose wash over me. The stage had opened a door, and we were all eager to walk through it together. I envisioned a community showcase, a chance for each dancer to share their stories and the journeys they had undertaken. The idea filled me with exhilaration. We would not only celebrate our achievements but also create a platform for others to express themselves, fostering an environment where creativity thrived.

The days turned into weeks, and the energy within the studio was electric. We choreographed new pieces, drawing inspiration from the stories of our lives. The students brought their experiences to the forefront, each narrative adding depth and richness to our performances. We rehearsed tirelessly, laughter echoing in the air, the dance floor alive with the sound of our footsteps.

As the showcase approached, I reflected on how far we had come. My heart swelled with pride as I watched my students transform from hesitant beginners into confident performers, each one radiating their unique light. They were no longer just students; they had become a family, bonded by a shared love for dance and storytelling.

On the night of the showcase, the community center buzzed with excitement. Friends and family filled the seats, their faces glowing with anticipation. The energy was palpable, a whirlwind of hope and dreams intertwining in the air. I stood backstage, watching my students prepare, their nervousness melting away as they shared jokes and encouragement.

As the curtain lifted, we stepped onto the stage, the spotlight bathing us in warmth. I looked out at the sea of faces, and my heart raced, but this time it was different. I felt a sense of belonging, a profound connection to the moment and to the dancers beside me. We were not just performing; we were sharing a piece of our hearts with the world.

With every movement, we poured our souls into the performance, weaving our stories together in a tapestry of joy, resilience, and love. The applause that erupted at the end resonated deep within me, a reminder of the power of dance to connect us all.

In that moment, I understood that my journey was not just about pursuing my own dreams. It was about empowering others, creating a space for voices to be heard, and allowing hearts to express themselves through the beauty of movement. I felt a wave of gratitude wash over me, knowing that I had found my path—not just as a dancer but as a guide, a mentor, and a friend.

The future stretched before us, a vast expanse filled with possibilities. We were ready to embrace it together, hand in hand, hearts open, and spirits soaring. The world awaited our stories, and I was determined to ensure that we would tell them—one dance at a time.

Milton Keynes UK
Ingram Content Group UK Ltd.
UKHW040638131024
449481UK00001B/42

9 798227 693440